TWO GRAVES

FOR MICHAEL FUREY

BRUCE

FERGUSSON

Lucky Bat Books

A Lucky Bat Book

Two Graves for Michael Furey
Copyright 2015 Bruce Fergusson
Cover Design: Nuno Moreira

ISBN: 978-1-943588-00-8

LuckyBatBooks.com
10 9 8 7 6 5 4 3 2 1

TWO GRAVES

FOR MICHAEL FUREY

BRUCE

FERGUSSON

CHAPTER 1
FADO

Noon, Friday, July 13, 2007

WHEN THE MAN emerged from the forest, Helen Sommers stopped weeding the furrows between the tomato plants in her garden. She leaned on the hoe, watching him wade through the ankle-high grass and wildflowers of the meadow that sloped gently down to a creek and the palisade of firs and cedars beyond.

She visored a gloved hand over her brow. It was odd he hadn't used the footbridge that spanned the creek and led to a path into the dense woods. He carried no rifle so at least she wouldn't have to tell him firmly that her property was posted for no hunting.

Lost hikers happened out here on the wilderness fringe of the Mt. Baker-Snoqualmie National Forest, though deer were the most common visitors—why she'd fenced the garden. She got the occasional foraging bear and once saw a gray wolf pad across the meadow, but it left quickly and she'd been inside the cabin anyway. She'd never seen a cougar on her property but they were out there. Whenever she hiked into the forest she took the .22 pistol she kept by the door to her cabin, in the top drawer of a burled maple chest Michael made in a high school shop class second semester senior year.

If this tall, husky man was a lost hiker, he was a foolish one. He had no walking stick or day-pack to carry survival essentials for a hike in this area of dense second and third-growth forest, rocky hills, ravines and abandoned mines. Even a twisted ankle could be fatal if you were out there alone—and Helen saw no companion. Yet the man seemed to know where he was going, away from her, toward the old logging road that began not far from the other side of the cabin she'd named Fado; an Irish word, one of Michael's favorites. The road was the only way in—or out.

She walked outside the garden gate to keep him in sight; the root cellar where she kept her perishables had momentarily blocked her view. He was halfway through the meadow and still hadn't shouted an apology for trespassing.

She called out: "Help you?"

The man waved and kept trudging through the grass, veering closer to her. "Are you lost?" she shouted again, though he should have heard her the first time. He neither stopped nor answered her.

"If you don't need help, you'll have to leave," she yelled, louder still. "This is private property." She pointed beyond the cabin, to her right: "The way out is over there, an old logging road; follow it out for a mile."

When he said, "No, more like two," she realized the mistake she'd made in assuming he was walking off the meadow toward the road since he had to pass by the cabin to get there. He was almost closer to the porch steps now than she was.

"Stop right there!" she shouted, edging toward the cabin. The scythe she used to cut the meadow grass leaned against the porch railing. The .22 was just inside the door.

"Not now," he shouted back. "We need to go inside Fado."

She bolted toward the side of the cabin where she kept Michael's Mustang covered in a tarp. Stop at the back corner, surprise him with the hoe?—slash at his groin, not the face; she could easily miss that. *No…* She'd just have one chance. He could block her swing, grab the hoe. Even if he didn't, a fucking garden tool wouldn't hurt him enough.

She flung the hoe away—it would only slow her down—and sprinted for the road. Three choices now: keep on, outrun him; scramble up the little ridge alongside the road and into the forest; or disappear over the other side. *No way…*The slope there was too steep—the tops of the trees rose to the level of the road—and she might tumble down, hurt herself badly. If he didn't see her on the road, he'd know she was down there. Outrun him? She was fast but couldn't risk that he was too, and in better shape. *No, up the hill…*Farther up, around another twist in the road beyond the bluff, the hillside was eroded more. She could lose him quickly once she got up to the ridge and into the forest—places where he'd never find her.

She glanced back as she reached the sharp bend in the road. The flimsy hope vanished that he might not be coming after; that he'd just been someone who'd stumbled lost out of the woods upon a woman alone by her cabin and thought better of the easy pickings once she took off.

He was thirty yards behind, running easily, matching her pace.

She maxed it out around the bend. When she saw the white SUV she shouted for help, waved as she ran—before she realized there was no one in the car.

It's his…

He'd left it here, then sneaked around to surprise her. And how he knew the name of the cabin; he'd seen the sign coming in.

She had to slow down to get past the car that blocked most of the narrow road. She veered off, leaped over the shallow gully at a run—too fast. She skidded down, scrambled up again on all fours, grunting, digging her gloved fingers into the scree—she still had on the garden gloves—kicking back rivulets of dirt and gravel, forcing herself not to look back to see how close he was; that would only slow her down. *Get up…come on…*She grabbed at a root, then a straggly madrona angling out from the slope. She could hear his breathing behind her, scuffling feet.

She almost made it.

He snagged an ankle, pulled her back. The madrona branch snapped in her hand. She kicked back, trying to loosen his grip. A root caught in her hair, snarling it out to length as he kept pulling…pulling…on both of her ankles now. She loosened a fist-sized rock, twisted around, launched a blow to his head as he leaned close. He jerked back, avoiding the strike but also lost his balance—and her ankles. She scrambled away.

She never made it out of the ditch. She tried to hit him again with the rock, but he caught her wrist and prised the rock from her grasp, tossed it away. He had a bizarre tattoo on his left forearm.

She screamed as he flipped her over, using his weight to pin her and got a roll of duct tape from a pocket of his hunting vest. She heard the rip of the tape then the sudden constriction on her wrists as he cinched them together at the small of her back. She kept kicking with her legs to no avail. Within seconds he'd taped one ankle, pulled it to the other, and wrapped both together.

More tearing sounds. From behind he slapped tape over her mouth and around her head, then picked her up easily, draping her over his shoulder and carried her toward the rear of the car. He put her down on the gravel road and kneeled by her side, smiling, catching his breath. The taped sucked in and out with her breathing. She chuffed through her nose. She felt like she was going to suffocate. Her right eye watered—dirt in there—but she could see him now: close-cropped hair, blue eyes and a burned splotch on his face that began at the side of his lips and spread, as if the redness was seeping out from his mouth. And that tattoo: a skull with vanes like a windmill.

He got up, opened the back of the car, shoved stuff to make room for her—boxes, a hunting bow, jugs of water—so much that she couldn't see but could hear someone in the back seat saying: "I'm sorry...I'm sorry."

"Too late for that, Sean," he said. "Here she is, close as can be, just like you wanted." Then, to her: "Watch your feet, Lennie."

As he closed the car's gate, sealing her inside, she thought that she must have not heard him right. No one had ever called her Lennie except for her sister and Michael, who said it first and thought the cabin should be named Fado.

CHAPTER 2

KATIE

July, 2004

I MET HER at the first baseball game I went to seven years after I blew my chance at a major league career.

Malloys have a way with one-eighties, degrees that is. With the exception of my father the reasons have usually been apparent.

My brother Sean lit out for the territories, taking his baggage train with him. We only knew he'd gone to southern California when we got the Mission Beach postcard.

My mother bought cigarettes for the first time in her life two weeks after my father said he was going to Tollgate, a five-minute drive from our home in Slingerlands, New York, to get some take-out burgers for dinner and a half-gallon of banana ice cream—the family favorite. He never returned. His car was never found. A year later, before she got breast cancer, she quit smoking just as abruptly as she'd begun.

My older sister Marcy called me up one morning in early March and asked me to help her move some 'things' at her home in East Greenbush: her husband's table saw, riding lawn mower, golf clubs, leaf blower, everything that was more his than hers. She had found out he'd been cheating on her. When he came back from a business trip in Chicago, he found a late snow covering his woodworking bench in the driveway and walnuts she'd cracked in the bench vise. He wanted to go to couples' marriage counseling; she told him to go fuck himself.

Me? I'd played baseball through college, then beyond in the Red Sox organization, hitting over .300 at every level—well, .294 one year with the Single-A Michigan Battle Cats of the Midwest League—but one night changed all that, the same day I got called up to Boston's Triple-A Pawtucket affiliate club. After that night I still had 10-15 vision but my left wrist and hand—the lead hand that pulls you through if you're a right handed batter—were never quite the same after the operation and rehab. I could still run down balls hit into the outfield gaps but I couldn't catch up to low-90s fastballs, or wait and rip on the breaking stuff.

Until the game where I met Katie Walsh I hadn't set foot in a ballpark for seven years. The game I almost didn't go to became my turn for a one-eighty.

Marcy said her son, Davy, wanted only one thing for his upcoming birthday and that was for his uncle to take him to Joe Bruno stadium to see the Tri-City Valley Cats, the Houston Astros Single-A affiliate in the New York-Penn League. As it turned out, Davy got sick the day before, was running a fever that morning, but I decided to go anyway, if only to get him a red and black Cats' cap for a birthday present. I'd already covered my Saturday night shift bartending at Emmett's, a restaurant near the Mall in Albany.

Located in Troy, at Hudson Valley Community College, "The Joe" was only a half-hour drive from where I lived in Delmar a few miles south of Albany, a slick new stadium fronted with glass and brick and a lot sleeker than most of the parks in which I'd once played.

After a day hot enough to soften road tar it was tempting to sit on the grass berm beyond the right field fence, but I chose the aluminum bleachers along the third base line, thinking that would help, getting as close as I could get to where I once was—on the other side of the foul lines. It didn't. For three innings, among a full house of perhaps 4,000, I didn't know if I could do it, go the distance. Part of me wanted to just get Davy his cap and get the hell out. And I did, made it to the concessions, but I came back, drawn by the sudden roar of the Cats' doing something good.

She sat three rows down from me but I didn't notice her until Oneonta's lead-off guy hit a foul ball that veered wickedly toward her. Everyone else ducked but she made a stab at the ball. I heard it smack into her palms. She couldn't hold on; the ball glanced off and up to me. I caught it with one hand. She turned, rubbing her hands and I saw her then: a pretty blonde without streaks, wearing a black *Just Do It* T-shirt. She waved at me—more of a shaking-of-the-head because of her hands. The sting had to be there; so was a big smile. She turned back, said something to the woman sitting beside her, who looked at her hand.

I went down to give her the ball. Nearby, a few people clapped. "You did the hard part," I said.

"Yeah, but you caught it," she said.

"Well, you keep it."

The next inning I went down to buy Davy his cap and I saw both women at the concessions, and we got talking. Her name was Katie Walsh; the friend, Ellen DiGiulio. I joined them for the rest of the game.

Both had played softball in high school: Ellen in Oswego and Katie at Shaker High School in Latham. Both were finishing up grad school—Ellen in nursing at SUNY-Albany and Katie at Albany Law. I told them I bartended at Emmett's and that answered Ellen's question—"I know I've seen you somewhere"—since she'd gone there occasionally for the Pisco Sours.

The conversation had its teasing moments since I had also played football at Bethlehem Central High School. The Eagles were an arch-rival of the Shaker Blue Bisons. After the game ended, as we walked away from the stadium lights toward our respective cars, Katie gave me back the baseball.

"I really think you should have it," she said. I shrugged and took the ball, thinking I could give it to Davy, along with the hat and an autograph I got from the Cats' center-fielder because I wanted to wish him good luck. That had been my position all the way through to the end.

Then, in my car, with the overhead light on, I saw that she'd scribbled on the ball: *Nice catch—for an Eagle!*

She'd also written her phone number.

Katie had beaten me to the punch; I'd been planning on calling her. I did a day later and asked her when exactly she'd done the deed. I mean, I'd been with her and Ellen for the rest of the game, right next to her.

"I didn't do it," Katie said. "Ellen did."

She couldn't talk much; she was heading out the door, some family shindig, but said, "I'd love to," when I asked her out for that weekend. Over dinner, after a movie, I got the details.

"I slipped Ellen the ball, a pen and a look when you were into that nine pitch at-bat in the seventh. Ellen was a pitcher on our team at Wesleyan and I was the catcher, so she was used to taking signs from me—when she wasn't shaking them off, anyway."

I laughed. "I'm glad she didn't this time."

I asked her out again that night after I kissed her in front of her apartment door in Colonie. I kept the ball on the shelf over the desk in the living room, where I did my writing every day from 11 a.m. to 3 p.m.

TWO MONTHS AFTER we met, Katie came to pick me up for a date: *Brigadoon* at a summer stock theater down in Chatham. We were using her BMW, a college graduation gift from her father. My beater was in the shop. When I came out of the bedroom, tucking in my shirt, she had our ball in hand, tossed it once and put it back on the shelf. "That's one lonely ball," she said. "Maybe you could show me your other baseball stuff sometime. We haven't done scrapbooks yet."

"It's ancient history, semi-ancient anyway."

"Still counts. You have it all here?"

"At my sister's."

"Why there?"

"She has the house, more room." As if I couldn't fit in a couple boxes or shelves here.

She sat on the edge of the parson's desk I salvaged from a de-flocked Lutheran church's going-out-of-business sale.

"So what've we got here, you think?" she said. "Fastball, curve or change-up?"

I sat next to her. "I think neither of us wants to iron out the creases in the other, which is a great start. And I think if we don't get out of here we're going to miss the curtain."

"Was that a curve?"

"Okay, what I really think?"

"Yeah."

I didn't want to answer her with more baseball, but I did think this: *what can you ever do but hit the ball where it's pitched?*

"I think we're long overdue for scrapbooks," I said, and kissed her and pulled her off the desk. "Come on. One of the actors is wearing the kilt I borrowed from a buddy at work. They put out a call. I didn't tell you. It's how I got the tickets."

WE WAITED ANOTHER year, long enough for Katie to finish law school and for me to finish writing the first draft of a novel called *Angel's Share*, which had more or less equal measures of restaurant and baseball in it.

That year was long enough for John Walsh—Papa John—to get worried about what his only daughter and her bartender boyfriend might be planning to do.

He phoned me one weekend, in July of 2005, while Katy was away in Boston visiting Ellen, who had moved to Boston. Katie wouldn't be back until late Monday night. John Walsh said: "You've been almost a part of the family for a while now, but you and I haven't had a chance to really sit down and have a chat."

It was sneaky of him to call when he knew Katy was gone, but I couldn't say no to the guy who would likely be my father-in-law. He suggested the following Monday for lunch at Vincent's, near the old Delaware and Hudson building. "I think they make pretty good drinks there. I'd be interested to get your opinion."

Since I was only a bartender?

I said: "Monday's fine, Mr. Walsh."

Over the weekend I wondered—not for the first time—whether my ongoing opinion of Papa John might have something to do with my own father, also a John. You need a walkabout, some time to think about things, reset your sails, okay. But you're supposed to walk back if you have a family. My father never did. We never knew if he was dead, alive or re-married, much less where the Slingerlands short-circuit had been. Foul play wasn't likely—not when you're over six feet, 220, and had only a five minute drive along a leafy suburban street to get to a restaurant which never did sell you any banana ice cream that evening.

I'd be lying if I told you that my anger had mutated into not caring at all what had happened to him because it's hard to give up on someone you loved a lot. Sean took it even harder, maybe because he was two years older and closer to Dad than I was. I put the blame on what happened to Sean—and still what might happen—at our father's feet.

A lot of kids might wish their father would take a hike and keep hiking, but it wasn't like that with Dad. It's safe to say that if he had stuck around he wouldn't have done what Katie said her father did: keep detailed graphs of all three of his kids' academic progress through high school and tack them up on the wall, side by side.

I decided to cut Papa John some slack. I wouldn't be marrying the guy or his expectations. I'd try to get along with him. He was Katie's father, and she loved him in the way you still want to swim on a hot day even if the water's murky. Still, I wasn't looking forward to dealing with a man who was still trying to pull the strings on his grown-up children. But maybe that was a perverse kind of bond I had with Katie: my own father was still pulling the strings—especially with Sean—even though he'd cut them a long time ago.

On the way to Vincent's that Monday, I figured Papa John would probably do one of three things, maybe all of them. The first? Offering me a job in his specialty gas business. You couldn't miss all the *Walsh Specialty Gases* vans driving around to tech businesses and hospitals. He had the lock on that in the Tri-Cities area but lucrative as that was, you don't own a five bedroom vacation home sitting pretty on three acres on Vinalhaven off the coast of Maine with just that. Walsh was born into wealth and Katie had two large trust funds from aunts. Which was the second thing, though he probably wouldn't tell me about it: putting up legal roadblocks so a mere bartender like me couldn't get my hands on Katie's money.

The third? A liege-lord like Papa John was used to issuing edicts: you hurt or abuse my baby girl in any way and you're going to be very sorry.

I had my answers.

No thanks.

Keep your money.

Threats are abuse, too, Mr. Walsh, and not the best way to begin, don't you think?

But there was a fourth, which blew Papa John far off the scale.

VINCENT'S HAD THE air of a men's club: deco light fixtures, mahogany paneling, cut prism glass windows, waiters in white jackets. We sat in a booth. A small brass plaque adorned the rim of the table: *Walsh Specialty Gases.*

So Papa John came here a lot.

He was taller than I, in his mid-fifties, had a Rushmore cut to his chin and most of his hair which he kept short. A light blue pastel shirt enhanced the marquee of his summer tan. Katie had many of his features—the high cheekbones, hazel eyes, blond hair—which reminded me of what this was all about: taking Daddy's little girl away from him.

I knew he ran 10Ks, played golf—a game baseball players were supposed to like though I never much cared for it. He also found time to grow prize-winning bonsai trees. Katie once showed me his greenhouse. I've never been a fan of bonsai trees. Maybe it was my wicked-witch third grade teacher who had one on the corner of her desk. They might be exotic works of living art, but consider the means to the impressively stunted end—incessant cutting, constriction and deprivation. Never mind they're only plants.

John Walsh was the kind of guy who puts his initials on everything, and over the past year I had seen them on shirts, cufflinks, tie clasps, sweaters, his golf bag—everything except Katie and her two brothers. But here was a new one: the expensive fountain pen sticking out of his shirt pocket.

He ordered a Stoly martini; I ordered a beer. We talked baseball first, which seemed common enough ground. Walsh had played in high school though he added, flashing his brilliantly bleached teeth, "There was never the possibility I could have gone on and played like you. Katie tells me you were pretty good. It's a shame what happened."

"Katie told you?"

"Not exactly—look, James, we're man-to-man here. What happened…"

"I'd like to know because Katy said she was going to wait on that, though I didn't care when she told you."

Walsh shrugged. "Very well, let's bring it out. Fortunately, I have the resources to have made inquiries. I think it's worthwhile for parents of a young woman who is obviously in love and thinking of perhaps marrying the young man, to know that he was arrested for assaulting a policeman and not so very long ago. At any rate, you make my point. Of course it's something my daughter would have been reluctant to tell me or her mother."

"It's more to the point for her to know about it, and she does."

"It's human nature to present one's best side about something like this, as it is for a young woman in love to perhaps not be as objective about the matter as her family would be.

"Objective as in…a private investigator?"

Walsh waved it off. "It doesn't matter."

"Well, I'm thinking what does matter is that you don't seem to trust your daughter. The facts are these and Katie knows them. It was a turning point in my life, and it scared the shit out of me. I paid a steep price for something stupid I did seven years ago—which isn't that recently, but never mind that. If it happened again I'd walk away. I didn't at the time. The guy was an undercover cop…"

"That doesn't matter in court."

"True, but I didn't know he was a cop at first. I was sitting in my car waiting for my brother to come out of this place off Central Avenue, Rovers. I'd just come home for a day before reporting to the team in Pawtucket, and sure I'd been celebrating but Sean was doing more since I was driving. This guy backs out of his parking spot real fast and creams the side of our car and almost hits Sean. Sean's pissed, bangs on the car; who wouldn't? I get out, the guy gets out, and I take a look, telling Sean to cool it. I ask for the guy's name, insurance information, like you do."

"James…"

I held up a hand. "Please, let me finish. So now the guy tells me to just move my 'fucking car,' and says 'take this asshole with you,' meaning my brother, and shoves Sean as he gets back in his car. That's when I punched through his window. Twice."

"You should have let it go."

"You bet I should have, but I didn't. When he pulled his service revolver I said: 'Why don't you put that away and we'll settle this around the corner of the building.' And we did."

"He said it was two of you against him. That was in the report."

"Sure he did because it wasn't going well for him, even with me only using my right hand. No, it was just the two of us. Sean was there but he wasn't part of it. What he did do was tell me we had visitors right before I heard them shouting behind me. I turned to see two cops pointing their guns at me.

"That was it. I'd broken my left hand, ripped up tendons. Screwed up my wrist. Two operations. I used the last of my signing bonus on the best lawyer I could find and even then I was lucky to get off with probation and a ton of community service. I had no previous record, though Sean had had some problems, but he wasn't the one who put his fist through the window or laid a hand on the guy, and I told them that. My lawyer told me I was very lucky because the judge had a kid playing in the Orioles organization. I was finished with the Red Sox and maybe baseball and the judge knew that, probably felt that was more punishment than his being a hard-ass with me."

I felt like walking out now but I didn't only because that's what Papa John Walsh probably wanted me to do. *See honey, he did it with me, spinning out of control. See what will happen later if you piss him off down the road? I shudder to think what he might do alone with you...*

He said: "You told Katie all this?"

I turned my hand so he could see the scars. "Hard to hide these."

The food had come a while ago. I didn't feel like eating. "So this means you won't be offering me a job," I said.

Papa John still seemed to have an appetite for his Cobb salad. "What would you have said if I did?"

"No thanks."

He mulled that over. "What makes you think I was going to do that?"

I shrugged, thinking of his monograms.

"Shall we move on?" he said. "Katie tells me you're something of a writer. Trying your hand at a novel."

"It's something I've wanted to do for a long time. If this one doesn't go, I'll do another." For some reason I was glad I hadn't told Katie I was also thinking about going to SUNY-Albany for a Master's, then teaching; something to do besides bartending while I was writing. That might have gotten to her father and probably would have pleased him. I wasn't in any mood to please the son-of-a-bitch.

"Well, James," he said, "I'm all for ambition…but writing novels is not what you'd call a real job."

"Depends on what your ambition is. When you were in the fourth grade, did you dream of going into specialty gases?"

Give the man credit, he took that with a smile and surprised me with this: "You know, you really could have a future in business."

Then he began telling me a story of how he had once almost lost his life saving a drowning man years ago. "They'll pull you under, but as you said about the undercover cop, I didn't know that at the time. It's not their fault, understand. They're struggling desperately to survive. But you have to be careful or you'll get dragged under, too."

He was talking about Katie and I, of course, and it was clear who he thought was drowning.

"I'll assume the moral of that story is…not to go near the water."

"Look, I know you've been through a lot—your father, and the problems that caused. Your mother. I understand Sean has had difficulties, attempted…"

"Please leave my family out of this."

"I admire your loyalty…but look at it from my vantage point."

"Yours? This is about Katie and I."

"What I mean is…there's a difference in our worlds, yours and mine."

"What worlds are we talking about? Your bank account versus mine? Cro-Magnon and Neanderthal? Upstairs, downstairs? Your daughter and

I love each other very much. Isn't that enough of a world for you? Is there a time warp here? I don't believe I'm hearing this from you a week after we got back the latest pictures from Mars."

"Calm down, now. My concern is for my daughter; that down the road those differences may not wear well, even though you're a smart, good-looking fellow—and feisty, too, I might add. No wonder Katie likes you. I like you too, but that's beside the point now."

He pushed away his salad and from his jacket took an envelope, slid it toward my half-finished pint of beer. "This is a gift," he said. "I think you understand what I would like you to do if you take it."

I made no move to touch the envelope. "Is this a test?"

"I told you, it's a gift."

"I think I'd like you to be more specific, put the words on the table along with the money in that envelope."

"That isn't necessary. Take a week to think about it if you want."

"That isn't necessary either. You're a piece of work, Mr. Walsh." I scraped back my chair, dropped a twenty on top of my uneaten jerked spice tuna melt, and left.

I COULD DO nothing else for hours afterwards except think about it, especially since I wasn't bartending that night. Not about whether to take him up on his offer to get the hell out of his daughter's life. No. I was thinking about what, if anything, I should tell Katie when she got home. I felt like I should check the calendar, to make sure I'd been sitting across from John Walsh in the right century.

Tell Katie? *Baby, your father just offered me a shit-load of money to dump you...*

What would happen if I did that? I'd never seen her angry, but I sure would for this. She'd be furious and the wound wouldn't heal for a long time, if ever. She'd lose her father, such as he was. Just as I'd lost my own son-of-a-bitch.

Papa John Walsh would likely claim it was a misunderstanding. He'd been careful about not specifically asking me to take a hike. *Sweetie, James misunderstood me. I did talk to him but all I wanted was to get to know the man you're thinking about marrying. Sure, I have doubts; no guy is ever good enough for a father's daughter. But I'd never do what James says I did. It was a gift to celebrate your coming engagement. I think perhaps he's a little sensitive, maybe too proud, you know—a family like his—about financial help…*

He'd turn it into a father's word against mine. And the thought of it would be so incredible that Katie might have doubts. She might have rolled her eyes relating "Papa John stories" in the past, but in the end he was her father. She'd known him for a lot longer than she'd known a washed-up ball player currently tending bar. She might even think I was shifting around the baggage on my personal carousel.

Was this the wedge her father was really after, a fallback plan? Hoping I'd tell her, and with luck sow the seeds of a break-up?

I decided not to tell her. How badly did he want me gone? Let him be the one to go to her, directly, and tell her he didn't want her marrying James Ahrens Malloy: the guy everyone, from Little League through Double-A, always called Jam.

It bothered me that Katie and I might be starting out from the get-go with a secret. My own father must have harbored one because his sudden departure came out-of-the-blue. There had been no slow descent in my parents' marriage that I remembered and believe me I'd tried, even wondering if it had been something I'd done to make any matters worse. No, the day before he went for the ice cream, my mother happily spread out brochures on the dining room table for a trip to Italy, and my father had been the one to bring them home from the travel agency.

I saw the bottom line as saving Katie from a world of hurt, a betrayal on par with the worst.

They say that's what you try to do when you love someone.

SHE CAME BACK at 9 p.m. to my place in Delmar, and we went out for a few drinks so she could tell me about her weekend. We 'fobo-ed'— fucked-our-brains-out—like it had been three months instead of only three days, and then again when the birds began for the day. She liked to wake up and have me inside her. The air-conditioning didn't work well in the Four Corners duplex where I lived behind Andriano's Pizza. We'd gotten used to drying ourselves off with a towel at my place afterwards and we took our time with it, like we did when we'd take turns washing each other in the bath. She called all of that 'babooning,' which got me laughing the first time she said it.

We lay facing each other on the bed. She hummed a few bars of a favorite song that she said her favorite aunt used to sing to her when she was younger: an old Chad Mitchell song called "Quiet Room" or something like that. Then she stopped and whispered in my ear:

"You're just in this for the sex."

"Yup."

"Tell me what you're thinking," she said, and snapped her finger against my forehead.

"That we're going to kill ourselves with lack of sleep."

"Nice try. You've been kind of quiet since I got back. Like the way you get after we visit my family."

"I like your Mom. She's a peach."

"She should have divorced him a long time ago. But at some point, I guess, staying in the basket seems less scary than going out on the shelf. Promise me one thing?"

"Let's hear it first."

"If you ever fall out of love with me, you won't stay in the basket."

"Now where the hell did that come from?"

"Things pop into your head. I couldn't stand it, or respect you if you did. Promise?"

"Okay. But that goes for you, too."

"Never happen," she said.

"Hey, you're not playing by the rules. First rule of the basket, you have to play fair, especially when we fight."

"We haven't had one yet, not really."

"We will."

"Because of all my bad habits?" she said. "What's the worst? Oh, I know: eating off your plate. I'm working on that."

"That's annoying enough but asking me a question and then answering it for me is near the top of the list."

"But I talk quicker than you. And you're a slow eater. Drives me nuts."

"It's healthy, macushla."

"What's that?"

"'My young colt' in Gaelic; something like that, anyway."

"Fucking law texts; you don't learn shit."

"And your mouth."

"Christ, you're no fucking better."

"You're impatient."

"I'm impulsive. Sounds better. You're not. That's one reason why you did so well in baseball. Stay back on the ball, blah blah. Wait for your pitch, blah blah. Stand out there in center-field…waiting…waiting… *ohhh-deee-dohhh—look, there's a dandelion!*"

I laughed so hard her breasts jiggled. "Yeah, but when you gotta move, baby, you gotta *move.*"

I moved all right, right on top of her and kissed both of them.

She snapped my forehead again with two fingers this time. "Time to let it rip?"

"I'd say."

"So it isn't just about the sex then?"

"I didn't say that." I gave her a belly-bob—sort of a Whoopee Cushion sound I made on her stomach. "But while we're on the subject…"

"Which would be me…"

"…how many do you want?"

"Hmmm, maybe three—that seems to be the mold for our families—but it'll be hell on the law career. Then again, you'll have sold the book to the movies so you can stay home, take care of the kids during the day and write by night. How's that?"

"You forgot the part about fishing the manuscript out of the garbage, like Stephen King's wife did when they were living in the trailer."

"A deal then, even the trailer, but I don't think that'll happen—can you kiss the other one, please?"

I did.

"Then they'll be gone," she said. "We have to remind ourselves they're only on loan to us—you know where that's coming from."

Did I ever. "On loan, got it."

"So let's see…our football player joins the ballet, and our daughter runs off with a rapper and…"

"…who cares so long as they phone once in a while. It'll be just you and me then, sitting on the porch, rocking away, and we can't tell if it's the chairs or our bones. And you'll be saying to me"—I gave her my best old codger-ette voice—'Jimmy, it wasn't all about the sex, was it?' And…"

"And that's when you'll pop the blue pill, or whatever color it is then, and jump my bones."

"Okay, it's a plan," I said. "I'm ready. But I don't think your father is. I think he had a Yale-educated doctor in mind for you."

That was the closest I came to telling her about the lunch at Vincent's.

"Hey, Papa John can think what he wants," she said. "He'll come around. I'm not going to lose you."

But she did. And I lost her, two months after we were engaged to be married.

If I'd done what her father wanted, it never would have happened.

CHAPTER 3

FADO

1 p.m., Friday, July 13, 2007

ERIC LANE CASTER took possession of the cabin, bringing with him a thick coil of clothesline rope from the Explorer. He cut the rope in quarters with his knife, put two lengths on the bed in the larger of the two bedrooms, and the other two by the door to the smaller.

He used a fireman's carry to bring Sean in first, dumped him near the wall and shelves filled with books and mementos—hers and probably this Michael Furey from the artist's book she'd written and illustrated.

He left the tape on Sean's ankles and wrists, added the rope, wrapped tape around his mouth. Now that Sean had served his purpose showing Caster the way to Fado, there was no reason to listen to him anymore, hear his mewling, the protestations that he had no idea where his brother was, that he was stalking her solo; or have him shout at Helen that he hadn't intended on doing anything to her; or that he didn't want to die. But the tape wouldn't prevent Sean from weeping all he wanted to, and as Caster left to go get Helen from the Explorer, Sean seemed to be on the verge of doing just that.

Helen was so light a load. Katie had been a tad heavier; Lissa too, but he'd never carried her this way. There was nothing Helen could do except club his legs with her taped hands, kick her legs. All she accomplished was knocking over a vase of flowers from a chest by the door. That got Sean's attention. He sat up, back against the wall, a rug scrunched up around him, wet around the eyes. He squeezed them shut again, as if he didn't want to see her after all, the closest he'd been to her—except for the Explorer—since he waited on her at that restaurant, or so he claimed.

Caster slid her off onto the Mission-style bed. She bucked and twisted but he used his weight to rope first her ankles to the footboard rungs and then her wrists to the headboard's, and that was that. He went to the kitchen, came back with a pint glass of water from a big jug dispenser and drank some before ripping the tape from her mouth. He offered her the rest of the water.

She shook her head.

"What, cooties?"

"Not thirsty."

"If I'm thirsty, you must be. You gave us a run out there." He put the half-filled glass on the flat of the headboard above her head, then trailed his hands through her black hair, drawing it out, the last of it almost long enough to reach the big book that lapped over the edge of the bedside table.

"Do you have a gun here?" he asked.

"No."

"A woman all alone out here in the boonies?"

"I'm not...someone's coming here very soon, so if..."

"Michael?"

He thought he'd get more surprise from her, even shock, but she kept looking at him, scarcely blinking her blues, reminding him of the game he used to play with Lissa: Turn-Off-Your-Eyes. She was giving him nothing: no pleading, little fear. She had to believe he was going to rape her right now. He wanted to know where that unusual composure came from. He made a mental note to remember this moment.

"It is not much of a guess," he said. "A wall out there is filled with his stuff. Your artist's book here has his name on it."

The mention of the artist's book got him something. He could tell she wanted to ask him how he knew what it was. Still, all she said was: "He's coming with a friend of his from college. We were all going to hike this..."

He put a hand over her mouth. "Shhhh…He would have been here for his birthday just a few days ago and that was not the case. Remember? The carriage ride you began alone but finished with company—of a sort."

That got her, all right: the parting lips, a hard swallow. She was about to say something but she couldn't get it out.

He said: "What you did was one of the most remarkable things I have ever seen, and I could make a long list for you. Perhaps you would like that someday." She stiffened when he brushed away a tendril of her hair from her throat.

"You still have on the gloves," he said. He leaned higher over her and took off the soiled garden gloves, loosening one finger at a time. "Just these…for now," he added and placed the gloves in the vale between her breasts. Her hands were sweaty, but clean, unlike his own. He'd wash his thoroughly, of course, but for now a clean dishtowel would do and that's what he brought back from the kitchen.

"I'm wondering," he said, "about the sign you have on a tree at the beginning of the road. Do you pronounce the name *Fah-DOH*?" He took out the roll of tape from a pocket of his vest, and ripped out a length. "At least tell me what it means."

"Look it up."

"I will." He tapped the artist's book. "Perhaps the answer is here and I missed it. Oh, by the way, speaking of names, I told Sean—and his brother too—that mine is Shadden. But for you let's make it Eric—Eric Lane Caster."

He wrapped the tape around her head and mouth. "Michael is not coming, we know that. But someone else might this afternoon, so we cannot have you hear tires on the gravel and start making a fuss." He draped the cloth over the book, and picked it up carefully. It was the size of an atlas and almost as heavy.

Halfway to the door, the book tucked under his arm, he had the feeling he'd done this before, and then the memory coalesced: that one time in church, when his mother, Marla, thought it might do him good to read a passage—Jeremiah, was it?—in front of the congregation, make him feel important as a pastor approaching the pulpit, carrying a Bible high and tight.

He was glad he remembered that because he'd forgotten to tell her the most important thing, so he told her in the doorway: "Sean would have hurt you, done what you thought I was going to do just now. He was watching your house, following you; he even followed you up here, though not all the way to the cabin, but he would have if I had not stopped him. That is how I knew where you were. He showed me the way. Before we leave tonight, he shall get what he deserves, trust me."

CASTER PUT THE swaddled book on the L-shaped table opposite the kitchen area. He could see why she'd chosen this part of the cabin for her working area: the light from a window on the side wall and the larger one in front, one of two that faced the meadow.

He found a broom, swept the pieces of the broken vase and most of the spilled water out the door, because the mess bothered him. He tossed the flowers out as well. He figured she'd keep a gun where it would be handy when she hiked in the forest, with or without Michael Furey. And so it was. He found the gun in the first place he looked: the chest from which she'd knocked off the vase. The .22 wasn't loaded but he found a clip in a bottom drawer of the chest and took care of that, placed the gun on top of the chest, setting aside the decision to use it or his hunting bow to kill Sean later.

Jimmy Malloy's brother stared at him from across the room.

"Not yet," Caster said, thinking maybe he'd use the bow. He was a little rusty, could always use the target practice.

He washed his hands in the kitchen, dried them thoroughly, and sat down at her desk, sliding the book directly in front of him on the towel. It took all of his self-discipline not to scrape back the chair, go to the room, to Helen. But when you've found your One, when you know you are going to be with that someone for the rest of your life, you don't start out like that. When you have someone as beautiful as her you put on the gloves so you won't mar the beauty, like the woman in the gallery asked him to do with her artist's book. You put on the gloves first if you want to turn the pages, even though the gloves the woman had were far too small for his hands.

"You see, Sean, it makes all the difference if you know everything you can first. It is what you were doing, following her, maybe even taking photographs of her, getting to know her. Maybe we are not so different, you and I."

She'd been working on a rough sketch; it looked like one of those locks that raise and lower boats so they can move from one body of water to another. She had everything here she needed to work on the book: jars of pens, paper, rulers, design templates.

Her book was the most beautiful thing he'd ever seen—except for the necklace. From a zippered pocket of his vest, he took out the blue, drawstringed Crown Royal pouch he'd gotten from a waiter he'd robbed who kept his change and tip money in it, then the necklace from the pouch.

The necklace of gold, emeralds and pearls used to be Lissa's, though Katie had liked to wear it after a while, as would Helen in time, the last one who would ever wear it, ask him where he got it and how, and...*is it really 2000 years old? Who wore it do you think? She must have been someone very special...*

As special as the book before him now.

Helen Sommers was an artist and sometimes artists did these one-of-a-kind books. Give it the same age as the necklace and it would be the equivalent of one of those illustrated manuscripts, what was the most famous?—*The Book of Kells*, that was it. Of course, if he tried to sell it, he might get a whopping few hundred dollars from someone who collected these things. It wasn't like she was Picasso, anyone like that, though she was a wonderfully gifted artist; he'd seen that at the gallery. And the necklace, if he ever sold it—which he never would—could be worth ten times the price she and Michael had paid for this property.

His hands had seeped out sweat and he dried them on the edges of the towel, before brushing his fingers over the cover of Helen's book. She had inked the triskell motif—so the gallery woman had said—in swirls of blue, green and gold; impossibly intricate, a maze with three dead-ends. The blue predominated, and he was tempted to go in the room and see if that blue matched her eyes.

Not yet...

He opened the cover and began to read.

THE BOOK OF MICHAEL

WHAT IF ONE of us had to make a choice that Friday in July, when dolphins swam in Lake Shendego? That's the one thing we've never talked about since because there should have been the three of us together, as always.

That summer Michael worked for Wick Houser's best landscaping crew, Petra as a lifeguard at the town pool. I taught beginning art classes at the local Y. On the Friday it happened I was late leaving the clinic. Dr. Pennington was overbooked, running almost an hour late, and because of that I arrived home much later than I expected, around 5:30 p.m. on that hot, muggy day.

The plan was for Michael to pick Petra and I up at home in the Mustang at 4:30 p.m. so we could go together to the shindig at Bannerwood State Park at Lake Shendego. Petra had gotten the okay to leave work early and so did Michael from Houser. As senior class president, Michael had to be there to get things going. Petra and I said we'd help. The three of us had been a package deal for a long time. If Leary Falls hadn't been such a small town, people would have assumed we came from the same family. Anyway, habits are hard to break, especially since two of us would be heading off to college in little more than a month.

I came home to an empty house. Dad wouldn't be back from business in Albany until late that night. Since Mom's car was there I assumed she was giving our German shepherd, Ruckus, a walk along the towpath of the Erie Canal which runs close enough to our front yard for Michael to have once flung a Frisbee onto the deck of a passing motorboat.

Michael had left a note on the kitchen table: *Lennie—Pete and I waited but??? Had to go. Take your mother's car? See you there!*

P.S. Got your home run trot? Since I'm doing the batting order for the game, you're cleanup! Love ya, baby.

He didn't sign his name but drew his usual cartoon head—four or five squiggly lines with a circonflex eyebrow for attitude.

Those were his nicknames for the Sommers girls: Lennie and Pete. He thought our real ones too fancy for a couple of tomboys, one of whom—me—could run faster than he could; well, before he turned fourteen anyway.

I didn't feel like batting cleanup or running now—except to the upstairs bathroom next to the room Petra and I shared even though we didn't have to, and threw up near but not quite in the toilet. Then I turned on the fan, took off my jeans and T-shirt and lay down on my bed.

The sky grew dark, began rumbling. The thunderstorm broke before long, and I had to get up to close the big window overlooking the canal. I suddenly wanted everyone here in the house; my mother home from the storm, and my Dad, but most of all Michael and Petra. I wanted everyone to turn around and come back home.

I waited a few minutes at the window, hoping to catch sight of Mom but maybe she hadn't been with Ruckus on the towpath. I wanted Petra in the room with me so I could tell her about the doctor's visit.

She and I had friends who never understood why we insisted on sharing the room, always had, since our home had once been a rooming house long ago. When we came here to the big house by the canal, there were other bedrooms we could have chosen for our own, individually, but we were certain ghosts resided in them. It stood to reason, the house having once served countless lodgers who brought with them—for a day, a week, a month—their pasts, their secrets, their dreams and nightmares. There may have been a few true stories that came with the house but Petra and I imagined a lot more.

The house hadn't been a fancy place back then. The first time we saw it, we thought: yup, haunted house. When our parents fixed it up with money Dad got from an inheritance from Uncle Tally, we were not convinced the remodel had evicted the ghosts.

Petra and I were excited, of course, to be closer to where Michael lived. It really was a fluke—Dad had had his eye on the property for a long time, but Petra and I thought it was fate with a capitol "F" to be closer to Michael. He'd been a constant presence for our entire lives, ever since Mom agreed to let the newly-hired nanny, one Mary Furey, bring along her two month-old son when she came to care for one-month-old Helen. Petra came along two years later.

Michael believed that one of his ancestors, Callan Furey, who had emigrated from County Clare to work on the canal, might even have stayed at the house, located between two canal locks. In those days the locks were where the action was, Michael said. That included women; sometimes wooed, more often bought. Callan supposedly had charm as long as the canal—and a bit more money to spend since he was a foreman, not just a navvy. He disappeared one day, never to be seen again. Maybe, Michael said, he was murdered by one of his ladies' husbands or lovers.

He spun all this out when he was ten, and on his eleventh birthday the three of us stayed in the spookiest rooms to test them out for ghosts. On the last night of the weekend, in the biggest room overlooking the canal, Petra and I woke to a rustling, a scratching and a raspy voice, just loud enough to hear over the wind and rain of a summer storm.

"Callan Furey, you mick bastard! You're gonna die for what you done, you son of a bitch!"

I don't know who was more terrified—Petra or I—for those few moments. Michael was gone from the camp cot in the room. Then the voice began laughing so loudly we knew it was him out in the storm, and sure as hell he'd wake up our parents on the other side of the house and they'd know he knew swear words like that and wasn't afraid to use them.

I rushed to the window first, opened it up, and with a shriek that prompted a "ssshhhh" from Petra, oblivious to the rain and wind blowing in, I tugged the stick with which Michael had been scratching at the window from his perch in the oak tree. Oh, he was way up there, one arm crooked around a branch, leaning out over nothing to get close enough to that window to tap on it and scare the dickens out of us.

I don't know why I wanted to tug on the stick. Payback? Well, Michael being Michael, he was delighted by the contest. Petra kept whispering: "Lennie…stop…stop! You'll pull him off, he'll fall." I wouldn't let go. Neither would Michael, until the stick broke, ending the tug-of-war, the both of us laughing

He climbed down, tromped into the house sopping wet. I put his clothes in the dryer. Petra fixed the hot chocolate. Wrapped in a beach towel, Michael got the cinnamon for us; he knew our kitchen as well as we did. "Admit it," he said, grinning. "I had you going for a minute."

I nudged Petra with a toe under the table. "The 'son of a bitch' was good, sure," I said.

"I liked the 'mick' part," Petra said. "That's a bad word for Irish, right?"

"But the accent—naah," I said.

"Right, like you've even been to Ireland," Michael said.

"Neither have you."

"Okay, but I watched *Ryan's Daughter* and I wasn't supposed to."

The three of us sat at the kitchen table, like it was our house in some future. Petra went on about how Michael and I were both crazy. She said to me the next day: "You two are either going to be married someday or you'll kill each other."

"Maybe it will be both," I said. "Anyway, it will always be the three of us, Pete, just like last night. Count on it."

I GOT UP about 7 p.m., feeling better after a short nap. The sky to the south had cleared while I slept and I was tempted to head out to the lake to catch the last of the game and picnic, though the beer would be all gone by now.

The phone rang but got picked up downstairs after two rings. So Mom was home. As I dressed I thought about what I had to tell Michael that night, and Petra too.

Mom shouted up to me in a voice that got me out of the room quickly.

Petra and Michael never made it to Bannerwood State Park. They'd been in an accident and were at the hospital in Leary Falls.

The full story of what happened came later, after the police made their rounds with everyone, but that evening it was enough to know that Michael and Petra were going to be okay. She was in intensive care with a collapsed lung, skull fracture, broken collar bone. Michael had a possible arm fracture, a severe concussion and a bruised kidney. Doctors picked out windshield glass from his forehead. Both had almost drowned after the Mustang—with Michael driving—skidded from the highway and off a low bluff and into the lake. There was a wide shoulder to the road there but no guardrail.

This was during the thunderstorm. The police said later there had been a construction-related gravel spill on the highway earlier that afternoon that hadn't been adequately cleared. During the storm a motorcycle skidded, overturned, and Michael must have swerved to avoid it, lost the curve of the road. The Mustang plummeted twenty feet into Lake Shendego where the water was deep enough that divers had to be called in later to get the car out.

Jack and Mary Furey arrived at the hospital shortly after we did. Mom and Mary held hands for a long time in the rooms. The doctor and nurses wouldn't allow us much time with Petra. Michael was unconscious, his head bandaged, one eye swollen shut. He'd broken a wrist, too, but I held his other hand long after I stopped crying.

I didn't know at that point that some of our friends saw the accident; at least saw the car plunge from the bluff in the distance. The closest witnesses were in a boat on the lake and told police they saw a young man in the water go back under twice—and on the third attempt bring up a girl he brought to the shore.

I didn't think about the dolphins then. They came later that night, on the porch, when I was alone again.

MOM AND DAD had been talking for a long time in the kitchen, and then they came out to the porch, gently closing the screen door. Neither sat down in the swing with me but Dad came over, squeezed my shoulder, gave me a kiss on the top of my head and went back in.

"Bad as it is, they're lucky," Mom said. "We're all lucky, honey."

"Remember all the warnings you and Dad gave us about the canal when we moved in," I said. "We couldn't swim then but within a month we'd learned."

"That was at the top of the moving-in list."

"Michael already knew how to swim."

"Thank God he's a good one," she said.

"That doesn't cover what happened, what he did."

"What do you mean?"

"Oh, I don't know." I let it drop and for a few minutes it was just the crickets and us. Then Mom said softly: "It's maybe not the time, but it's been a helluva day and it isn't over yet so we might as well talk about it."

"Talk about what?"

"You're pregnant, aren't you?"

After a moment I nodded. "How did you know?"

"Maternal radar. Does Michael know?"

"I was going to tell him tonight, and Petra."

"What's that little smile for?"

"Your assumption. That it's Michael's and not some secret flavor-of-the-month's."

"That's hardly an assumption, honey. With you two it was never a matter of if, but when."

She leaned over, making the swing move, and kissed me where Dad had. Before she went in she said: "I never thought I'd be grateful to hear my eighteen-year-old daughter tell me she's pregnant two months before she goes off to college."

"Why, because it's Michael's?"

"No, because we could have had you in the hospital along with your sister. But we have to talk about this again, like...tomorrow."

"I know." We could talk but nothing was going to be decided until I told Michael and that wasn't what my mother had in mind.

The door closed and I thought about the dolphins. I know, dolphins in a lake in upstate New York? Still, I couldn't help it. I wondered how many there were in Lake Shendego, and whether there would have been enough to help Michael, if he'd had to save the two of us and not just one, or whether he would have had to choose. Or if I was the one who had to make a choice.

I don't think I could have done it.

WE CAME INTO the world so closely, Michael and I, that our mothers diapered us together. Petra too, soon enough. We were often breast-fed together, learned to pee and shit on the same toilet. In time we often ate at the same table. We never had a choice about each other. There was never a before-and-after with Michael and I, always the present. His existence was as elemental, as constant, as the phases of the moon.

He was Jack and Mary's only child. He always said that when the time came he wanted a large family—which secretly thrilled me. But it was also another way of saying that he always thought Petra and I were lucky to have each other, squabbles and all. For an only child he was adept at keeping his feet between our sibling gauntlet. Petra and I might have, later, compared ourselves, preening and frowning, in front of the full-length mirror in our room, but we could never pull Michael into taking sides.

I always thought Petra was maybe prettier than I was; she had the blonde hair, and I was envious of her legs which I considered more shapely than my tomboy sticks. Petra would joke that I'd been left as a baby at the doorstep, since neither my backside—"you're working on a black woman's ass, Lennie"—or my bust seemed to run in the family, at least so far as Petra and Mom were evidence.

I told Michael what Petra had said, hoping to hear him tell me a big ole booty was a great thing to have.

He held up a finger, like he had to think about it, but I heard him ask my mother for a magnifying glass and she produced one from my father's study. He used it for his stamp collection.

So Michael lined Petra and I up behind the tree, with the tree-house above us, and ran the glass all over us, front and back, like he was hunting for ticks.

"Nope," he said. "I'd say what you have going on there, Lennie, is an Assyrian body; Pete's is more Zoroastrian."

"What the hell are those?" I said.

"Look 'em up," he said. "Now I gotta go to baseball practice." He handed me the magnifying glass. "Give this back to your Mom. We might need to get our story straight so if she asks you two, tell her we were looking at bugs."

"At fifteen?" I said.

"Hey, bugs are beautiful."

Mom once told us that Michael being an only child would likely make him a wonderful husband for some lucky woman—or a terrible one. Either he would always have that need for companionship, which was good for a marriage, she said; or he would always be more comfortable alone, which was not.

But with Michael it wasn't one or the other. He loved to be the center of attention but didn't insist on it, didn't seem to have the need. He could go it alone, do what he called 'hamlet-ing'—which had something to do with processing what was going on in his world. Occasionally that amounted to a day or weekend off in the woods, or in his book-filled room in the house where he lived above the town, writing in his journal. Close as we were then, and still are, he's never showed me the journal. I've never asked to see it.

I've known him all my life, but I still couldn't tell you from where his confidence came. I could talk about his intelligence, his instinctive problem-solving. He had many other friends besides Petra and I. Can you be mysterious at such a young age? He was. I mean, how do you figure a guy who loved to swim, play football and baseball, work on his car and brush the Sommers girls' hair?—mine black, Petra's blonde.

Physically he had a combination of size, grace and strength that drew athletic scholarship offers from Division I schools like Syracuse but he chose Amherst. It was the best college he could get into that was the closest to where I was going to go. I'd chosen Mt. Holyoke for the same reason. We made our picks together.

But the biggest thing about Michael was his will—and that's where his equation runs off the chalkboard. Michael had this kind of…passing lane, and I'm not talking about the Mustang and how he got it from Houser. Michael had an ability to smoothly accelerate to where he wanted to go, in the shortest amount of time. He could work as hard or harder than others; you just didn't notice that. Perhaps even more of a puzzle is that while many people envied him, few resented him, possibly because things happened when he was around: the things people wanted to remember, not forget.

He was invariably the youngest to do those things—certainly getting the Mustang was one of them. The exception was with me, when we first had sex, losing our virginity in the treehouse of all places, that he, Petra and I built one summer in a beech tree that hung over the towpath not far from our house. Michael called it our 'cherry tree,' of course.

We were sixteen. Some of our friends had already taken 'Route 66'—as he called it. I have no idea why he merged sex with that that old TV show, which I doubt he'd ever seen. Everyone had always assumed Michael and I would be the first. We could have, even at thirteen. Maybe it was this unspoken thing that we both knew we were in this for keeps, so what was the rush? I don't know. There were times we might have, like the time I wanted him to give me a spanking—again up in the treehouse—because I'd come across some books my mother had hidden away and I was curious about something that had never happened to me. Oh, was I curious! Maybe even as much as Michael. But we didn't take Route 66 then or other times. One or the other of us would start giggling or laughing and it never happened until it happened.

It started with us laughing about the water balloon fight we'd had with condoms up in the treehouse the first time Michael showed them to me at thirteen. We hadn't been up there in a while and we went up for good this time at sixteen and we used a condom all right, but the last time we used one—when Petra was away at a friend's house and my parents were out for the evening—it must have been defective. A pre-owned rubber, a retread, a loser of a condom that caused a big-time glitch that was going to have to have a name.

Michael didn't know yet and I still had a choice, I suppose, to tell him or not. He'd never know. The accident could have been the excuse not to tell him, and do the thing that my parents wanted me to do. But Michael and I had never had secrets and I wasn't going to start now and keep it for the rest of our lives together. He had to know. We would decide things together.

I TOLD HIM two weeks later, the Tuesday after Petra came home from the hospital and we spent the rest of the afternoon talking about what we were going to do. We'd pretty much talked out the accident, all except for the dolphins. I didn't mention them exactly, but I came close enough.

A year before, he had spent the summer traveling in Europe, with money he'd saved up from the job with Houser. Major getaway time, he said. I'd taken mine the year before, if you could count going with my family.

Michael went first to Ireland to visit the Fureys' ancestral village, Inchmahulish, in County Clare. In the middle of a lake near the village there is an island with a ring-fort where the Fureys supposedly took refuge from Viking raiders coming up the Shannon, so Michael said. No one knew for sure. He was probably imagining that. What guy could resist the images of Viking longboats, broadswords and axes and his brave Celtic ancestors defending stony ramparts? When he came back he promised Petra and I he'd take us there someday.

He bummed around, hitching or taking trains, getting all the way to the Dalmatian coast where he met a Brit named Tony and a Swede named Per, both in their mid-twenties. Michael was seventeen but it was his idea, evidently, to free the dolphins.

The three spent a lot of time on the Bodrum Peninsula which sticks out between the Aegean and the Mediterranean, and in Turkbuku they heard about the penned dolphins. Russian black-marketers wanted to sell them to the Turks or anyone who had money in Turkbuku, for saffron, looted antiquities from a new archaeological dig near Ephesus, whatever they could get. They even had a polar bear in a cage with ice and blowers on their shabby freighter. Word also had them hiding Siberian tigers below decks but Michael said he never saw those, if they even existed. The dolphin net was slung alongside the ship.

So Michael, Per and Tony rented scuba gear, practiced one night, did it the next—swimming out to the ships, cutting the nets and letting the dolphins go. They'd expected more than the two but figured the Russians had already sold some. Michael saw only the two. He said they—and he swore this was true—swam back. The dolphins could have kept going but they came back. Michael felt the dolphins graze his legs, and then they left.

"They were thanking us, Lennie," he said. "What else could it have been?"

The caper somehow made the Reuters wire. I didn't want to think about what the Russians or Turks would have done if they'd caught the trio. But Michael? He never once thought they couldn't pull it off. He'd never used scuba gear before, though Tony evidently had.

That afternoon I drew two things on his cast that he couldn't see until the damn thing came off. He never said anything about it later, so maybe he never saw them, just chucked the plaster.

I drew two dolphins.

They're not in Lake Shendego, anymore. I know…I know. But I'll always believe dolphins were there for Michael when he needed them, that third time he went under to get Petra. I have the dolphins with me now in—or rather on—one of his favorite places.

Les Deux. I had them done at a tattoo parlor on Central Avenue in Albany.

My idea, his name. He has a knack, always had, for coming up with the right word (even if he mangled the French a bit in this instance), the right name, the one to remember. There was an exception to that.

I was the one who named our son.

CHAPTER 4
THE NECKLACE

October, 2005

NOT LONG AFTER Katie and I got engaged we rented a two-bedroom house on Fernbank Avenue in Delmar, for the fireplace, big back yard and proximity to our jobs in Albany. She'd been working for three months already at Stauffer & Kline, a firm specializing in environmental law. She loved the job.

Two weeks into September I took a sort of pre-season bachelor party—a four-day hiking trip in the Adirondacks with a couple of ex-teammates from Penn State with whom I'd kept in touch, Bennie Branson and Chulu Jones.

Now it was Katy's turn: a long weekend in the Boston area. She was going to help Ellen and her new husband, Peter Cunningham, move from their old place on Trapelo Road in Belmont to Westwood, a leafy suburb southwest of Boston. Two other friends were going to help, one of whom had just gotten engaged as well. Katie billed it as sort of a Fellowship of the Rings—with packing boxes.

She left on a Friday, around 3 p.m., with a wave and a honk of the horn. She hoped the local forecast of warmer weather would extend to Boston.

Ellen called the following morning at nine, waking me up. I usually slept until 11 a.m. after I had closed the bar the previous night.

Katie had no-showed.

I dropped the phone as Ellen began asking me if there had been a mix-up in plans, if she was sick—and hurried downstairs, blasted awake, snakes squirming in my gut. Maybe she'd come back too late for bed, maybe she was in the kitchen. She wasn't downstairs. I looked outside. Only my car was in the driveway.

Ellen was still there when I got back to the phone—"*Jimmy...Jimmy, are you there...what's going on?*" We tried to stay calm about it. No, Katie hadn't mentioned any stops she wanted to make but maybe she'd had car problems. Ellen pointed out the obvious: Katie would have called either her or me if that was the case.

After a shaky goodbye I quickly called Katie's parents, then her brothers Tim and Brad. She wasn't with any of them. I called the New York and Massachusetts state police: no reports of any accident, a disabled or abandoned vehicle matching Katie's Honda Civic. I wanted to get in my car and start looking myself but at this point that's what the state police were for. I decided it was better to be here, by the phone, when Katie called. She *would* be calling, with a simple explanation to account for the missing hours.

By late afternoon I was way past worry: the police still hadn't located the car.

There was no way I could work that night.

Or the next.

I couldn't stand the waiting any longer, had to do something to get away from the feeling of helplessness and dread. It might have been useless to go looking for her, with the police in two states doing that now, but I did anyway at seven in the morning that Sunday. Wherever Katie was she hadn't arrived in Boston.

I crashed for the night with them amidst all the boxes, talking long into the night in useless speculation freighted with longer silences about what could have happened. I drove back early Monday, giving in to the hope that Katie would be home, greeting me with: *Jimmy, you wouldn't believe what happened...*

That afternoon I called her father. He had already filed a missing person report but I went ahead and did the same after the man hung up on me, as if Katie's disappearance was my fault. The attitude of the police dismayed me but I understood it. They were never initially serious about adult disappearances that didn't carry a strong whiff of something worse. It wasn't a crime if an adult didn't show up where she was supposed to. For all the police knew she could have had a nasty quarrel with me, or run off with an ex-boyfriend or taken a…walkabout to reconsider one of the biggest decisions of her life.

I GOT THE initial attention when an investigation did ensue. I wasn't the husband—always the first stop—but as her fiancé I came a close second. By the time I'd finished with the New York State Police Bureau of Crime Investigation and then the FBI in Albany, Katie had been missing for over three weeks and the NCIC computers hadn't delivered any matches given the information put in about her.

I told them everything I could think of—including John Walsh's lack of enthusiasm about the engagement, leaving out the money part only because Walsh would have relayed his dim regard for the guy who once had a fist fight with an undercover Albany cop. They knew about that, of course, but I didn't wait to be asked.

I stayed on three lists though not long on the official one. A neighbor, Bill Carlson, who had been mowing his lawn next to ours, had seen Katie and I kiss on the front porch, seen her leaving, seen her wave, heard her honking the horn. Half an hour later he and I were chatting about the NFL Giants' prospects for the coming season as I stretched on the lawn prior to going for a run. My car had been in the driveway until I drove to work that night.

The second one? John Walsh's. He needed someone to blame.

The third was my own.

Katie had wanted me to go with her that weekend. I'd said no. I wanted to work on the book.

MONTHS FOLLOWED.

On my days off I drove to Boston and back, taking exits along the way—Stockbridge, Lee, Springfield, Worcester, all of them—talking to people at gas stations, convenience store clerks, anyone who might remember a pretty woman in her late twenties, with shoulder-length blonde hair, stopping in a forest-green Honda sedan with stuffed animals crowding the back seat ledge.

Christmas came. I didn't hear from anyone in her family, nor did I do anything to keep the connection. What do you say?

I bought presents for Katie, one of them a Welsh miner's lamp from an importer out near Seattle, of all places. One night the summer before, Katie and I had polished off a bottle of wine as we talked about what makes things last—year in, year out—and how we might deal with the inevitable familiarity, the ebb and flow of desire. We knew there would be some days, weeks or even months when one of us, or both, might even wonder if it was going to last. What kept things going? Maybe it was like a lantern, I said. The flame within might be bright or dim but either way it was the lantern that let it shine through, protecting what was there. Well, bad as the Welsh miner's lantern analogy was, at least I hadn't offered a baseball cliché.

I put her presents under a small tree, as if that might do it, and she would wake me up, smiling, wait for me to come downstairs before she opened them. We'd been together long enough to know holiday patterns. I'd become a night owl, sleeping late, and probably would have even with the kids that would never happen now...*Let Daddy sleep a bit longer, okay? Then you can go pounce on him and wake him up...*

That Christmas day was no different than any other since Katie disappeared. I left the house hoping that when I came back she'd be there. I went to Marcy's for dinner and when I came back Katie's gifts were still under the tree.

I began drinking more than I ever had before, telling myself it was only to help me get to sleep, get away from the thoughts that kept floating out there in the deep water.

Maybe Papa John was responsible. His own daughter? But who knew what lengths a man like him would go to be...right. A control freak like that might do anything to prevent his daughter from making the mistake of her life; he had no doubts about that. Katie always had said she didn't give a shit about the family money, the trust funds, but when faced with a father who said he'd cut her off if she married me, maybe she blinked. She loved the sun; summer was her favorite season. Maybe she was in San Diego now, set up by Daddy, and still working up the courage to write me.

Or maybe she'd had second thoughts about the coming marriage and never mind Papa John.

Or maybe she simply met someone else. She'd been in that law office long enough to see all the Ivy-bird plumage, and decided on her own that her world and mine wouldn't work after all: *this is my husband Jim, he's a bartender but he's working on a novel.* Me and a hundred thousand other bartenders from Portland, Maine to Portland, Oregon.

Those months after she disappeared I was out there, all right, treading in this deep water. You think you know a person, but you really can't. I thought I knew my father. I loved him. We all did. Pipe, model train set up in the basement, sports pages and all. A guy who never raised his voice. And one day he disappeared too. Sean took a baseball bat to the HO scale trains one day a year after, smashing them all to pieces except one I saved, a Great Northern caboose, with the goat-on-a-rock logo. It's at Marcy's, too.

Of course the theories were nuts, though I took a little pleasure in the one about Papa John, because I could blame him and not myself for not going with Katie for that weekend. I knew they didn't make any sense. Even if there had been someone else, or Katie had gotten wet feet about marrying an ex-ballplayer still struggling to work himself back in the lineup—any lineup—she would have told me, face to face. Closer to shore, away from the deep water, I truly believed that. She would not just have…taken off.

So the theories were useless, except for one thing, the alternative: she was dead. Caught in the wrong place, wrong time.

I kept hoping. I bought her a present for her birthday, March 7, which came and went but I put the present on our bureau anyway. I kept our house spotless, in better shape than before, a private deal. If I'd let other things slide since she disappeared—including my sobriety—I'd keep our place like it was before, better even.

When my sister came over to visit, she said nothing about my living like Katie was still there, just out for an errand. She saw the fresh-cut flowers I kept on the dining room table, changed every other day like Katie used to do, and said nothing.

Katie presence...

One Saturday she came over with Davy and found the tea kettle on simmer, the water boiled off, the stink of burnt metal in the kitchen air, and me upstairs, still sleeping. I had gotten up earlier, hangover and all, to put the water on, like we'd do, Katie and I, taking turns with having the coffee ready for the other. And I'd gone back to bed.

Katie presence...

Marcy might have told me it was time to move on, but all she said was: "You better be more careful, kiddo, or you'll burn the house down."

She saw the profusion of phone messages I kept tacked up on the kitchen bulletin board, all for Katie, from peripheral acquaintances who hadn't heard yet. No doubt my sister wondered when I *would* be moving on. She saw how clean the place was, and maybe she remembered those months after our father took off and never came back. My room had always been a mess. But after Dad left, I cleaned up my act, kept it that way. When you're that young you think that maybe your pigsty of a room had something to do with it.

At some point in the months after, this idea had taken root: that I could *will* her back, in a mutation of what I had often felt I could do in a ball game—conjuring up the late-inning base hit with two strikes, two out. So what? Or better yet, a walk-off home run. I'd had two over the years. If you can't at least believe you *can* do it, you never will.

For a few minutes late one night in May I thought I had done.

That Friday I was the early guy off in the bar. I should have gone home but I went down the street to the Triple Door and should have stopped with the three pints of Guinness, but I followed that with two shots of Red Breast that were more than singles because the bartender was a friend and I always poured heavy for him when he came to my place.

When I got home I flicked the light on, kicked off my shoes at the door, like Katie and I always did coming in...and there it was, the first thing I saw walking into the living room: the green dragon on top of the TV, the thick spiky tail hanging almost to the DVD recorder below.

It was one of Katie's stuffed animals, the last one I'd given her to add to her collection. I won it for her at the Altamont Fair a month before she disappeared, knocking down the bottles, one after another, until the barker cut me off. I loved it that Katie—a future partner at a top-tier Albany law firm—collected stuffed animals, had that side to her, like H.G. Wells with his toy soldiers.

I yelled: "*KATIE?!*"

She'd come back. Wherever she'd been—Costa Rica, Mexico, wherever the hell—with money she'd saved up, not Daddy's, she was back from her walkabout. I spun out the story: *Somewhere between Albany and Boston she'd decided she needed time away from both men in her life, her father and I, before she settled down once and for all…*

She owed me and a lot of people big-time for what she'd done. But maybe it didn't have to be a deal-breaker.

"*KATIE!*"

Her car wasn't out front. I kept spinning: *She sold it for cash, took the stuffed animals from the back seat ledge of her car…*They were the last thing I'd seen when she drove away.

I raced to the foot of the stairs, shouting her name again, then louder, expecting her to appear, sleepy, from our bedroom.

"*KAATIEE?*"

I took the carpeted stairs two at a time, ran to the bedroom.

The bed was empty.

I checked the room I used for my study, then the bathroom. Maybe she was sick…*she came back sick…*She would have heard me but I checked anyway.

I stopped at the top of the stairs, hearing only the hum of the refrigerator compressor kicking in downstairs.

Who had left the dragon then? One of the Walshes? Brad or Tim, sent by Papa John? Maybe one of them had left the stuffed animal, bought a look-alike. Why? A sick reminder? *Fuck what the cops think. We know you did it…*

No, not even John Walsh would do something like this, pretend to bring her back as a way to punish the one he wanted to blame for her disappearance. Someone else, a neighbor, friend of the family, convinced I was guilty and wanted to make the point? When my Irish-Yankee grandfather lived briefly in North Carolina, he used to get hate mail and bags of shit on the front porch from people who thought him too friendly with "the coloreds."

So someone broke into the house to deliver a message: *The cops are letting you off scot-free but we know you did it...*

But it had to be her. I hurried downstairs thinking: *She's left again, why her car isn't there; she's gone to get some things...the all-night supermarket a few miles away...be back any minute now and...*

And we would try to reset the calendar, see if we could get beyond all those months she'd been gone without letting me the fuck know where she was; and we'd make love and I'd trace every inch of her Costa Rican tan lines before we made love again.

I went into the living room again but I couldn't keep the delusion going any longer, waiting for the echo of her name to come back with mine.

She wasn't back. Her car should have been here. More lights in the house should have been on, not just the one. I hadn't noticed what lay under the dragon because all I'd seen from halfway across the living room was the stuffed animal, and what I'd wanted to see was Katie, sure I would see her in this house again. But with the truth came a different acuity, things as they are...such as the small, light blue card the dragon held in its tiny furry claws.

Closer now, right in front of the TV I could also see the transparent tape that held it in place, and see what Katie had written on the piece of card: *HI, JIMMY!*

Even then I thought she'd come back with the dragon, left this as a way to explain, an apology by proxy, unable to face me after all the months, but cruelly casual, as if nothing had ever happened...*Hi, Jimmy!...*

I put the dragon on the floor.

There was another note on the same blue card: *I HOPE YOU LIKE THIS, BABY! LOVE, LISSA.*

It occurred to me not to touch the slim plastic case enclosing the silvery DVD within. But I was going to watch it, would have to watch it—in the police station on Division Street here, or in the federal building in Albany, in the company of FBI agents. Not doing so now was like trying to fight a magnetic field…because Katie was on that tape, with the answer to what had happened to her.

I didn't know any *Lissa*.

But I knew Katie's handwriting, just as I knew that whoever had left this was not the woman I loved. I tried not to touch it.

Take it to the cops. Take it now…Don't watch it, don't do what he wanted… For the love of Christ don't watch what he wanted you to watch…

He?

I tried to walk away—what I should have done, too, before, even after the undercover cop shoved my brother to the ground. I should have just lifted Sean up and said, *Let's get out of here.*

I tried and maybe that's why the towel in my hand surprised me because I couldn't remember going into the kitchen to get it. I picked up the DVD case with the towel, opened it up, took the DVD out. Sometimes the last thing you want to do is the only thing you can do. I kept the towel in my hand to smother the shaking. It didn't help.

I sat on the edge of the couch to watch because I couldn't stand; my legs wouldn't let me.

Katie lay on a bed in a brightly lit room devoid of other furniture except a bureau and a captain's chair facing the corner of the bed. Nothing adorned the white walls. Cut flowers rose from a blue vase on the bureau. She had arranged the stuffed animals on the bed, as if she had not yet begun to play with them. The light blue cards—the same ones in our living room—were arranged neatly next to a marker on a yellow legal pad at the foot of the bed.

Her blond hair was much longer now. She knelt in the middle of the bed, sheets and covers bunched up to her breasts, wearing only a black slip, and a necklace of gold, emeralds and pearls, a necklace only her father could have afforded to give her.

She was thinner, paler, gaunt, the circles under her eyes dark as bruises. She smiled at me, as if she didn't know how terrible she looked. Maybe she didn't. She pouted her lips.

"Jiiimmmy, where have you been?"

That's when I lost it, squeezed my eyes shut, wanted to keep them shut, turn the thing off but I had to look again. She was here...here again after six months, bouncing a little on the bed, like she was excited to see me. Then she stopped, drew a forefinger in an arc around her neck, tracing the necklace.

"Thank you, Jimmy. It's the most beautiful gift I've ever received."

She glanced to her right, where he was, whoever was doing this to her: "May I sing it now?"

I heard no response. There must have been a nod. She curled, uncurled her fingers, nervous for this...audition. "Okay, here goes. Break a leg." She cleared her throat, and began softly.

"They're gonna put me in the movies...they're gonna make a big star outta me..."

Her left hand splayed on her breasts with the first *me*; her right on the second.

"I'll play the part, and I won't need rehearsing...all I gotta do is...act naturally."

Katie looked to her right, looking for approval and beamed when she got it: a loud clapping. I felt as a stab in the gut.

"*Now* do I get the mirror?" she asked. "You said I could have one, Jimmy, after I did the cards for Lissa and sang the song."

The screen dissolved into blackness, but came back, the camera focusing on the window, then panning to the bed where Katie lay now on her side, in a hurdler's pose, legs separated and bent, one arm outstretched, the other behind her resting on the crumpled ridge of blankets and sheets. Her black slip rose above the swell of her belly.

She was pregnant.

Katie...oh, Jesus...Katie...

I slid to the floor from the edge of the couch, wanting to keep going, keep falling away from this. I kept looking because I wanted to see her move, wanted to believe she was only sleeping. But the abrasions around her neck were still red. Her hazel eyes, hugely open, stared at the window across from the bed at snow rimming the panes of glass. The camera went that way, leading me to the window, focusing on the falling snow, the only movement in the frame, until the screen dissolved with more clapping.

I waited for her killer to show himself, a face hidden by a mask, to say why he'd taken her, kept her for months, to tell me why murdering her wasn't enough, why he'd come here to deliver this.

No one showed. The screen was still black.

I couldn't move from the floor.

Jimmy, where have you been?

I still had the towel in my hand, which made me think of the gun I kept wrapped up in a cigar box in the cellar, a .38 I'd found among my father's things a year after he left. I never told Sean about it—nor had I told Katie.

Get it. Call the cops…Get the gun…in case he comes back.

But wherever he was now, he wouldn't come back to the house, not with the cops here soon.

Jimmy, where have you been?

And tell them…*oh Christ, Katie…*tell them I had no idea who he was, why he had done this, why he'd left a note…

…I hope you like this baby! Love, Lissa…

…with the name of a woman I didn't know.

Get it now…get the gun…

I almost made it up from the floor.

He stood three feet away, his back to the kitchen, face hidden by a camo mask. All I saw before he punched me was a tattoo on his arm. A skull in the shape of a windmill.

I got my arms up but was off balance and the fist came right over. He wore thin, padded gloves. I'd never been hit so hard in my life.

The back of my head hit the edge of the coffee table by the couch. I tried to get up but the floor tilted crazily. My arms slid through a pile of magazines and books. He grabbed my arm, spun me around, threw a short punch to the side of my head and the last thing I remembered was the holes in the mask, the flash of eye-whites and teeth.

CHAPTER 5

FADO

4 p.m. Friday, July 8, 2007

SEAN HEARD NOTHING from the other room where Shadden stashed her: no screaming or shouting. If she was crying, she was doing it quietly or maybe he'd taped her mouth, too. Breathing through his nose, sucking on the tape, he could not quite mask the rustle of the turning pages. For a while Sean counted, then gave it up at fifty-seven. What was the point?

The psycho fucker was an incredibly fast reader, always turning the big book's pages with his left hand, the left arm tattooed with the black windmill/skull and blood-red vanes, that marked him as the man Jimmy told him about, all Jimmy had seen that night at his home in Delmar.

And what was the point to keep berating himself—*you stupid fuck*—for not telling Jimmy; for not tracking him down through Marcy when he saw that tattoo, saw the guy. But he'd wanted to wrap the ribbon on Shadden, put him in a box and give it to his younger brother. He had it all worked out: *See what I did, Jimmy? Now maybe you'll forgive me after I tell you something I should have a long time ago.*

Shadden turned another page, a slight rustle.

He'd screwed up for good this time; no second chance, no time for any kind of confession. Jimmy—and Marcy—would never know.

He had to piss, and his legs and arms were stiff and ached like hell, but at least his eyes could move around the room. The circuit began and ended with that gun on the chest by the front door, opposite the room where Helen was, near the kitchen area and a wood stove. He wouldn't kill her immediately, maybe not for a long while; he hadn't with Katie. Was that any better than knowing you were going to die later rather than sooner?

Another page, another rustle.

The big hearth separated the two bedrooms, faced the couch. There was no window on the wall to Sean's right, only the shelves of books and mementos, and above them plaques and sports awards, a #*25* football jersey, a diploma, some framed newspaper articles. Sean still had his 20-20 vision—not as good as Jimmy's 20-15 last he knew—so he could see the name on the diploma from Leary Falls High School: Michael Furey.

The guy had to be her husband. Sean had seen the ring at the restaurant where he'd waited on her, ages ago it seemed. And where was he now? Getting groceries in Pattison? Doing an errand in Bellingham?

Sean had to piss real bad now; he couldn't hold it anymore and let go, drenching himself, feeling the wet warmth. It wasn't like there was a puddle after; his pants soaked it all in, but he moved away and that gave him the idea, the only one worth a damn now. What if he kept moving, closer to the window? So that…if someone, maybe even this Michael Furey, came here, there was something he could do, even if he couldn't scream.

He scrunched ahead, inch by inch, on his side toward the window. A sliver from the wood floor needled into his hip, a big one. The tape muffled his grunt of pain but not completely. Shadden didn't glance at him. Whatever was in that big book of Helen's had him good, like *he* was the one bound hand and foot.

Sean snaked halfway across the room, the time it took Shadden to turn another twenty pages. He figured another six or seven feet and he'd be close enough to the window when a car came; close enough to get up…and before Shadden could stop him, crash through the window, panes and all. Michael Furey—whoever it was—would realize something was very wrong in the cabin. Of course he wouldn't quickly leave to go call the cops. His wife was in the cabin. Shadden had the gun right over there, would kill him too.

Still, Sean decided he'd do the only thing that might give Furey a chance to get away.

It wouldn't be the first time Sean crashed through a sheet of glass.

He got another two feet, then heard a slightly louder sound from the desk where Shadden was reading, and it wasn't the whisper of a turning page but him patting the cover of the book. *Oh God, he's done…*

Shadden sat there, staring at it. Sean waited for him to look up, see him not where he'd left him by the door to the room. A minute passed before he looked over at Sean. Then he smiled, as if he'd remembered what had to be done now.

Shadden scraped the chair back, came over to Sean and pulled him back across the room to the bunched up rug, and walked away. Sean closed his eyes. He didn't want to see the fucker pick up the gun, come back over with it…

He heard the scrape of the chair again and opened his eyes to Shadden at the desk once more, talking about "a little change of plans," then: "You should know something about her and where you are going to die, where your brother will find you sooner or later, outside in the meadow, with the crows picking away at you; or maybe you will draw something else out of the forest, wolves perhaps. But for now, Sean, would you like to listen? Think of it as a reward for leading me here."

Sean Malloy looked away from him, toward the window, listening for that car he knew would never come in time now to save Helen and him. He closed his eyes as Shadden began to read from the book. When he opened them again, the book was closed. Shadden wasn't reading from it.

He was reciting:

> …So going up to Fado was like going back in time, to a very real, yet secret lover. It's the place where I began *The Book of Michael* as it exists now, anyway, and continue still, often in dawn hours so fresh with dreams—always my favorite hours for making love; a time when it does seem possible to wade into the same river twice.
>
> Only a few friends know Fado exists. Of course, there have been the men who built it, five years ago, and those who've done

the few things I didn't want to do myself, like dig the privy, or the root cellar—the "spring house" as Michael prefers to call it. I've served up hot coffee to my snowplower and once a lost hunter who shouldn't have been out there in the woods alone, much less on Christmas Eve.

But no one close to me—no one except Michael, Petra and Callan—has ever been inside and it's not because I'm afraid of what friends might think about what's inside, or the Mustang I keep under wraps and drive only on the best days in summer, taking the road at a pace as slow as a walk so gravel doesn't ding the car.

Fado is a place for just Michael and I—and our child. And Petra. She's the reason for the second room. Anyway, who brings friends, or lovers, back to where you honeymooned? Well, Michael and I never had one, so I created one for us here, with his help.

He is most at home in Fado—or so he says. A home away from home, with much of his stuff around him, including the Mustang. No, not the same one that was taken from Lake Shendego. But it's the same color and year, has the same LF Spartans decal on the back. And it runs as well as the original.

I don't think friends would understand our arrangement, because they'd have to know entire lives. Alone of my friends, oddly enough, it is the oldest, Barbara, who might understand how I could have chosen to leave my son in Leary Falls with Michael, yet no one could really know him as I do, what a wonderful father he is. Nor could they know that Petra, with her more practical, quiet way, is probably as good a mother to my son as I. Maybe better. All of them are always here, even when they're not. This is their home away from home. They visit here and I go back to Leary Falls once a year, to see them all.

Michael knows I have had lovers, and these lovers have known—I've told them up front—that whatever we share is finite. Beyond that there is Michael. Some have wanted to know his name, who he is; I won't tell them. Michael and Petra have been lovers, of course. Who but we could understand how I can accept that, or Michael my occasional lover. Petra and I never shared Michael then, but we do now. It is our universe, almost from birth, with its peculiar gravitational field and natural laws that nevertheless are supremely balanced for us. Why should that change? To change that, you'd have to alter the axis of the earth, the phases of the moon.

This might be the most difficult thing for others to understand: why Michael remained in Leary Falls, and why I chose to leave. Everyone assumed he would charge out into the world and possibly change it, but he stayed in that small Mohawk River valley town on the Erie Canal. Why? For an answer they would have had to have known Michael as I did.

His imagination opened doors to the world—some he created, some he didn't—when we were young. In the end, that imagination was enough for him. I mean, they say that Isaac Newton never saw the ocean and never got laid.

Anyway, after you've risked your life saving dolphins in Turkey, or swum in Doon Lake in County Clare, racing Petra, wee Callan and I (in the rowboat) to the shore (and winning!) where else can you go?

Why did I leave? Perhaps because I never had Michael's imagination and always wanted doors of my own. Sharing his and being the beneficiary proved insufficient ultimately. There is a kind of claustrophobia attendant to that. Perhaps even Michael couldn't give it a name. So if I couldn't see, as he could, what was out there, I had to see for myself. He understood. He knew he would never lose me, just as I know I will never lose him. We've known that all our lives.

His imagination included Fado, of course. I may have had it built, but the idea was his. He said everyone needed a refuge. He said that in our fifteenth summer, well past a kid's prime treehouse years, but he said it in the treehouse and he sounded like—the way he said it—a guy pushing fifty and knowing what he was talking about, consequences and all, and never mind he was soaked from the water balloon fight we'd had and still had a smear of his beloved peanut butter on his T-shirt from lunch.

Petra had just climbed down the knotted rope to go change her clothes, though she'd gotten soaked the least. There was no ladder. When we built the treehouse Michael insisted there be only a rope to get down and up, so our arms would get stronger. The knots in the rope were my suggestion and Petra sided with me. Michael was outvoted. I think he secretly liked it when we ganged up on him.

He was fifteen, always and forever a month older than I. And fifteen feet off the ground we sat close enough for our knees to touch. It was easy for me to think it was just as likely he was talking about…us…as the refuge. He sounded so old when he said it, and I had the quick picture then—maybe because my grandparents were visiting at the time from "Narch" (Norwich, N.Y.)—of Michael and I growing old together. There would be no treehouse, just canes and walkers, so there'd be no doubt about this place he wanted.

He had his mind on a piece of land even then, and the cabin we'd build. As I recall, he first mentioned it when he came back from Europe—with the Irish harp tattoo he got done on Grafton Street in Dublin. Maybe seeing the old Furey sod in County Clare got him thinking. It had probably been on his mind a while, though, since his parents had always rented and occasionally were forced to move within the town. They were going to buy a home once, but Mary had a serious illness—meningitis, I think—and the money they'd saved had to go help pay her medical bills so that never happened. Jack and Mary refused Dad's offer to help out.

Michael said we should get "a piece of the rock" somewhere and build a cabin from scratch, using timber from the property. He always carried the ball, whether on the football field or off, and he did so now, getting books from the library. We drew up plans, the three of us. I loved the sketches from one book in particular from the '50s by Conrad Meinecke.

Here's a confession: we kept that book. My story about what happened to it was better than Michael's, we agreed, so that was the one we gave Mrs. Parks at the Carnegie library, and we pitched in to pay the fine years after she died. It's at Fado now, of course, on the shelf.

I bought the land after I came out to the Northwest and sold two paintings to the same buyer. I refined the cabin's design, with Michael and Petra looking over my shoulder, here or by phone. Petra once said: "But there won't be electricity or indoor plumbing." To which Michael replied: "Well…yeah, Pete; that's what it's all about."

He was a big help. We couldn't have done it without him, even though he and Petra couldn't do some of the physical work—they still have physical problem from the accident, and probably always will. So Mt. Baker Construction built it for the most part, using nearby firs and cedars for the shakes and siding. I later got handy with a chainsaw, cutting down trees to increase the southern exposure, and had a guy remove the stumps. We wanted a garden and space where Callan could run. The trees weren't that big, mostly second or third growth; the old fellas had been logged many years before, about the time the gold mines in the area played out. There's still a few of those you can enter, if you dare.

I split some of the log sections myself, cutting them up until the blisters got bad but then I paid Barb Hollner's boy to do the rest. You need a lot of cords of wood for the stove and hearth in the winter and you have to begin the cutting in the summer.

Even when Michael's not here, there's much to explore and do: go to Bellingham for a fancy meal, browsing at Village Books, tending the garden and polishing the Mustang, and always hiking. When I go out, just in case, I always carry a handgun for the cougars and bears—and now wolves.

There's also swims in the small lake beyond the rapids chute by the escarpment and old mining track and smaller lakes if you go east a mile from the creek bridge. Birthday-Suit Lake...Lizard Lake...Moonlight Lake. Michael named them all, even though they already had names on the map. He always does the naming, even now. The shelving rock of Lizard Lake is perfect for sunbathing in the buff, or doing the same at night under a full moon. The three of us did that once at Lake Shendego. Moonbathing, Michael called it. Here, at night, when we do that, I can't see the scars from the accident but he's kept his wonderful body in shape. It's taken a lot of work, but he says now he's as strong as he was before the accident, and I have to agree...

"I THINK THAT'S enough, don't you, Sean?"

He didn't remember much of what Shadden recited. He was left with what Shadden wanted to leave him: *I can read every word she's written here, just once, and I have it all.* He could have made up a lot of it, but Sean knew that couldn't be. The man recited without a pause, like he was reading it off the page yet the book stayed closed. If he had winged it that only made him more of a freak…

…A freak who now got up and went into the room to get Helen and bring her out because it was time now, the little "reward" over. When Shadden was finished with her…

Sean couldn't stop the shakes, couldn't breathe right with the tape over his mouth, kept sucking on it, in and out, snuffing through his nose. He tried closing his eyes, but that only made it worse, seeing the rape in his mind; he couldn't help it. And after, he saw this too: Shadden backing off her, getting the gun, poking the muzzle at his head…

There was only one thing he could do, that Shadden couldn't *make* him do.

Sean had seen Helen Sommers kneel down in front of the bum, the carriage stopped behind her on that busy Seattle intersection a block from the restaurant; and on the ferry he'd seen the seagulls line up to be fed from her outstretched palms. But he was not going to watch Shadden rape her now on the couch in front of her cabin's hearth. He would hear that, hear whatever he said to her as he was doing it; he couldn't prevent that. But he was not going to witness it, none of it. He turned away, fixing his eyes on Michael Furey's maroon football jersey, before he closed his eyes on the white number **25**.

Soon, he heard the door to Helen's room creak open, then steps, heavy ones, but nothing like a man carrying a woman, no sounds of struggle or pleas. Or was she resigned to what was going to happen? The front door opened—the rattle of the door knob. Was he taking her outside for this? Which meant Shadden would come back for him. The door clacked shut.

Sean rolled over.

The gun was missing from the chest.

Shadden had been gone for about ten minutes. What was he doing? Taking a shit in the privy? Setting the stage? All Shadden had to do was leave Helen and the gun out there and come back him. He sure as hell wasn't leaving; Sean would have heard that.

Then: tromping steps on the porch. Shadden came in with an armful of firewood, dumped the load in front of the hearth and kneeled to begin making a fire with kindling and smaller pieces of wood from a nearby bin. He lit the fire with stove matches from a box on the mantel and blew on the first licks of flame.

"Nothing like a little fire. I imagine it gets a little chilly up here, even in the summer. By the way, the Mustang is out there, just like she wrote, under a tarp by the side of the cabin. You should see that car, Sean. Good as new. Cherry."

Shadden lit the lantern on the corner of the desk, then went into the kitchen and returned with a bottle and a short glass. He came over to Sean and ripped the tape from his mouth, saying: "See if you take to this whiskey any better than your brother did the Maker's Mark I poured down his throat. It is Irish—Red Breast. Ever heard of it? No doubt it is Michael's but he should not mind sharing."

He shoved the bottle into Sean's mouth, poured for a second. He gagged but some of it got down, burning his throat. Sean turned on his side and as he puked up the rest of the whiskey, Shadden said: "No one is coming, Sean, not today. It gets dark earlier here in the mountains and no one is going to drive that road in the dark, so the tape can stay off. Lennie's too. I will get you both food and water soon, but not now; I have something to do."

Sean's eyes were watering, blurry, but at least he could breathe better now. The hearth fire crackled and spit out a tiny, glowing cinder that didn't last long.

Shadden sat at the desk, poured three fingers of whiskey into the glass and raised it at Sean. He held a necklace in the same hand and it tinkled against the glass as he took a sip. "Slainte, I think they say. To having everything one needs here. To beautiful artifacts." He set the glass down.

Sean watched him as he began writing at Helen's desk. A memory came back: what he and Jimmy used to do when they were kids eating at the dinner table. They liked to keep a baseball in their left hand while they ate with their right, rotating the ball without looking, feeling for the seams, going through grips for various pitches, over and over.

Shadden wasn't looking, either, at what he held in his left hand as he wrote, wasn't feeling for the seams of a baseball with his thumb and fingers, but rather the jewels of the necklace.

THE BOOK OF ERIC

LENNIE, THERE IS no better place to begin than on a night in early April when I became a rich man. First, however, a question for you: why did you write and illustrate *The Book of Michael*, that wondrous testament?

I asked you in the room just now; you refused to tell me. The answer to that question is not the kind that can be forced from one who believes she is going to die anyway, or from someone who refuses to ask who I am, though I can understand why you did not. What does it matter? I could have given you the name I use now, Eric Lane Caster; or Shadden—the one Sean knows me by and the one I gave his brother when I met him at his home in Delmar, New York. Neither name matters to you, of course. But perhaps there will come a time after we leave Fado when you'll think of a better name for me than either of those others.

There was a man named Shadden whose name I took—you will learn about him soon enough—who had a place not as fine as Fado but with many, many more books than you and Michael have on those shelves near where Sean awaits his fate when I am finished with this—why not call it my own testament? I asked Shadden why all those books were written, and he said that sometimes the life one lives is simply not enough proof of one's existence; that others feel so estranged, at war, with their lives that they have to alter the campaign more to their liking. A testament is needed. Is that one of the reasons for your *Book of Michael?*

I scoffed at Shadden when he suggested I should write mine down, give it the weight that only an artifact can bestow. I asked him: "Do you know who you are talking with? A nobody. The kind of person people make a conscious effort to forget." When I met

Shadden I could scarcely read. I had nothing then; not Lissa, not the necklace. Shadden persisted, reminding me of stories I had told him because there had been no one else who cared to listen. He said he would write it all down for me—if his eyes were not so bad. What he suggested seemed impossible to me. How do you document impermanence? How do you describe shadows? Who would care to read it? "Oh, you give up too easily," he said. "Ask any artist, great or small: shadows are what defines the light; you cannot paint one without the other." He was right, was he not, Lennie?

I had forgotten all this until I came here and realized I have everything I need to finally do what Shadden suggested, and not only the means but also the inspiration which lays before me on your desk. Well, inspiration mixed with a hefty measure of jealousy that you would devote an entire book to one man. There will come a time when you will create the illustrations to go along with my modest effort. You did it before, with your Michael and Petra and your son. Surely you will do it again, for us, when they are gone.

I LAY BELOW decks in Jacob Califf's gently rocking yacht, my feet hanging over the edge of a starboard berth. I took out Shadden's pocket watch, the one he used to mark time when he gave exams to students at the college where he taught. The old Elgin timepiece was not an affectation; my wrist was too thick for a normal watch band.

It was 9:30 p.m. Soon, the houseman would come outside to sit on the steps leading up from the courtyard to smoke. He would, of course, reset the alarm system after going back into Califf's mansion after his cigarette. Two nights in row he had come out for a smoke at 10:30 p.m. and tonight he'd probably do the same.

The house in East Hampton, New York had not been hard to find with the local map I got at a grocery store. I did not want to be seen hanging around this kind of neighborhood, my size easily remembered and certainly my face—the splotched left side—where long ago my mother's boyfriend spilled the skillet of hot bacon grease, his arm knocked by my brother Kurt backing from the refrigerator as he drank the last of the chocolate milk from the carton. Later, she would smear on some of her makeup to cover it up. I still do that, keeping a tube of whatever is cheapest in my pocket.

At the grocery store I also bought enough food and bottled water for several days, put it all in a plastic bag with handles, left the car in the village, near that windmill they have there. I had stolen the car from under the Alaskan Way viaduct in Seattle, and before I got to the end of Long Island I broke my last twenty dollar bill washing the car and cleaning the interior of all the detritus from the cross-country trip. I could not risk a passing cop getting suspicious and running the plate.

I had timed my arrival at 223 Tory Hole Road for after dark. This was not one of the 'goldilocks'—as Lissa used to call the house invasions—that she, Kurt and I did when we were in our early teens. Summer was the best time to check the good neighborhoods. If, after a couple of days, a darkened home stayed dark, chances were the owners were away on vacation.

A wall shielded Califf's mansion from the shore road. I could not loiter by the gate, of course, where there would likely be security cameras. But the wall ended at a hedge separating his property from the much more modest home adjacent to his. I needed a roost, from which to safely observe Califf's home for a while. A mansion on the water surely had a boat; otherwise why bother? And surely Jacob Califf would not be using the boat in early April.

I walked along the neighbor's side of the hedge, straight down to the water, saw what could only be Califf's power boat, a forty-footer at least—the *Betcha Kan*—tied up alongside his dock. A toy for summer, not early spring. The boat was still shrouded with a winter's tarp. I cut only two of the ropes, crawled in, jimmied the lock to get below and made myself at home for two days.

I had never been on a boat before, not even in Seattle, where every other person seemed to have one.

I slept by day, watched by night. There were two floodlights in the back, one by the pool and the other by the steps leading up from the tennis court. The basketball net concerned me—evidence of children. But Califf was old enough now for any children to be out of the nest, and what a nest it was.

His fake Italian villa had the requisite tile roof, archways and Romeo and Juliet balconies. Shadden had books on architecture so I knew what I was looking at: Califf's crass version of a Roman emperor's villa. The L-shaped wing on one side of the property framed the covered pool. The outdoor furniture was covered also. Steps led down from the pool area to a lower courtyard and more floodlit steps to the tennis court.

I had seen Califf occasionally through the windows at night when I came up from below decks to watch, mark distances and domestic rhythms. The L-shaped wing was for guests and I had seen no activity there. That narrowed possibilities. Califf would likely be somewhere upstairs in the main block.

It was time now to meet the man I had last seen when I was a boy.

I left the berth, taking a coil of rope from a locker. I weighted the plastic bag of my garbage, tossed it overboard, retied the tarp. No sense in giving the police any reason to check the boat immediately after. Someone would find the jimmied lock but not for a while.

I kneeled on the dock, feeling good about my dark clothes, sure that no one could see me in the night, and waited for the house-man to appear. I saw only a few lights on the ground level of the mansion, just one from upstairs. This night, a Thursday, would not be a party night at 223 Tory Hole Road. This night was a good choice because the weekend began tomorrow and that could bring guests, or Califf might leave for some other social excursion.

What if the servant did not come out tonight? The day then. Someone had to go out for errands, wash the cars. I would have to do it then, when the alarm system was not set. Not a first choice but doable. The mansion was set back from the road. The wall and trees in front would help. But if Califf was the one who left, I would have to go somewhere and come back and people would see me.

A door slid open: someone passed across the glare of the floodlight. I moved closer, careful with the creaking dock.

There he was, right on time, sitting on the steps, facing the courtyard, his back to the light at the corner of the mansion.

I fitted the fabric mask, left the dock, keeping low. The coil of rope—a bonus from the yacht—slid off my shoulder. I slung the rope over again, moved along the near, long edge of the tennis court, away from the floods, went around the chain link fence at the end, staying close to the hedge. Ahead: the raised portion of the courtyard and the swimming pool beyond.

I stopped twenty feet behind the servant, hiding near a cluster of outdoor furniture, and checked the annex balconies even though the windows were dark. I could heard the faint rasp of a match as the houseman lit his cigarette.

He brought a cell phone to his left ear; a minor glitch. I could not move closer now, risk the man deciding to get up and pace while he talked and then see an intruder ten feet away and the person on the other end becoming alarmed and calling the police.

I waited, listening to the man talking in Russian or a similarly guttural language. The man turned a little, cigarette in his mouth. He laughed, gesturing with a straight finger, a screwing motion: the crude gesture of rutting. Califf and his wife or girlfriend? I had not seen a woman anywhere around the house or through a window.

A minute passed. The houseman ended the call, sat there, finished the cigarette and threw it carelessly away and from somewhere came a yearning for a time when I could have put him to death for that minor transgression, had I been his lord.

Instead of the knife I had, I took a hardware store scratch awl from a duct tape sheath on my ankle. The awl would provide the same—and less messy—result. I moved closer, seeing in my mind what was going to happen to make sure it would; then closer still, close enough to smell the man's cologne, the wisps of cigarette smoke.

Five feet away.

I rushed him before he could sense my presence, snaked my left arm around his neck, cutting off his wind, drove the awl into the base of his skull, yanking him back as I jammed the five dollar tool up into his brain. He struggled but not for long. He kept twitching, shoe heels tapping the brick. He shuddered, went slack. The cell phone clattered on the brick, the loudest sound of any of it.

I pulled out the awl, released him, wipe it off on his sweater, and wormed it back under the tape at my ankle.

Entering the mansion, I heard the music immediately though I did not recognize it. I have never had the chance to listen to much music. Not with Shadden, who preferred his books, and so then did I. But I followed this music, through the big kitchen, the dining room with a table set with twelve chairs, deeper into the mansion. The huge living room had shelves of figurines, including miniature versions of those pursed-lipped, big-eared giants from Easter Island, which made me think of Shadden's big ones.

The music seemed to be coming from the east end of the mansion, near where I remembered the four-car garage to be. I moved cautiously, pausing frequently to listen for additional sounds because the music could mask the presence of others. I came to a suite of rooms and the music now was loudest behind the second of three doors to the rooms. And more from that room: slaps... moans.

Rutting: probably not Califf enjoying his wife or girlfriend. Not downstairs.

I checked the other rooms. Empty.

The music welled louder as I opened the door to the one I wanted, enough to see a man with a ponytail, a scar on his back, basting the woman from behind on the bed.

I dropped the coil of rope in the corridor, got the awl again, pushed the door open and walked up to the end of the bed. The man leaned over the woman to cup a pendulous breast, shouting over the thumping music: "Say it again. Who's your man?" I pushed him hard, flattening him, so if he screamed he would do it into her flesh. As she collapsed under him, I reprised the awl with Pony-tail, stick-shifting it. He stiffened, tried to turn his head, but I pushed his face harder into the woman.

"Kenny, what're you doing? Get off me."

I did it for him. He was dead but his phallus did not know it yet, bouncing like a little buoy as I yanked him over the side of the bed. Before the woman could scream I clapped a hand over her mouth. Her eyes widened to the size of quarters.

"No screams."

She nodded, staring at the awl in my other hand. I slipped my palm off her mouth, pressed the point of the awl across her lips, the point pricking her upturned nose. "All I want is Califf. Tell me where he is and you will live." I brushed away the hair over her forehead, feeling the dampness, the way Lissa did for me after the grease burned my face. She would cool me off with a towel she dipped in ice water before putting on the Vitamin E salve.

"I know he is in the house," I said.

"He's...he's..."

I kept stroking her blonde hair. It had been a long while since I had touched a woman. "It is going to be okay. Just tell me."

"Uhh...upstairs."

"I know that. Where?"

"In...the last I knew...his office."

She had a Southern accent, maybe Texas.

"Good," I said. "Now where is that?"

"Go...up the stairs. Straight ahead."

"Anyone else in the house?"

"Just Sergei."

Who was dead.

"I will find out if you are lying."

"Please! Mr. Califf's alone. He always is in there. His office."

"Who was that one?" I asked, nodding at the side of the bed.

"One of us...the staff. I'm the maid."

"What is your name?"

"Rachel."

"You are very pretty, Rachel," I said, making her think she would be all right if I took her now. "That is a lovely tattoo on your shoulder."

So it was easy for me to turn her over. Or perhaps she was merely resigned or did not want to look at my mask any longer. I ran my hand over her buttocks, careful not to nick her with the awl.

Such a waste, but it could not be helped. I stroked the back of her head one last time, thinking it a pity they all could not be Lissa, and then shifted the awl to my right hand.

THE ROOM WAS directly across from the landing at the top of the stairs. The door was closed although the one to the left was open. I checked it—from the size the master bedroom. The other rooms down the corridor were empty as well.

I slowly turned the door knob. Locked. What was Califf doing inside a locked room, while Kenny and Rachel were fornicating downstairs? If I tried to force my way in, he would be quickly on his office phone. He also probably had an intercom in there. I hoped he would not be using that to call for a nightcap and wonder why the help was not fetching. Still, the man had to go to bed sometime.

I stayed by the nearest room, ready to duck in yet close enough to move quickly on Califf when he came out. Fifteen minutes later I heard the faint slide and click of a dead-bolt, which told me he had something in there he wanted to safeguard very much.

He was dressed casually—khaki pants and sleeveless black sweater over a red shirt. He had a paunch now, thinning hair but still the big ears and big rings on stubby fingers. He walked into the master bedroom in a splay-footed manner. *Duck-man...Quackerjack*, Kurt had called him then.

He left the bedroom door open so he probably was not going to bed yet. I heard him in the bathroom, the intermittent pissing somehow reminding me of the stutter I used to have. Lissa's hands ended that for me long ago when she tended the burn on my face before her parents moved, taking her away from me. The scarring of the burn remained, but somehow my stuttering, that verbal disfigurement, vanished.

It was not likely there was someone else in the study. Not in his office this time of night. I stepped back into the empty room and shouldered the rope as Califf came out of the bedroom.

Office or downstairs?

Seconds now, for either.

Office.

I moved quickly, shoved the door hard just as Califf was closing it. The door smacked him in the forehead, stunning him. I hooked a foot around his ankle, pushed hard. He fell back against a chair, skidding it against another. I had the rope out now and quickly wrapped his ankles. I slapped him to stop his huffs and squeals, turned him over, snagged a wrist with part of the rope, then the other, slapped him hard again before I tied it off.

Three chairs, book cases behind the large desk, and the lack of a window all made the office seem smaller than it was. Underneath shelves of figurines and ancient pottery opposite the desk was a long slim table of pictures and more artifacts, and a silver tray filled with bottles of liquor. A humidifier hummed in a corner.

Califf scuffled on the floor, slackening the rope binding his wrists and ankles. It would do for now. He blinked rapidly from the floor, his chest heaving. "What do you want?"

What I wanted was to take the mask off, cool my face. Not yet. I wanted him to think for a few more minutes that this was merely a robbery.

"The others are dead. Whether you join them is up to you, so make this worth my while."

"Please…I will…there's $5,000 in a strongbox in the lower right hand drawer of my desk. It's locked. Both are."

"Where are the keys?"

"The African basket on the upper shelf over there, and the lamp at the end."

I went over, found the keys. "You will have to do better than $5,000."

He snuffled, licking then swallowing the blood trickling from his nose. "Take the lamp. It's Roman, worth another five."

"The rest of it?"

"Sell them. New York, London."

"Not enough."

"It's worth a lot. Just take it and go."

"How much?"

"Twenty at least. You won't have a problem. It's mostly no-questions-asked."

"You stole all of it."

"I paid for it."

"You bought from people who did."

"My God, this matters to you? Call it what you want. Just take it. What's downstairs, too; whatever you want."

I unlocked the drawer and strongbox. I glanced at Califf looking past me, then quickly away.

I stuffed a thick wad of 100 dollar bills in my pocket. "What are you looking at?"

"Nothing."

I turned from him, slowly, curious now, and heard him groan—a little whinny.

Books crammed two floor-to-ceiling cases lining the wall behind the desk, with a foot of space between them. They were not aligned. The right-hand bookcase stood flush against the wall, but not the left which stuck out perhaps six inches. Preoccupied with Califf I had not noticed the difference.

I pulled on the left one and it came to me as easily as a jar of pickles from the pantry shelf. I opened it more, hearing the soft rolling of bearings underneath. I had to stoop through the low, narrow entrance.

The room beyond was larger than any walk-in closet I had seen goldilocking with Lissa and Kurt. On one side two comfortable chairs flanked a small table with a stack of notebooks and bottles of liqueurs set on a glistening silver tray with swan's neck handles. A bottle of Drambuie was opened next to a half-filled tumbler. An uncapped fountain pen lay atop an open notebook. Over-sized books lined a single shelf above and behind the chairs and table, and above that small spotlights illuminated the opposite wall of black shelving.

Some of the artifacts neatly spaced on that shelving were pottery. But all the rest were golden, jeweled, presented dramatically on little white rectangles—some vertical, some horizontal—and shining brightly in the focused light.

I walked out of the vault. His eyes were shut but his cheeks gleamed with tears—this East Hampton pharaoh mourning the breaching of his treasure-filled tomb.

I dragged him by his shoes around the desk and into the vault, checked to make sure the ropes were secure, cut the phone line, then went downstairs to the kitchen to find plastic trash bags. I took four from under the black marble-top sink. When I returned Califf had squirmed almost to the door. I hauled him back, lifting him onto one of his chairs to witness the looting of his hoard, but he closed his eyes again.

I doubled the trash bags. Two would suffice, given the small size of most of the artifacts. I was about to toss in the notebook, to look at later. I would need that to know what I was selling. But I could not wait, and scanned the entries under a heading—*CURRENT COLLECTION*—and the date. Then a subheading—*South American*:

—*Moche fantasy death scene on rectangular pottery vessel. Skeleton presiding over ceremony, playing drum. 7" high. Red on white.*

—*Gold pendant, Tairona style, representing crocodile god. 4" high.*

—*Matching pair of gold and turquoise mosaic ear disks, Moche-style. 'Running messenger' figures. Diameter 2".*

—*Gold pendant/pectoral, Cocie-style. Leaf-nosed bats as warriors. Single-piece casting. Diameter 4".*

—*Nazca-style hammered gold mask. Diameter 7".*

—*Gold crown with plumes and bangles. South Ecuador highlands. 14" high.*

—*Quimbaya style gold flask. Worn around neck. Contents analysis: traces of lime powder consistent with chewing of coca leaves.*

There was not much under the subheading of *Middle East*, just... *a ceramic oil lamp from Caesarea. Volutes flank the nozzle and on circular discus two men play a board game.*

A volute? I had memorized most of Shadden's dictionary, but I could not remember coming across the word "volute." Now I knew.

"That one should stay, Jacob," I said, turning to him. "Pottery will just break in the bag and I should leave you something to look at, no?"

He opened his eyes. My using his name or the hint of his coming fate?

I read on: *Europe*.

—*Gold chain, fastened at shoulders by disc-brooches, bearing Byzantine coin of Theodosius II.*

—*Gold brooch with four double-headed serpents in cloisonné, looped to form a quatre-foil against a gold filigree backround. Possibly Kaupang, Norway?*

—*Gold crozier head. Irish. Found in Honess, Norway.*

—*Headband of gold wire. Aristocratic gift of bridegroom to bride? Krefeld-Gellup, lower Rhine.*

—*Gold penannular or ring-brooch. 'Three-wolf-heads.' 4"x 3". Birka, Sweden.*

—*Braided gold neck-ring. .5 kilo. Tisso, Denmark.*

—*Silver and gold pendant. Viking 'gripping beast' motif. Diameter 3". Varby, Sweden.*

—*Matching golden horns, with runes and human/animal figures. From Kallhus, Denmark.*

—*Gold ribbon necklace decorated with mother of pearl collets alternating with emerald prisms. From Pompeii. Belonged to favored wife/concubine of noble/wealthy landowner?*

That necklace adorned a mannequin's neck on the middle shelf, the light of one spotlight directly on it. "I will not sell that one.

I will take good care of it. I have a use for it. Does that make you feel better?"

"Fuck you to hell."

"Such bravado, Jacob. Here I am, feeling this bond with you, and you insult me. Given a choice between gazing at that necklace or basting the maid—as you could have done no doubt—I might choose as you have. I have never seen anything as beautiful as that necklace, not that I have ever had the leisure time for museums. But I read somewhere that Romans had a thing for emeralds. Is that true?"

"You know nothing."

"Oh, I do."

I took the mask off, tossed it away, and scratched the side of my face, the glazed scar in the shape of Mexico, more or less. As I began taking the artifacts off the shelves and putting them into the bags, I wondered how long it would take him to remember. I said: "Are you wondering how you are going to enjoy your pharaoh's afterlife without all of this around you. They did that, you know."

He had a stack of soft polishing cloths neatly folded on the table. I took two and wrapped the necklace and put it in the bag, then the gold flask, the crozier.

"You're her other one," he whispered.

"If you can remember my mother's name I will leave this," I said, and held up the Nazca gold mask for a few moments. "No? Too bad." I put it in the bag. "Marla never called me Richie or Ricky. Always Richard. As if the full name would make a difference. You would think she would have saved the formality for you, a man she had not known for long. But you were always Jako, never Jacob. She would always say, 'I'll be going out with Jako later tonight, boys. I won't be late.' But she always was."

"You're fucking nuts."

"No, merely lucky for a change. So there I was, in Seattle, a long way from those days, at Market-Time at the north end of Fremont, not far from Woodland Park where I sometimes spent the night. Not to rob the store; there are much easier and less risky ways of getting money. I just wanted a sandwich and the tiny grocery store was even more crowded than usual so I picked up one of those celebrity magazines while I waited in line, and there you were, right next to Billy Joel in the picture of you at a benefit party for the Nature Conservancy—right here I bet."

"It wasn't here."

"Close enough to look you up. You had your arm around him and I remembered your wee hands and the golf-ball nose. A long time ago, but you do not forget when you are fifteen and see the guy who gave your mother money at the door. There had been others, of course, other generous gentlemen; maybe one reason she took the summer waitressing gig at Lake George. We needed the money; she still had her looks. But you were the last froggie to come a-courting that summer when the three of us—Marla, Kurt and I—shared that crappy motel room half an hour from the resort where she worked. Remember? How many times did you take her to your fancy summer home on the lake? She said you had one, and I wanted to see it and she said she could not do that."

"It was a business associate's, not mine."

"How many times did you take her there? Had to be a dozen."

"Look, she got what she wanted and so did I."

"As did your business associate. Or perhaps there were others, too, for a gang-bang-by-the-lake?"

Jacob Califf said nothing to that.

The first bag was full. I opened the second, and began emptying the second shelf, talking straight at what was left, loud enough for him to hear me.

"After you had not shown up for a while, Marla said she had to go on a trip; no big deal, she was not going to be gone for long. She said: 'Richard, you're a big guy now, and you can take care of yourself until Kurt and I get back. There's food in the fridge and I left some makeup for your face.' She would not tell me where she was going with Kurt, but she did tell me not to go near the lake, since I could not swim.

"I figured later, after she and Kurt did not come back, that you had gotten her pregnant and since the only business I ever saw was you handing her money at the door to our apartment, I figured you were the business. So what happened to them? I have come a long way to find out."

"I didn't do anything to them."

"Yes, you did. The last time I saw Kurt—the day he left with our mother—she had given him a haircut and new shoes and one of my better shirts since he was almost as big as I though younger. Did she ask for help? You had to have some of this then." I jiggled the bag. *Chink...chink.* "Did she ask for too much? Did you use some of your petty cash to have someone take care of the problem? Cheaper than your wife divorcing you and taking you to the cleaners—I assume you were married then."

"There's a price for everything. Go ahead, take it all and kill me. But there's a price."

"Yes, there is. You are going to pay it."

"I didn't kill them, but I'll tell you what *did* happen. She came down to *sell* your brother to me."

"That will not work. Almost time for me to go."

"It's *true.* My wife wanted a child. I...couldn't give her one. She didn't want one from Korea or Bosnia, wherever. She wanted a blond, blue-eyed kid. You know how hard they are to find? But I knew where I could get one."

I had almost finished filling the bag.

"And it wasn't you!" Califf shrilled. "She took the money. She left you knowing she was never going to go back to you and that shit-hole. Wherever she is..."

"All done, Jako."

"And if you hadn't come here, you never would have known. Sleeping dogs. Take it all, but it's sleeping dogs. You tell me now, is it worth it? *Is it?*"

I hefted the bags. "Santa is taking back the toys." As I carried them past Califf he shouted: "Proof, you want *proof?* Go check the second room down the hall; that was his."

I dropped the bags by the desk chair in the office. *Chink... Chink.* Califf was still at it: "Go on, check the room! See for yourself. I didn't kill them. His stuff is still there."

I dragged Califf to the back of the vault. He was crying again. "Check it...*please!* He played lacrosse one year. The junior-varsity letter is there."

He did not seem to notice me taking the rings off his fingers. I put them in my pocket to pawn later. "Where is he then?"

"Boston, I think. Last I knew..."

"Last you knew?"

"It…didn't work out. I had to send him away to school."

"What about your wife?"

"She left before. We're divorced."

"She got tired of the puppy after you brought him home? Handsome but a handful, right?"

"Please…you have to believe that I didn't…"

"She never knew about what you had in here, did she?"

"No—I didn't kill Marlie or your brother."

"It was Marla, not Marlie. I like the part about the sleeping dogs." I turned him over and punched the awl into the back of his head with a hard smack from the heel of my hand, a simple workman's effort. I left it inside him. As he fell to his side, the awl's wooden butt tapped on the floor, marking staccato time to his convulsions.

I flicked off the spotlights, left the vault and closed the bookcases, carried the bags out to the hallway. Back in the office I put everything back as it should be, made sure everything looked normal. I had to hand it to him. Unless one knew the vault was there, one would never guess what lay behind the bookcases.

I wiped down everything with my shirttail, including the tumbler of Macallan after I downed a shot and clinked a toast on the bottle: to myself and to Lissa.

I closed the office door, wiped the handle. Let the police think whoever did that wanted to make sure, maybe someone with prints on file in computer vaults; maybe even Kurt's, who had some problems it seemed. I had been on my own since Marla left and never came back. There had been close calls, but I had never been forced to put thumb to ink. I considered that as much of a miracle as what Lissa had done, exorcising my stuttering.

I left the house the same way I entered, went around the side, pausing near the front to make sure about passing cars or late-night joggers. Within an hour I would be back at the car parked by the windmill, checking to make sure all the lights worked. I obviously could not be stopped by the police for any reason, not now.

And nothing could be more suspicious than a man carrying two garbage bags over his shoulder at this time of night.

Hey fella, what've you got there, grass clippings?

I had passed garbage cans set out on Tory Hole Road for the morning pickup. The next residence I came to I placed my treasure by a couple of containers. They would be safe until I drove the car back here. Plenty of time. I noted the name and address on the mailbox: *Andrews*.

I could afford the laugh now: two bags of artifacts worth... what?—several hundred thousand dollars? Lying next to rich folks' garbage. There had been times, and not only in Seattle, when I had sifted through garbage cans for the treasure of something to eat.

But just in case, I took the necklace and the crocodile pendant with me.

I felt like another person and it was time for another name to begin again after I found Lissa. Richard Lampron, the one I started out with, was gone. There had been others. Shadden once called me a resurrectionist, a fade-artist. He used to talk about two buddies of his who never made it home from World War II: Eric Caster and Lane Davidson. The names were as good as any to use now: Eric Lane Caster.

I had never breathed better air than the sea air off the Long Island Sound that night. There was a lot to do and I spent the time walking back to the car thinking about it. First, I wanted something to mark this night, something I could always look at and remember.

Califf would eventually be found. At some point his stink would seep through. There had been two chairs in the vault so it was reasonable to think that he had shared the glory of his hoard with a co-masturbator who had his own to hide. Show me yours, I'll show you mine. That person might anonymously tip the police, but probably not before Eric Lane Caster—the garbage man—cashed in Jacob Califf's hoard. Until that person did, Califf would have disappeared, his body dumped in the Sound by the man who killed Kenny, Rachel and the Russian.

By then I would have Lissa at my side again, the necklace around her neck. Wherever she was I had the means now to find her. I had no doubt she would come with me, even if she was married. I had all I needed to persuade her, whether she was...a favored wife or a pimp's concubine. I could take her away now to a place all our own, give her the only things I would never sell; things you would not find at Walmart where I had once stolen candy while Marla strolled with Kurt in the next aisle over, looking for the rice and beans.

CHAPTER 6

SHADDEN

May, 2006

I FELT A kick at my feet, then a voice came out of the darkness: "Where have you been, Jimmy?"

It took me a moment to remember. *Katie...*

But this was a man speaking, in a mocking tone.

Another kick to my feet: "Oh, come on, Jimmy. I did not hit you that hard. We have to talk; I do not have all night."

He'd blindfolded me. My jaw hurt, but not as badly as the back of my head. My ears were ringing, and I felt like I was going to puke and that panicked me because he'd taped my mouth. I couldn't move my hands or feet. I tried, bending at the waist, but I couldn't get up; he'd taped my ankles together. I stretched back, letting the wave of nausea pass. I lay on the floor, feeling the tight pressure of the blindfold, the edge of the couch.

"Can you hear me, Jimmy?" The voice came more distantly, from the overstuffed chair facing the couch. I remembered sitting in that chair, tired from moving in. Katie came over and whispered in my ear: *Let's christen the place.* We moved to the couch—the only space not crammed with boxes in the living room—to make love ten minutes after the Mayflower van pulled away.

He went on: "Did you like the midnight show? *My* name is not Jimmy, however. Tonight, for you, it is Shadden. The *Jimmy* was for Katie's bene- fit, and for yours."

I lay there on the floor, trying not to throw up, choke on my own vomit, trying not to see again on that dark screen the last moments of Katie's life.

"There is another name," he said. "You knew Lissa's name before you came back and dragged her away from the campsite with your hand over her mouth, until you were far enough away in the woods. She must have told you she was pregnant; she must have begged you just to take the pendant, and in the end she must have pleaded with you not to kill her. But you could not do that, could you?—leave her alive because she knew your name and where you lived."

He kicked me hard in the side and for a moment I saw white light.

"I am not going to kill you, not tonight. I have decided on a better idea that will keep on ticking for the man who took my Lissa away from me.

"Getting into this house was easy; I have had practice with that. You should have looked in the cellar: that is where I waited for you. But I could still hear Katie's little song, my cue to go onstage.

"I have taped your mouth because I do not want to have you screaming and waking up the neighbors, or squealing about how you did not do it. I know you did. Katie did not deserve you. Engaged to be married and you betrayed her in the most sickening way. I even thought you might have given Katie the pendant, with some story about where you got it, but you did not even make a gift of it to the woman you were going to marry. Maybe you have it still, maybe you sold it; I do not care. Katie was compensation enough for me, as you saw."

I reeled with these lies. There had been a woman at a campsite on the trail my buddies and I took going back to the trailhead. She complained about the black flies and mosquitoes, and I gave her the netting, the hood I wore. I could do without now; the hike was almost over. She said her name was Elisabeth…Lissa?

I didn't kill her.

I turned away from him, found the bottom edge of the couch frame, began rubbing the tape binding my wrists. It would take too long but it was something…something to focus on besides hearing this insanity. If

I could get my hands free and quickly rip off the blindfold, it would be enough: a lunge in the dark, a chance to get my hands on him.

Maybe he saw the pale shadow of my face disappear, heard the change in breathing, because he said: "That will not do any good. I will not be here that long. Before I go, however, I want to tell you about Katie.

"Our women are gone. Neither will be coming back because of you, so listen carefully.

"It was easy, watching you both, getting your movements down, waiting for just the right opportunity—and that happened when she took off for Boston. When she left and kept going this time—not to the store or work—I was not far behind. We are talking a straight arrow shot on I-90, following her and those stuffed animals in the back of her car. It was so easy, maybe as easy as it was for you and my Lissa. I had Katie for a lot longer than you had Lissa, and she told me everything after a while. Maybe if you two had parted earlier in the day I would have thought twice about taking her in daylight.

"She stopped in Stockbridge, locked her car, went into the Adams Inn for a bite to eat. It was not yet dark when she went in but it was when she came out. I parked next to her car a minute after she went in, backed in, to match our drivers' sides.

"I waited. I counted exactly sixteen stuffed animals. When she came out, approached her car, keys in hand, I got out of mine too. She glanced my way. I said 'hi,' pleasant as can be, gave her my best smile and she smiled back—that is our Katie, Jimmy. She said something that surprised me. Such an innocent and also observant. So good-natured. That is our Katie. It is such a pity you forced me to take her because of what you did to my Lissa. She said: 'Did you leave your keys in your car?'

"See, she had noticed the one empty hand and the other held—as she saw it—a balled-up rag of some sort, but no key, nothing to worry about. I told her, 'oh I know, but thanks,' and pointed past her to the inn. 'I will not be long. Pit stop.'

"As I passed her—as she unlocked her car—I got the chloroform-soaked rag over her face, brought her down, held her down and abracadabra, within two minutes I was driving away with her in the back of my car, tinted windows and all. I came back later for the stuffed animals, and left her car where it would not be found for a long time, if ever. Are you listening, Jimmy? You are breathing a little harder now. Still trying to get that tape off?

"The Indians used to do this sort of thing in those parts. You must know that. Katie said you were a writer, maybe thinking of teaching instead of tending bar while you're at it. The Deerfield massacre happened not too far to the east; Indians killing the men, taking the women back to Canada, never to be seen again, except for a very few, I believe. Some women even went 'native' during their captivity. One could say the same thing about Katie, I suppose.

"I had taped her up, too, so she was not going anywhere when she regained consciousness. We drove a short way south. Her mouth was taped but she talked a lot later. She was very good later about answering questions about you, even though she cried buckets for a while. I wanted to find out all I could about you, and over time she told me. Said you took her to Tanglewood once to hear Eric Clapton and to see *Brigadoon* at the Mac-Haydn Theater in Chatham, which I've been to as well. So I told her, '*what a coincidence!*'; that Lissa loved the theater also, as much as I did. We both enjoyed *Wicked* so much.

"What else? I won't go into it all, but she said you once played baseball, told me the sweet story of how you two met. Said your teammates at Penn State called you *Jam*. I got the *J* and the *M*, of course. But the *A*? She said that was your middle name, Ahrens, but the initials were not the main reason why they called you *Jam*. That was because your batting average was higher with men in scoring position. What a guy! A sweet-as-jam hitter when it counts."

I wriggled further up the couch, trying to find a nail, a splintered edge to the frame, anything to work the tape better, but it was smooth all the way down. I tried the other direction. Useless. But anything was better than just lying there, listening to him.

"I had her for months. I told her the first day my name was Jimmy, too. Yet another coincidence. Was this fate or what! After several months that is what she began calling me, though in the beginning she did not believe me. She tried not to, she really tried, bless her heart. When I kept telling her, over and over, that this was happening because of what you did to Lissa, she refused to believe me.

"But do not think too badly of her that she eventually did. Doubt is like infection, is it not? You had gone away, you did not want to go with her to Boston, her father did not approve of you or your family, she admitted, and she had not known you for *that* long, had she? Something had caused this to happen to her. Sometimes it takes a while for an often-repeated truth to sink in.

"I did not so much wear her down as bring her to the point where the stress of her reality—her world shrunk to one room—simply gained enough weight to tip the scales. We all have our thresholds. Eventually most people wind up choosing the least stressful path.

"Lissa cured my childhood stutter with her hands. K-K-K-Katie was too pretty to waste. She did not have Lissa's figure but she was prettier and just what the doctor ordered. It helped me to think of Lissa in that room, you know, with the lights out. Did you ever do that with Katie? Pretend she is someone else?

"Soon enough, Jimmy, the pretense was all but gone. After four months it was all aboard the train and in the end she was showing her ticket without me having to ask. You cannot blame her. We talked about Lissa a lot and the baby she lost along with her life. Katie came to think of herself as Lissa's successor. You should have seen the smile on her face when she told me she was pregnant."

I tried to shut it all out as I kept going…trying to free myself and get at him.

"The last few weeks? If I had left the door unlocked to her room upstairs, she would have stayed there with all her stuffed animals. I understand you gave her some. So thank you, they helped a lot. Early on she wanted a mirror, perhaps because she could shatter it, use a shard to try and kill me. So I never gave her one until the very end, when all she would have done with it was look at herself for the first time in many months.

"They are both gone now. Four, if you count the unborn. All where they will never be found. My two are still up in the Adirondacks. What did you do, bury Lissa up there, or weight her body and dump her in a lake? So many of those up there from which to choose. I never got a chance to show her real mountains, where the cougars sometimes come into the towns, and the bears cuff steelhead or salmon returning to spawn, where you can sail in the morning on a mild winter's day and ski in the afternoon; not that I ever did either. But we could have out there, Lissa and I. Now, stop what you are doing, and pay attention to the last of what I shall tell you.

"I would not marry if I were you. Do that and your new woman dies. If you have a child, he or she dies too. I have the resources now to be able to find you, wherever you might go. You can change your name, drop out of sight, move to Manitoba, but I will find you.

"It may be two months, or a year, or three years in between—what shall we call them?—visitations? You will not see me. But you will know I visited because you will get another of Katie's stuffed animals—in your car, at the door to your house or apartment. Perhaps the time between visitations will be even longer; long enough for you to think I am done with you, moved on. You may meet someone else, and think that something must have happened to him: a cement truck, cancer, whatever.

"That is always a possibility, of course. But would you want to risk the life of Mrs. Jam and Jam Junior? What are you going to tell the new love of your life? You really should tell her. You cannot keep such a secret, even though you were going to keep a big one from Katie. Sooner or later she would have found out. I merely happened to provide the sooner. So I would confess this time. How else to explain a cute stuffed animal on top of your car that Jam Junior wants to take inside and hold while you read him a bed-time story? I can do that if you would like. What is this if not a bed-time story for you?

"Then again, I may kill you the next time I see you. Are you ready for your new life? Our life? We have so much in common; call it the void. It has to be filled again. We shall do our best."

I heard him get up from the chair. I thought he was going to leave now. But his breathing was louder, much closer. He gripped my hair—I felt the padded glove. I tried to shake it off, twist my head, but I couldn't move.

"Lissa should not have been drinking that night, but she said she had a lot on her mind. Never mind the baby she was carrying; if she had not been drinking from the bottle of Maker's Mark, she might have sensed you behind her."

He ripped the tape off my mouth and shoved the bottle into my mouth—before I realized what he was doing, before I could clench my teeth.

"Slainte, Jimmy."

He poured it in my mouth. Some of the whiskey flowed down my chin but I couldn't move and too much got in. I choked on it, bucking to get it out but he kept the bottle there, the glass clacking against my teeth, until finally it was gone.

I rolled over, face to the floor, vomiting the burning whiskey back up, and kept puking it up. I heard the door close. He was gone.

I forced myself up, puked again as I hopped to the window, fell down by the chair where he'd sat, got up again. Even if I could get the blindfold off there wasn't much time to get the window, see the make of the car or a license plate. I rubbed the back of my head against the window sill, trying to get the thing off, wondering why I didn't hear a car starting up outside. Then I realized he wouldn't have parked in front. There wouldn't be a car to see, even if it had been daylight, even if he hadn't tied the blindfold so tightly I couldn't remove it without using my hands.

I threw up again, spit out the last dregs of whiskey, shuffled toward the kitchen, knocking into the couch, walking into the bookcase by the far wall, sliding over into the kitchen finally. I tipped over the knife block by the sink—a clatter of spilling knives. One fell to the floor. I skidded it to the base of the counter, slumped down with my back against the wood, smelling my whiskey-soaked shirt, and managed to get a chef's knife in my hands. I worked the blade for ten minutes, dropping it several times and cutting my wrist before finally slicing the tape. I ripped off the tape, then the blindfold.

The house was still dark. I hopped over to flick on the kitchen light, sliced the tape at my ankles and went into the living room, telling myself to leave everything as it is—the DVD, the bottle of Maker's Mark on the floor by the couch, the stuffed animal.

I picked up the kitchen wall phone to make the 911 call.

And put the phone back.

By the time the police came, a man I couldn't describe would be long gone in a car I couldn't describe either.

Tell them what happened?

Seems like you've been drinking Mr. Malloy.

He made me. His name is Shadden and he broke into my home, with a DVD showing the murder of my fiancée, Katie Walsh, who disappeared last year.

He made you to watch this DVD?

Not exactly.

Is this man on the DVD?

No, but he had it, he had to be the one who murdered my fiancée.

Why would he do this?

It was payback. He thought I raped and murdered his wife or girlfriend up in the Adirondacks and disposed of her body up there somewhere.

Were you there, Mr. Malloy?

Yes, but I didn't do it.

Did you know this other woman?

No.

This…Shadden?

No.

How did this man find you?

I…I don't know. I spoke to the woman on the trail. I must have given her my name, address.

So you did know her then. Why would this…Shadden…leave the DVD, the evidence, for us, Mr. Malloy?

They would watch it, and they would hear Katie say words I would never forget.

Jimmy, where have you been?

They would know about my assault charge. They might wonder why my fiancée called me Jimmy in the DVD which, for all they knew, could have been taken in some room in Albany. But they would know I didn't, couldn't have done that to Katie. They would know I hadn't set the whole thing up. They would know it wasn't a sick game I was playing: here's the proof of what I did but you'll never make it stick.

I couldn't make the call now. I should have but I couldn't. I noticed now he'd cut the phone cord near the jack, but even if he hadn't, I wouldn't have made the call. I didn't have a cell—disliked the things—but even if I had I wouldn't have made the call.

Nor could I watch the DVD again, and hear those words again, see what he'd done to her over the course of those months, and witness her last moments. Not now. Not until I had to do it with the police.

I told myself I'd go in the morning, when I wouldn't stink with booze.

It was too late to go after this Shadden. He could be anywhere. What could the police do, stop every car in the Tri-Cities, all the way to Massachusetts, if he was going there? Check out all the red houses in the Berkshires, look for a man with a tattoo on his arm? I had no other description to give them except that he was bigger than me, with hands, wrists as thick as bricks.

Where have you been, Jimmy?

I found where he had gotten in: a window by the back porch. A square of glass he'd cut out leaned against the railing.

I went down into the basement to get my father's gun, loaded it with rounds I'd bought for the one time I'd taken it to a practice range.

I turned off the lights in the house and sat against a wall in the living room, to wait for him to come back, because he'd left the DVD, the evidence. So consumed with his revenge for something I hadn't done, and delivering his threat, he'd forgotten about it. He had to be closing on the house, hurrying to get back before the police arrived. Perhaps he still thought I was trying to get free.

More than anything I wanted to kill him for what he'd done to Katie.

Light from a street lamp filtered through the front window.

Any minute now.

He wouldn't bother with coming in the back. I listened for the sound of his steps on the front porch, gun in my right hand. The bottle of Maker's Mark lay nearby. I spun the top of the bottle with the muzzle of the gun—a *tink* of glass. It wound up pointing at me.

It was so quiet I could hear the ticking of the kitchen clock. The refrigerator compressor kicked on.

After five minutes I began wondering why he hadn't coming back for the DVD. He wasn't shown on it, but he had to know the state police or FBI could do a lot with it.

Twenty minutes must have passed, more than enough time to tread in the deep water again with thoughts of John Walsh, who couldn't take no for an answer, who knew I'd been up there for a hike with two friends, who had plenty of money to hire someone to do this, tell him all about his daughter and her fiancé, and spend more to find and hire an actress who looked a helluva lot like his daughter.

No. Not even John Walsh would—could—do something like that. And where was Katie all this time?

She was on that DVD, which I was going to have to look at in the morning, with the police. What I wanted was for them to arrive at the house, lights flashing, and Shadden's body lying near the front door, and I'd never have to watch Katie on that DVD again, or wonder if his threat was real or not, because they'd have her killer, whoever he was.

Come on…come back for it…

It was like he knew I was waiting for him.

I waited for an hour, then longer still, even though I knew now he wouldn't be coming back.

And then I had to quit believing he would return so I could kill him for what he'd done to Katie.

You walk out of your house, anything's possible. There are people who make a lot of money telling you basically just that; the people who chide you to say *make* a great day instead of the passive *have* a nice day.

I thought of taking the gun, but…either he would have returned for the DVD or he was long gone.

I left the house Katie and I once shared, leaving the gun because it was possible I would walk to the police station and get it over with. My father had left the gun, too, walked out the door to get banana ice cream from Tollgate, and that wasn't the only thing we shared. He knew he'd never sleep another night in that house and I did, too. He kept going. Anything was possible. I could keep on walking, night to day to night and on and on; stopping where I had to for day-work and money when the cash in my wallet ran out. There was a $150 in there. Toss the wallet. Credit cards, license, everything, all the bread crumbs Shadden needed to follow the trail.

Even in this day and age it was possible to disappear if you were willing to abandon the lifestyle for which everyone else strived. Eventually you could piece together a new one, picking new names and burying old ones. *Right, Dad?* That's how you do it. Keep saying the new name over and over, and you'll eventually come to believe it, and so will everyone else. It's what Shadden did with Katie.

Keep on walking. Sean did it. Runs in the family. He went west; maybe my father did too.

I could walk east, to Marcy's. Take me a day. But I didn't want to bring her into this, not yet. Shadden said nothing about…family. Yet it would be an easy thing for him to do that, pull another string. I had to put as much space between her and me, if he really was going to make good on his threats.

Let them think what they wanted: Jimmy Malloy left everything in the house—his unfinished manuscript, his life, a gun on the floor, a little blood in the kitchen, scraps of duct tape, a stuffed animal and a note and a DVD of his pregnant fiancee's murder.

I walked three blocks, past Hamagrael Elementary school. Anything was possible if you kept on walking, including never seeing that DVD again, never having to look at Katie on that bed in that room, not the quiet room she sang softly about when she was happy. And maybe if I kept on walking long enough I wouldn't hear her last words anymore.

THE BOOK OF ERIC

LISSA WAS THE one before you, Helen, or even Katie for that matter. Jacob Califf—and antiquities dealers in half a dozen major cities—made it possible for me to find her again. Over the course of six months I dressed for and practiced the part of one Eric Lane Caster, an identity I paid well for in New York.

It was a starring role that Kurt, ever the supporting actor, would have exchanged his good looks to get, had he known. And it is one I never could have pulled off had it not been for the time I spent with Shadden in his house of a thousand books, in the lee of the Olympic Mountains.

The path to you began some time ago when I left the streets of Seattle, left the dumpsters and the underground warrens below Pioneer Square where the tour guides never take tourists, to go to the Olympic peninsula. This was before I went East to Califf then Lissa; before my brother Kurt's subsequent betrayal that brought me west again, and finally to you and Fado.

I could survive on the streets but out in the woods, deep in the rain shadow of the Olympic Mountains near Sequim? Something pulled me out there. I did not know what it was then. When I came to Shadden's place at the end of a gravel road I was thinking only of another goldilocks, except this one turned out to last not for a night but for two years, long after Shadden was dead. And then back to Seattle and the miracle of seeing Jacob Califf's picture in that magazine.

All of it is linked wondrously, like one of your paintings or sketches in *The Book of Michael*. An artist's brush strokes may seem random, but that is not always so, is it? Something moves the hand to bestow color and perspective, something that pre-exists and directs the creation.

The man I hired found Elisabeth in a week. She was married to a William Dolan in Lansdale, Pennsylvania. He was a loading dock supervisor at Merck. It did not surprise me she was married. Even at fourteen, when her parents moved—to get her away from Richard and Kurt Lampron—Lissa had been pretty, teased about her figure by envious girls.

I checked things out for a couple of days, then showed up at the place where she worked—Etta's Restaurant in a shopping mall off Sumneytown Pike—and took a stool at the counter, keeping my sunglasses on and the left side of my face away. She did not recognize me as she poured coffee. I wrote a note on a napkin:

That's the last cup of coffee you will ever have to serve. Take off the bistro apron and meet me outside in five minutes in front of the Rite-Aid. The black BMW sedan.

Richard

I wrapped the note in a hundred dollar bill.

I was sitting in the car with the AC on when she knocked on the tinted passenger side window and got in, grinning like it had been only a day instead of almost twenty years.

"Wherever you've been," she said, "you got there."

"It has taken a while."

"I'm married."

"I know. Does he treat you well?"

"Not anymore."

"I can take care of that, if you want."

"I was planning on leaving him anyway, the son of a bitch. I got some money saved up he doesn't know about."

She touched my face. "It's better, Richard." She, too, always called me Richard. Not Rich or Ricky, like Kurt did. Always Richard. Like you, Lennie, always have done with Michael, never calling him Mike or Mick.

"You do not know how better it is."

"You talk like you've spent some time in England."

"No, far from there." I shrugged. "Sometimes you pick things up without realizing you are doing it. But all that began with you."

"Look…I have to know what…I mean, is this for keeps or just old time's sake?"

"Both." I handed her a bag containing a thick envelope and a box of Godiva chocolates. "You always had a sweet tooth. There is $10,000 in the envelope. Meet me in Philadelphia in a week. I booked a room at the Westin." I gave her the name.

"Eric Lane Caster?"

"For now."

"I like it."

She went to a friend's house in Perkasie that weekend, gave me the keys to hers. I walked a mile from my car to her house in the middle of the night, and interrupted Charming Billy from his snore-fest. We went for a one-way ride into the Poconos in his own pickup. He made it easy for me, saying things he should not have said about Lissa; how he may have hit her some but only because she was catting around. The truth is, Lissa could have been happily married and it would not have made a difference to me. I had come back to get her, one way or another.

You are thinking now, Helen, that this was a test for her. Perhaps. The money meant little to me, yet the amount was enough to tempt her with other ideas.

She was there, room 436, as instructed. She did not ask me once about her husband; it was like he never existed. She did, though, ask me what I would have done if she had taken off with the money: "That must have crossed your mind."

"I would have found you again," I said, and left it at that.

We could have rented a much better place than the two-bedroom house in Haverstraw, New York, but the money had to last. Still, from the deck in back we could see barges and sailboats on a bend in the Hudson. However, the house was not far from a pizzeria careless with garbage, hence the rats that found their way across the street and into our house. We caught them with poison or smashed them with a spade left by previous renters. I would take the rats over to the pizzeria late at night and pile the tiny carcasses at the front door, a present for the opening manager.

I cannot bear rodents ever since the time, two years on my own, when I was hired under the table at an Agway feed plant because they could not find enough Mexicans to pour a reeking chemical additive into the hopper, night after night, in the summer heat of upstate New York, with the stuff melting on my skin like molasses; or load fifty pound sacks of feed onto trucks, tossing away the bags that were nests to squirming mice.

I told Lissa about Jacob Califf. Now you, Helen, are the only one who knows what happened in East Hampton. You have seen my tattoo and must have wondered about it. Lissa had a talent—nothing like yours, of course—for drawing. She drew a sketch which I later took to a tattoo parlor in Kingston: a black skull in the shape of a windmill, the vanes blood-red.

It was our secret, hidden in plain sight, as they say. Your paintings are on display in homes, lobbies and galleries for all to see. I display Lissa's creation. She was so proud of it, and proud to wear the gifts I gave her; the necklace one day, the crocodile god pendant the next. I saved only those two artifacts from Califf's hoard. They were a measure of our long-delayed resurrection, the only adornment to our fornicating.

Here is a question for you: does resurrection exist if there is no one—no disciples—to bear witness, as Sean will to our beginning when I have finished this mirroring of your masterpiece?

Now, Shadden had me read occasionally from the Bible though he was not otherwise religious, as I am sure you are not though your home in Washington state is behind that church on Mercer Island, close enough to make faith a matter of convenience. What is the Bible if not a record of witnesses and disciples, or at least the words of those who were told the story?

So I think, yes; others are needed.

Lissa was the first witness to my resurrection. When you read this in time, please do not laugh at the word; there is no other. I wanted another witness, you see: my brother Kurt. You must understand why I desired this. If what Jacob Califf said was true, Kurt was living in a waterfront mansion while I was heaving mice-infested bags of feed into dumpsters; showering in homes I broke into and stealing whatever I could take; living under the streets of Pioneer Square or under I-5 overpasses; but always *under* in some way. For many years the only worthy shelter was the memory of Lissa, before her parents took her away.

I used a different man to find Kurt, who took less time to find him than the other had with Lissa. As she and I pulled into the driveway of the red house on Byron Road, near a private school on the outskirts of South Linfield, Massachusetts, I assumed a reunion of a day, a week perhaps, the three of us again. He clapped when he recognized us after we removed our matching sunglasses. I did not expect the long embrace. He whispered into my ear that he thought I was dead or in prison, and then: "She left me, too."

He clapped again, this handsome blond fellow with the big Lampron hands. In the time we spent at the red house I came to see his sudden claps as kind of a physical tic, some sort of necessary release, or perhaps he merely thought the moment insufficient without applause.

Here is a riddle for you that I thought of as my brother later told me his story, before I gave him one of mine:

What will decay, yet has no form but will last forever; is so fragile it can never be moved, yet cannot be broken; is brilliant yet can never be shown or exhibited; priceless yet not worth a penny to its creator because it can never be sold?

The answer?

What I felt as I listened to Kurt.

Call it triumph or revenge or even the moment before you create another's death. Shadden would agree with me: the accumulated knowledge of a thousand years could not match the incandescence and power of that single moment.

I knew more about Kurt's once-gifted life—the more recent, significant events anyway—than he did because I made them happen. Jacob Califf, my brother's stepfather, had not yet been found where I had left him in his hidden lair behind the book-lined wall of his office. Whoever had occupied that second chair within, to gaze with Califf at his hoard, had not come forward, though the house, devalued as the sight of well-publicized murders, had been sold to a prominent Manhattan attorney named Kanski. Remember the yacht, the *Betcha Kan?* What are friends for if not to allow a hoard-buddy to moor his boat in East Hampton? Betcha Kanski must have thought he was also buying the treasure of his

still-missing but presumed dead friend—but instead found a de-
cayed body he had to dump from his boat into the Sound.

Kurt, of course, knew of the friendship between the men—if it
was just that—but nothing of what his step-father had hidden, nor
did I tell him. Califf left Kurt nothing in his will. He was, however,
left with answering questions from police about what he was doing on the night I paid Califf a visit. Luckily for Kurt he had been
working at the nearby school and then that night as a stage hand
for its Spring musical. He occasionally had bit parts in plays elsewhere, but his specialty was operating ropes, pulleys and various
stage effects. He also fancied himself a film-maker.

The last time Kurt saw Jacob Califf was in East Hampton,
shortly after Deerfield expelled him for infractions he would not
specify but were obvious enough once we saw the room upstairs.

Califf had used old-boy connections to send his bought, blond
headache—the puppy the ex-wife soon tired of—away to the private school, and he used more to wipe the record clean. He gave
Kurt a thick wad of severance—as if Kurt were an employee and
not a son, however ill-gotten—and told him he never wanted to
see him again. I like to think that Kurt got his walking papers in the
same office where I gave Jacob Califf his. That was the closest I
came to telling Kurt. Had I done so surely he would have clapped,
but I didn't trust his applause.

Kurt wound up back to the Berkshires, lived on the money for
a while, bought better video equipment, went through a succession
of day jobs as he became a playhouse rat; as if his looks, his East
Hampton party pedigree and private school plays qualified him.

He also had the room upstairs. It is just a guess but I think he
has kept his current job as a groundskeeper and maintenance
guy at the Taconic School down the road in part by not bringing home seventeen year-old coeds to star in his home movies,
though he seems to have had no problem with older townies from
various Pioneer Valley hamlets.

I told him my story to explain how his older brother, who had
once lived in a shipping container on the Albany docks, had managed to arrive in a black BMW, with Lissa wearing a gold crocodile
pendant as old as the Magna Carta and worth as much as the
BMW. She lay against me on the couch in the living room that first

day, her head on my shoulder. Halfway through, she whispered in my ear: "I like this story better than the other."

The Maersk shipping container was a start. When I closed the doors the only light came in through a gash near the floor, where a forklift had ruptured the metal. The container was abandoned, useless, but the security goons kicked me out anyway, telling me I was not even worth the trouble of a phone call to the cops.

I made my way out to the Northwest, where it rained a lot, so I had heard, at least on the west side of the Cascade Mountains. I had always liked the rain; it made the left side of my face feel better, the skin less tight somehow. When I told Kurt about the years on the Seattle streets, sleeping under overpasses, under the sidewalks of Pioneer Square where the old level of the city used to be before the fire, taking goldilocks showers for a night in homes on Queen Anne hill and in Wallingford, he perhaps was expecting the explanation for my money to end there.

But I took the story out into the woods, to a man named Shadden who lived under something called the "blue hole" of Sequim where it hardly rained at all, thanks to its peculiar siting east of the Olympics. I was looking for a place to build a cabin, I said, where I could stay; a refuge much like Fado, Lennie.

On the Bear Creek trail a few miles west of Lost Mountain I heard moans and a snarling and came upon an old man about to get mauled by a cougar. I chased it away, waving my arms, making a lot of noise like one is supposed to do with the big cats. The old man had fallen, hurting an arthritic hip, I found out later.

I carried him a mile back to his place, offered to go get some help for him but he declined, and I soon found out why. Here was Grampa with a gray pony-tail, growing weed behind a cabin bigger than Fado, with a roof covered with moss, green icing on a cake.

His name was Carl Shadden. He said he had once been a college professor, back East at Bowdoin, though he was originally from the Northwest. He came back after his wife died and moved first to Port Townsend, then to the 'hunting lodge' here, as Shadden called it. And now I had one, too.

Both of us got a bargain. Shadden could read but not well because of cataracts, so I read to him, badly at first, but with his help I got better—a lot better. He showed me, as best as he could, how to shoot the hunting bow and I became proficient at that, too. I helped him grow the weed and sell it, in Port Angeles, Port Townsend and Seattle. He smoked a little of it—helped his eyes, he said. He had a lot of money from that, stashed away, he said, in surplus army ammo boxes.

Shadden never trusted banks, did not trust some greedy CEO to run off with his money and never go to prison for it; said he had to see the money or it did not exist for him. So he stashed it. He told me that when he died he was going to give it all to me, for saving his life, and caring for him in his last years.

When he died I was supposed to go to a lawyer in Port Angeles. He had it worked out with this fellow, so I could get the okay to take what was in a P.O. box—the location of the ammo boxes he hid in the woods. A few days after I buried the old man, I found the ammo boxes and the money, five boxes worth. In one of them he kept a medal from WWII: a Distinguished Service Cross, a laurel one shy of the Medal of Honor. He was one of only six in his platoon who were not killed, wounded on D-Day. There was also the necklace and pendant in that same box. Shadden had told me about those, said he got them toward the end of the war from an SS officer who had looted them from a museum in Paris. The Nazi wanted to barter them for his life, but Shadden bayoneted him anyway. Shadden's wife wore the artifacts once a year on their anniversary, for fifty years.

Lissa and I showed Kurt the pendant and the necklace—which I always kept on me except for those times I gave them to Lissa to wear. But Kurt seemed more interested in what I had told him about the bowhunting. "The old man really teach you how to hunt with one?"

By way of answering him, the next day I bought a bow; cost me $600 with the target arrows. I had not used one since I left Shadden's, but I put the second arrow into the hole of a birdhouse above the door to the barn out back, from thirty yards away, then gave the bow to Kurt.

He learned quickly. Four days later I woke up from a nap to clapping outside. Not Kurt's. Lissa's. When I came out she said: "There was a crow sitting on the arrow you put in the hole and Kurtsie got it." He had pinned the crow to the birdhouse.

The impaled crow was still there three months later when Kurt and I got back from the Adirondacks, ready to go after James Malloy. Other birds had pecked away most of it.

I stayed at Kurt's red house longer than any other place besides Shadden's. Lissa liked it there. She had moved around a lot and I think she thought of it as home, the three of us together as we had been long ago. She liked cooking for us, though Kurt was the better one. She liked the evenings together on the porch, when we all were not off watching Kurt in one of his productions, talking about what might have happened to Marla and what we might do if we ever found her again—if she was alive. She asked both of us if we could remember who our father was but we couldn't. Marla never talked about him.

One night after we had been drinking Maker's Mark, she and I were upstairs and Kurt came in and said, "Don't mind me, keep going," and began filming us. Lissa said to me: "It's okay. It's like before, remember? It's like that French word, when you've been there before. It's just the three of us, like always."

It was true. Kurt had only been only seven when he saw us doing it the first time in the house in Gloversville, New York, with Marla away at work and probably not coming home that night. We let him watch. "He has to know how it's done," Lissa said then, or something like that. Years later, when I found out later that she had showed him "some things" herself, all she said was: "Better me than someone else." I did not talk to her for two weeks after that, but she brought me around. She always had.

Later we watched what Kurt filmed. "You two are something else," he said. "The necklace makes it work big-time."

Lissa especially liked it at the red house because she got pregnant there. She had always wanted a child; Charming Billy kept shooting blanks. I began reading to her when she began to show a little, and sometimes Kurt—he called himself Uncle Kurt when Lissa broke the news—would read to her, too, from some play. *Our Town* was one of his favorites. Lissa liked us both to do that. She said she had read somewhere that if you read to your kid while they are inside, the kid will turn out to be good with words. "Just like you turned out to be, Richard. And Kurt, too."

Kurt talked a lot about moving to California, getting into films for real; just go, the three of us. But with Lissa pregnant that wasn't feasible. Still, she wanted to get away before she got too big, because once the child was born, things would change. California was not an immediate solution but maybe someplace closer. She got the idea of going up to the Adirondacks, maybe find that place Joe Piersall's family used to have near Saranac Lake. Do a goldilocks, one last goldilocks. Maybe it was still there, she said, the place Joe took us to back then, Joe being eighteen so he could drive. "Remember?" Lissa said.

I remembered. Joe had other things on his mind, namely her. He did not know the Lampron boys, but to get to Lissa he had to take us. He thought we would not be a problem. Kurt and I beat him to a pulp for what he tried to do to her up there. We left him senseless, drove his own car back and got in trouble but not so much as Joe did. What he did was bad enough but the worst came from his father, a town cop embarrassed that his eighteen year-old son got the tar beaten out of him by kids younger than he was.

Lissa said we could do some bowhunting up there, too, since it would be the start of the season in September, or close enough anyway. I would kill a deer and show everyone how to dress it and cook it, like Shadden showed me.

You must know how this is going to end, Helen.

It began well enough.

We never did find Joe Piersall's place; I do not know why Lissa or any of us thought that a possibility. But we made do with a campsite just off the trail, and four miles from the trailhead where we parked the car. Loon Lake was less than a quarter-mile away, close enough to carry water to boil and, as it turned out, a good place to hunt. The doe lingered too long by the shore, sensed my presence too late. She bolted right into it: a perfect lung shot from twenty yards away in the late afternoon.

I carried the doe back myself since Kurt was in camp, not feeling well, and Lissa was taking a nap. I slit the deer, hung her up to drain behind the tent. We were going to have venison for dinner the next day.

We never did.

That evening Kurt and I were in the tent; Lissa was out in front by the fire we kept smoky because of the black flies and mosquitoes. They were bothering her a lot, and the smell of insect repellent made her feel sick.

Three men came down the trail wearing netted head gear because of the insects and I heard Lissa say something about one of those hoods being "just what the doctor ordered...these damn flies are eating me alive." She was laughing when she said it, serious but not really. The last guy of the three stopped and took the hood off and gave it to her. He and Lissa got talking. I did not hear what they were saying but just as I got up from the cot to end it, the man left, hurrying to catch up to the others.

By the time I got out Lissa had put on the hood, the bottom edge covering the pendant she had worn the whole time we had been camping. She went on and on about this nice guy, name of Malloy—Jim Malloy—from Delmar, not far from where she moved to Voorheesville after she and her family left our town. Small world, kindness of strangers.

She looked like some kind of wolf-lady with that thing on.

I yanked it off her head, tossed it into the fire. The wolf's hood crackled and melted in a minute.

"He was breathing into that," I told her. Kurt had come out by now and he said: "You don't know he wasn't sick or something. Not a good idea."

"He looked healthy enough to me. He said he didn't need it anymore because they're heading back home. Go fuck yourselves, the both of you." I had never seen her so angry.

She went to sleep with her back toward me. I woke up in the middle of the night to see her by the rekindled fire and asked her what she was doing out there—before I saw her reach for one of the two bottles of Maker's Mark Kurt had brought. It was a party of one. She giggled, saying she could not sleep, had a lot of things on her mind.

She pointed the bottle of whiskey at me, Kurt in the tent, and then somewhere off in the direction of the trail: "Eeenie meenie minee mo..."

I grabbed the half-empty bottle from her and threw it into the darkness.

"You know you should not be doing that."

She slurred the words: "Why did Kurtsie bring it then?"

"Not for you."

"You talk like a fucking preacher—hey, catch a preacher by the toe…"

"Lissa, that is enough…"

"Blah, blah—Mr. Blah-blah." She lifted the pendant like it was a comic book amulet. "Back, back I say!"

She giggled again as I went back to the tent. "And if he hollers let him go…"

Kurt had woken up: "What was that all about?"

"Nothing. Go back to sleep." It was a while before I could. When I woke in the morning Lissa was not in the tent. I got the fire going, waited for her. Maybe she had gone for water, or to relieve herself. After twenty minutes she had not returned. I woke up Kurt.

Six hours later we had not found her. She would not have gone far in her condition. If she had fallen, hurt herself, we would have heard her cries or the whistle, part of our gear for the woods. We all wore one around our necks. There were only two other possibilities. And when we hiked back to the trailhead and did not see her by the car, that left just one.

I asked Kurt: "What did she say his name was again?"

"Malloy. James Malloy. From that town…Delmar. He was going back home."

"He did it. He saw what she was wearing, the pendant, when he stopped on the trail. He came back for it."

"I bet he came back for a lot more."

Kurt said something else but I was not listening to him. I was seeing this James Malloy on the trail, watching her by the fire, the fire crackling, masking his approach; and Malloy thinking this would be easy, seeing as how she was drunk. Her back had to be turned to him. Then he crept close enough for a quick arm around her neck, so she could not use the whistle. A quick hand over her mouth.

Helen, surely you realize Sean Malloy might have done the same to you if I had not prevented it from happening. I could not with Lissa. You are alive now because I learned my lesson. But this Malloy, he dragged Lissa down the trail while Kurt and I slept.

James Malloy, from Delmar, New York. Just south of Albany.

"Ricky?"

I heard him now.

"Ricky, what are we going to do about it?"

"We will talk about it in the car."

"We're not going to go to the police then?"

"No."

"That makes sense," he said, "if we're going to do what I think we are."

CHAPTER 7

SWITCH

I WOKE WHEN someone said, "Hey, Coach, there's someone in here."
Boys in blue and gold uniforms clustered around the entrance to the dugout, gloves hanging from their hands. I heard a clunk behind them: someone dropping an equipment bag.

"What's going on, guys?"

One boy, taller than the rest, pointed with his bat at me through the chain link fence of the dugout. "Uh, he was sleeping on the bench or something."

I knew the coach, Phil Giacone, a classmate of mine at Bethlehem Central. He'd taken over Andriano's Pizza, helped run the town's youth baseball leagues. Every now and then I'd run into him at the Owl & Thistle, a tavern next door to Andriano's, and he'd always asked me—before Katie disappeared anyway—about coaching a Babe Ruth team. He wasn't going to be asking me again. If I could smell my whiskey-soaked shirt, he and his players surely could.

Phil told them to go warm up. They didn't move far. Watching a drunk stumble out of the visitors' dugout at Schuyler Crest Park was a lot better than throw and catch.

"What's up, Jimmy?" Phil said.

"I took a walk, couldn't get to sleep. I guess I did here."

"Looks like it…you okay?"

"Yeah. Sorry about this…the kids."

He coughed a little, looked away to his players, then back. "Things happen…take care of yourself, all right?"

As I walked toward the gap in the outfield fencing, the kids were still watching, no doubt talking about the guy they found sleeping it off in the dugout. They were old enough to know what that meant. I doubted Phil Giacone would be telling them that the guy in that dugout almost made it to the one at Fenway Park.

Schuyler Crest Park was three miles from the house, and I'd stopped there to lie on the grass, remembering something someone had said at work about meteor showers, and I'd wanted to see them and tell Katie again what I'd told her when she asked me once: "What if our kid wants a telescope instead of a baseball mitt?" She had laughed. "Hey, it's a possibility," she said. "Stranger things have happened."

I told her: "Then he—or she—gets a telescope. When the kid's older we'll talk about how time slows down the closer you approach the speed of light—which is a lot easier to explain than the infield fly rule."

But the sprinklers went on, and I went into the dugout to lie down there instead because there was no place else to go until the morning when I had to go back to the house.

An hour after I woke up in the dugout I saw Brad Walsh, looking pissed from half a block away, and I realized now I'd forgotten he was going to be coming over to get some of Katie's things.

Brad was stocky, blond, lived in Latham with a girlfriend he'd met at Skidmore. He went straight from Tufts to his father's business, played fly-half for an area rugby team, the Patroons, and once had tried to get me to play on the team after I'd gotten lucky horsing around with drop-kicks at the family compound in Maine. They had a lawn big enough for that, these Kennedy wannabes. Brad—or possibly his father—had marked a big W on the football, as if there was a chance someone would creep onto their property and steal it.

He saw me soon enough, timed his sigh with precision—he on the porch and me below at the steps. "It's 11:00, Jimmy. I've been waiting for you for almost an hour."

"Door's open, Brad." I didn't remember if it was or not. Probably not. What was the point?

"I'm not going to just walk in, for Chrissakes. And anyway, I don't know where you put Katie's stuff."

"In the cellar, near the stairs. A few boxes. I haven't finished packing them."

"That's why I called you last week, to give you time to do it."

"So you did."

He sighed again, shaking his head. "I'll take what you've done then." He stepped aside as I passed him and walked in, thinking I'd just let him do his thing and leave me to do mine. Maybe it was better that none of the Walshes saw the DVD. Let the police tell them after I'd done the last thing I wanted to do and the one thing I had to.

"Where's the cellar," he asked.

"Off the kitchen, first door on the right." *Can't miss it. A guy named Shadden waited for me there while I watched a DVD of what he did to Katie …*

Stepping over the bottle of Maker's Mark he looked back at me. "You're a piece of work," he said, stealing the words I'd told his father. Then he saw the gun on the floor, not far away.

"Tell me that thing isn't loaded."

"It's loaded."

"What the fuck is wrong with you? The door's open and you have a loaded gun?"

He was at the cellar door, ruining the fingerprints, if there were any. There wouldn't be; Shadden had worn those padded gloves so he wouldn't hurt his hands knocking me out cold.

Fuck it…

I disliked Brad but he was here and the family had to know sooner or later.

"Forget the boxes," I said. "We have to talk."

"About what?"

"Katie."

From outside came a sudden blaring of music; a car stereo, a neighbor pulling in.

"All right, let's talk."

Brad sank into the overstuffed chair where Shadden had sat.

"What, you have to stand up for this?" he said.

"Yes, I do." My hands were shaking; I shoved them into my pockets.

He saw the stuffed dragon. "That one of Katie's?"

"I had a visit last night from the man who brought it…the one who abducted her and…Katie's dead. He was the one…he murdered her."

It wasn't the long overdue confession Brad probably expected to hear.

He leaned forward, elbows on his knees, and said very slowly: "What the fuck are you talking about?"

"He said his name was Shadden."

"And you say he killed Katie?"

"That's what he said." I told him everything else—almost everything. He interrupted me before I could tell him about the DVD.

"Hold on, just hold on. Let me get this straight. You're saying this big guy, some weird tattoo on his arm, surprised you here last night, had this mask on, and he told you he killed Katie because he believed you…murdered his wife or some woman up there on that hiking trip you took last year. And he wasn't satisfied with the payback of…Katie…so he threatened you about what he would do to you and your family in the future. Then he left, leaving that whiskey bottle over there. But not the gun; that's yours?"

"I thought he might come back."

"Katie know you had a gun?"

"Brad, are you hearing what I'm telling you?"

"Oh, I'm *hearing* all right; I'm just not believing a fucking word."

It had been a mistake to tell him and it would probably be another to let him see the DVD now. But he had a front row seat now; he was Katie's brother and I admit it, I wanted to wipe his *you're-Looney-Tunes-Jimmy* smile off his face.

"He also left something else," I said and pointed to the television. "A DVD. Katie's on it. It's…" My lips began trembling and I thought I was going to lose it, right in front of him.

"It's what?"

"You might not want to watch it. But if you do, it's there. Right now I'm going to get ready to go to the police with it."

I went upstairs to shower and change clothes.

When I came back down he was passing through the living room, carrying two boxes of Katie's things to the door. He kicked the whiskey bottle out of his way, sending it spinning to a corner. The television was on: the scene from *Unbreakable* where Bruce Willis is leaving the hospital, walking the gauntlet between relatives of the train wreck victims.

"Brad, that wasn't…"

"You're sick, you know that? A sick joke."

I kept waiting for Katie to appear on the DVD—what I'd seen—but the movie kept going and then Brad came back, stood in the hallway, arms folded.

"He must have switched DVDs while I was out cold," I said. "He took the one with Katie on it, and left that one. It's the only explanation."

He smirked. "Explanation?"

"Brad, listen to me. Why…"

"Oh, I'm listening all right. And you know what I'm hearing? A lot of…*he*. Who is *he*? Just who the fuck is this Shadden guy you never saw?"

I looked away, to the low table where Katie and I kept family pictures and the baseball—the foul ball we caught—our icon, with her old telephone number on it: *275-4299*. I could see the tiny numbers clearly. Chulu Jones, one of the buddies who went with me on that hike, once told me he would have given his left nut for my 20-15 vision. Not now he wouldn't.

And what was Brad Walsh seeing? Brad, who came here still half-believing I had something to do with his sister's disappearance, was seeing things that *could* be explained. The bruise on the cheek, cut on the wrist? *Hit himself, cut himself to make it look good.* The gun, the bottle of whiskey? *Props.* Why bother with the story about the switched DVDs? *Very creative. The would-be novelist had to have some story, didn't he?* The stuffed animal? *Took it from Katy's car.* The point of entry into the house? *Anyone can break a glass window.*

Bruce Willis was talking to his son now.

Brad said: "I wouldn't take that to the cops. Then again, maybe you *should* go, tell them a different story, the real one. Or you could tell me now. Let's both sit down this time and you tell me what *really* happened."

"He took it. He took the one with Katie on it."

Brad stared at me, then shook his head: "You need some serious help."

He slammed the front door on his way out.

I heard the squealing tires, the gunning engine, an angry shout. I went to the window. Brad's car sped away, much too fast for a quiet residential street. A neighbor had managed to give Brad the finger while holding a garden hose. He glanced at the house with obvious disgust: *what next from that place where the woman disappeared...*

Before the day was out Brad would be on the phone to his father, who might not just be pleased that I was obviously cracking up, delusional; he might make a few more calls himself.

I suggest you interview James Malloy again. My son had a very disturbing talk with him, last Saturday morning...

There was nothing to take to the police now to back up a wild story; no fingerprints to lift, he had worn gloves; no DVD with Katie on it; no description of the vehicle he'd used; nothing of himself except what I'd seen on his arm: a bizarre tattoo of a black skull with windmill vanes. But I couldn't be sure. It had been the flash of a moment. How many men with criminal records had tattoos on their left arm? Thousands? Hundreds of thousands? And he might not even have a record.

For everyone except me—and a man named Shadden—last night might as well have never happened.

I put away the gun, carefully bagged Katie's stuffed animal, the DVD and the bottle of Maker's Mark. Then I sat down at the kitchen table with a pad of paper and wrote everything I could remember about what Shadden had said, and did my best to sketch that tattoo on his left arm. The handwriting was almost illegible; it was all I could manage now.

I got in my car, drove away and stopped abruptly at a crosswalk for two boys on bikes. The kid behind rode into the other in front because he was staring at a guy who was talking to himself with no one else in the car.

I waited until they sorted out the little collision, turned on Delaware Avenue, toward Albany, to look for a new place to live.

THE BOOK OF ERIC

LENNIE, IF MICHAEL FUREY was at the core of your triskell, Lissa was with mine. She was my capstone. When James Malloy took that away, the arch collapsed.

For a time, however, there was a reprieve, while Katie remained with Kurt and I in the red house. Surely you can understand what had to be done with her, given what Malloy had done. She could not live and have her child, no more than Lissa could. That may be Old Testament but so be it. Kurt filmed her last minutes in the time it took him to finish the bottle of Budweiser he brought upstairs.

My brother and I planned the visit to Malloy together, choreographed the play. The script was mine because Lissa had been mine, but Kurt was at Malloy's house with me, content with silently filming the man's well-deserved humiliation and letting me do the talking, as I had insisted. Ever the stage manager, he switched the DVD while Malloy was unconscious and he clapped as we walked back to the car two blocks away, pleased with his work. As ever, Kurt was his own audience.

After that, back at the red house, the unraveling began. Kurt was impatient; he wanted to kill Malloy soon. My brother has no conception of what a stalking hunt truly is much less the patience it requires, but then he did not come from the same depths as I. He prides himself on his filming but he has neither the imagination nor intellect to conceive, as I did, a work of art without form: the pursuit, harrying and gutting of James Malloy's life, year after year, until I tired of it and killed him.

We came back to an empty house after that night at Malloy's, to acidic emptiness. Kurt began to bring in women to film while he fornicated with them. I could hear what he was doing to them upstairs. Twice I heard him tell two different women that while she was in the room he was going to call her Lissa, because… "every star in my movies needs a stage name."

He desecrated that room with women no better than whores, and one of them stole Katie's engagement ring and a Kokopelli pin she had been wearing the day we took her from Malloy. I keep the necklace on me at all times, so that was not taken, but I thoughtlessly had kept the ring and pin in the bureau, with everything else I had saved to remember her. I suspect Kurt may have used the ring and pin as props, making it easier for the woman to simply walk out the door with them while I was in my room.

Kurt was angry when I told Kurt to get those artifacts back. He was away for two days, but he brought them back, then told me he wanted me to leave, return to the Northwest, wherever; he did not care as long as I got out of his life and stayed out for good this time.

He said this was his house, the special room upstairs his room, that Katie had been as much his as mine, that he had fornicated with her when I was away. He claimed she had been carrying his child, not mine. He raved on and on about that. I did not believe a word of it. Katie would have told me.

It was a performance, perhaps his best; a final act before the curtain call. I said I would leave in the morning. When he said he was leaving for the night, I assumed he was fearful of what might happen to him if we both remained in the house before I left. But it was more than that, as you shall soon see.

The next morning I loaded up the car with some clothes, my hunting bow and little else except a few pictures of Lissa and I that Kurt had taken. I went out the back fields, past the tiny skeleton of the crow Kurt had skewered to the bird house, heading toward the forested ridge line and the stone fence and the hiding place where I kept the money I'd gotten from selling Califf's hoard of artifacts. Like Shadden, I had to see the money, touch it, know that no one else knew where it was except for Lissa; where I did not have to ask anyone for a key to what was mine.

That is how they catch you. Go into a bank, tell them you wanted to deposit the cash equivalent of Jacob Califf's hoard—or do you like the other story better, Helen, as Lissa did?—and the cameras are all over you, everywhere, recording you for someone behind a wall to see you. Blond, handsome Kurt, without a mark on his face, liked to be seen; that is why he did his plays. I did not. Perhaps that is why I moved best at night, liked the forests and stayed so long at Shadden's. But in a bank…Someone behind a wall, a partition, pushes a button or whispers to a superior and it is all over.

The hiding place was less than a mile from the house. I walked along the crumbling stone wall that meandered through younger maples and oaks, evidence that this had once been farmland. In the four times I had been through these woods I had yet to see anyone, though twice I spotted deer—always reminder to give myself a tick check when I returned to the red house. Now, I saw a cardinal flitting from a branch.

I passed the overgrown ruins of a farm house which meant I had less than a hundred yards to go until this stone wall met another at the juncture of what had once marked a far, rising corner of the farm. From there, I could see across a gentle swale, to a development of homes under construction. Today, the morning mist obscured the development when I got to my cache.

I had chosen the place for several reasons: I could come here at night, easily following the stone wall until I came to the juncture; and also because the rise and thinning trees here gave me a clear view of the surroundings. I could make sure no one approached. I could easily heft the stones with both hands, though a boy or a woman might have difficulty, as Lissa did the only time I brought her here.

The wall had crumbled to one side of the juncture and that is where I had hidden the surplus ammo box a day after Lissa and I arrived at the red house, while Kurt was away in South Linfield. I had buried it under two stones resting on a third to keep it off the ground.

When I lifted the first stone I knew something was wrong. I should have seen a wedge of olive-drab steel. I tossed away the stone, frantically gripped the second, dropped that.

The ammo box containing $280,000 was gone.

I tore at the stones, hurling one after another against the top of the wall, dislodging more, and picked up a fallen branch, broke that in two on the spot where the ammo box had been. I kept half because I needed something in my hands to break again. I hurled those pieces and began running back.

Of course it had been Kurt. Who else? I always looked around when I came to the hiding place. There was no reason for any-one else to poke around an old stone wall. But Kurt, if he had followed, staying back in the woods, would have wondered. Why follow me? Because he knew the money had to be somewhere. He knew I never went to a bank.

Had Lissa told him, betraying me? Or was it just Kurt, who knew the money had to be somewhere, so he tracked me, using the cheap binoculars with which Lissa used to watch the cardinals out back. And he saw me—or Lissa and I that one time—and wondered if we were going to fornicate in the woods, brought his camera.

So he saw the place, came back at night with a flashlight while we slept. Put the box away in a safe place, his own hidey-hole like Shadden had. He might have thought of killing me, but Kurt...Kurt liked to manage the stage, move the people around. Now, though, he would try to do it. If he was simply going to take the money and disappear, he would already have done that. He knew I would go get the money. He was timing his return to the house, to wait for me.

The only question was whether I could get there before he did—and wait to kill him.

I sprinted past trees, pushing it harder along the stone wall, thinking only of the gun in the car, and getting back before he did, and killing him—but not before he told me where he had hidden the money. I pictured this: shooting out his kneecaps, setting him up as a target in the back, a living prop, and crucifying him, one arrow at a time, arms then eyes. Bull's-eyes at thirty yards, death of a scavenging crow, like the one he killed with a lucky shot.

Where is the money, Kurt? Right eye first, then the left. *Where is it?* Then his crotch. One through there and he would be finished fornicating behind my back, if that was true about Katie...*Where is the money?*

When I came to the fence at the back of the yard I circled around, keeping in the bordering trees. I stopped, panting, fifty yards from the driveway and the barn.

His truck was parked behind my car.

I had the keys in my pocket but I had forgotten the spare set I kept on the rack in the kitchen. I saw him now, coming down the steps, heading for my car, his .22 rifle—the one he used for crows and squirrels—tucked under an arm.

I took a step. Rush him, take my chances? No, he could get off three shots, hit with two. I might make it, but not in good enough shape to finish him when I got there, and not if I took one in the head.

Kurt fired the rifle at a rear tire of my car, swiveled and fired again at a front tire, same side. The blowouts echoed. The car was not going anywhere now. Kurt looked around as he placed the rifle on the roof of the canted car and I instinctively kneeled, though he did not see me. He unlocked the car, leaning in, and I almost went for him then. But within seconds he backed out with the gun, like he knew it was there.

Had Lissa told him? How could she have betrayed me? I had taken her away, given her a new life, the gift of the necklace.

I watched Kurt take out my bow, bring it to the porch.

I considered my options. Leave, go buy a gun? I had less than $100 on me—and the necklace. But I would not sell that, nor will I ever.

Stay in the woods, wait for the opportunity to sneak back up on the house at night and kill him in his sleep? Kurt would not be that stupid, stay in the house alone, not knowing if I was out there, waiting for my chance. Wherever that dog lay down for the night, it would not be at the red house, not for a while. He had all my money now to go anywhere, for as long as he wanted, and friends in the area whom he would undoubtedly ask to keep an eye out for his brother.

He stayed on the porch, sipping a beer, cradling the rifle, my gun within easy reach on the closest of the three chairs, waiting for me to show, figuring there was little I could do now. He knew the money had a past, whether or not he believed what I had told him. He must have seen the car's registration, seen the name—Eric Lane Caster—and figured there had to be a reason why I was no longer Richard Lampron.

I left.

I had enough money to get me to…Syracuse? Steal a car to sleep in and head west. Stay long enough in the bigger cities to mug waiters flush with tips on their way to their cars after a busy Saturday night shift. I did that occasionally in Seattle. One could spot them a block away in their livery of black and white.

I kept to the woods for a few minutes, walking south, then where the road took a turn hopped the split-rail fence, coming out just past the entrance to the Taconic School and continued along the shoulder, stepping over a dead raccoon that had lived only long enough to crawl from the middle of the road.

I figured it would take me a day to get to Great Barrington and a local bus north to Pittsfield and then west, plenty of time to think about why Kurt did not kill me after he took the money.

Perhaps Lissa had indeed betrayed me. Perhaps she was still alive. Told Kurt the location of the cache, and he and I could not find her because she had simply left that campsite, as she and Kurt planned? Perhaps she was even now waiting for him in Los Angeles, where she would star in his first film, bankrolled by my money. She had loved it, after all, when he filmed us fornicating. The only condition of her betrayal? That Kurt kill me, to make sure I would never find them.

Or perhaps Kurt was the one frightened that I would ultimately find and kill him.

Perhaps.

Was Lissa's campsite Maker's Mark drunkenness a bravura performance?

What do you think, Helen?

What is certain is that I will never know for sure, so they will all have to die, sooner or later—Malloy, Kurt…and Lissa. Then, as now, I would bet the necklace it was Malloy who began it all, taking Lissa from me. But I would never do that, Helen, not with your necklace. So they all have to die.

You shall be a part of it, I promise you. And another promise: you shall resume your painting. We will find a place for you to do that. In time, I will not have to sell them for you; in time I will be able to trust you to do that yourself. There will be many paintings besides the ones you have already done—those displayed and many already bought from that gallery in Pioneer Square, not too far from where I used to live under the streets, where I first saw your *Book of Michael*.

We will have our fortune again, thanks to you. There will come a time when, if anything happens to me, you will find Malloy and Kurt and Lissa and do what I could not. Who would not let a woman such as you get close enough to do that? Such will be our bond, surpassing even the one you have with Michael Furey.

And should anything happen to me, you will always have this testament, this one-of-kind artifact. Is it not so different than what you have done for Michael, who lives far from this cabin, with yours? Promise me only that you will show Kurt and Lissa the necklace before you kill them for me. I am sure you would think of something equally special for James Malloy.

Do you know there was one other person who saw the necklace, besides Kurt and Lissa? It happened on the road, perhaps three miles from the red house after I left the brother who stole my resurrection from me.

A girl of ten or eleven was in a swing in her front yard, digging her feet into the air as children do, as Lissa did in the red house; as you did, Lennie, in the canal swing you sketched in your book, with Michael pushing you to get you started.

This little girl did it all by herself; there was no one behind her. She saw me and waved at the top of one arc, her feet high over her head, her long hair brushing the grass. Such a bold and fearless girl, to release one hand, instead of holding on.

I stopped, took the necklace out and the girl saw it on the next arc and waved again. I put the necklace away, the secret shared, and walked on. The girl's black hair streamed out behind her as she swung, the same color as yours, Helen.

I did not know it then, of course, but it was a sign, another miracle perhaps, for you to have aged so beautifully in the time it took me to cross the country and find you.

CHAPTER 8

LARK STREET

TWO MONTHS INTO the new apartment I was still waking up from the nightmares, but toward the end of the summer they became less frequent. And I began thinking that it might be okay. If he had found me once, he could surely do it again, just a few miles from the house in Delmar. But it was also possible that a man like Shadden could wind up dead himself, or in prison. Katie couldn't have been the first for a predator like Shadden. Even so, I resolved to move again in a few months, to Boston or New York. And perhaps one more time before I could stop looking over my shoulder.

The second floor apartment was on Lark Street, one of Albany's brownstone neighborhoods west of the state capitol Mall. I did my running there in Washington Park a few blocks away, starting and ending at the Robert Burns monument which had an inscription that John Walsh wouldn't have understood: *The rank is but the guinea's stamp/The man's the gowd for a' that.*

I changed jobs, found work as a night bartender at Jason's Steak House near the bottom of the State Street hill, not far from the old D&H building and the riverfront park. The restaurant was only a twenty minute walk from the apartment.

I added a better lock, always looked before unchaining the door so I wouldn't be surprised on the way out, and kept the gun loaded in the top drawer of the bed-side table. That drawer was partially open at all times. I also kept a baseball bat in my car and one by the door. A bat wouldn't be much use if Shadden came with a gun, but it made me feel safer anyway.

I altered routines. Sometimes I'd walk to work, sometimes drive. No matter how late it was, I first made sure when I left work that no one was following me. Occasionally I left Jason's through the kitchen, out the back-alley exit. I never went directly to the apartment, took the extra few minutes to watch from a block away, in my car or not, to see if anyone lingered suspiciously close by. I developed the habit of stopping abruptly, wherever I was, and looking behind me.

I spent a lot of time on my days off at Kells, a tavern across the street from my apartment. I'd take my time drinking a few beers, enough to justify a window table while I wrote, pad and pen. Sometimes I did get work done on *Angel's Share* but not much because my attention would invariably wander to the street, looking for a big man with a tattoo on his left arm.

Once the weather turned too cold for short-sleeves though, I was left with only the hope of seeing a car that didn't belong in the neighborhood, a big guy in a car that kept coming back—anyone who seemed suspicious enough for me to follow. Because the one thing I wanted more than Shadden not to find *me*, was to see *him* first, follow him and watch him leave a red house, wherever that was, and break in and find the stuffed animals and then make a call to Hal Penders, the FBI Special Agent whom I had talked to twice in the months after Katie's disappearance, and tell him I found the man who killed her.

Marcy knew where I lived but I wouldn't let her come over, and risk Shadden seeing her and getting the wrong idea. Nor had I gone over to her place since the time, not long after it happened, when I went to see her and tell her what had happened. She was a clinical social worker at Albany Medical Center. She knew how to listen. We talked for two hours about it on a Wednesday night, after Davy was asleep.

She believed me. Of course she did. I was her kid brother. But before I left she gave me a piece of paper with the names and telephone numbers of three people: "Just if you need someone else to talk to, Jimmy."

Shrinks.

It was an asterix to belief—a well-intentioned asterix since she was my sister.

Someone to talk to *because* it had happened?

Or someone to talk to because I was way out in the deep water of delusion or paranoia?

I thanked her, hugged her. Two minutes after I drove away from her house I crumpled up the paper and threw it out the window.

I didn't need shrinks. They couldn't see the DVD because for them it didn't exist. All they could do was filter what oozed out of me. I didn't need to hear them tell me that *quite possibly* the 'Shadden episode' was the black, gooey residue of my father walking out the door and never bringing home the banana ice cream; that Shadden was the manifestation, the sum of it all: my father's skedaddling, my mother's early death, the erosion of the close relationship I'd once had with my brother, and Katie's disappearance—*Oh, God, Katie*—and the end of my dream of making a flat-out diving catch on a sinking liner in center field in front of a full house at Fenway.

They'd call that a kind of death, too. They'd tell me…ouch, you're one angry fella, but we see no overt self-destructiveness, unlike what you've told us about your brother who also chose to flee from the unseen…dark riders, we'll call them. But you've chosen to conjure them for real, focus them to a point, like lasers do with light, and give them a single name—Shadden—because if it has a name, if it exists, then perhaps it can be dealt with, banished, and your hurt will go away. Do you understand how this Shadden's threat is particularly revealing since you will have to live the rest of your life, too, with the legacy of all that has profoundly saddened you, hurt you, disappointed you? They're one and the same, do you see?

I didn't need to hear bullshit. What I needed was to find Shadden and banish him from my life and make sure he would not take anyone else's. One way or the other. I needed to get on with my life somehow with this…creature out of it. Or I needed to see a man with that particular tattoo on his left arm, and let Hal Penders do the rest. But if I had a choice I'd put a bullet in his head for Katie—for us both—and not lose a night's sleep over it.

I KEPT AN unlisted telephone number I gave to only a few people—Marcy; my manager at work, Carl; Peter Crary, a good friend with whom I'd worked on the Penn State newspaper in the off-season. He was now living in Binghamton with his wife Monica. I brought no friends or co-workers over to my place. So far I'd had only two visitors.

Victor Vitelli was one—my baseball coach at Bethlehem Central. One evening as I made dinner I heard heavy steps on the stairs. Those steps weren't what I usually heard. The person who lived next to me was a woman who couldn't have weighed more than a hundred pounds, including all the makeup she wore. I grabbed the bat by the door. Shadden wouldn't be paying a visit at the dinner hour, but I gripped the bat anyway as I slid the grate open, to see Coach V, red-faced and puffing from the single flight of stairs.

I let him in. The first thing he saw was the bat I leaned against the wall.

"Good," he said. "Still taking your swings."

VICTOR VITELLI HAD taken over a .500 team halfway through the season after the previous coach, Arnie Schlicter, left abruptly for personal reasons. In reality he'd lost control of the team. The jury was out for this one but one thing was certain: this guy wasn't a bantam-weight screamer like Schlicter and he knew the game better. The feeling on the bench for the first game was that if you pissed off Vitelli with a lack of effort, the guy was big enough to knock you from first to third.

I was fifteen then, the only freshman on the varsity.

We won that first game under Vitelli, beating top-dog Shaker High at home by six. After the game, I sat reading on the curb behind the dugout, waiting for Marcy to pick me up. She was late; the other guys on the team had already left. Maybe she'd had a fight with Sean, telling him yet again he couldn't just stay in his room listening to music, or watching television. Then again, he probably wasn't even around. Sometimes he'd take off after school—if he'd even gone that day—and not come back until midnight. Mom didn't know what to do anymore. None of us did.

Coach V came by, metal bats clinking in the canvas duffel he carried. They clinked more when he put the bag down—Santa Claus in May, sweats and all, arms almost as thick as our shortstop's legs. Word was he'd once been a catcher in the Yankees organization but that didn't come from Vitelli.

"You know what you did today?" he asked.

"Uh, three for four," I said.

"I mean the head first slide. Listen, you're fast enough for spikes first, and doing that also might make the guy covering the bag a little more nervous; so maybe he screws up the double play. Do your more valuable extremities a favor and cut that stuff out."

"Got it, coach."

"You know, they told me about you when I came aboard and so far it hasn't been a mistake to move you up. You're one of the few I've had who could do it, go all the way, and against my better judgment I'm telling you now. So don't mess it up."

"I won't."

He tipped the cover of the book I was reading: *The Stand.*

"That's not a book, it's a backstop. Worth it?"

"I won't ruin the eyes. I mean…well, I hit the guy's curve for a single today, a change-up for another and his fastball for the triple."

"Just keep it up," he said.

I figured he was still talking baseball, maybe a warning about the eyes.

"I just had them checked, coach. The doctor said I could be a jet pilot I wanted. 20-15 in both." Sean came in with 20-20. Marcy had to get glasses in fourth grade—go figure—and it still pissed her off she had to wear them and her brothers didn't.

"I meant the book," Coach V said.

WE'D KEPT IN touch over the years, through college and then minor league ball. He knew I'd messed it up after all. I hadn't seen him for several years. He was pushing seventy now, with a hitch in his breathing that didn't sound good.

I was making pasta with meatballs, offered him some and a glass of wine but he took a pass on the food. "I just got off that stuff. My doctor has me eating like a rabbit, but he says a little wine's okay."

He said he'd contacted Marcy, wondering what the hell had happened to me and she gave him my address and phone number and the hint I was going through a tough time. He'd been in Albany visiting his eldest daughter, Vicky, decided to stop by.

I put away the food for later; I wasn't going to eat if he wasn't. We had two glasses of wine apiece by the time I finished telling him what had happened. He got up from the table, put a hand on my shoulder.

"I'm sorry," he said, kept the hand there for a moment, then walked to the window, as if he, too, was looking. Then he asked if I wanted to move in with him. "It's only me and Maryellen now that the girls are on their own. No one'll find you there. Everything would go through us, less for this psycho to trace."

"I couldn't do that."

"The extra eyes could help. It's not like I got a golf game to take up my time and Maryellen just has her bridge tournaments. We might see something when you don't—it's what has to happen so you got something to take to the police. You should have gone before but maybe it's too late for that now. Anyway, think about it. You can tend bar anywhere, get on with things, work on a book. I think I remember something about you wanting to be a writer."

"Just getting back into it."

"One of those thick ones?"

"We'll see."

"What's it called?"

"*Angel's Share.*" I pointed to the desk near him by the widow, the manuscript. I always printed out the pages from the computer as I wrote them, to see the pages piling up in three dimensions. The manuscript was an inch thick so far.

Coach V went over. "This is it, hunh?" He lifted a few pages, saw the dedication. *To Victor Vitelli, who saw the book behind the backstop.*

"Jimmy…that's a heckuva thing to do."

"I have to finish it first."

"You will. It means a lot. But me? You got a lot of people to choose from."

"Not so many."

"There'll be more."

He said he had to go. "Think about the offer, okay? You need a place where you're not always at the window to see if that fucker's outside."

After he left I went there, thinking that was the first time I'd ever heard the man swear. I saw him pause on the sidewalk below, catching his breath maybe, but also looking around. He glanced up, catching his breath. He gave me a wave, which I returned. His right hand moved across the chest, then down his left arm, shoulder to elbow. For a moment I thought he was giving me the steal sign from long ago.

He'd always put the game in motion. Advance the runner. Hit behind him. That's what he'd told me to do. You won't always get home standing on the bag, waiting for a home run that might never happen.

I wished it had been a sign. But he was just scratching himself over his heart, maybe feeling that hitch in his breathing while he paused to get his wind back after the stairs.

THE ONLY OTHER visitor I had was Beverly Curtiss, a cocktail hostess I worked with most nights at Jason's. She was 28, married to a guy who'd been the lead mechanic at a car dealership on Central Avenue and now was halfway through a second stint in Iraq with the National Guard, repairing Humvees instead of high-end imports.

Beverly was working on a degree in computer animation at SUNY-Albany during the day. Occasionally I'd walk her to her car after a closing shift and once drove her home when her car was in the shop. She was a big fan of the Wallace and Gromit animated films, had a bumper sticker that said: *May I someday become the kind of person my dog thinks I am.* I kidded her about that because she didn't have one, but she said they would, she and her husband Bill, once he got back for good this time. In the meantime I gave her *Marley and Me* as a birthday present. She was a slim, pretty redhead, who never lost her composure during the hectic Happy Hours, early and late.

I was off the night she showed up at my door at 1 a.m., looking anything but composed. Through the grate I saw her hands nervously twisting the strap of the shoulder bag she always carried. She asked if she could talk with me about a personal problem, something that had just happened at work.

I hadn't gone to bed yet but I must have looked reluctant to let her in. You work in a restaurant you know everyone else's business and Beverly knew I wasn't seeing anyone. Maybe she thought I had a one-night stand in there because she suggested the morning if it wasn't convenient for me now.

She was obviously upset. I let her in. We talked until 2:30 a.m.

Daryl Huston, an assistant manager on the job for a month, had closed the restaurant that night, and he'd hit on her in the employee dressing room upstairs, next to the office, in a way that went far beyond the usual flirting and raunchy talk that always goes on in restaurants.

It had been a rough night, Beverly said. She'd gotten a complaint and Huston had kept her late, after everyone else had left, to talk about it. That wasn't so unusual, discussing a matter after a shift, but in retrospect he obviously had wanted the restaurant empty for what he had in mind.

The hero turned out to be Francisco, the closing dishwasher, who had gone out for a smoke in the alley, padding his hours by twenty minutes before coming back in to punch out. He'd heard Huston, and Beverly's protests, peeked in, and that stopped Huston from going further.

I offered to drive her home but she said she was okay. I gave her my phone number on a slip of paper, in case she wanted to talk more. When she left she was still undecided whether to quit or file a complaint as I urged her to do. When I went back to work a day later, I found out she had indeed talked to Carl, the GM, who fired Huston.

The last time I saw Beverly was on a Tuesday night, at 10 p.m. She was doing fine, considering what had happened, happy to be off early for a change. I paused in the middle of making a French 75, to give her a thumb's up, which she returned on her way out.

The next morning I slept through the phone ringing at 11 a.m.—too early for a bartender—but I got up and answered at noon when the phone rang again.

It was Carl, and he told me what happened to Beverly.

"We're closing for the day; no way any of us can work."

I went in anyway; so did everyone else.

She had been found that morning, in a corner of the parking lot of a Days Inn, two blocks from the entrance to Union College in Schenectady, by a father and son from Pennsylvania who were checking out of the motel prior to the son's 9 a.m. interview at the school. Police identified her through a medical bracelet she always wore.

We found out that Huston had been in New York City the night Beverly had been strangled. Two detectives interviewed some of us at the restaurant, in the private dining room, but I wasn't one of them, which surprised me because they must have run the records of all the employees.

I almost walked in there anyway, but what could I have said? *I think the man who murdered Beverly was the same one who abducted, murdered and raped my fiancée, who warned me he would do the same to others I chose to bring closely into my life, because I had supposedly done that to a woman named Lissa on a trail in the Adirondacks near Saranac Lake...*

I should have gone in there anyway.

I didn't. What could I have given them except a story they would not believe because there was no evidence, no description of the man, just a name that likely wasn't his and a tattoo on his arm. And maybe my gut had it all wrong. Beverly was just a work-place friend; she'd spent less than two hours at my apartment. There were plenty of others out there like Shadden, I told myself.

Two weeks passed. Her husband flew back from Iraq. There was a memorial for her at the Holy Trinity Catholic Church on Union Street, not three blocks from where she had been found on Nott Terrace. It was just enough time to make me think that what had happened to Beverly was a random event—terrible but random. A robbery that ended tragically. She'd been seen leaving work that night with her shoulder bag. It hadn't been found near her body or anywhere close by.

Two weeks to the day she was murdered, I saw the folded white sheet of paper on the floor as I was about to go out for a late-morning run. I didn't think for a moment the landlord had left the note for some reason. I knew it was from him. I hurried to the window, hoping to catch sight of a big man, hurrying away, glancing back, and finally...seeing his face.

The immediate vicinity of Lark Street was empty except for an elderly lady pulling a shopping cart that bounced on the uneven bricks of the sidewalk.

I read the note by the door. The handwriting was small but very legible:

Where were you, Jimmy? I knocked but no answer.

I apologize for taking so long to return but some things have happened and I had to go back to get one of Katie's stuffers for you, the smallest one she had. She said her father bought it for her years ago at Disney World, if I remember correctly. Anyway, go have a look outside your door and bear witness, again, to what you have caused. I warned you, and you chose not to believe me. Moreover, she was married, Jimmy. Taken. Surely you knew that. Once again you took another's One.

You could bring what I have left to the police, like a good Scout, but rest assured, that would do you as much good as the DVD of Unbreakable. *My timing could have been better—perhaps when you were not working at Jason's. But between you and me, the last thing I want is for you to wind up in prison. No stuffed animals in there.*

This is goodbye for now. I am going away for a while; I miss the rain on one side of the mountains and the bowhunting on the drier other. I am lighting out for the territories; maybe roughing it, my wannabe writer friend, but our twains shall meet again.

S

When I opened the door, Beverly Curtiss' shoulder bag swung into the room. He'd hung it from the door knob, twisting the strap. A silver Kokopelli brooch was pinned to a furry brown ear sticking out of the top of the dark blue leather bag.

The Kokopelli brooch was Katie's.

Which time had it been, which of the few times I'd walked her to her car had he been watching us? Or had he seen her go into my apartment building and not come out for two hours?

I used the handle of the baseball bat to free the twisted strap of her shoulder bag and put it in a small plastic trash bag I got from the kitchen.

I left it by the door, sat down at the kitchen table, but not to decide what to do now. I knew that the moment I read Shadden's note. I needed to think of the words, the shitty lies to go along with the decision.

Five minutes later I called Carl at work, told him I had just gotten news of my brother's "attempted suicide" and had to go be with him, take care of him. Didn't know when I'd be back.

"Family first," Carl said. "Your job will be here when you get back."

I pulled my old baseball duffel bag out of the closet, stuffed it with everything I'd need, including Shadden's note, the gun, two pictures of Katie and I, whatever I couldn't leave behind. I put my manuscript and notebooks in a black, fabric briefcase—a gift from Katie.

I'd already paid a last month's rent but I wrote out another one to my landlord to cover the cost of outstanding bills, disposing of everything in the apartment, computer, the works. I left a note—the same lie. I couldn't give that story to Marcy. I had to give her another, so she wouldn't wind up calling the restaurant. But I really didn't care at this point about the consequences of mismatched lies.

I knew she was at work and I could have called her there but instead I left a message for her at home. Call that what you want, but I didn't want to get into a long talk with her. She was persistent; she was my older sister and she would ask the questions whose answers I couldn't give her.

Better this way, to let her think I just had to get out of town for a while, lighting out for the territories, like Shadden had written, like Sean had done a few years ago, and let her think that her kid brother preferred the open road to the phone numbers of the shrinks he never called.

Whether she understood or not, she would probably think—*first Dad, then Sean and now Jimmy*. I told her in the message that I'd be back but that was a lie too, because that wasn't at all certain: *I'll be in touch, Marce; I'll write. I love you. Make sure Davy doesn't practice throwing a curveball like I shouldn't have shown him how to do last year; he's still too young for it and might hurt his elbow.*

I used kitchen gloves to squeeze Beverly's plastic-wrapped shoulder bag in a small box—small enough to pop into a mailbox—and typed up her name on the computer, printed it out and also the address of the Schenectady Police Department, Investigative Services Bureau, 531 Liberty Street—and sealed it all up with her name inside.

I left the apartment keys on the table with the check and note, walked to my car, making sure no one was following me, threw the duffel in the back seat and drove the three blocks to my bank to cash out: exactly $7,345. It would be enough to last me until I found another job.

Maybe the police would find something. Maybe this would help. I doubted it.

Half an hour later I was doing 70 on I-90, heading west. I stopped at a rest area near Utica, backed into a spot, watched the cars coming in, looking for one that would have a man, a single driver. Shadden wouldn't be paying for two people to follow me, whatever he'd paid for one to find me on Lark Street if he'd hired out the job.

Practice, that's what it was.

Practice with my father's gun would come later.

Six cars passed—two with families, three with two passengers, and one with just the driver. I pulled out; the singleton didn't follow. I watched him go inside the building and took off again, pointing my car toward a...guess.

A far-away guess. But that night at the house in Delmar, he'd said this—I remembered like it had been the day before: *I never got a chance to show Lissa real mountains where cougars sometimes come down to the outlying suburbs, and the bears cuff steelhead and salmon coming back to spawn; where you can sail in the morning on a decent winter's day, and ski in the afternoon, not that I did either. But we could have out there, Lissa and I...*

And he had written this: *I miss the rain on one side of the mountains and the bowhunting on the drier other...*

You see, when I was twelve my parents sent Sean and I out west to visit my maternal grandparents. What can happen to two boys, you see them off at the airport gate and have your folks meet them at the other end? We got seasick on Grandpa Ben's boat, fishing for steelhead on the Skagit River.

Later, I remembered asking Sean why Grandpa winked at Grammy when he said: "Lucky fish, steelhead. They're sea-run trout, really. Now, they taste a lot like salmon but unlike kings or sockeyes, steelhead get to do it again. Spawn that is." She gave her husband a look. Sean answered my later question with an older brother know-it-all: "What do you think Grandpa meant? They're still old, but they still do it."

There was only one place in the country I could think of where you could sail in the morning and ski in the afternoon on a decent winter's day, with the sea being so close to the mountains; where the hunting was good on the drier east side of the mountains, real mountains that blocked the rain coming in from the Pacific.

There was no one else to go after him, and stop him from taking someone else.

That's not true, of course. I could have passed off what little I knew to the pros, hunker down somewhere, keep looking behind me every time I went out, day after day, month after month.

The difference was keeping an eye ahead, looking out instead of waiting to be found.

The truth is I wanted to find Shadden myself—I had to. For Katie and for Beverly. If it took the rest of my life, then so be it.

The Book of Eric

MOST MEN WITH a priceless necklace as their sole possession would sell it for food and shelter. I would not do that, Lennie. Perhaps your Michael would not either, if his sole possession was something of yours. I came back to Seattle with the necklace still in my pocket, and survived as I had before. James Malloy—or Kurt—took Lissa from me but not the belief that I would find someone else who would wear it as she did.

Then I saw you.

I was in downtown Seattle one evening, anticipating the opportunities of nightfall, walking down Spring Street toward the intersection with Western Avenue. The scene began to unfold from half a block away.

The homeless man—he had to be by the looks of him—had just crossed Spring, as if late to some imaginary appointment. Head down, talking to himself, he bumped into people, ploughed through a family, raising his head at the husband's angry words. That's when he must have seen the carriage passing him on Western, heading toward the intersection with Spring. You must have seen him blow you the kiss and start skipping sideways back in the direction from which he had come, back toward where I stood near the intersection. The carriage driver had to stop for the light and this streetie danced into the middle of the crossroads, arms outstretched, shouting: "Wait! Wait!" He kneeled ten feet in front of the blinkered horse, gesturing like the Pope with little lifts of his hands.

The carriage could not go anywhere, certainly not up the steep one-way slope of Spring Street. The driver could have turned around, but that would not have taken care of the problem—the crazy homeless man could have followed you the other way. The light had already changed. Cars were backed up two, three deep. The transient seemed oblivious to the honking. Some people by-passed the standoff, gawking as they crossed behind him and the stopped carriage.

I watched from the corner, unable to take my eyes off you, the woman in the carriage. Two men stood next me, one of whom said: "He may be a bum but he still can pick 'em."

The other, younger man quipped: "She's his old prom date." His grin vanished when I told him to shut up. He stared at me long enough to decide not to escalate matters and moved on, perhaps thinking that here was another bum sticking up for his own. I turned back to you and the ditchlicker kneeling in the middle of the intersection.

He made fists with his shiny, blackened hands, then spread his fingers wide—a fallen wizard casting a spell. He was not old, but had a long beard of dreadlocks that made me think of a castaway with nothing else to do except braid and re-braid the hair he could see. There was a cardboard note tied to one of the dreads with a grimy red ribbon, as if he was a child and someone had written his name and address on it should he wander from the playground.

Only one of his sneakers had laces. He wore a ripped Kalakala T-shirt—the name of the old streamlined aluminum ferry that used to cross Puget Sound. Kalakala means "flying bird" in the now extinct Chinook language. This man was not Native-American, however.

The scene had the air of an execution—Flying Bird kneeling in the street, arms out for mercy.

The carriage driver kept shouting at him to move but was ob-viously reluctant to physically confront the transient. Still, he had to do something and was about to get down, but you leaned forward, touching him on the shoulder. I couldn't hear what you said to him. You got out of the carriage, calmly, your long legs sheathed in jeans, your long black hair contrasting with the pale blue of your blouse. My hand went into the pocket of my light jacket, closing on the necklace. For a moment I thought of Lissa, who could fill out a sweater and jeans too—but nothing like this woman.

You knelt in front of Flying Bird, brushed your hair away from your face. I saw your eyes then, blue as a Cascade alpine lake. I wondered: *does she know him? Is she a social worker who cannot stay off-duty?*

I was ready, at the curb, in case Flying Bird got nasty, or if the chinless swine in the pickup, head hanging out the window, decided he could not wait any more for this "bullshit."

I kept asking myself: *why is she alone in that carriage?* There had to be a reason.

I hoped the police would not arrive soon, or anyone who might try to intercede. I was ready to prevent anyone from interfering in your evident purpose: to talk to him, persuade him firmly to let the world go on as it was now that he had stopped it momentarily.

You could not have known that you had someone on the sidelines, ready to do this for you, or help you if Flying Bird turned violent. We were in this together, even then, and it was as if you were doing this for me, a performance on a stage with a true audience of one. The coincidence was too great to ignore. I had walked down Spring Street and…here you were. Why were you alone?

I had the answer now: for me.

I had found someone deserving of the necklace. My fingers were sweating, moistening your gift-to-come.

I edged forward, over the curb now, close enough to hear you say to Flying Bird: "You'd better not wave your arms anymore, okay? You're scaring the horse, and it might bolt and trample both of us. Now, we can't stay here; we have to go before the people in the cars get really pissed off and do something bad. The police will be here soon, too. So why don't you finish out the carriage ride with me, if you want."

I had to give you a round of applause for that. A few others who had heard you also, followed my lead. You deserved it, my One.

You got in first, held out your hand, pulled him up, not caring about his grimy hand. And off you went, with the clop-clop of the stamping horse, just as the bicycle cops arrived, two of them, with no problem now to solve. Flying Bird waved at them and slyly glanced at you, as if to say: *I'm getting away with something. See what I did? See?* I was watching you all the time and you were watching his dervish hands, perhaps expecting him to flip the cops off but he did not do that. He waved like a monarch.

Silently this time, I clapped again as the carriage passed. The crowd had dispersed but I slowly followed, pacing the carriage. You did not notice me. Oh, I am sure you were thinking: *what if this bum gets weirder, tries to do something?* But I was there, Lennie, in case anything happened. If he had hurt you and fled, I would have found him because I knew where to look in the city. There would have been one less meal handed out at the Memorial Plaza on Saturday afternoons.

I followed you, pausing at storefronts when I had to, keeping an eye on you and Flying Bird all the while. The driver had his job, his back to his riders, so he would not have been able to react quickly if anything happened. I could. You could have handled it, of course. Then again, Lissa could take care of herself, too, and look what happened to her.

Flying Bird could not sit still across from you. When not waving at passersby curious about this mismatched pair in the carriage, he tapped his knees to the slow clapping of the horse's hooves. He slid from side to side on his seat, peering down at the pavement, as if the carriage was a boat riding over the waves, and he was dipping his hands down into a phosphorescent wake. After each time he did that, he would wipe his hands on his shirt, glancing at you furtively. Evidently, you were not supposed to see him doing that.

You have to believe me, Lennie: the only other time in my life I felt this euphoria was when I walked out of Jacob Califf's house with a fortune slung over my shoulder. That and seeing Lissa again for our all too brief resurrection.

I shadowed the carriage as it made a loop, coming back along the waterfront and finally to a garage opposite the old Federal Building on Western. The driver said: "Okay, pardner, time to go." Flying Bird jumped off, gave an exaggerated bow to you, then skipped away across the street, shouting "Did it! Did it!," and wiping his hands on his shirt one last time before turning a corner.

I waited for you to finish up with the driver and then followed you to your car parked in the lot in front of Nijo's. I had no intention of approaching you now. That would have been like taking a shot in the woods before knowing it would bring the animal down. No, I just wanted to see you safely to your car. If had had a car then I would have followed you home, but for now it was enough to see you drive away up Cherry to First, in a green Toyota Highlander.

I walked back to Western, sighting the back of the green and gold carriage—Emerald City Carriages—and the driver in his graying pony tail and wide-brimmed leather hat, heading toward the waterfront for more business.

One way or the other I intended to get what I needed from him.

I hailed him from the sidewalk, took all the money I had from my pocket—four twenty dollar bills. The driver pulled up on the reins, clearly hesitant about getting down and opening the carriage door for this particular customer, and relieved when I waved him off: "Not this evening, thank you. I have a favor to ask."

"Okaaayy," he said.

"I saw what happened a little while ago, with the woman in your carriage and that…man in the intersection. Did she happen to tell you her name? I would like to meet her and tell her in person that she made my day."

The driver looked me over and I had to turn away momentarily to hide my anger. Grandpa drives horses, empties the bag of excrement dangling behind the horse, and he was looking at me like I belonged there.

"Well," he said, "She did tell me her name but you gotta understand I'm not comfortable giving it to you."

When he just stared at the two twenties I offered, I had to fight the urge to pull him down from the seat and get your name another way.

"We will come back," I said, "if it is okay with her, get another ride from you, the two of us, all right?"

"That isn't the point, fella. Look, here's as far as I'll go. She's an artist, she said, has a showing at a gallery in Pioneer Square. Andrews/Chase. Why don't you introduce yourself to her there, maybe even buy a painting."

This drover was pushing it. Though he seemed confused at the disparity between my clothes and my words, he still had a look on his face like: *buy a painting? How about some decent clothes first.* He said: "Now, if that's still worth forty bucks to you, I'll take your money."

I handed him the bills. "Oh, one more thing."

He sighed. "Yeah?"

"You get another forty if you tell me why she was going for a ride in your carriage all by herself. Did she mention that?"

"She said she was celebrating a birthday. I said 'Happy Birthday' and she told me it wasn't hers."

I gave him the last of my money. "Thanks, brother." I even winked. Man to man. Remember how it was, old fella?

I assume the birthday was Michael's or your son's. Am I right?

I began walking toward Pike Place Market, heading toward Queen Anne Hill and maybe more luck in that toney neighborhood. I hadn't yet read about Michael's 'passing lane,' but that's what I felt I was in then. I walked and kept seeing you again, the way you brushed back your hair with your left hand as you kneeled in front of Flying Bird, taking care of the problem so calmly, as if no one else was watching you.

In time we will take a carriage ride, you and I. You shall be wearing the necklace. Whoever wore it two thousand years ago, I have no doubt that someone else was doing the driving for her too then.

CHAPTER 9
SEATTLE

THE RUSSIAN KID was out there as usual, throwing the safety ball against a wall of the courtyard through a gap in the bushes. Dimitri had marked a strike zone onto the brick with white chalk. I'd added the black chalk on the inside and outside edges, explaining to him what 'painting the black' meant.

His mother sat on the stoop across from the one that led up to my second-floor apartment, drinking tea, smoking and tapping the ashes into a tuna fish can, the cell phone hidden by her blonde hair.

Kira Petraznik waved at me as I came up the walk at 6 p.m., after a day of re-sodding part of a playing field in Magnolia. I scooped up the ball that had rebounded away from her son, tossed it back to him.

Dimitri's mother worked in a bank downtown, spoke English well and we'd talked enough for me to know she'd lost her first husband, an electrician, in the *Kursk* submarine tragedy. He had been one of the lucky ones, she said, because he hadn't lived long enough to write a note. I told her I'd lost my fiancée in an accident. She'd asked me once up to her apartment for tea and I declined and that was that—though she may have wondered why, since she was pretty, intelligent and hadn't seen a woman come up to my apartment in the four months she and her son had been at the complex.

I got my mitt and a baseball from inside. I'd picked up the glove at a neighborhood garage sale for ten bucks; the smell of oiled leather around the apartment was a bonus.

Dimitri was a good kid, big for his age, a leftie like my nephew Davy. He was warmed up but I needed a few easy tosses first. The ritual had begun after Dimitri broke a window out there by himself—my window. We fixed it together without the apartment manager finding out. I began taking a half-hour after work to show Dimitri how to throw and catch properly, oil his glove, swing a bat. I showed him the game of Porky Pig, which Sean and I used to play: whenever you screwed up a catch or throw you had to say "Porky Pig"—rules of the game. I got a kick out of the way Dimitri pronounced it: *Porky Peeg*.

We went at it, back and forth. He mixed in the change-up I taught him with a fastball, always grinning before he threw it so I'd know it was coming. He was getting better—still wild but better.

Kira stood, telling him it was time for dinner. The boy and I ended on three consecutive good pitches—we always did that, even if it took a few to get there. He gave me a wave. "Later," he said. I nodded, and as I always did when we were done, I glanced back at the street, just in case.

At the top of the stairs to my apartment, I put food in a bowl for Jack Two. I didn't much like cats, least of all one who had pissed and scratched the carpet in front of my door until I began putting out food. I had no idea why he chose me for his provider. He reminded me of one I'd seen in a newspaper photo that showed a cat sitting on his haunches looking up at a black bear he'd treed somewhere in Oregon. The newspaper cat's name was Jack, and he'd done this not once, according to the caption, but twice before.

I'D ARRIVED IN Seattle to a renter's market so I managed to find a small apartment complex in north Seattle that would accept additional security, two extra months' rent and two references. I used Coach V and one of my baseball buddies for those. I didn't want my Lark Street landlord getting a call from his counterpart in Seattle, since it would be an easy thing for Shadden to get that information from the guy.

I needed a job right off, but restaurants and bars would be the first places Shadden—or a hireling—would be looking. When I wasn't playing baseball during high school summers I'd done some free-lance landscaping work, so I thought that might be worth a try. I got a job with Eden Landscaping, based in Ballard, a gentrifying neighborhood in northwest Seattle where the Alaskan fishing fleet was based. The owner had immediately offered me the job, under the table. He said he preferred to have at least one guy on a crew that could speak English he could understand. He smiled when he said it; the guy was Hispanic.

The plan was not to stay in one place too long, keeping only enough possessions to fit in my car, and dumping the rest. My time at this apartment was almost up. I'd be moving on in few more weeks.

I used a sleeping bag and air mattress for a bed, kept the gun underneath the rolled up blanket I used for a pillow. Everything was either scavenged or bought at garage sales: a folding chair, lamp. For a dinner table I used a piece of plywood supported by cinder blocks, covering the wood with a folded bed-sheet. The dinner table doubled as a desk. After a few months I returned to *Angel's Share*, writing longhand.

I had no phone, no television, had all my bills sent to a P.O. Box. I couldn't tell you which movie was grossing the most, which politician ahead in the polls. I worked on the book, oiled a glove I didn't need except to play catch with Dimitri, and read Patrick O'Brian novels and all the Faulkner I'd misplayed in college.

Since I'd been in Seattle I'd called my sister only twice, once from San Francisco when the plane fare was too low to pass up a weekend visit to see the Giants' at AT&T Park, and the other time from Coeur d'Alene, Idaho, where a thousand bowhunters had gathered for a convention at the big resort on the lake.

Truck stops along I-5 and I-90 became my post offices. I'd ask a trucker to mail the letter when it was convenient for him, just so long as it wasn't in the Northwest. Some were suspicious—you couldn't blame them these days. Money usually persuaded. One long-hauler at an I-90 truck stop in Cle Elum asked me: "So what'd you do?"

This was smack in the heart of the Cascades, a few exits past the one leading to the secluded spot where I practiced with my father's gun.

I shook my head, handed him a twenty. "Any place past Montana will work."

The trucker took the letter, pushed away the bill: "I was there once."

The letters to Marcy and others were short and mostly lies, with inspiration gleaned from Sunday newspaper travel articles. I couldn't yet bring myself to tell her I was in Seattle. But at some point I'd have let her know; the way things were going, it could be years before I found Shadden.

A few months after that call to Marcy from San Francisco I had just gotten off work and was driving on Leary Way in Ballard, glanced to my left and there was Sean, not fifty feet away at a Shell station, wearing a waiter's uniform of black pants, shoes and long sleeved white shirt, filling the tank of a blue beater.

At least I thought it was him.

I slowed so suddenly the guy in back almost rear-ended me. A Hansen Brothers moving van pulled ahead of me on the left, blocking my view. By the time I managed to turn and drive by the gas station, the car was gone. I made no attempt to race after him—if it had, in fact, been my brother, which was unlikely. The last I knew he'd been working at a Chart House in San Diego.

I hadn't seen him in a long while, and we'd spoken only a few times on the phone. During the last call I told him about what had happened that night in Delmar.

"Wish to fuck I'd been there," he said, the closest thing to belief I'd gotten from anyone, maybe even Marcy. Then he went on about something only the two of us knew about, something I hadn't even told Katie.

"Remember that guy in the parking lot?" Sean said.

It was the last time I'd seen him. He'd surprised us all and came home for Marcy's birthday. We were going to pick up her birthday cake at a supermarket. A guy with two earrings in one ear and a rag around his head went postal on an old fellow who'd dinged his new pickup. Sean and I tried to calm the asshole down, which didn't work and then the jerk told me to fuck off—mind my own business—and threatened to get a wrench from his truck and put a dent in the old fellow's head. Seanie was holding the box with the cake. All I did was step in between the two of them—at first.

Sean laughed, recalling it. "Captain Kidd was so rattled after you put him on his ass that he left without his rag."

We were almost an hour late bringing the cake home, what with the cops, witnesses who confirmed that the jerk swung at me first. Marcy got me an ice bag to put on my hand, and I wonder now if she wasn't thinking about that incident—and the others—when she gave me the list of shrinks.

Was it my brother there at the gas station on Leary Way? Probably not but it sure looked like him. Still, it was still the closest thing to any kind of hope I'd had in finding Shadden.

Because if I could run into my brother in a city of half a million, maybe there was a chance I could find Shadden, and I went through the list again: *a bowhunter, probably his thirties and living alone; who possibly had enough money to hire someone to find me; liked going to the theater, so a Renaissance type with his plays and bowhunting; who talked in an oddly formal way and had on his left arm a tattoo of a skull with windmill vanes.*

I used my days off and most nights, in the warmer months of the year, looking for a man with that tattoo. I prowled beaches, Seattle Center, the malls—wherever there were crowds. I spent a lot of time near the major Seattle theaters—the Rep, Intiman and ACT—watching from a careful distance the men leaving after a performance. Seattle was a casual place, and I saw plenty of bigger guys coming out in short-sleeves or even T-shirts. The married men were easy to spot. I doubted very much Shadden was married.

I was suspicious enough to follow only four men who'd gone to the theater alone—two from the Rep, and one each from the others. I hadn't seen any tattoo since the men had worn either a jacket or long-sleeve shirt, but they'd been alone and the right physical size. I eliminated all four soon enough for various reasons. One drove in a hybrid car to a very large Craftsman-style home near Volunteer Park on Capitol Hill. Shadden might have money but returning to a home like that in a small hybrid didn't fit.

Another man had an Amnesty International sticker on his car. A murderer and rapist offended by torture? Another had kids' toys and a play structure in the front yard of a Phinney Ridge home. The fourth? I heard music blasting on the car stereo before he shut it off in the driveway of a

Madison Park home that had a wind-chime on the front porch. Whatever music and home decor Shadden liked, it probably wasn't James Taylor and wind-chimes.

Every time I felt it was useless I reminded myself of what was worse: sitting around and waiting for him to find me first.

I frequented the better restaurants in the city, on the assumption that a solitary man, possibly with money, probably went out to eat a lot. I couldn't afford these places so I'd find a spot in the bar where I could keep an eye on the traffic, nurse a beer for an hour, and move on to the next.

Always there was the thought that I'd guessed wrong about this part of the country. But I reassured myself by remembering the camo mask he'd been wearing that night. I'd seen similar ones in bowhunting magazines. There were plenty of places in the country to hunt with a bow, but none fit better than what he had told me and written in that note about the proximity of water to mountains, the dry and the wet. That's Washington state, a geographic schizo, with a maritime climate on the Seattle side of the Cascades, and a continental one on the other.

In the Cascades you could hunt for most anything—bear, deer, cougars. A month ago in Issaquah, a suburb nestled in the western foothills of those mountains, a cougar had made the news loping across the parking lot of a new Home Depot. Within an hour's drive of the Space Needle there were signs at trailheads warning hikers what to do if they came across a cougar. The idea was to let the big cat know you weren't prey, a deer, so you were advised to wave your arms and make a lot of noise. In other circumstances I'd consider that good advice for living your life in general.

I thought of getting into the sport myself, joining one of several bow-hunting clubs in the area, but decided that was too risky. Shadden might see me or otherwise find out someone was asking questions. I didn't see him at the 'Bow-Con' in Coeur d'Alene, but I went back repeatedly to Roslyn and Enumclaw, towns within two hours of Seattle where there were bowhunting clubs. I didn't go into these places, only watched from a distance those who came and went.

I was more direct at sporting goods stores, especially the few that spe-cialized in bowhunting equipment, working in the "friend with a tattoo" in various contexts. He had to buy his arrows and equipment somewhere, and somehow I didn't see him doing that on-line. He probably moved around a lot and wasn't facile with a computer. I drew blanks in stores from Bellingham to Tacoma; Seattle to Wenatchee.

He was out there somewhere and by now I had to assume he would start looking for me if he hadn't already. Whenever I got to feeling that he would have as much difficulty in finding me as I was having in finding him, I thought of Beverly Curtiss.

ON A WARM Thursday in July I got home a little early from a job in Laurelhurst—laying a brick patio for the varsity baseball coach at the University of Washington, no less. I showered, didn't feel like making dinner, so I decided to get something at the Fiddler's Inn before hitting a few restaurants on Seattle's waterfront. Then back to the apartment and an hour's work on *Angel's Share*.

I had a riff I used in restaurant bars. I'd steer the conversation to tattoos, surprised no longer at how easily you can tack the conversation around to your bearings. So I'd say something like: *What's the strangest looking tatt you ever saw?* Then I'd mention my nominee: *Saw a guy once with a windmill on his arm, looked like a skull...*

And hope the guy on the stool next to me, or the bartender, would say: *Now that's weird. Guy came in here just the other day, had one just like that on his arm. Has to be the same guy you saw; couldn't be too many of those running around.*

And the haystack would suddenly get smaller, or the needle bigger. If I couldn't get anything more, I'd stake out the bar every night for Shadden to show again, whatever it took.

It hadn't happened.

Not yet.

The Fiddler's Inn was a fifteen minute walk from my apartment. I took a route through the complex, past kids splashing in a pool just large enough for the management to boast of having one, then cut over to NE 75th.

When I got to the Fiddler's, a low, shambling tavern sided with fake logs, I ordered a burger and a Guinness. The Mariners were playing the

Red Sox at Fenway. Marcy, an avid Red Sox fan, was probably watching the game with Davy. Maybe that was the reason why I suddenly wanted to call her, besides the fact that I hadn't written or called her in a while, and wanted to know she was okay. When I finished the burger and paid up, I walked to the back for the pay phone, used a $25 calling card I'd bought for the last time I'd called my sister—and telling myself that she was a continent away from the guy I was looking for here.

"Hello?"

"So you think the Sox will do it this year?"

There was a pause, then: "*Jimmy?*"

"Hey, Marce."

"My God, where *are* you?"

"Getting a bite to eat in a tavern, watching your lefty heartthrob, Ron Mahay, about to give the game back to the Mariners. He should've stayed an outfielder."

"That doesn't tell me much—east, west or fly-over?

"Seattle."

"You're in *Seattle*?"

"Passing through."

"I was just about to call the police there."

My gut clenched: "Are you and Davy okay?"

"No, no…we're fine here; it's Sean. He's in Seattle."

Someone watching the gamed whooped.

So it was him at the gas station…

"Is he…all right?"

"That's just it. I don't know. I got a call from the manager of the restaurant he's working at. He hasn't shown up for three straight shifts. Didn't return any calls."

"Anyone go over to his place?"

"Two co-workers. Got no answer. The manager—Carson something or other—thought he should inform the next of kin Sean listed on the job application before calling the police. I was Sean's emergency contact, 3000 miles away."

"He probably hadn't been in Seattle long enough when he got the job to list anyone else. Did they notice his car there?"

"Shit, I didn't ask. That...wouldn't be a good sign if his car was still there."

"No, but we don't know yet."

Seanie had attempted suicide once before, with pills; twice if you counted the time a week after high school graduation when he crashed his car into a tree near Colonial Acres in Glenmont. He hadn't been drinking and a witness said the driver seemed to swerve deliberately toward the tree.

I said: "I thought he was still in California."

"Same here. I didn't know he'd moved on to Seattle."

"Last time I talked to him he sounded okay, said he was getting into photography."

"I'm worried..."

"Marce, he probably just got fed up. A guy at the restaurant I worked at in Albany wanted to go to the Burning Man Festival, couldn't get his shifts covered and never showed up."

"Yeah, but some people at your place must have known he was maybe going to stiff them."

"Well, you're right about that. Listen, I'm here, I'll handle it."

"What about the police?"

"I'll go over there first," I said. "Right now, they'd just tell me to come back when it's clearer he just hasn't taken off to Vancouver, or wherever. He moves, that's what he does; makes him feel like he's on his way to somewhere better. Wasn't he in Phoenix for a few months before San Diego?"

As soon as I said it I realized it could have been Seanie and Marcy talking about me. Maybe they had once. Marcy was probably thinking the same thing, given the moments of silence over the line, punctuated only by her clearing her voice: *First, the old man, then one brother, now the other...what the fuck's up with our family?*

"I'm just worried is all," she said. "I mean, he would have called into work if he'd gotten stuck somewhere, his car broke down, or even if he was just...fed up, like you said."

"I'll find out. I'm…here. We'll wind up having a few beers together. We're way past due."

"That makes three of us."

She gave me Sean's phone number and address. It was in the Crown Hill neighborhood in north Seattle.

"Jimmy?"

"Yeah?"

"No, never mind, it's silly."

"Try me."

"Well, Davy's doing what Sean used to do."

"What's that?"

"The point and scoop thing he did when he was a kid. Remember? Whenever he saw something he liked—didn't matter what or who it was—he'd point at it and then curl his hand back to his chest."

"I'd forgotten about that."

"You were pretty young. Sean was maybe six. You copied him for a while. Mostly you guys did it when Mom was around. She'd just roll her eyes, but it annoyed Dad for some reason. He'd brush Sean's hand away, like it was a bad habit, like biting his nails."

"So you're thinking…you're worried maybe you'll be getting a call twenty years from now that Davy's missed three shifts of work and no one knows where he is?"

"Of course not. I told you it was silly. Forget it."

"It's your mom-prism, that's all. Maybe that's what Sean has just done."

"What?"

"Well, point. Except now he's old enough to grab it, whatever it is— listen, I got to go. I'll call you when I find out what's going on, okay?"

"All right. Thank God you're in Seattle.

If only you knew why…

Which she would have to, sooner or later.

I said: "Love you, kiddo."

"Me too. One more thing…You've got to be tired of the roads and those day-job gigs you write about. Think about Christmas here. We haven't had one in a while, all of us."

"We'll see."

"And bring him back with you. I'm pointing at you both."

I walked out of the Fiddler's Inn. Sean was so close I could have kept going west and in an hour I could have been at his apartment. I hoped like hell his car wouldn't be at his apartment when I drove over the next day.

THE BOOK OF ERIC

IT WOULD HAVE been easier to stay for the night in one of my Pioneer Square hidey-holes since the gallery was there, but Queen Anne Hill was where I had to be, to watch the sun go down on what I was sure would be the last day before a new beginning.

You must have been to the little elbow of a park on Highland Avenue, at an elevation almost equal to that of the Space Needle. Such a panorama of the city to the south! There once was a mate to Queen Anne Hill I have heard—Denny Hill—but a hundred years ago the city fathers thought hills bad for business so they sluiced the hill into the harbor to extend the city in that direction, working around recalcitrant residents and marooning their houses on pinnacles of land, until they gave up. There once was water where I watched you in the carriage.

I went to that pocket park on Highland Avenue, where on weekend afternoons the wedding limousines pull up. Happy couples disembark for picture-taking, perhaps hoping that an unrivaled view will mean an unrivaled marriage. Million dollar mansions rise across the street.

It would have been an even more wondrous end to the day to have stayed for the night in one of those and never mind its security system probably costs more than your carriage driver makes in a year. As it turned out I found a much more modest place yet a minor miracle nonetheless.

I continued farther into the neighborhood. Night had fallen by now; a gibbous moon hung over the Queen Anne playfield. Across from it, a row of homes stepped back high on terraces. Residents had to take angled flights of steps to get up to the big porches rarely found in modern homes. I didn't know then that you had such a porch in your childhood home in Leary Falls.

An airport Shuttle Express van pull up in front of one of these houses, and I stopped at the end of the block to see if the van was letting off passengers or picking them up.

When the driver got out and ascended the steps two at a time, I knew I would have a place to stay. From the amount and size of the luggage the driver soon brought to the van, I could have stayed a week. But all I would need was the night—to shower, get some clothes that might fit just enough; the man who followed presumably his wife into the van was almost as tall as I, though skinny.

I waited ten minutes after the van left, then broke into the house from a rear cellar window next to the doorwell. People think that makes a lot of noise and it does but only if you are impatient and smash it. You have to pressure the glass, fracturing it before removing the shards.

The couple had a dog, some kind of terrier—not like your Ruckus. I had to do something about the yapper. After removing the kitchen oven rungs I cornered the wee beastie, slapped its muzzle hard, grabbed the pink collar, stuffed the dog in the oven and closed the door.

The woman of the house had left a note on a kitchen counter:

Janet—thanks for looking after Sophie. Her food's in the box and her pills. Give her two a day—important! After you put the pill in, rub her throat like I showed you how and she'll swallow. She's used to a.m. and p.m. walks. We walked her before we left so she'll be okay until tomorrow when you come over at 11 like you said. Feel free to use the Explorer while your car's in the shop— keys and leash are on the hooks. Here's some gas money if you take Explorer to go on that hike with Sophie and Milo—otherwise treat yourself! See you on the 5th and thanks again for taking care of my furry baby.
Love to you and Bri,
Mom

I had never had a goldilocks quite like this one, not even with Lissa. The house smelled like eucalyptus and there was plenty of food in the refrigerator—probably left for the daughter. I used the microwave to heat up some kind of seafood casserole, complementing it with the last of a bottle of Clos du Bois chardonnay.

From magazine labels and a few bills left on a table by the door, I found out their names were Margery and Tom Carlisle—not that it mattered. But I derive pleasure from knowing whom I should thank, in absentia, for their hospitality.

I did not have to go through the closet trying to find the best fit of clothes and shoes because in their bedroom they had a large aquarium half-filled with one, five and ten-dollar bills. It must have been Margery who had pasted the note on the aquarium: *One year to go—the Bahamas and Atlantis!*

I took the aquarium into the living room, poured myself a tumbler of Macallan from their stash of liquor in a dining room sideboard. Whatever the amount of bills, it surely would be enough to stop by Nordstrom's downtown and kit myself out in attire suitable for an upscale Pioneer Square gallery tomorrow afternoon.

Before I began counting and stacking the bills, I picked out a CD for some music, and chose someone named Eva Cassidy. I wanted to hear a woman's voice. Her rendition of "Over the Rainbow" was exquisite. She sang her song as I counted the Carlisles' vacation money. Given another few months they might have had plane fare for all of us. With what Margery had left with the note, I had the most money since Califf.

I put it all in a bag, and replayed "Over the Rainbow," because I liked it so much and because it could not have been a better song for a day like today.

Have you heard of Eva Cassidy? She is dead now; I am sure of it, reading between the lines of the cover notes. She was blonde and attractive but nowhere near as beautiful as the woman in the carriage, whose name I still did not know. Did Eva Cassidy know she was dying when she sang that song? Was that what made it so transcendent for me? Such a stunning and sensuous voice and she is singing from the dead.

I went to bed in my clothes; old habits die hard. I set the alarm for 9 a.m. Before I fell asleep in Tom's and Margery's bed I thought about the idea of singing from the dead.

Is that what drives artists, Lennie? Why they do it? Creating something for others to hear or see or touch long after. Certainly the person who made the necklace—your necklace—was an artist.

I made a mental note to ask you about that. I did not know your name yet but that did not matter because I would find out tomorrow, and by this time tomorrow it would seem as if we had known each other all our lives.

CHAPTER 10

A GLOVE FOR SEANIE

I CROSSED 35TH, on my way to find out which *fuck-it* my brother had chosen—suicide or moving on. Up the hill, near Eckstein Middle School I could see part of Mt. Rainier—or Tahoma, what the Native-Americans called it. If there was ever something that might make a kid point and scoop, the mountain was it.

For all I knew Seanie had headed north from California to see it and stayed. At fourteen he knew all about that mountain where, in 1947, Kenneth Arnold saw, thought he saw or lied about seeing the things flying around Mt. Rainier that were soon dubbed "flying saucers." On a clear summer day like this one, anywhere you went you could see the mountain to the south: 14,000 feet of active volcano, still capped with snow at the top and still claiming the lives of climbers most every year. It's a stunning sight for a guy from the East Coast, where the mountains are foothills compared to the grandeur of Rainier.

Sean had been obsessed with UFOs, the alleged government cover-up, Project Blue Book, Donald Keyhoe's books on the subject, Roswell, the works. And I'd followed him in that for a while. We "incorporated" ourselves as The American Space Research Organization, wrote and drew pictures of aliens for a five-page "magazine" called *The UFO Inquirer*, and "published" it with the help of a teacher. Sean browbeat a few of our friends into buying copies and organized backyard sleepover vigils, camera at the ready, to scan the night sky for saucers with the help of a small

Unitron refractor telescope, a shared gift we got for Christmas. When the saucers didn't materialize, some of us would swing the telescope around toward Betsy Friedman's house in the hopes of seeing Betsy—who was developing early and bountifully—through her bedroom window. These sleepovers and my partnership with my brother dissolved, ending in discord, as Sean accused me and the others of not being "serious" enough about UFOs—meaning we began to have other things on our minds, like girls.

I GOT CAUGHT in traffic around Green Lake, a much-favored mecca for bicyclists, joggers and strollers. I took 85th across Aurora Avenue, the most direct route to the Shilshole beaches and the view of Puget Sound, Bainbridge Island and the jagged Olympic Mountains beyond.

I checked the address Marcy had given me and there it was: a small apartment building on the north side of 85th where the mixed zoning begins, tucked behind a row of business, including the Fredd of Switzerland European-style hair salon.

The Patrician Apartments. Number 6.

I parked, found his apartment number on the row of twelve mailboxes in the entryway, and walked down a short stairwell. I didn't hear any bell or buzzer when I pressed the button, so I knocked, waited, listening to the shouting in the apartment somewhere over Sean's—a squabble about the television.

I knocked again, more loudly, got no response, and went back upstairs, found the manager's apartment near the front entrance, buzzed the door—this one worked—but got no answer either.

A guy came in and said: "Help you?"

I told him I was looking for the manager.

"That's me. Sheldon Watson." He had a tiny American flag pinned to his red golf shirt. His belly sagged over a ring of keys. It was a toss-up who was fatter, pound for pound—the lord of this twelve-unit realm, or the basset sniffing at my ankles.

The dog didn't budge an inch when Watson yanked the leash. "Don't mind Sheila," he said. "She just smells something on your shoes. They oughta have more dogs working the airports for terrorists, my opinion. If you want to rent, there's no vacancies."

"I'm looking for Sean Malloy. I'm his brother."

"Just missed him; saw him when Sheila and I were setting out for the walk—you look like that's good news."

"That's very good news."

The dog strained on his leash and this time it was Watson who couldn't be budged. "There's not a problem, is there?"

"Not now; I just hadn't heard from him in a while. I'm visiting in town from back East."

"Never been there myself, unless you count Chicago."

"Did he have a suitcase with him when you saw him, like he was going on a trip?"

"Not that I noticed and that would be hard to miss. Probably just going to the Safeway. Well, maybe not, since the store's just down the street and everybody walks. Always a selling point to tell people who want to rent from me these days with gas what it is."

"Did he seem to be doing okay? Like I said, I haven't seen him in a while."

"Well, it's not like I'm one of those—whaddayou call them—conseergies; I just manage the place. But sure, he seemed fine. He was eating a cookie big as a dinner plate almost, broke off a chunk to give Sheila. He also gave me rent money, which was late, but what're you gonna say he shares his cookie with your dog. Not that she needs it."

"Thanks for your time, Mr. Watson."

"Hey, don't mention it."

I backed up almost to the corridor wall to let them both pass to their door, with Sheila leading the way. She was inside when I asked: "By the way, would you happen to know the kind of car Sean runs, so I know what to look for?"

"Some small import, blue I think. Dent in the side."

That fit what I saw at the gas station on Leary. Watson let the dog go, leash and all. "You know," he said, "it's crossed my mind maybe he's in trouble and you're something else besides his brother."

"I'm his brother."

"I know, but I gotta ask. Sheila didn't growl at you. Dogs are something else. She doesn't growl at Sean either, about the only tenant she doesn't. Anyway, doesn't matter who you are I suppose; I got my rent."

I had to smile. "I think maybe the both of you should work at the airport."

"Naah. When the shit hits the fan, people won't be flying but they always got to live somewhere this side of Park Avenue."

I STAYED IN my car, waiting for Sean to come back. I figured that by the time he and I had finished catching up it would probably be late, too late to call Marcy who went to bed early and got up early. So tomorrow morning then—for the good news.

Sean probably didn't have the job any longer, but whatever the reason he'd bailed, it didn't seem like he was in deep trouble. If you're on the edge, you don't stop to share a cookie with your landlord's dog.

I thought about just going back to my apartment, call Marcy with the good news, tell her I'd be moving on, would catch up to Sean some other time now that he was all right. Go back to my one-bedroom, with Sean on one side of I-5 and me on the other, with him never knowing I was here; and better that way because…what if Shadden saw us together, decided to riff on his threat, do something to Sean?

And hope that *he* wasn't the one, next time, to see *me* filling my car at a gas station. Seattle wasn't that big a city. The thing was, I wanted to see my brother before he moved on, if that's what it was about.

Yet it was more than that. If I saw him now I'd have to tell him I was living here and one question would lead to another: such as why I didn't contact him, and why I was working as a landscaper under the table, had no phone and hadn't told Marcy. Sean would figure it out. He'd said on the phone before, when I told him about that terrible night: *I wish to fuck I'd been there…*

But I wanted to see him. I realized now that I wanted us back where we used to be, before the axis shifted and our father left. I wanted to be able to go over and say to him, *c'mon let's throw a little…*

Most likely he wouldn't have a glove. You move around like that, you don't carry one around, and especially if you hadn't played in a long time.

He quit after Dad took off, just like Mom had quit the smoking. I wished he hadn't quit. He was the one who told me first, when he was still playing to…*keep your hands back, and wait on it, see where it's going…it's not what you see in the beginning, it's what you see at the end and trust your hands to bring the bat through the zone level and fucking quick…*

I never got the chance to ask him why he didn't follow his own advice, or even if Dad had told him that first and he'd just passed it on to me. I never got the chance, for a lot of reasons—some of which were my fault—to ask him why he'd turned off the switch long ago. We could have pulled together, gotten even closer after Dad walked off, but Sean flicked a switch off; the light left the room we shared, and it wasn't long before I was driving him to the hospital after he'd swallowed the bottle of aspirin because Marcy and Mom were in New York seeing a play, so it was me running lights and stop signs, the two Malloy brothers in the car with only one driver's license between us and it wasn't mine.

He wouldn't have a mitt. I'd have to borrow Dimitri's. Sean was a lefty too. Maybe he'd ask me why I had one. *What, you play catch with yourself in the car, doing all the highways?*

That's how it would begin. I'd think of something to tell him as we tossed it back and forth, seeing if he still had the curve he taught me, the same nose-to-knees curveball John Malloy—who'd played semi-pro— had taught his eldest son first.

And then, fuck it, maybe more.

Two pairs of eyes are better than one…

If he's here, Jimmy, we'll find him…

You and me, just like before…

I waited in the parking lot behind the Patrician Apartments for a long time but Seanie didn't show. I wrote a note with pen and scrap paper from the glove compartment and tucked it in the crease of the door to his apartment:

Seanie—I'm in town, been trying to get a hold of you. Hope everything's okay. How about a few beers at the Blue Moon on 45th? Friday at 8 p.m. okay? I don't see you there, I'll keep trying. We have some catching up to do.

Jimmy

THE BOOK OF ERIC

I WAS A good houseguest, Lennie. I let Sophie out, amazed she'd lasted the night in that Kenmore kennel. I took the note which Janet could not know her mother had left. With any luck she might think she had gotten the departure day mixed up, that her mother and father were doing an errand in the Explorer. She might not even see the empty window out back, the empty aquarium in the bedroom, if she even knew it existed. All in all I left a small wake behind me; likely I would have considerable time before Janet called the police.

Closing on 1 p.m., I parked Tom and Margery's white Explorer in a garage to keep it off the streets. I wore what I had bought downtown and put other purchases—including a hunting bow and arrows—in the back of the SUV.

On 1st Avenue, near the Bread of Life Mission, with the neon 'Come Unto Me' sign, I passed a group of sneakered tourists with their guide, taking the Underground Seattle Tour. I knew a few ditchlickers—Crosswalk and Raff—who lived down there in what used to be the old level of the city before it burned down in the late 1800s. Instead of clearing away what was left, the city burghers built over what remained—which perhaps is what I have personally done. Of course, only a small portion of the Seattle Underground is suitable for taking Ma and Pa from Omaha down to gape at, and that is not where Raff, Crosswalk and I used to squat.

I confess that this idea once appealed to me: living your life unseen, coming up only when you had to score food or a bottle of cheap booze. But I had risen from that and this day was the first time I had been back to Pioneer Square in a while. I did not miss the drips, dampness and rodents—you know I have always hated them—or the police. Pioneer Square draws them like rats. Never mind the occasional Fat Tuesday riot, there are always a lot of police around to keep an eye on the bikers at the Central Tavern, and denizens like Flying Bird who defecate in alleys and drink and squabble in Occidental Park, frightening the tourists, curdling the cream of Old Seattle.

Still, Pioneer Square is popular because there is a lot going on and it is a favorite place for artists and others from bigger cities, for whom the area can only seem tame. But people in Pioneer Square are also wary; I had always had better luck in the greener residential parts of the city where the likes of Tom and Margery, bless them, were not expecting trouble, where police do not walk a beat.

Who knows, Lennie, we might have crossed paths before, near the gallery on the corner of Jackson and Occidental. Flanking the doorway, posters touted the Thursday evening Art Walk and artists Darcy Bank and Helen Sommers.

Inside, the young woman at the reception desk looked at me like I was a Seahawks' linebacker who had gotten lost trying to find the locker room at the stadium two blocks away. I certainly was dressed well enough. Perhaps it was my face, not merely my size.

I glanced around at the scrubbed brick walls and exposed piping overhead. A curving black metal staircase led to a second floor, a kind of loft added for more display area. I saw no brochures or pictures of the featured artists at the reception desk and, of course, I did not see you. I did not want to have to ask anyone, match one of the names with the woman of the carriage, but I would do it if I had to.

I went upstairs to check out this Darcy Bank. Her work was décor-art, the kind you see in lobbies; paintings that matched the color of rugs and walls, vertical and horizontal bands of mushed-up color. I could not imagine my woman doing these, not the woman who had let a ditchlicker ride with her in a carriage.

So you had to be Helen Sommers.

I went down the iron stairs, shivering the steps, caught the receptionist looking at me again. I knew after only a few minutes of looking at Helen Sommers' watercolors that she was the one.

There were red SOLD stickers on three of the paintings. The largest, *American Aqueduct,* had sold for $18,000; the next, *Tow Path*, for $12,000; the third, *Canal Swing,* for $14,000.

Lennie, for that kind of money you could have bought your own carriage.

You had people in your paintings. I liked that. There was something else I could not put my finger on, looking at your work, especially *Canal Swing*, the one I liked the best. There seemed to be more in the paintings than what was actually there. Was that why you had sold, in this gallery alone, three paintings for $44,000? None of your subject matter was drawn from around these parts. So I wondered: were you visiting here or did you live back East?

I stopped at a small, waist-high table, set diagonally in a corner, hoping there might be pictures of you, information I could use, an address. I saw only a book, about an inch thick, and easily twice as large as a regular book, but not the kind I ever read at Shadden's. Next to the book lay a tray of latex gloves—like those I had used at Califf's—and a creased card that said: NOT FOR SALE. Another card: PLEASE USE GLOVES.

I knocked a wastebasket a little as I peered over to see the title: *The Book of Michael.* Your name was not on the green cover, just the title and a Celtic motif. But this book had to be yours, surrounding by your paintings. I opened the book to a random page, and read:

It was his birthday, and my parents were talking about him, but he was looking at Petra and I, though mostly me, back and forth. He must have been thinking about how he and I were going to be celebrating his birthday that night. If I could see the bulge in Michael's jeans, they surely could, but they kept their eyes up, sort of gazing past us at the window, expecting to see the top of a canal barge gliding through the land.

Dad was asking about Michael's plans for the future. I kept staring at Michael, only lower, totally amazed, even if Petra (perhaps because she was still a virgin) wasn't; amazed that a guy could get an erection just by looking at his girl from ten feet away. A word came to me to describe that—telepenisis—and that's when I laughed. Dad said: "What's so funny, Helen? Everyone has plans, even when they've turned seventeen. I'm sure Michael has big ones."

And, of course, I laughed again. Michael—finally, my God!—crossed his legs so his stiffie wouldn't show anymore. (I asked him later, patting his crotch, if it was painful to cross his legs with his cock in the way). He said: "I sure do, Mr. Sommers." And that's when I said: "So do I, Dad." And he said: "Well, I hear you two are going to apply to schools near each other."

I heard a chirpy voice behind me. "Don't forget to use the gloves."

I turned around to see a tiny woman with glasses perched at the end of her nose.

"So sorry. I'll make sure to just look."

"Not a problem. That's fine." She introduced herself as Meg Chase, and said: "It's exquisite, isn't it?"

"It is, indeed." I pointed at the NOT FOR SALE card. "Is that for real or can we work something out?"

"For real, I'm afraid. The book is on loan from the artist. It's an on-going work, actually. We requested biographical information and this is what she gave us. It's beautiful, must have taken her Lord knows how long just to write the title and do that Celtic motif—the triskell. It's all handwritten, of course. Gorgeous—though I wouldn't want my ten-year-old to read it."

"The artist is…local?"

"Oh yes, Mercer Island. She's one of our own, though most of her subject matter is from upstate New York—the Erie Canal region just west of Schenectady, actually.

"So…definitely not for sale?"

"I wish it were. We've had more offers for this book than her paintings. One collector wanted to write out a check on the spot for $50,000. The craft is extraordinary even for these sort of things; artists' books they're called. Look at the clamshell cover she's done. There are not many artists who can do script that tiny, either, with the legibility of type. The sketches are done with colored ink, even the smaller ones in the margins, so you get the impression of one of those old illustrated manuscripts, like *The Book of Kells*. Are you interested in artists' books specifically?"

"To be honest I did not know there was such a thing—the category, I mean."

"Well, personally, what I think is most appealing about artists' books—in addition to their sensual aspects, the heavy pages you

can feel as you turn them—is the artistic purity. They're done sole-
ly by the artist, for the artist; or at most a very limited circulation.
They're one of a kind, with no expectation of commercial reward."
She laughed. "Of course, Ms. Sommers obviously can afford what
you might call..."

"A labor of love?"

"If there ever was one. If you're—excuse me, I didn't get your
name."

Which one to give Meg? Lampron? Shadden? Or the latest?
"It's Caster. Eric Lane Caster."

"Pleased to meet you, Mr. Caster. If you're interested in looking at more of these, the University of Washington has one of the
preeminent collections in the country. They're not for sale but you
could arrange a viewing. The curator, Sandra Sykes, is a good
friend of mine and I'd be happy to..."

"No, thank you. I will not be in town for long."

What I wanted to do, Lennie, was take your book and read it
from clamshell cover to cover.

Meg Chase kept on. "Well, if you're looking to buy while you're
here, Leiberman and Wessel has a nice selection of artist's books.
Their store is only a few blocks from here. But I daresay you'll find
nothing more beautifully done than this one...anywhere."

I wanted her to disappear. Was Michael the husband? That did
not matter. It had not mattered with Lissa's. I said: "Leiberman and
Wessel you say?"

"On 1st Avenue."

I could not wait any longer, and turned the cover of the book.

"Please, don't forget the gloves if you want to page through,"
she said, pointing at the tray.

I forced a smile. "Right. I keep forgetting. No telling where peo-
ples' hands have been, hunh, Meg?"

She blinked, taken aback by my using her first name. "Well, it's
not so much that..."

"I understand. If everyone did it, over time..."

I tried the gloves, but they split. I peeled off the shreds, dropping them into the wastebasket.

"My, you do have large hands," Meg Chase said. "Maybe I
have bigger gloves in the storeroom."

I watched her go—eagerly it seemed—to a room at the end of a short corridor at the back of the gallery. Not the office, I noted; that door was open and I could see another woman at a desk, on the phone. There were two other people in the gallery at the moment, besides the receptionist, a man and a woman with their backs turned to me, looking at *Canal Swing.* The woman said: "She sure's got a thing for threes. This one, too." When the woman pointed at another of your paintings I noticed the camera above them, in the corner.

It would have taken only a few seconds to scoop up your book, bolt outside before anyone could do anything. Wee Meg? The receptionist? Hardly. By the time the police arrived I would be back at the garage. Then I heard the door open. Three more people came in, pausing at the desk right in front of the door. The moment was lost.

Meg Chase came back from this storeroom and mistook my frown as disappointment with her empty hands.

"Sorry," she said. "Nothing bigger."

I held up my hands. "What am I ever going to do with these?"

For the first time she let her gaze linger at my face. She cleared her throat.

"But you could do me a favor," I said.

"Well, of course," she said, without a shred of enthusiasm.

"Let me have one last peek at what I cannot buy," I said, giving her another smile she did not return. Another potential customer came in and Meg Chase looked past me as she slipped on a glove I handed her. She flipped the pages back to the first.

"Who is this Michael, of the title, do you suppose?" I asked her.

"I haven't read all of the text, Mr. Caster, but I'd imagine he's someone special to the artist," she said. "Now if you'll excuse me, we seem to be getting busy."

"By all means. Thank you."

So I read the first words of your book:

What if one of us had to make a choice that Friday in July, when dolphins swam in Lake Shendego? That is the one thing we've never talked about since, because there should have been the three of us together, as always.

Eager-to-get-away-Meg had her back turned when I flipped to page 57, the number penned in blue ink. No writing on this page, just a sketch, in black ink, of some lake, with two women and a boy in a rowboat, with someone else swimming alongside. As I read later, it was that race with Michael—which he won. Did he ever not win, Lennie?

The sketch seemed to me like it was alive, given the way you drew the movement of the water, the way your hand gripped the shirt of the fearless boy at the bow. I could not imagine creating something this well done, what it must have felt like to sit back and gaze at what you had done. The only thing I had to measure this with was the euphoria after Califf; and seeing Lissa again; and witnessing what you did with Flying Bird and the carriage. And what I would feel like when I had you, alone, to gaze upon. I felt the necklace in my pocket. Your book was another treasure: I had two now; soon you would be the third.

Meg Chase was busy with the new customers, verbally annotating your paintings, the motif of threes—that triskell—chattering about the boldness of the watercolors. "Very unusual for the medium," I heard her say.

I turned more of your pages—I am a very quick reader—and marveled at your impossibly small handwriting which was as easy to read as newspaper print. Page 64 began:

We talked about it, this concept of settling down and I don't know which of us mugged the worst face. Michael could raise the corners of his lips grotesquely high, making them quiver, showing one canine then the other. Neither of us wanted any part of what that seemed to mean: settling down. We didn't see any reason why that should happen to us when we got older.

That we'd be together was a given; we weren't just tiptoeing around the idea of other people. We just didn't want to be the sort of people—years hence—who measured the quality of life by what didn't happen.

I suppose the weight of years can cause that—too many phone calls that weren't the kind you wanted, too many newspaper headlines. My parents were like that—good people, rock-solid, proud of their marriage—but they were definitely of the no-news-is-good-news school.

Michael and I didn't see it that way. Maybe we were too used to things happening when we were together—he and I, and Petra.

Michael was someone who didn't walk around puddles, figurative or otherwise. He still isn't. Either he leaped over them or stomped, to see how far the splash would go. He'd expect you to do the next one; me anyway. Petra wasn't a puddle-stomper but she giggled when we did. Sure, you'd get wet occasionally, hanging around Michael, but it was worth it. I knew in my core it would always be worth it. That's a reflexive, instinctive assessment, not a conscious one. It was all I'd ever known.

Take the Mustang, for instance.

Petra and I were biking around with him one day, a week before his Pop Warner football practices started, when he first saw that car in Wick Houser's driveway. Petra and I had seen it before; he had three other cars. He was one of the wealthiest men in town, with construction and plumbing businesses as well as the landscaping company.

Michael had undoubtedly seen the red Mustang, but he acted like Ford had just made a parachute delivery of Houser's classic car, smack onto the man's curving drive. All the rest of us pulled in and backed out of our driveways; Wick Houser could do it like you'd check into a fancy hotel in the Finger Lakes or Saratoga.

Michael told us flat-out he was going to own the Mustang someday. Not one like it. This one. "It's in great shape," he said. "'Don't be corralled. Get a Mustang. Mustang for '65.'"

"What?" I said.

"It's a slogan."

"We weren't even born then," Petra said.

"So? I just thought it up—what they should have come up with if they didn't. Not that they needed to. You could probably park all the ones they sold, bumper to bumper along the canal, Albany to Buffalo and..."

"Okay," I said, "we get it; they sold a lot of 'em."

Petra rolled her eyes. "Why would he sell it to you?"

"Why not?"

"For one thing, it's not your favorite color," I said.

"I happen to like green 'cause I'm Irish but red's okay for a car. Anyway you like red, Lennie, those bright colors that contrast with your hair. When I get it, I'm not gonna ride around all by myself."

He rode his bike right up to the front door, leaned it against one of the river-rock columns, hiked up the stairs to the porch you could almost play tennis on. From the road, Petra and I heard the faint ring of the bell. I sat on my bike, arm out on one of the lamp-posts of the gateway, balancing myself. Petra straddled hers, two feet on the asphalt. It was so hot that day you could smoosh road tar.

Michael didn't look back at us like any other boy would do for the girls. He was all business. He tucked in his shirt. The door opened. He talked for a minute with a woman, a maid, since she was too young to be Mrs. Houser and they didn't have an older daughter. Then he went in, taking off his Seattle Mariners baseball cap. He liked that team, Lord knows why; it sucked. I think it was because it hadn't been around long and the city was so far away.

We thought he'd be in and out in five minutes.

Fifteen passed. Then half an hour.

Petra and I were hot out there, but I didn't even think of leaving, and I'm sure she didn't either.

It must have been close to noon before he came out, the door closing behind him, his grin big enough to see from the road. He had two cups of something, which he held by the rims with one hand and rode his bike back without spilling—as if the 'interview,' whatever you wanted to call it—wasn't enough off a trick. I knew he hadn't spilled any because the cups were full when he handed one to each of us.

As we gulped the lemonade, he told us Houser had been pretty surprised all right and it was a lucky thing to catch him at home. He agreed to sell Michael the car when he got older and even named a price—which Michael wouldn't tell us, though we did our best to get it out of him.

That was proof, Petra said, that he was bullshitting us. I didn't think so—he'd been gone too long—but I still thought maybe Houser was just humoring him. But then Michael said that Houser had offered him a summer job with his landscaping company when he was older.

Petra was still not convinced—until Michael said he wouldn't be biking back with us. "I gotta go mow his lawn. He asked if I wanted to mow his lawn for the rest of September and then do the leaves every week, and after that some snow shoveling. I said sure, 'cause I knew it was probably a test."

We saw him that evening, grass-stained sneakers and all, and he showed us the four bucks Houser had paid him. "It's a start," he said.

"You need something to put it in," I said. So I got him a Mason jar from my Mom.

Wick Houser kept the Mustang cherry for Michael, waiting to sell it to him and no one else. Every other person in Leary Falls came to know of the handshake deal Michael Furey made, at eleven years old, with maybe the richest man in town.

Not long after, Dad said he went into his favorite watering hole, the Lockspot & Barrel, one night and heard some guys wondering aloud how much the Furey kid had saved so far—tossing it back and forth like they did about football or baseball; like they would do later about Michael when he was playing in high school—how many yards had he gained so far that season? How many more home runs did he need to break the school record?

So now: did Houser ask too much for the Mustang? Too little? They asked Dad about it, since they knew, like most people did, about the Sommers sisters and Michael. Dad told me he said: "Helen tells me he's got a jar and it's filling up fast."

That was the thing: no one I heard ever wondered if Michael could do it.

I didn't. I just kept giving him the jars, even after he got the bank account, and if he ever wondered why the jars were filling up a little faster than he thought, he never mentioned it to Petra and I. We were pretty sneaky about it, all of us were, including Mary, who knew where he kept the jars in his room in their small house beyond the heights above the town.

MEG CHASE HAD not seen me turn any pages but she must have seen me reading and glared at me, so I decided that was enough for now. I nodded, smiled at her for the last time and walked to the back of the gallery where she had supposedly gone for the gloves. Of course she had known there were not any larger sizes; she was just going through the motions.

I opened the second door on the right, past the office. It was not the rest room but that is what I would have said I needed, if anyone asked. The storeroom would do just fine—plenty of crated canvases, partitions, stacked portable chairs, a display case. Plenty of clutter to hide behind, lying on the floor, below eye level.

So eager was I to possess this book of yours I briefly considered doing it now. But it was too early, and I had to match your name to an address in the area. Better to come back shortly before closing time, wait to come in with others, drift toward the back, slip into the storage room and hopefully they would assume the big man had left with everyone else. And then after they closed up and left, I would emerge from hiding, putting on the fabric mask from my pocket to spite the video camera, and walk out into the night with another treasure tucked under my arm this time instead of over my shoulder as I had done on Tory Hole Road in East Hampton.

Of course it did not turn out that way.

Meg Chase did not see me when I left; perhaps she was upstairs as I timed my departure for the brief moment when the receptionist had turned away to answer a phone call at the desk. So perhaps, if worse came to worse, I would not have to do to either of them what I had with Jacob Califf's man in the mansion's courtyard.

First, your *Book of Michael* and then you, Lennie; so much the better plan than you first. Surely you can understand how I could not take you away before reading all of it. Is there any measure to account for fateful beneficence—that you, who did not know yet that I existed, would give me such a gift before I gave you mine, both one-of-a-kind, when all I had hoped for going into the gallery was the name of the woman in the carriage.

CHAPTER 11

VIGIL/HELEN

I COULD HAVE gone straight to Sean's apartment but the Blue Moon tavern was on the way from mine so I decided to give it a beer, see if he showed up.

The scruffy tavern was older than most everything around, including I-5 a stone's throw away, but students at the nearby University of Washington kept it going. No one cared if you scratched your opinions on the tables. *Nixon's an asshole…9/11 was an inside job…Bush has a small dick…*It was all there. The sign outside showed a leggy blonde riding a crescent moon, and they sold T-shirts with the same.

Now, same as the last time I'd been there, the bartender asked me if I wanted one. He'd seen me staring at the sample above the backbar—just about Katie's size.

I left twenty minutes later without one, passed a night game at the new field at Lower Woodland Park off 50th, caught the scent of cut grass baked from the day, and the hot-electric smell of the big lights above. Years before—in that other life—when rain began to fall, the lights of the ballparks I'd played in would sizzle and steam, but not tonight, not here. There hadn't been rain for two weeks.

Sean's car wasn't in the lot in front of the Patrician Apartments. The note was still in the crease of the door where I'd left it. Wherever he was he hadn't stiffed me, anyway. Sheldon Watson let me in, though I suppose he could have refused, brother or not. Maybe it was the dog. She greeted me like we were old pals.

"She thinks you're going to give her a cookie like Sean did," he said.

It had been only a day since Watson had seen him leave in his car; even so, I felt a little relief to smell only the mustiness of the basement apartment and cigarette smoke. He'd started with the cigarettes years ago, stealing our mother's, as if that would help her quit.

I suppose I was looking for evidence of where he'd gone, if not why he'd 86'd his job. I expected some kind of *fuck-it* bachelor pad clutter. What I found was an apartment tidier than any place I'd ever abused, even when Katie and I were living together and I cleaned up my act, not that she'd ever been a neat freak. Maybe he had a girlfriend, had cleaned up his so he wouldn't bring her back to a shit-hole.

He didn't have a picture of any girlfriend in his bedroom, or any of us for that matter—Marcy and I, or a favorite photo of our mother. He'd lined up his shoes, all two pairs, in the closet, made the bed. It was almost as if he expected someone to visit here.

A couch, small TV in the corner, and his gaming hobby took up most of the living room—something called Warhammer from a box on a work table near the sliding doors that led to the outside. Strewn about the large table were fantasy figures, small pots of pain, cans of spray paint, detail brushes, tubes of glue. He worked with two extension lamps and his current project seemed to be painting a model the size of my fist, called a Steam Tank. On the wall nearby were a dozen close-up photographs of models he'd painted.

Sean had always been good with his hands, and not just the eye-hand coordination that ran in the family. Our father, too, liked to go small. Dad hadn't much choice; he'd hurt his knee and a shoulder playing ball when he was younger, couldn't last long playing catch with his kids.

I wasn't as good as Sean with the small stuff—or any of the other things Sean was interested, like astronomy, UFOs, and photography. I often bailed out on afternoons in the cellar, working with Sean and Dad on the HO scale train lay-out. I preferred the outside, where I could crank up the gross motor engine; ride my bike to collect friends for a pickup baseball or football game. Sometimes I could cajole Sean into going along, but often as not he preferred to be inside, working with Dad on the trains.

The police had never found any evidence that foul-play had been involved with Dad's disappearance. After it was apparent Dad was not coming back, a sort of disbelief and fatigue set in—after the worry had mutated to anger, and again to hope he might return, and then to a kind of numbing pain that you woke up to and walked with. Sometimes the marker was the most banal: how could he have abandoned that model train world he set up on the ping pong table. He'd worked on it for years, his refuge from the excesses of domesticity, I suppose, but also a way to connect with his two sons, especially Sean, since Marcy wasn't interested. His passion for the hobby made Christmas and birthday gifts easy for us all.

Seanie had come full circle with this stuff and I was amazed at the artistry of the figures he'd painted and arrayed on that table-top—the scenery of forests, a stone bridge, sections of a beautifully done river and waterfall coursing down from an outcrop of rock and cliff made from insulation foam.

There were cigarette butts in an ashtray on the small dining room table, a few scattered bills, a folded magazine he'd been reading called *White Dwarf*. He'd been here recently. The feeling I got here was that he'd been planning on returning.

I'd called Marcy to update her, and we'd agreed that the most probable explanation was also the most likely—he'd just gotten fed up with schlepping the dessert tray to customers at the restaurant and decided he needed a break, and a week in the Gulf Islands in B.C., or wherever, was just what the doctor ordered. Restaurant jobs were a dime a dozen; he could always get another.

Or maybe he'd gone out into the mountains with the intention of never coming back. Last week a body had been found in Gordon Lake, west of Chelan in the Cascades. The guy had roped himself to a backpack loaded with 150 pounds of rock, walked into the water and let the ballast do the rest.

What else was there to look for here? Some indication—a brochure, reservation phone numbers—of a destination, a place he was driving to after he gave Sheldon Watson's dog a cookie?

There was a crammed bookshelf, and on a cheap desk in the far corner of the living room a lamp, a phone. There was no answering machine. If he had some other messaging arrangement, without his personal code I couldn't access any that might provide a clue to where the hell he was. He had no computer—unusual for a guy his age; then again I didn't either anymore. It occurred to me that the reasons might not be so different for us both.

I went over to look at two small photographs pinned low on the wall over his desk.

One showed a tall woman with long black hair getting into a green mid-sized SUV in front of a carport. The second: the same woman at a city intersection, waiting for the light, glancing to her left, toward the camera. Sean must have used some sort of zoom lens because she didn't seem to be aware she was being photographed. He'd caught her eyes— bluest of blue.

These weren't the kind of shots you take of a new girlfriend you're so smitten with you up and quit your job because she doesn't live close by. And—*fuck it*—you just have to be with her.

These were something else again.

I opened a folder that lay on the desk: more photographs of the same beautiful woman, younger than Sean by perhaps three or four years. He'd gotten better light for a half-dozen pictures showing her standing, arm outstretched, with a taller man sporting a pony tail, at the railing of a ferry, surrounded by a line of sea gulls. She seemed to be feeding them and she was smiling, as was the man who stood very close to her in all the photographs. If she looked around thirty, he was easily pushing fifty, with a receding hair-line, flecks of gray visible even at this distance.

These were something else, all right: surveillance photos.

The next few showed the woman alone, with two young boys.

There are terraces that step up from the Chittenden Locks near the Shilshole marina and beach in northwest Seattle. It's a busy and favorite place for picnics, with the nearby formal gardens and succession of sailboats and working vessels making the passage between Lake Union and Puget Sound. I'd been there occasionally to scan the crowds before or after I made the rounds of all the restaurants in the area, as always look-ing for Shadden. Sean must have been at the top of the terraces, shooting down at the woman near the railing and trees bordering the edge of the concrete embankment of the canal and locks.

He caught her kneeling, the boys standing behind her, as she reached under that railing for a ball or perhaps a Frisbee that almost skipped over the edge and into the lock. The woman was retrieving it for them, obvi-ously. Her own children? My brother obsessed with a woman with kids?

There was a notebook underneath the folder. On the front page Sean had written—and crossed out *Vigil*, and substituted a name: *Helen*.

On the next page was a story, or so it seemed because he'd made cor-rections, crossing out words and replacing them with something better, like you would in a story and not necessarily for a journal. I began reading:

It was safe because he wasn't the only one taking pictures of her and the man.

He'd never seen anything like this before. She leaned over the rail on the top deck of the ferry, her hair flowing almost horizontally from the wind and the ship's passage, her right hand extended for the seagulls lining up, seemingly motionless, to take the bread crumbs from her palm. Other peo-ple watched them, but if she was aware of that she gave no indication, no hint of self-consciousness or performing for the passengers.

He knew her name from the credit card she used at the restaurant, and he wondered if she would recognize him, should she turn. Not a chance. Who fucking remembers the waiter? He'd been careful, too, though he'd pushed it when he followed her to the Locks.

He counted twelve seagulls. When one took her offering, it wheeled around to get in the back of the undulating queue. The next glided toward her hand, pecked at the morsel and moved on. The only break in the rhythm and symmetry was her dipping her feeding hand into the bag of crumbs and offering again.

He heard her laugh at a particularly greedy bird; the man with her laughed, too, and he wondered why the man hadn't been riding in the car-riage with her days before. But if this man had, instead of the bum, they would have been like any other couple taking a carriage ride through the

West Edge streets of Seattle on a beautiful summer evening. He would have given her more than a passing glance, of course, but he would have walked on to his car and back to his life, such as it was. And he would not be here, taking pictures of her, his life suddenly turned around, his vices—self-pity, self-destructiveness—routed and on the run.

He had done this before, of course, but this time was different. There was a name for what he was doing but he couldn't have cared less, so long as he was careful. He intended to follow this—and her—to the end. There was a name for that, also. And as before, this time would have to remain a secret, but this time it would be one to which he could return.

When the ferry berthed at Bainbridge Island, he followed her green Toyota Highlander to the Bloedel Reserve. He couldn't enter as they did; the private nature park required reservations. All he could do was park on the shoulder of the road and wait for them to come out.

They did, an hour later, heading straight back to the ferry terminal for the half-hour trip back to Seattle. He followed the car to a house in the Wallingford neighborhood. The man got out, went right in, without a look back or a wave. Something had happened between them. He wasn't the same man who had been looking at her more than the seagulls, smiling, laughing.

She took five minutes to leave, as if she was thinking about what had happened. A delay of rumination, dismay, sadness…what? He felt a lift of happiness—or at least possibility—as if a rival had been eliminated. A foolish thought—fuck yes—but the feeling persisted as he followed her back to her home on upscale Mercer Island, where they had few homes like the one the man had entered…

What the hell was Sean doing?

I had to sit down for the rest of it:

Did she have to get away? He thought of that after he followed her the next afternoon to an art gallery in Pioneer Square. He matched her name with the one on a poster on the gallery window. So she was an artist. She'd gone in empty-handed, came out with something in a white plastic bag carrying it carefully. Was she religious? She did live behind a church, but he had to believe—wanted to believe, perhaps—that that was a coincidence, even if she was only a minute's walk from a Sunday sermon, across the gravel parking lot between her home and the church.

Then north on I-5.

After an hour he wondered if he would wind up in British Columbia; if so, he would follow her. What else did he have to do? Nothing else mattered since he'd seen her, because where she went HE would likely be following and not the man with her on the ferry.

She left the interstate south of Bellingham, took him around Robin Hood's barn near a podunk town called Pattison, then on to a road, higher up in the mountain foothills that turned to gravel and only then, just before that ended, did she stop at a barrier blocking a logging road. She swung the barrier open and drove in.

No wonder she drove the Highlander SUV; she needed it for this, and perhaps the cargo space to take her artwork to galleries. She wasn't the usual soccer or lacrosse Mom, though in the way she followed the horse-play of those boys at the Locks—before and after she retrieved the ball for them (where was their mother?)—it occurred to him that perhaps something had happened to her own children.

What was this place to which she'd gone? A vacation cabin-in-the-woods at the end of a roughly carved track on the hillside? A refuge, to be sure. Everyone needed one. Hers was out in the sticks. His? Being alone, except on the game nights; and the cigarettes, drinking too much; and his Warhammer guys on the table. But he realized now that solitude was not the refuge everyone thought it was.

He spent the drive back puzzling what that carved sign mean on the tree near the barrier.

FADO.

It was obviously the name she'd given to her refuge up there, and he knew what it meant. He debated whether he should have gone ahead earlier, to see her destination, whatever it was. But he couldn't have done that, much as he wanted to keep close to her, keep feeding from her hand, like she had done—sort of—from his own at the restaurant, when he delivered the half-loaf of French sourdough, the blackened steelhead, asparagus and a tumbler of Jameson's on the rocks. No frilly, sugary Cosmo for her. And she delivered pleases-and-thank yous, like he wasn't just a peon waiter. So many others had that dismissive air. Give them the food and drinks and they say nothing, keep on talking like you didn't exist. She looked him squarely in the eyes.

The restaurant GM had needed a space to fill on the wall near the restrooms in the back so he'd bought one of his photographs, this one of Snoqualmie Falls, and for some reason she'd mentioned it, as if she knew it was his and that led to a brief chat about not only his photography but to that ground the native tribes had once considered sacred, and then to the importance of the concept of the potlatch in Northwest Indian culture. He'd been neglecting his other tables; he didn't care.

All of this came after he'd asked her if she was doing a film in town. Lots of actors and celebrities stayed at the Alexis down the street. She laughed and seemed to be honestly flattered. But no, she wasn't an actress. He quickly mentioned all the ones he'd waited on—the Bridges brothers, Tom Hanks, Dennis Quaid, Rosie O'Donnell and Drew Barrymore who was sweet; Meg Ryan, not so much. Stupidly thinking that mentioning stars would somehow elevate his own status.

He'd wanted to go down that logging road to see the refuge she'd created. He couldn't because she might see him. Yet he knew he could find the place again. Maybe go up again when he knew she wouldn't be there. Spend the night—on the porch if the refuge was a cabin and it had one. Or if he had the nerve, break in, and really get close to her, touch what she had touched, smell her presence, and take something she wouldn't miss.

And if he really had the nerve…

Back at his apartment he cleaned up, though his own place seemed stale, a relic of a past life, as if he'd been away for months. But he did intend to go out to Mercer Island to continue the vigil, the best name he could think of for what he was doing…so far. Then, if she hadn't returned, back up to Fado, until the opportunity came and he did what only he could do now, and shed the chrysalis of the past. The closer he stayed to her the better. She didn't know—how could she?—that she was some sort of…bait? Could one life balance another? He had no doubt about that, not in this case. And he knew this as well: he had been fated for this vigil, this purpose. Otherwise he would have been dead long ago.

SEAN HAD WRITTEN nothing else in the notebook but the snakes in my gut told me he intended to be back to it, to continue…to finish. There was something else tucked in the notebook, however, a folded piece of paper, with just a small bent corner showing, as if Sean had book-marked another passage.

Sean hadn't written anything else. But when I unfolded the yellowing piece of paper, I saw who had.

Our father.

THE BOOK OF ERIC

PERHAPS I MISSED it, but I do not believe you wrote about what position Michael played in football. He was obviously a very good athlete, so if he had been a running back, he would have been naturally adept at a spin move: transferring the shock of a tackle into lateral energy, spinning away from the collision and with a runner's balance keep going forward. The most important thing is to keep the legs moving. If another tackler awaits, at least you have survived the first and perhaps gained a crucial first down.

I have watched but never played the game. Forgive this crude analogy, Helen, but this running back's spin move is how I have survived: never staying in a place long enough to be targeted, crushed and brought to earth; never staying with that one name and identity long enough so that it enveloped me as surely as a tackler's arms.

I did not get *The Book of Michael* as I planned; we must have just missed each other at the gallery. Another employee, not Meg Chase, told me: "Oh, that's a special arrangement; the artist needs it back for a while. It's an ongoing biographical work, you understand, but she's promised to let us show it again for the last two weeks of the exhibition, ends next month."

So I spun away, and by 6:30 that day I was at the north end of your Mercer Island. I had everything we would need: bags of non-perishable groceries, jugs of water, duct tape, rope, blankets to cover you with, two sleeping bags—one for you to lay on and one for me, though I would do my sleeping outside during the day, in secluded, shady places since I would be driving at night. I bought static windshield screen at an auto supply store and spread it around the rear windows of the Explorer so no one could see you inside.

I wore a fisherman's vest, the necklace zippered safely in one of the many pockets. I had a full tank of gas and expected that most of the money I had would be going toward fuel, since we would not be stopping at motels on our way across the country.

I got your address easily enough: 6005 Island Crest Way, at the south end of the island. I did not as yet have *The Book of Michael*, but I would soon after it grew dark, when I would go get you, take you away. I was not worried about the car; white Ford Explorers abound, and I had exchanged the plates in the garage in Pioneer Square, with those of a Taurus station wagon.

I picked up a couple of sandwiches, fruit, a bottle of water at the QFC supermarket, got back in the car and drove around looking for a place to eat my dinner, and wait until the hour. I passed the entrance to I-90—marveling at the lid over the interstate that cuts through your island—thinking it could not be any easier: after getting you and driving back north on Island Crest Way all there was to do was turn right onto I-90 and at the other end, in the Berkshires, take another right south off the same interstate and we would be only an hour from home. Or what would become our home, after I disposed of Kurt. I'd come to believe that he hadn't left the red house after all.

I followed signs for Luther Burbank Park. In the immediate area of the parking lot there were too many people so I locked the car, took my dinner with me and followed a path past tennis courts and an old brick manor with some kind of power plant with a smokestack, evidence that at one time this had been more than a shoreline playground for islanders. Children horsed around a flag pole rising from a lawn that spread down to the water.

I paused by the concrete ruins of a building, listening to a couple asking each other what it might been used for. That seemed obvious enough to me given the large openings, the rusted broken piping leading to rows of troughs: a milking barn for cows.

I kept on. Dogs frolicked in an off-leash area, their owners clustered by a fence. The path ended at the water's edge. Boats vectored on Lake Washington which stretched for miles to the north. Somewhere up there Bill Gates had his mansion on the eastern shore.

I sat down on a log, and as I began to eat I noticed off to my left, past the bushes and a swampy area, an eagle perched in a high snag of a dead fir, surrounded by even taller trees. Beyond, homes with expanses of glass faced the water. Every one had a slip for a boat.

The eagle took off suddenly. I watched it glide over the water, then swoop down, talons scarcely making a splash as it found its prey—not a salmon; nothing that big yet dinner nonetheless. The raptor swerved around back to its perch, looking around, protective of its kill.

I swiveled on the log, raising my own half-eaten sandwich as a toast and watched my companion begin ripping the fish to shreds, marveling that the eagle, even with its marvelous eyesight, could have spotted the fish from so far away. No doubt the lowering sun had helped. The eagle flew off again, the mutilated fish still in its talons. To the nest it shared with its mate? They mate for life, did you know that, Helen?

Hunting with my bow in the woods, I have seen hawks and ospreys high above, riding the thermals, but never a bald eagle catching its prey in the midst of an island suburb. This was much better than hiding in the store room of the gallery, which was where I would have been if things had gone the way I had planned.

Things certainly didn't go according to plan for Sean. Next month, you may not even remember the name of the man who will soon witness our consummation at Fado. You and I will be far away, with the books, yours and mine, and Kurt will be no more. Perhaps my belief that he is still in the red house has more to do with my desire to kill him for his betrayal.

I can put an arrow through a target the size of a bread plate from fifty yards away. Perhaps I shall have you lure him outside, so that I can shoot him in one leg, then the other, and watch him try to crawl up the porch steps. I will drag him back, out into the yard and tie him to a tree and put two more arrows into him—one for each eye—and then take him away to where he will never be found. His few friends may wonder where he has gone, and I will tell them: *Kurt? He said he was going to Seattle for a while. He wanted me to look after the house while he is gone.*

Finally, I shall have a place of my own—a piece of the rock, as Michael said—the goldilocking gone forever; finally, a home to share with someone who will never be taken away from me, as Lissa was. In time, Lennie, you will think of the red house as your home. All it will take is time; Malloy's Katie proved that. Enough time so that when you begin painting again and selling those paintings, you can put another name on the canvas—or I can do it for you. For a while I will have to be the one going to galleries, but in time you will do that yourself.

Now, in the park, I waited for the eagle to reappear, hunt again. I wondered where the nest was; perhaps in Pioneer Park, very near where you lived. I had seen it on a map of Mercer Island. How the park remained wild and not corrupted into playfields—or worse, a golf course—seemed a minor miracle.

I stayed at Luther Burbank until the shadows deepened with dusk; it was time to go get you. The eagle had made me curious about this place. Near the entrance to the manor I stopped to read the visitor placards and look at old photos encased in plastic.

The manor housed offices of King County Parks and Recreation, but for over fifty years, from 1910 to 1963, it had served as a home for juvenile delinquents and troubled orphans. There was a photo of the couple who ran the facility for most of that time, and others of boys gathered around the flag pole for a long-ago Fourth of July celebration and working in a garden, an orchard and the milking barn.

I had read somewhere that the first bridges connecting the island to the mainland east and west had not been built until after World War II. So for most of the time this place had been isolated, the perfect exile for youths who still might be resurrected.

When I got back to the Explorer I could not remember having walked from the visitor placards to the parking lot, so entranced was I with the before-and-after of this place. See what I mean about spinning, Lennie? You changed my plans and yet I found this place and saw the eagle.

But why was I drawn to Luther Burbank Park? How had I immediately known the purpose of those concrete ruins?

All of what had happened, from your taking the book to coming here, seemed fated—as much as finding Shadden, or seeing

Califf's picture in that magazine, or seeing you riding in that carriage. One after the other, these gifts have led me to this place before the final journey we shall take together. That part of Mercer Island was where I once would have been sent for the beneficial effects, so they assumed, of fresh air and hard work and raising the flag in the morning, lowering it at dusk.

Perhaps I *had* been sent here.

I sat in the car until well after darkness had fallen and all the other cars had left the lot. I was reluctant to leave, when only hours before I had been eager for the sun to set. I could not stay, of course. It was time to go—the others with me said so: two voices.

Oh, they did not want me to go because I had become like a son to them, of all the boys. They called me by another name. And in Tom and Margery's Explorer, hearing them, the coincidence stunned me.

We're sorry but you have to leave now.

We've done as much for you here as we can.

But you can't stay with us any longer; someone else is coming to take your place.

You know where to go now, don't you?

He should follow the eagle, shouldn't he, darling?

I would say so, yes.

You know where your final home will be and what you must do to get there. We've talked about what's necessary.

We think you understand—you do, don't you, Michael?

YOUR HOME WAS hard to find; I almost missed the number and the tilting arrow nailed to a fir that pointed the way to the rear of the Grace Methodist Church. But I parked in the small front lot of the church, not far from the illuminated reader board that asked: *Is the Son's light in your eyes?* The plan was that after I had secured you inside the house, I could back the Explorer right up to the front door, tuck you in, and we would be on our way.

I locked up, took one of the three rolls of duct tape with me and walked around the side of the church, where the short driveway expanded into a large gravel parking lot. The full moon revealed stables to my left, beyond a split rail fence bordering the parking lot. Horses rustled, sensing my passing presence.

The smell of the stables faded, replaced by the scent of cedars sheltering your home at the far end of the lot. A few lights of neighboring houses peeked through the trees surrounding this clearing in the woods. The carport was empty, so I assumed you were out for the evening. I figured an hour until you returned, maybe more; time enough to enter your home and later surprise you from within.

I went around behind your split-level, noting the high plank fence smothered with climbing roses that separated the narrow back yard from a neighbor's. The door to this lower level had a glass window which I broke, reached inside to unlock the door.

I waited for fifteen minutes at the side of the house, in case you had a silent alarm. But I did not expect the police and none came. A woman who offered to share her carriage ride with a ditchlicker was not a woman who worried about intruders lurking on affluent Mercer Island. I heard no barking or growling so you did not have a dog, another Ruckus, who might present problems.

Inside now, I crunched some of the glass underfoot, a reminder to listen for tires on the gravel lot in front. I took the stairs up to the main floor and went from room to room, turning on lights just long enough to bring your home to my eyes and senses: roses in a vase on your dining room table, bookcases but no television, fruit in a bowl on a kitchen counter. I smelled a whiff of garlic from the chopping block island. Your pots and pans and pans were arranged in descending size, your Mission-style bed neatly made with a yellow spread. The better to contrast with your raven hair? Those bright colors Michael mentioned? A book lay on the bedside table, a page marker sticking out. You were halfway through a novel, *Cold Mountain*.

Two framed photographs rose from the bureau. One showed your parents with Ruckus? The other was of you and your sister? flanking a young man with unruly hair dark as yours. He had to be Michael—of course it was Michael. Who else would be in the middle, draping his arms like that over the shoulders of the Sommers sisters? The three of you, peas in a pod, had big grins and leaned against the red Mustang.

I risked keeping the light on the longest in your studio—a large sky-lit annex off the bedroom—because here was your soul. I breathed in your work: the aroma of paint, pine and canvas. As a precaution for later, I hid the staple gun you used to fix canvases to the frames you evidently made yourself, since nearby on another table lay a miter-saw and assorted tools.

Your current painting was half-finished, a watercolor like the ones in the gallery, but this was of a place I knew: the Locks in Ballard. I had been there only once, on my way back from my home for a week in the woods below the Shilshole bluffs, across the train tracks from the beaches. I had done reasonably well there as a thief, able to see parents leaving their cars. Occasionally, distracted by children eager for the beaches, they would forget to lock up.

Most other artists would have chosen the perspective of the terraces above the Locks, that preference for height. You chose to place three people on the lowest terrace, having a picnic in the foreground, looking out toward the adjacent canal and the seeming impossibility of sailboats and tugs moving through the land itself, their masts and funnels rising from the rim of concrete, grass and trees.

I knew you might be coming back any minute, notice the light in your studio as you drove across the lot behind the church, but seeing all this was worth the risk. I heard no sound of tires crunching on gravel.

I thumbed through some of your large portfolios stacked on another small table near a drafting board. The portfolios gave me a glimpse of where you sketched out ideas for paintings, did studies of perspective, landscape, anatomy; faces and hands in particular. I thought one drawing—of hands on a steering wheel—as impressive as any finished work of yours I had seen. Another portfolio contained rough sketches of sailboats and rowboats which you perfected later for paintings of canal scenes.

Yet another portfolio was devoted to studies of animals—mostly dogs, horses and birds—which reminded me to make sure I told you about the eagle. Someday you will do a painting of the eagle, at the moment its talons skim the water just before snaring its prey.

After opening the last portfolio, I had to pull over a chair and sit down. What began with drawings of nude men and women ended with the corruption of dozens of pages of erotic sketches as graphic and salacious as any in the stash of DVDs that Kurt tried to get Lissa and I to watch.

I could not believe it. Was this the same artist, the same woman I had seen in the carriage? I was disgusted, Lennie, I have to admit. Part of me wanted to toss these in the trash, but I closed the cover on them, the last of their kind you will ever do, and in time you will forget they even existed. Kurt would have appreciated them, but he was a voyeur.

I turned out the lights in your studio, wondering if Michael had inspired you to sketch these disgusting images. I even considered another way to finish the night, and move on to another One more worthy of the necklace. But no, it would be enough to excise this part of you and time would take care of the rest. I had come too far this time, All signs pointed to you. If Michael had been the inspiration, as he surely was, he would not for long remain such. He has to go, Lennie, surely you realize that.

I went to the kitchen, turned on the light long enough to find a bottle of Jack Daniels in a cupboard over the telephone and sipped two fingers' worth in the dark. The phone's answering machine kept blinking a green 3. I pressed the play button.

The first two messages were from a woman named Dana, who had questions regarding the website she was updating for you; and a message from a Roger at Island Books, to let you know the books you had ordered had arrived.

The third message came from a man slurring the words, pausing in between them:

Helen, s'me. So…whadda we do now? I had any more wishes left I'd fucking turn myself into a seagull. Shit. You were too nice about it, thass the problem. No, I'm the problem. F'I had logs anna maul I'd chop your winter wood in a weekend, save you the sore hands but maybe better not do that right now, hunh? Probly cut my fucking foot off, 'scuse me. This is…listen…can we talk about maybe a plan B sometime? I'll be okay by then. No more…surprises, I promise. Call me, all right? Please. Or I'll call you. 'Kay, I better go.

Had you shown this loser the book, too? Was he Michael? No, not a chance in hell this drunk could be Michael; you had obviously dumped this guy. First the obscene sketches I found and now phone call evidence that you were dallying with some guy who wasn't Michael. I know the reason now. I did not then. I had not yet read all of your book.

The round black kitchen clock, that had MoMA stenciled in the middle of it, ticked off 10:25. I wished I had brought the Eva Cassidy tape to listen to again while I waited for you. But music was out of the question. I had to be able to hear the approach of your car outside.

I decided the best place to be for your arrival was on the stairs leading down to the lower level of the house. I would leave the door open, so I could hear your movements—kitchen first, perhaps, then the bathroom or bedroom. Once I knew you were in that part of the house, I would emerge, blocking the hallway and the quickest exit.

Would you be alone? Or would you be bringing a lover home after a date, after just having rid yourself of another: that pathetic drunk bleating on the phone? Were you keeping another on the string? Not likely. Then again, you had not seemed like the kind of woman capable of doing those obscene Michael-inspired sketches.

I finished the whiskey, waited, kept glancing at the MoMA clock.

Then, at 11:05, I heard faint crunching of tires on gravel.

I thought it was you.

I grabbed the roll of duct tape, was about to head for the stairs to the lower level of the house, then realized I should make sure you were alone. If you were not, I would need to know just who it was—a man or a female friend, perhaps. The knowledge would be helpful, if not crucial. Either gender, they were dead.

I lifted the window blinds in the dining room to see the carport, just enough. You would not notice that. Dark outside, dark inside.

The car had stopped a third of the way into the lot, was backing up, headlights off, toward the sidewalk leading to the rear entrance of the church. The blinds crinkled as I let them go. I lifted them again for another look, saw no one getting out, no pastor coming back to the church to retrieve something he had left in his office. Whoever was in the car was sitting there in the dark; he or she wasn't lost or merely turning around in the lot.

Teenagers wanting a secluded space to drink or fornicate? More likely, since from the street you could not see the large parking lot behind the church, and there was nothing back here but stables, a lonely house and surrounding trees.

But if they were kids why back up facing the house? Teenagers would just pull in and get on with the party. Police were the ones who always backed in, so they could leave quickly if they got a call. Yet this was no police cruiser.

If you back in like that, there is only one thing to look at—the house at the far end of the lot.

Where I was now.

Had someone followed me here? That could not be. For one thing, the car had just showed up. And who would be following me? No one knew I was here.

For fifteen minutes I waited for the car to leave. I could not wait any longer. You might be arriving any time now, and I could not have the car there, the driver witnessing all, including bringing the Explorer to the house.

I moved quickly, tape in hand, back down the stairs and out the door, over the picket fence at the side and into a neighbor's yard, jogging between the trees, keeping an eye on lighted windows, skirting a patio. I jumped off a low embankment and onto a lane that had to curl around back to Island Crest Way, thinking I would circle around to the front of the church and approach the car in the lot from the rear.

It did not matter who was in the car unless there were more than two. Two I could handle. Three or four, and I had better wait until they left. Once you arrived, I figured I had all night, though I was eager to get on the road.

I jogged up the road leading to Island Crest Way, then cut across in front of the church and into the nearer of two entryways flanking what seemed to be an office between the two halves of the church—one the chapel, the other a social hall. I needed nothing from my car, only my hands and surprise.

I could not go right up to the car, tell the driver to scram, pretend I was the owner of that house and was suspicious of a car here at this time of night. I could not risk the watcher getting offended, perhaps going to the police to report a man who had hassled him.

Whoever the driver was, he was drinking his last beer, smoking his last cigarette. No one would see what happened here.

I had the duct tape ready; you never knew. I slowed to a walk coming through to the rear of the church. The moonlight cast a sheen on the car's roof. The right rear wheel was missing a hubcap. The side was dented. I looked ahead to make sure you had not yet arrived and stopped twenty yards away from the car to listen. A night like this the windows might be open, so if there was more than one person in there, I would likely hear conversation— or more.

Nothing.

Ten yards now. I glanced to my left, to where you would be coming in, tires crunching gravel, thinking: *not yet, Lennie. Not yet. Let me take care of this watcher first...*

I could smell the driver smoking. The elbow poking out of the window unhinged and the driver flicked the butt away. At five yards I was close enough to see only one person in the car, that driver; was ready to move on him but stopped again when I heard the talking. I checked again, closer. There was no one else in the car. He was talking to himself, propping his elbow out again.

I kneeled by the left rear tire, leaving the duct tape on the ground, kept low and rose up toward the door. I yanked it open so quickly the guy did not have time to scream. He had his weight against the door, so he almost fell out. I grabbed a fistful of hair, then his shirt, and dragged him all the way out, hauling trash.

He screamed now but that stopped when his face hit the gravel. I still had him by his hair, swung him around, smashed his head twice against the car's door sill as the tinkling bell sounded the open door alarm: *ding...ding...*

He slumped, his head lolling near the wheel, almost underneath, giving me the idea. I glanced around to make sure no one else was in the lot. I filched his wallet, stepped over his legs into the lighted car, started it up, the car idling for the last second of this interloper's life.

He had sixty dollars. Then, my hand on the gear lever, I saw his license in the wallet, twisted to get a better look at it from the overhead. And checked it again, to make sure, even as I heard the groaning underneath the car.

I took out something else from the wallet. I could not have been more surprised, Lennie, if I had seen Kurt riding in that carriage with you.

So two of us were waiting for you to come home.

I killed the engine. Time for the tape.

CHAPTER 12

GOING AFTER SEAN

THE NOTE WAS written on the train-themed *Chief Engineer* stationary we had given him as a gift one Christmas. He loved it. He was a textile engineer, after all, for Albany International, who had had to learn new tricks as the company became the world's largest manufacturer of papermakers' felt, whatever the hell that was. He used the stationary to design his train layouts, scribble errand requests to Mom, and to leave notes of encouragement or congratulations for his kids about school, sports…whatever.

This time he had used it to say goodbye.

Staring at the sheet of paper now, my heart galloping, the whole of the house he'd left came back, all the forgotten territory. I wondered where he had left it so only Sean would find it. But that was just it; he couldn't have safely—if that's the word—left it anywhere in that house on Devonshire Drive. Then I knew: the cellar. The train layout. Mom and Marcy never went down there. I did occasionally but nowhere near as much as my older brother.

Sean,

I have to leave. You know why.

I always told you and Jimmy and Marcy that you always have a choice, that there's always a way out if there's a problem, if you make mistakes. I once believed that, but not now. I made a big one, and so did you because of it.

The only way I see out of this—for you, for me, for us all—is to leave, and leaving only you and I to know what happened, so everyone else can go on.

For what it's worth, I love you, love you all.

Dad

I DON'T KNOW why I left everything as I'd found it in Sean's apartment because everything had changed. I don't even remember if I locked the door on my way out.

The game at Woodland Park was over. The lights flicked off, fading to amber as I passed the field. I stopped at a 7-11 on 50th to fill up the tank. I must have seemed suspicious to the clerk: here's a guy who'd come in to pay, and now wasn't leaving like he should, was looking around the store as if he had something else on his mind, like maybe waiting for the only other customer to pick his beer and go.

"Anything else?" the clerk said, to my back. I turned to him. He pushed up his glasses with one hand; the other was hidden under the counter.

What else do you need to drive up into the sticks at night to find your brother and pull him back from…doing it again? Doing what?

What was the big mistake he'd made, following Dad's?

Anything else? Maybe the flashlight in the car needed batteries. Maybe it wouldn't the fuck matter. Whatever I found up there, chances were it wouldn't be at night. "No," I said. "Nothing else."

"Okay, well, if that's the case…" the clerk said, pointing past me at the guy holding the six-pack of Miller and a bag of potato chips.

They both glanced at me as I left, the guy shaking his head and saying, "What's with him?" The clerk sighed, something between annoyance and relief.

I checked the flashlight anyway. It worked. If the gun hadn't been in the glove compartment, I wouldn't have put in. The gun was for Shadden, not for my brother. But it had to stay where it was; there was no other place to keep it now.

I have to leave. You know why…

I had everything I needed except an exact destination—some place east or south of Bellingham, someplace...*near a podunk town called Pattison*...and a sign at the beginning of a logging road that said...*FADO*.

An hour and a half up to Bellingham then...

...*around Robin Hood's barn.*

There was time enough to wonder what my brother and father had done long ago, what mistakes...

I made a big one, and so did you because of it...

...they'd made to send one off, never to be seen again, and the other to keep a secret, carrying it to an of exile of his own.

And plenty of time enough to wonder what the hell Sean was doing, following...*stalking*...a woman he'd waited on in the restaurant.

Wondering was useless until I found him. No, not completely useless, because it also served to distract me from merging all of us together in my mind—my brother, my father, and I.

Sean couldn't have killed someone. Something like that would have surfaced in the days and weeks after my father's disappearance.

Or had he?

I switched on the radio as I turned left from 50th onto I-5, merging into light traffic heading north.

The chances of finding Sean, even if he was up there at this...FADO... at midnight, were slim to none. But I didn't consider for a moment going back to my apartment, to wait for the morning before driving up there to find him and prevent him from acting on the answer to his own question that he'd posed in that story, or whatever it was.

Had he? Had it been an accident?

Can one life balance out another?

I had to find him tonight, or at least get a good jump for the morning. Otherwise it might be too late to help not only my brother from making another big mistake, but also that woman, an artist who had a way with seagulls and didn't know she was bait.

Bait for whom?

THE BOOK OF ERIC

IT WAS A Utica Blue Sox baseball card, Lennie. Utica is not far from Leary Falls, am I right? One side had all the facts, the stats, except those that mattered to me: what he did to Lissa.

#16
James A. Malloy
Position: OF Throws: R Bats: R
Height: 6'2" Weight: 200 Born: 3/6/73
Hometown: Slingerlands, New York

*Malloy was selected by the Red Sox in the 4th
round of the June 1995 draft. He received a B.A.
degree in English from Penn State where he
was a varsity starter for three years, and MVP
his senior year, leading the team in hitting (.358),
RBIs (41) and stolen bases (13), and collecting
15 doubles, 3 triples and 11 home runs.*

I still have the card that his brother kept in his wallet. Before I toss the card into the fire later, take a look at his picture on the other side, the cap tilted up and askew just enough for attitude. Know your enemy. You would not think that this young man holding the bat on his shoulder is the one who took Lissa from me but he did. His brother's presence here surely confirmed that. And thus #16 deserved retribution. He raped her and would surely do the same to you if he came here and somehow killed me. Just as his brother would have done that had I not prevented that. Need I state the obvious, Lennie? I saved your life, just as Michael saved Petra's.

So here was Sean, the smaller brother; Malloy Lite. I taped him up before he fully roused—mouth, wrists and ankles. I dragged him over the gravel by his ankles, to a utility shed behind a towering fir. I used the last of the tape to cinch his ankles to the padlock chain on the shed. No one would see him there in the short time I would be gone.

Two cars in the lot would be suspicious so I drove his to the nearby park, left it there and jogged back across the fields, then took a path that led through bordering trees and back to the church and my car, which I pulled around into the lot. I backed up the Explorer toward Sean and opened the rear door. I cut him loose from the shed, dragged him back to the car and lifted him up, rolled him in feet first, shoved him in far enough past the supplies and my bow, so that his head was close to the edge. If I had wanted now I could have yanked him by the hair as I slit his throat and his blood would have spilled onto the gravel.

But Sean and I had to talk. I was not worried about you arriving now. If you did, all you would see is that one car, and Sean and I could pause while you went inside your home. We would finish up, and I would take him to Pioneer Park not far away, where he would probably be found by a jogger. But by then you and I would be long gone.

I told him: "I am going to take the tape off. You scream, you are dead." I tapped the knife on his throat, snagged the skin. "Do you understand?"

He nodded and I sliced the tape by his ear, ripped it off. He sucked in air. I still had a fistful of his hair.

"Where is he, Sean?"

Undoubtedly he did not expect to hear his name. I asked him again.

"Where is who?" he said.

"You know who I am talking about. You had his baseball card in your wallet." I tapped the flat of the knife on his Adam's apple. "You get twenty seconds to tell me or I will bleed you out right here."

He took half that. "I...I don't know where he is."

"Not a good answer. I am sure he has told you all about me, but perhaps he has neglected to tell you what he did to someone very special to me."

"You're lying about that. Jimmy…"

"Is where?"

"I told you, I don't know."

"You are his brother. He told you about me." I showed him the tattoo. "Why would you not tell him you had found Shadden?"

"I'm telling you I don't know where he is…maybe back East. I'm here on my own. It's my—look, I just didn't want to tell him I had seen you."

"Where was that?"

"Downtown Seattle. I saw you following a woman in a carriage, down the street from McCormick's. I'm a waiter there. I waited on her earlier that evening."

"And you figured…what? You would use her to find me, is that it?"

Sean's silence was the answer.

"What would you have done if I had not been here tonight and she came home?"

His response was too quick. "Nothing."

"A woman like that? I do not believe you. Nor do I believe you have not told your brother." I pulled his head back tightly by the hair, scored his neck, carving shallow gills on this fish, my hand over his mouth to muffle his screams. Then off: "Where is he?"

"I don't *know!* I'm telling you the truth. Everything I've said. You have to believe me."

"Freelancing, is that it?"

"It's just me, it's up to me. My brother can't ever know."

I clamped a hand over his mouth again, and dragged the flat of the knife over his eyes, then made a cut over the bridge of his nose. And off again.

"Please, you…"

"I do not believe that you were just going to sit in your car here. Maybe you were thinking of doing what your brother did to Lissa—and tell him later: 'Oh you will never believe this, Jimmy; he did it again, a woman named Helen Sommers.'"

"*No!* I wasn't, I swear. I…how could I? She's not even…"

"Not even what?"

"She's…I…I don't think she's coming home tonight, so how…"

"Why would you be here if she is not coming home tonight? Because maybe I might show up? Looks like you got more than you bargained for." I tapped his eyes with the knife. "Now you *have* been following her. You know she is not coming back tonight so then you know where she is. You have another twenty seconds to tell me."

He did, with plenty of time to spare.

"She's...up...north."

"You will have to do a lot better than that."

"I followed her...east of Bellingham...then eight, nine miles... near a town...Pattison. She turned into a logging road. There was..."

"What? Keep going."

"There was a sign by the road."

"What did it say?"

"Just a word...Fado. Without the sign you wouldn't know any-thing's there."

"Then?"

"I turned back."

"Why?"

"I don't know...she would..."

"She might have seen you? Is that it? Where else have you followed her?"

"There was the ferry to Bainbridge. She was with a guy..."

"Was his name Michael?"

"How would I know his name? She fed seagulls on the boat. I followed them to a place on Bainbridge Island. When they came back out I followed them to the guy's house. He went in; she didn't."

"Where is the house?"

"In Wallingford, a green house on a corner lot, Wallingford Avenue and Johnson, just up from Gasworks Park."

"Did you get the name?"

"There wasn't a mailbox in front."

Of course I did not believe him when he said Malloy was not close. I have to admit, Lennie, that Sean was not stupid enough to think he was going to live, even though I told him he had done well; and maybe if he played navigator efficiently I might let him go. He did not plead for his life, promising to keep our talk a secret. I taped his mouth again with the second roll of duct tape, and shoved him further in the car and closed the gate with a click.

I could have killed him behind the church then, but you had to see him first, and know what I had done for you. So it is just we three here now, but soon there will only be you and I.

THE HOUSE WAS indeed on Wallingford Avenue that rose from the north end of Lake Union. I knew the neighborhood. Years before I had slept occasionally in the *Kalakala* that was berthed on the lake for a while. The old ferry never did get refurbished after being towed from a mud flat in Alaska. Sometimes I slept at nearby Gasworks Park, where they once squeezed gas from coal, then saved when they got the idea to leave the rusting industrial ruins as a kind of monumental urban sculpture.

One night I chased off a pair of taggers, claimed a dropped can of paint and sprayed Lissa's name on the tallest of the absorber towers, above all the other graffiti at the lower levels facing downtown Seattle and the Space Needle at the southern end of the lake, so everyone could see what I had done. It was worth it to climb high at night over rungs, piping and railings which could have broken off, sending me plummeting to my death if I was not impaled first on a snag of rusting iron.

I remember the feeling after doing that, though I did not skip away like Flying Bird. Painting your One's name high enough for all to see, stopping traffic at a downtown intersection, founding Alexandria, or writing this for you—is there so much a difference once you ascend or descend to a certain point?

I parked on a side street, made sure Sean was secure in the back, put on a long sleeve shirt on to cover the tattoo, then a nylon stocking I was going to use for the art gallery. I cut out eye-holes, took a roll of tape, went around the back of the house, and was delighted to find a window partially open, no doubt because of the hot weather. And more luck: thumping music that seemed to be coming from the front of the house. I raised the window, crawled into a lighted bedroom—clothes everywhere, single bed a mess, books scattered on the floor, stacked on the night table. On a bureau: a framed picture of you taken at what appeared to be a St. Patrick's Day party. You had a shamrock on each cheek.

I checked another room down the hall but it was used for storage. If this was the house of the Irish love-of-your-life he had fallen a long way. I wondered then if that was why you wrote and sketched his ascent, why you were not living with him.

It seemed no one else was either—unless he was fornicating in the living room. No, the moans were forced; the tawdry music gave it away. He was watching pornography.

The house smelled of fried food, mildew and liquor.

I saw him when I passed the kitchen. He faced away from me on a couch in the living room, slumped down, with only his head and shoulders visible. On the television, two men worked the same shaved anatomy of a woman.

For a moment I forgot I had seen a picture of you in the bedroom. Had I gotten the right house? Sean Malloy saw this swine with you? Was this your dark side, slumming with masturbators? Then I remembered the obscene sketches I had discovered in your studio.

I lifted a beer mug from the jumble of dirty dishes in the kitchen sink—the television masked the clinking dishes. I went back to the living room and from behind him, almost close enough to touch the rubber band cinching his graying pony-tail, I threw the mug at the television.

He jumped up, shrieking, as the screen exploded, underwear down by his knees, his penis bouncing up and down: a tall man, taller than I, but scrawny and older by ten years at least. He screamed again when he saw me, tried to pull up his underwear and move at the same time—and tripped over the coffee table, toppling a half-empty bottle of Beefeater's and an empty tumbler.

By then I had moved around the couch and shoved him down. I flipped him over, using my weight as he flailed away. I ripped off a length of tape, grabbed a wrist, wrapped it, then the other and bound them together, three times around. I secured his ankles and taped his mouth so he could keep screaming. He twisted around to look at me, tried to cover himself, but he could not do that, not with the tape.

I threw a couch pillow over his humiliation, not wanting to look at it, and then took in this pigsty.

I looked around because I still could not believe you would have been with this boozing loser. At least he was not masturbating with the help of your picture in his trashed-out bedroom. If he had, I might have killed him then and there.

He had framed pages on the wall—letters, newspaper clippings, a postcard. The television glass crackled underfoot as I went over to look, passing a big packing box, to see them closely. There was a postcard from the Venini glass factory in Murano, Italy.

I read one of the yellowed newspaper clippings, written by a Benjamin Stuckey, an art critic for *The Philadelphia Inquirer.*

...And then there's Robert Tiphook's twenty-inch high figurine of a nude woman, entitled 'Over Her Shoulder.' Of course, it represents a young man's voluptuous ideal, or fantasy of womanhood. That in itself is perhaps predictable, given Mr. Tiphook's age, and though beautifully rendered, the least remarkable aspect of a piece that marks his emergence as a glass artist of note.

Rather, it is the boldness of the woman's demeanor, at once mysterious yet inviting, with the wide and sensually wise smile, the insouciant tucking of her hands, the angle of her backwards glance that hints at her creator's confidence in his precocious ability, and the absolute certainty that there will be indeed something extraordinary to look back upon once the fires of his glory-hole have dimmed...

And another, from the *Seattle Post-Intelligencer,* three years later:

...Tiphook's 'Wilderness' sequence—the faunal equivalent of Chihuly's flora—is impressive enough. But in his most recent work, such as 'Prowl' and 'Wink,' this glass artist's ability to manipulate prisms to convey the appearance of movement gives his work a signature that so many others lack in a difficult medium...

The framed poster loomed over all. MoMA in big letters: The Museum of Modern Art—*The Glass Artistry of Robert Tiphook. May 1-20, 1992.*

The photo of the sculpture in the middle looked like something a child would put together with one of those connect-the-pieces toys.

What I had here was a…Glassman, a masturbating MoMA's boy.

And there was a framed letter from Bill Gates:

…You also mentioned at the reception that art will, at some point in the future, be the only thing that remains of humanity, defines it—distills the essence as you put it—once we have merged with our technological innovations. There's much to discuss on that score, of course, and my apologies for not being able to pursue it earlier. Perhaps another time. But should you prove right, Melinda and I would thus consider 'Frantic' one of the most exquisite definitions we have the pleasure to own and pass on to our children.

I turned to him. "If only Bill could see you now, Robert. Now, I am only here to talk with you, so please don't scream when I take off the tape. It would annoy me if you did and you do not want to annoy me. All right? "

He nodded and I yanked off the tape.

"Who are you?"

"Not just yet. I am curious about what Mr. Gates paid you for 'Frantic,' if you wouldn't mind telling me."

"Why do want to talk to me?"

"How much?"

"$95,000—if this is about money, I don't have any."

"My oh my—almost six figures for the Glassman. But you do not look like you are selling much to Bill—or anyone else these days. Where did it all go? Up your nose, down your throat?"

"What does it matter, it's gone. You can see that."

"Has Helen seen your Wall of Fame over there, or have you been too embarrassed to bring her in here?"

"Helen?"

"You know who I am talking about."

He gave it a moment. "What about her?"

"My name is James Malloy and I am—well, let us just say I am an old friend of hers from way back. I have come from New York, upstate actually, to catch up on old times with her and begin new ones. I know you and she were together on that ferry the other day. I know you called her afterwards, left a message, because I was at her home behind that church on Mercer Island."

"We're just...friends."

"I am here to make sure you understand that if you ever see here again, I will kill you."

"She never mentioned anyone named James Malloy."

"Did you hear what I just said?"

"Yes. Okay."

"Good. Have you ever fornicated with her?"

"That's none of your business."

"An intimate question, but then I would say we are rather intimate now."

"I told you...we're friends. And no, to answer your..."

"Friends with benefits, perhaps?"

"No. How many times do I have to..."

"What is in that big box over there?"

"Something I sent for."

"It does not look like that. No mailing labels. So what is it, Robert?"

"Nothing."

"Mind if I have a look?"

"What the fuck are you asking me for? You're going to do it anyway."

I gave your friend a round of applause, Lennie. I confess, I was having an amusing time with him. I slit the box open with my knife, plunged my hands into the packing peanuts, lifted out a glass sculpture of rods of black glass fused together with red seams. The impression was one of a bizarre animal. I turned the box upside down, showering the Styrofoam peanuts everywhere, placed the sculpture on top of the box.

"How many do you have here?"

"What?"

"These rods."

He sighed, his breath blowing peanuts off his skin. "Sixty-four."

"They look like little baseball bats."

"They're not."

"I used to play baseball, almost made it to the Show, as we say, so forgive me if I think they look like bats to me."

"Well, they're not—you don't talk like any baseball player I ever heard."

"Life is full of surprises, like finding a once-renowned glass art-ist living like a pig and masturbating in his living room."

"Fuck you."

"Such bravado, Robert. You give names to your work. So how about this one?"

"What does it *matter!* Jesus! Please, just leave. I heard what you said—it won't be a problem to do what you want."

"What is the name?"

"'Frenzy.' It's called 'Frenzy' if you have to..."

"Like the piece you sold Bill? 'Frenzy'...'Frantic.' Are they com-panion pieces?"

"What if they are?"

I clapped, smiling. "Oh, you bad boy! You went to the same well. You did it again, the same sculpture."

"No, they're...complimentary. You didn't see 'Frantic.'"

"And here Bill thought he was getting one-of-kind. What if he sees this?"

"You're wrong," he said. Then, after a moment he gave it up. "Anyway, he won't."

I tinked a glass rod with the knife. "No, perhaps he never will."

"Please don't do that..."

"You can do another, correct? Or are you that...dried up?"

"Of course I can do another but...it's...it's the first thing I've made in a while. I don't have my own studio anymore. I have to..."

"Go on."

"Nothing. I just brought it over."

"Why? To sit in a box?"

"No."

"Why, Robert?"

"Why do you *think*? To sell it. You can see I need the money."

"The same one? I think you made it for Helen."

"Okay, so maybe I did."

"That is a big gift for someone who is just a friend, wouldn't you say?"

"So she's a good friend."

"How long have you known her?"

"Over a year."

"That call you made. You were drunk. Something happened between you two."

"Please, I've told you I'm not going to see her anymore. You've made your point."

"A gift like that for someone like her? What, were you going to ask her to marry you?"

"*Leave me alone! Just go.* You've got what you want."

I tapped another glass rod. *Tink.* "So she said 'no.'"

"Please leave. I'm begging you."

"Oh Robert, what did you expect? They never want to fornicate with, much less marry men for whom they feel sorry. But you thought 'Frenzy' would help—proof that you weren't washed up after all. You were thinking younger women sometimes go for older men. But those men have to have the bright plumage and a lot of it."

"I'm not washed up."

"Hey, it happens to the best of us. Look at me. I never made it to the big leagues and I led my team in hitting at Penn State—did you get her a ring?"

"No."

"Yes you did."

"I'm telling you, I didn't."

I put a hand over his mouth, felt his muffled scream as I etched a thin red trail on his right leg with the knife, beginning at his ankle and stopping only at the pillow I had thrown over his privates. "Would you like to change your plea, or should I keep going?"

I let him have a minute to calm down. "I am not going to take the ring; I have something very special to give her myself, a necklace you will not find in any jewelry store, so for what do I need your bauble? Not the money. I was smart enough not to fritter away all of my signing bonus years ago. So where is it? Just a peek, is all."

"What the fuck does it matter now...It's in my bedroom; the dragonfly box on the bureau, next to her picture."

He had made the box—of course he made it—of red glass, soldered pewter seams. The blue dragonfly on the lid was the color of your eyes, Lennie. There was a folded note next to the ring within. I read:

There are two things of beauty in the world that I can't make. This ring is one of them. You are the other.

I took the ring back to him, squatted down. "It's exquisite, Robert. The note is worth another karat at least. Brings you up to, what, two? Did you really come up with the words yourself?"

"Just take it, you're going to anyway. I don't give a shit now. Leave me alone."

"I told you, I am not going to take the ring with me. But you do not need 'Frenzy' anymore."

He twisted up: *"No! No...please!,"* as I lifted the sculpture and smashed it to the floor. Shards of rods hit him in the feet, dozens skittering everywhere, a few all the way to the front door. He curled up quickly, like an insect, long like a dragonfly, scorched by a flame.

"Now," I said, "I am hungry and thirsty. You must have something for me in the kitchen."

He did not answer. I could have said more, but I did not want to play dentist, or hassle with prying open the Glassman's teeth with the knife, not that I cared if he lost any.

FIFTEEN MINUTES LATER I walked out the back door to the Explorer with two mementos. One was a glass rod I tossed in the back for Sean: something to talk about on the way up to get you at this place called Fado. There was a chance the Glassman knew you were up there, but he did not know that I knew and would be up there before he could call you, and warn you that some guy named James Malloy was looking for you; assuming you even had a phone that is, which was not likely. If you are at the end of a logging road, the last thing you want is a phone or cell within reach; otherwise what is the point of getting away? And he would not be feeling too kindly about you, Lennie. After all, you had just shown him the dumpster, not that anyone could blame you.

No, Robert Tiphook would undoubtedly be on his own phone to the police, to tell them all about what James Malloy had just done to him. I was hoping Malloy would not be out of reach too long because we still had a score to settle. But this would do for now.

"Hungry, Sean?" I flung the other memento—an extra piece of raisin bread—over the rear seat. "No? The guy in there was not hungry either, but you have to eat sometimes, whether you want to or not."

I drove north on Wallingford Avenue, then east on 45th to catch I-5 going north, thinking all the while not so much how long it would take the Glassman to expel the ring I had buried in a balled-up lump of raisin bread, but whether he would pick the glistening ring-worm from his excrement or flush it down the toilet.

CHAPTER 13

BARBARA'S BASKET

I FOUND PATTISON shortly before midnight, slept in my car, and got an early start the next day.

The hamlet, near the junction of Routes 9 and 542, had the tiniest Safeway I'd ever seen, a restaurant called the Alpen Hut, and Barbara's Basket—a general store with gas pumps and a contract postal station. In the surrounding hills, clear-cuts scabbed high hills veined with switch-back scars of logging roads.

Down the road—prophets versus profits—a white Adventist church faced off against the Nooksack Casino, whose main building and parking lot dwarfed the nearby high school/middle school complex—*Home of the Whatcom Wildcats*. Coming into Pattison on Route 9 I'd had the choice of sleeping in the parking lot of the school, casino or church. I chose the church, if only because there was less of a chance of getting rousted.

It took me two hours that Saturday morning to draw a blank in the little town, most of that spent at the casino lot, asking people if they'd heard of a place called Fado in the area. I followed Route 542, which par-alleled the North Fork of the Nooksack River, taking this road and that, getting deeper into the mountains, seeing one ramshackle house after another, their roofs edged with moss, cars kept in the yard for parts; and always the smell of woodsmoke. The best-looking house I saw had a huge Confederate flag draped over the front window, a Mary Kay sticker on an old Pontiac out front and llamas caged in a pen at the side of the house.

I stopped at those homes which had neither *Keep Out!* nor *Beware of Dog!* signs, to ask my question. By Saturday evening I had come full circle, somehow managing to run into Route 9 from the north, and wound up back in Pattison, the fuel gauge teasing empty.

I waited for a logging truck carrying skinny Doug firs to pass and turned into Barbara's Basket for a fill-up. The plan? There wasn't one, except maybe to keep calling Sean's number to see if he'd returned to the apartment. I'd already called once, from a casino phone. Failing that? Keep at it Sunday and perhaps Monday try my luck at a county office to see if anyone had issued permits for a woman named Helen something-or-other, from Mercer Island—and watch the clerk give me a grumpy *is-that-all-you've got?* stare.

Still, maybe a building inspector had seen a sign that said Fado. A woman as attractive as this Helen might be remembered. In the meantime, I had Sunday to prowl more back roads, and try to keep a lid on the feeling that asking about Fado might not matter anymore.

I got my gas, went in to pay and almost knocked over a tiny, plump woman who was flipping the sign on the door from *Open* to *Closed*.

She waved off my apology as I gave her the money, tucking it into a pocket instead of the till she'd presumably just emptied since she gave me change from a modest wad of bills—not something you'd want to do in the city.

"I shouldn't have been here anyway," she said, "but I'm closing up early."

I nodded, about to go back to my car but she kept talking as she locked the door. "It's my anniversary today," she said, as if more explanation was needed. She puffed out a little breath. "My husband goes golfing; I get my hair done on my lunch break—what do you think?"

"Congratulations."

"I mean my hair."

It was, well, too…black, with nary a gray hair for someone in her early fifties who should have some, and probably too long for such a wee woman.

I told her I liked it.

She wasn't buying it: "Well, Joe won't either. Oh, what the hell. At this point we're beyond gazing into each other's eyes. But that's not what it's about, don't you think?"

She walked toward a car parked near the air/water pump. I was half-way to mine, backing up from a question I had no idea how to answer.

She stopped and said a little louder since there was some distance between us: "I mean, they say it's about looking out together in the same direction—blah, blah, blah. Right. For Joe and me, that's both of us looking at his golf clubs—him wanting to get the hell to the first tee and me thinking about how nice that bag would look dumped in the Nooksack, with maybe his favorite driver clubbing a steelhead *he* could cook up for dinner for a change."

I had to laugh, the first in a long while. This lady deserved an answer. "What do I think? I think your husband has his hands full—and lucky, too."

"I keep telling him that—the last part, anyway."

I still had the change in hand, took a look—and hurried over to catch her as she was about to get in her car. "You gave me too much," I said, returning a ten.

"Why thank you! What I get for rushing. You're a sweetie-pie."

"Think of it as ten more bucks to lose at the casino tonight."

"Oh my, how did you know we were going there?"

"I've been driving around here all day and the casino seems like the only game in town."

"You're looking for property or something?"

"Sort of. You wouldn't happen to know of a place called Fado around here."

"Matter of fact I do."

I blew out a breath. "I was beginning to think it doesn't exist—I stopped here earlier in the day but the man…"

"That was Hank, my brother-in-law. He's from New Orleans and if that Katrina wasn't enough for the poor man, he just got divorced, so he's been staying with us for a while—it's tucked away near Mt. Union; you're not far."

"How do I get there?"

"Well, you know, it's not like I'd be telling you how to get to the Walmart, not that I'd *want* to tell you how to get there, place like that, place like the Basket. What I mean is, folks out here like their privacy."

"I've seen that."

"She's a good friend of mine, Helen is."

"I understand. The thing is Mrs…"

"Hollner. Barbara Hollner. You?"

"Jim Malloy—the thing is…" I wasn't about to give up now. What had Sean written? She was an artist, lived on Mercer Island, so she must have been doing well. I had to give Barbara Hollner something and hope she wouldn't ask me the woman's last name.

"The thing is, I'm a free-lance writer and I'm doing an article on Northwest artists. I tried to contact Helen at her home on Mercer Island but she wasn't there. A person at an art gallery in Seattle…"

"I know the place. It's in the old part of the city," she said, "Pioneer Square. I've been there but Joe won't go because they pee in the alleys, but I tell him that's not all they do there; people go to galleries, like you."

"The owner was sure she'd gone up to her other…home."

"It's not exactly a home."

"You would know—I thought I'd try to connect with her there. I was hoping to be able to see her today but as I said, I've not had luck—until you."

"Well, you've come a fair piece to chat with her, but it doesn't surprise me. Helen is *so* talented. I have a small painting of hers inside the store she did for me. They do that, you know, artists—bartering paintings for groceries and such. There was that fellow lived on Long Island, splattered paint on canvasses like you did when you were in kindergarten…what's his name? They made a movie about him."

"Jackson Pollock."

"That's the one. Not that Helen needs to do that."

"Bartering or splattering paint?"

That got a little laugh from her—which it looked like I might need. "Oh, neither," she said. "It was a Christmas present. I'd like to help you, mind. Too bad Helen doesn't have a phone out there or you could call her. I always tell her she should have a phone, some way people can get a hold of her but she doesn't like cell phones, not because they cause cancer, which Joe says they do. No, I tell her that because she's often out there by her lonesome and she always says, 'Barb, I'm not always alone, you know,' and gives me the wink. But I'll tell you what. Why don't you stop by in the morning and I'll fill you in—unless you're going to church."

"Uh, no."

"Me neither. I don't suppose Helen will be either since I happen to agree with her about what she said—last Easter it was—about that one hour on Sundays giving people an excuse to ignore the rest of the week. We don't just talk about frilly things, you know. Anyway, Joe will probably be sleeping in"—she gave me a wink—"but I'll be here at nine sharp. Can't ask Hank to fill in tomorrow like he did today, since he *does* go to church, not that it's done him much good."

"I appreciate it, Mrs. Hollner. Thanks."

"As a matter of fact, you *should* thank me. I could tell you now how to get there but you're a nice fellow and I wouldn't want you to try to get there now, leastways coming back at night on that road after you and Helen have a long chat. She's at the end of it and it's something else, that road. Blink and you're off and done for. My boy did some work for Helen after he got his license, but I wouldn't let him drive up there even in the daytime. Took him myself. I've never been inside her place, but she bought the lemons from me for the lemonade she brought out to my Charley while he was cutting wood for her, so you see how things always come around."

"Yes, that's always the hope," I said. "By the way, if you don't mind me asking, why haven't you been inside her place?"

"Oh, Helen's a sweetheart but you get the feeling she's there for a reason and that isn't to shoot the shit with me, pardon my French. We do that here at the Basket. Joe says I talk too much; well, he golfs too much. Sounds like the chicken and the egg to me, but…I do go on, I know."

"If you hadn't, I wouldn't be seeing Helen tomorrow, Mrs. Hollner."

"Barbara, please, and you're a nice man for a mind-reader—I can't believe you knew we're going to the casino tonight. You just be sure to write nice things about Helen."

I could only nod at that. "Congratulations again."

"Oh, that. Thank you. It's twenty-seven years. I just hope Joe had a decent round. That would put him a good mood when he hears what I paid for my hair."

"Don't tell him."

"I suspect you've never been married. Sooner or later one or the other of you finds out about everything. See you tomorrow morning, Jim."

I got in my car. Mrs. Hollner seemed to be waiting for me to leave first and I realized then what she was doing. She may have believed me, but she hadn't been just prattling on. She was jotting down my license plate, just in case. Helen-of-Fado may not have known it, but she had a gatekeeper and one old enough to be her mother.

I drove away thinking it was probably true the woman didn't have a phone at her cabin. At any rate, I hoped that was the case so Barbara Hollner wouldn't be making a call to her surrogate daughter, alerting her about a writer who wanted to interview her for an article. Even if I could have phoned the woman, what would I have told her? *My brother's been...stalking you and...*

And what?

Find Sean, get him the hell back before anything happened. He and I had some catching up to do all right, and a couple of beers at the Blue Moon wasn't going to cover it.

I went back to the casino to phone him again, hoping he would be back, so I could go back too, and let my lie to Mrs. Hollner become an odd bit of conversation for them to ponder over coffee at the Basket. Odd? More likely a close call. *He never showed up? That's very strange. There's no telling, is there, Helen? The man seemed so nice...*

Sean didn't answer.

I got back in the car and kept driving. Darkness came early in these highlands, so close to the Mt. Baker-Snoqualmie National Forest. Fado existed; it wasn't just a story Seanie had made up to match the pictures he'd taken of a woman, a fantasy to improve reality. Barbara Hollner was going to tell me how to get there in the morning.

Yet now that I knew Fado was out there, I couldn't wait. It wasn't so much any expectation of finding it now, but of having to keep moving—at least until I was too tired and had to stop for the night. If I couldn't find it tonight, there was always the morning. I had hours to go; I had to try to find it. Was Sean…out there, having survived the perilous logging road—going in this time—settling in, breathing the night air, to watch the cabin through the trees?

It's not exactly a home…

If somehow I got lucky, saw the sign for Fado, I decided I wouldn't drive, not at night, along that road Barbara Hollner warned me about. I'd walk it. How far in could the woman's cabin be? A mile…two?

And once I was there? I wouldn't be able to see Sean in the dark forest, but perhaps a light would be on in the cabin, and I'd watch that all through the night, waiting for a shadow to be silhouetted against that light, then move toward it, calling my brother's name, and bringing him back from the edge—this…vigil?

I turned on one road off Route 542 that I didn't remember taking before, feeling excited that this might be the one leading to Fado.

I knew what it meant and so did Sean.

When our other grandmother, Nora Malloy—Grammy Nor—came to visit us from Thiels, a little town along the Hudson near Poughkeepsie, she always began our bedtime stories with a single word. Her mother, who had been born in County Clare, had done the same with her.

That word was *Fado*. In Gaelic it meant…*in the beginning*. Or, *once upon a time*. Or, *long ago…*

That was what kept me going down the road, looking for the sign my brother might have passed, and not so very long ago.

The Book of Eric

I WOULD HAVE found Fado eventually, followed you to it some other time from Mercer Island, but Sean made it sooner rather than later. Would you be there? Most likely. Sean didn't know for sure, of course, so he'd chosen the most convenient place to wait for you—your home behind the church. Or perhaps he was going to come up here after you didn't come home.

But where else would you have gone for the weekend, with *The Book of Michael,* if not to your weekend cabin? I admit, though, I was pondering what to do with Sean if you weren't there.

We made the turn for Benson Road, drove past the entrance to the logging road, the headlights flashing past the Fado sign tacked to a tree near the barrier, and called it a night. I did not want to risk driving on that logging road in the dark; nor did I want to break into Fado as I had your home. There seemed a difference to me that night; and so there proved to be. Sean and I slept in the Explorer until mid-morning, when my late-night reluctance to drive that logging road was validated.

A road? Hardly. Its width was scarcely greater than that of the Explorer in places. One side offered a continuing rise beyond the ditch, but the other dropped off so steeply there were times I thought I was driving in the air and had to concentrate fully on the road and not let the magnificent view of the river far below distract me.

After two miles the road narrowed even more, then rose for another half-mile, before leveling out and turning away from the precipice, into dense forest.

I saw your Fado not long after that; perhaps five minutes: a sharp turn around the screen of an eroded bluff topped with trees and there it was.

I saw no other cars besides yours parked at the side of the cabin, and reversed mine—slowly, carefully, looking back and smiling at Sean. He was sitting up now. I said: "We have to leave the car where Helen cannot see it from the cabin."

I took the keys and, as always, the necklace. I doubted another car would soon come along from the outside and present a problem. Malloy? He had not been following; I made sure of that on the way up. I did not believe he could be *that* close. But if he was, I could deal with him should he arrive; I had his brother after all, the primary reason why I planned to keep him alive until the hour of our departure from Fado. I could deal with any other guest you might have in there. And I always had this as a last resort: disappearing into the forest and beginning again, as I had before, and coming for you.

The Explorer effectively blocked the road. Should there be a glitch in the minutes or hours to come, there was no way for you to escape. If you somehow fled into the wilderness I had the ability to track you down easily and bring you back, a legacy from my time with Shadden. Before him I had the city streets; he gave me wilderness, too.

I made sure Sean was secure, took the knife and more tape.

Though I had only seen your car, I could not be sure you *were* alone. You may have brought a friend to share Fado for the weekend. Or Michael. Perhaps he had flown in, and you picked him up at the airport and drove up here. Perhaps Petra, too. What a party we'd have, once I took care of him. Perhaps a better word might be reunion, given what I'd read so far of *The Book of Michael*.

I moved cautiously, keeping an eye on the cabin. A stone chimney, tapering up from a broad base, rose between two wings— bedrooms? This was the rear; the front faced away. High grass almost obscured the walkway around the near side. A split rail fence marked the edge of the property, rising to a modest ridge in a corner. The land did not fall off as sharply outside the fence and I gradually made my way around, keeping low.

The fence straightened out toward the back. I entered a gully, discovering a trickling creek coursing along the forest side of the fence. I stopped about thirty yards from the cabin, on a slight rise, among pungent cedars, taking in your two or three-acre Eden bordering the Mt. Baker-Snoqualmie National Forest.

Your meadow bloomed with dandelions and purple, white and red wildflowers. The fence rimmed the clearing, following the meandering creek. To my right a gate led to a simple planked bridge spanning the stream and a gravel path that soon disappeared into the forest palisade.

The high morning sun splashed the cabin and immediate vicinity with a brightness that ensured a visual mask; from the cabin, across the glare of the meadow, you could not easily see into the darker woods. I knelt by a cedar two feet in diameter. Closer birds ceased their calls.

If I had been given the choice of any place on the earth to be at this moment, I still would have chosen this one—listening to the rippling creek and the more distant birds; breathing in the mountain air, feeling at once the coolness of the forest and the warmth of the open meadow; and waiting for the moment to see you emerge from the cabin.

It was large enough but not fancy. Two paned windows interrupted the vertical, rough-cut planking and faced the meadow. The porch and its roof of cedar shakes spanned the cabin's entire front. Branches served as railings, adding to the rustic sensibility. Three pairs of snowshoes hung on pegs on the outside wall; three walking sticks leaned against a stack of firewood piled neatly near the door. A scythe also leaned against the railing. I assumed you used the scythe to cut the meadow grass. A splitting maul stuck out from a chopping log near the bottom of the porch steps. You had to be strong to handle the scythe and maul, unless another assumed the chores. I saw no power lines. Even if you had a cell phone, it would not work well here, if at all.

The creaking of the opening door carried across the meadow.

You came out, gathered up your black hair, let it fall, then descended the porch steps, moving fully into the morning's sunlight.

One can see things at a distance that are not apparent close-up. And so I noticed the grace with which you walked and turned, how you went about activity—not absent-mindedly, forgetting this or that; not indecisively but with purpose. You took possession of the day, still innocent of the fact that it was no longer yours alone here.

On the near side of the little hillock of a root cellar—I could see the top of the sunken door—you picked up gardening implements: a bucket and hoe. You put on gloves, your back toward the side of the cabin and what appeared to be a car covered in a gray, fitted tarp.

The garden was a rectangle of perhaps fifteen by twenty-five yards, and enclosed by a waist-high fence of wire mesh to discourage deer and other nibblers, no doubt. I could hear the faint click of the gate latch as you entered to get to work. You wore jeans and a yellow T-shirt which for a moment made me wonder if you were alone. Why choose Michael's bright colors to contrast with your sable hair, unless for him or someone else to notice and admire. Then again, why take a carriage ride by yourself, even if the purpose was to celebrate another's birthday?

I could have watched you for hours. I gave you ten minutes; time enough for you to look toward the cabin, or call out to whomever was in there, if anyone. I knew you would do neither. There was no one else, just you and I, with only the meadow between us now.

No doubt there exists in the world a lover who would still be sleeping or lounging in a cabin, leaving such a One as you outside in the sun. But you would not choose to be with that person. No, the extra pairs of snowshoes and walking sticks on the porch were for those who were not presently with you.

Time to leave the forest.

At that moment I felt kinship with countless others of the past who also emerged from darkness into light, to take away what they had to, wanted or could. Among the hundreds of Shadden's history books, I had read of those places and times. Remember how I told Katie about Deerfield, only an hour's drive from where you and I will begin our new life? At Deerfield, long ago, many were taken to Canada, never to return to what they once knew. What had once been been...faded; and faded still more, and then disappeared under the sediment of time.

In a past life I may have watched from the edge of another field, where there may have been another such as you; perhaps with a husband who, wary of what could emerge from the surrounding forest, kept a sword or flintlock nearby.

This field? You were alone, with only a hoe.

As I walked out, I saw you kneel, put something in a pail and then rise, move on, then stoop over a row of plants. Seconds passed…a minute.

Then you turned, saw me halfway across the meadow.

IT IS ALMOST time now, Lennie; this testament is almost done. Sean waits. He has wormed his way along the floor yet again, closer to the wall of Michael's things, giving me another idea for how to end his life.

When my hand has gotten cramped from the writing, I have taken breaks to prepare for our leave-taking. I uncovered the car—the Mustang. You must have recently polished the glistening chrome. There was not a scratch on the cherry red paint. How could you manage that, driving along that logging road, tires spitting out gravel? Anyone else might wonder how it could have remained in such perfect condition all these years. But I know. It is not the same car. You and Michael bought another, to replace the one dredged from Lake Shendego. I neatly refitted the tarp. We must take care of our artifacts.

Near the Mustang I found a full jerry can of gasoline and did not have to use much to fill the tank, since you evidently pay attention to that, perhaps in anticipation of a visit by Michael, Pete and your son, Callan—though it is clear now a visit is not imminent, that they are still in Leary Falls. You keep the keys in the ignition; and why not, out here? Perhaps it is merely the artist in you—the canvas always framed.

I am thinking now: after our consummation I will drive the Mustang to a place a short way up the road, leaving it angled at a decline, facing the precipice. Then I will walk back and sprinkle gas on the porch, leaving the can inside. As much as I would prefer your hand to be the one to ignite Fado, that will not be possible since you must be secure in the Explorer, along with Sean.

The three of us will leave Fado in flames. Everything will be destroyed, perhaps even portions of the surrounding forest, if not the places where you and Michael hiked and fornicated under the moonlight. All of it shall be ash: *The Book of Michael* and the belongings he brought here to remind you of him when he is far away; things that cannot be replaced, one-of-a-kind things. No more will he have here a home away from the one in Leary Falls; nor will Pete, with whom he sates himself when he is not with you. No, I do not understand the infidelity that must confuse Callan. That, too, shall be consumed in the pyre of Fado, replaced by our uncorrupted fidelity.

Sean? I will place him in the Mustang, the driver's seat; the dummy Michael's last and shortest ride, his wrists tied to the steering wheel. It should present no problem for me to push the car over the edge. With the engine running and a full tank of gas, the ensuing explosion will be spectacular, but you and I will be far away before anyone arrives to investigate a bright but distant flare.

The first Mustang ended with water. The second and last will end in fire. Nothing much will remain of Sean Malloy. He may or may not ever be identified. Either way, he will have been useful to the end. The connection with the ruin of Fado will be obvious.

I am considering not killing Michael when we arrive back east; not immediately anyway, as with Sean's brother. Perhaps I will also let Michael live for years, if not a lifetime—enough time for him to nurture the assumption that it was a lover you brought to Fado who did it: someone offended by his presence and power over a woman such as you who will of course have fled, unable to face the consequences of what she unleashed, breaking that gravitational field she wrote about.

And so I will remain a shadow, existing now only for you, my One.

CHAPTER 14
FADO

11 p.m. Saturday, July 14, 2007

H E CAPPED HELEN'S pen, set it aside, squared the pages of *The Book of Eric*, pleased that he'd chosen that name of them all to use, instead of Richard Lampron or Shadden.

He thought of other names now, too: Helen and Michael's Callan; and Joseph or Diana, the names Lissa had chosen for the child she never had, the one Malloy had murdered along with her. Toward the end, Katie had wanted to name hers Joseph, too, should it be male. Caster decided that would be fine for a male child he and Helen would conceive.

A girl? Michael Furey may have been good at naming, but there was one even he could not have dreamed of because he had never been to the deep, beautiful lake, whose 50-mile length extended into the wilderness of the Cascades. Caster had once trekked down from the mountains after hunting with his bow, to goldilock for a few days in one of the many vacation homes along the shore.

His eyes were an ordinary blue compared to Helen's. He was hoping the child would have hers, blue as Lake Chelan.

Thus the name: Chelan. *Sheh-LANN.* Close as could be to the mother's.

Could he deliver the baby himself? Of course. He could find a book on midwifery. And they would take care of the rest as the child grew.

Shadden had educated him. They would do the same for Joseph or Chelan. People would see the child and assume he or she had the usual trappings and crappings of existence, but that might not be the case. Did that matter so much? It had not with him. It might even be a gift to be deprived of what others thought so necessary but were not.

He brushed the back of his fingers over the top page of his book, sure that he would feel the same wonder and pride when he caressed the tiny head of his infant child to come—Joseph or Chelan.

Of course, the thin stack of paper before him could not compare to Lennie's book nearby on the table; but in time it would be, leavened not only by what he would add as the weeks and months and then years accumulated, but also by the sketches she would contribute.

He allowed himself a moment to list the possibilities, thrilled with the expectation of seeing her drawings bring his words to life: Jacob Califf's mansion and the secret room where he kept the glittering hoard of artifacts; Lissa and Katie wearing the necklace; the red house and Kurt; the carriage and Flying Bird; the eagle at Luther Burbank park; and Sean watching her house or prostrate on the floor as Malloy had been at his home. And, of course, Fado. In time, when she looked at that sketch, she would remember Fado not as the place where occasionally Michael and Petra and Callan came to be with her, but where she began her new life.

Caster scraped back the chair, got up, stretched, clawed the cramped fingers of his right hand, so tired after hours of writing. He found an envelope and cardboard from a shelf where she kept artists' supplies and sandwiched *The Book of Eric* with the cardboard and put it in the envelope. At some point in the future she would bind a thicker one, as she had done with hers, but for now this would do.

Helen proved as difficult coming out of the room as going in, but Caster managed the carry and laid her down between the couch and the hearth. He asked her to kneel, facing the hearth. He was not that surprised when she did so after a moment's hesitation. It was not so much resignation, he thought, though she seemed on the verge of crying now. She had to be thinking that as long as she was in that position he could not do what he had promised her he would, before they left.

He went back into her room to get what he needed from her bureau. She did not look at him returning; she was staring into the fire, the tape pulsing at her mouth. He glanced beyond her, at Sean facing the far wall, curled fetally under the shelves of Michael Furey's things.

Behind her now, he ran his hand over her, from neck to legs. She flinched, but that was all she could do. He was thinking of those dolphin tattoos—the two leaping dolphins she had done for the love of her life—when he said, slowly taking off the tape sealing her mouth: "He should have gone to Crete while he was in the neighborhood. He could have thought of you as he gazed upon the dolphin frescoes at Knossos. That is what I would have done. After 3,000 years those colors are still visible on the walls of the throne room of a king and queen. I have not been there, but Shadden had a book about the Minoans. Would you like to go there someday, Lennie?"

He tossed the tape away and picked up the silver hair brush he had brought out from her room, rubbed a thumb over the monogram S, waiting for her answer. "In six months you will be asking me when we can go."

She jerking her head forward, feeling his hand at the nape of her neck. He stroked the long black hair that almost reached the floor. Her jeans had ridden up her left leg and he saw now an anklet with a tiny gold medallion with the etched initials: *MF.*

Michael Furey. The man was everywhere: on the wall, in her book, on *her.* He decided then he couldn't wait. Michael had to go. And soon. They could not begin until he was gone.

Caster asked: "Did he use just the one brush? Or did Pete have her own, that he used on her?"

He stroked her hair again, and again she moved her head away from him. But she could not do it far enough. He whispered close to her ear: "Does he brush your hair before you two fornicate? Surely what began as a youthful ritual evolved to that. Shame on him if he has forgotten."

He said no more. He was not annoyed that she was still trying to escape his hand. Still, that wouldn't do, so he tightened his arm around her, locking her head in place with his hand, the left, his fingers and thumb like a vise on her throat and chin. He could feel a faint throbbing in her neck. She shuddered as he began brushing her hair and speaking so softly that even Sean might not have been able to hear him across the room:

…It became a weekly ritual. Petra and I had always kept our hair long, ever since we were young. But it was always better, more special, when Michael brushed our hair. He'd done it for years, ever since that day he came into our room. I was ten years old, Petra eight. We'd been reading Archie Comics as I recall. Michael just picked up my silver hairbrush from the dresser and said:"Okay, who wants to go first?"—as if this was yet something else we'd always done together.

I said I would. It seemed perfectly natural. We were used to his impulsiveness, his spontaneity, the sudden ideas. Michael may not have lived close to the canal where our house was, but he was around so frequently it seemed like he did live near—just up the canal. That became another of our code phrases for anything that was close, anything good, anything pleasing about to happen.

We groomed each other like a family of baboons. We liked the brushing, and Michael liked it when I cut his hair; I got to be pretty good at it. So we had these rituals going, though when we got older Michael brushed our hair on the front porch and not in the bedroom. The brushing made the bench swing rock gently and that became part of it too, with Michael and I later, when we would rock each other after making love. Then, Michael didn't care if his friends saw him doing this and certainly not the pleasure-boaters gliding past on the canal, a stone's throw away.

Poor Dad was disconcerted for a while, perhaps thinking that Michael was gay, or a budding hair-stylist. I heard him tell Mom once in the kitchen after a few instances of this hair-brushing: "He's a wonderful kid but… shouldn't he be out there with the other guys, playing ball, that sort of thing?"

To be fair, Dad was always a little out of the loop, away on business a lot in Utica, Syracuse or Albany. Mom said: "He usually is, dear. He's not with the girls all the time, you know. How could he be with sports all year round? Those three are not that inseparable. Michael made the honor roll at school last semester. You told me yourself he's on track to be maybe the best halfback Leary Falls has seen for years, never mind what he did as a pitcher last season. And Helen says his best sport might be swimming."

She'd begun to cry halfway through the brushing. He did not hear that so much—the fire was crackling, spitting. Her shoulders gave it away. He finished the hundred whispering strokes, felt her swallow hard one last time before he removed his hand from her throat and chin. He put the brush in a pocket of his vest and withdrew the necklace and draped it over his fingers before her. The gold and jewels glistened in the firelight. He was at her side now, not behind and he felt more of the heat from the fire.

"Perhaps it might help knowing this will be yours soon. As I recall, you never mentioned what gift Michael brought back for you from Europe. Whatever it was surely could not match this. Lissa—oh, and Katie after a while—would put it on themselves."

She closed her eyes and he closed his hand over the necklace and brushed the back of his fingers over her moist cheeks as he had just done with his book: "In time you will do that, also. Everything shall be better soon, you have my promise," he said, and drew her hair out to its full, sable length.

He pocketed the necklace. "If you like you can even pretend it is Michael instead of Sean over there with his back turned to us, since he undoubtedly could not bear to witness our consummation either. Now, I will be back in a minute with blankets for you to lie on, and you should be grateful to know that at least your ankles will be free."

He went to the room to get the blankets, thinking two, perhaps, to double up and spread on the bare floor in front of the hearth. He lit a lantern and found the blankets in a cedar chest at the foot of the bed. He had them in his hands when he heard someone whispering beyond the door which, out of plumb, had closed almost all the way. Helen? Had to be her—which seemed odd because she had still been crying when he left her, and now she had stopped abruptly.

Caster heard a *tink* against a window.

He turned, blankets in his arm. The window in this room?

No, the sound had been fainter, more distant. Had Sean gotten up somehow, was at a window out there? A branch tapping against a window pane? He listened more carefully, heard only the snapping fire. All was quiet now beyond the door.

Then: a scraping sound, more like a shuffle—not the sound of Sean worming across the floor, or Helen trying to get up.

Through the crack in the doorway Caster could see the lantern on the table, illuminating the folder of his book next to hers and also half of the couch, its back to the cabin door and one of the two flanking windows. What had it been? A bear or rummaging raccoons outside? There was no garbage on the porch.

He tossed aside the blankets, seeing it now, blinking to make sure he was not imagining it in the flickering light of that room: the door knob slowly turning, a half-turn and then back.

Bears were not frustrated by a locked door.

But there was an animal out there, all right.

James Malloy. Closer than he had thought. Who else could it be? Michael? No, Furey would not be hesitantly working the door knob. This was his home away from home.

So the police had not gotten Malloy for breaking the Glassman.

Caster stepped back from the door, focusing on the matter at hand. If he went into that room now the last thing he would hear was the shattering of glass as Malloy squared up on a window in the front and fired. He had light enough for targeting, and he would not have come all this way without a gun.

He blew out the lantern in the bedroom, in case Malloy was even now coming around the side of the cabin, wondering what he was doing in the back bedroom. The door was almost closed so Malloy would not see much of a change in light. Caster unlatched the window, pushing out the paned halves all the way, and peered out just enough to make sure Malloy was not there.

He heard no breathing, no rustling.

The fit was tight but he managed to squeeze himself through the window without making noise and dropped the three feet to the ground. He crouched at the corner of the cabin, going over in his mind what lay ahead. He could not risk knocking into anything in the dark, alerting Malloy on the porch. He would still be there, waiting for Caster to emerge from the room.

He could not remember anything in the way, only the Mustang at the side. There was plenty of space between the corner of the porch and the root cellar, no discarded planting pots or tools he could remember seeing.

He made his way carefully to the front of the car. When Helen and Michael used the car, they had to just drive it around the back of the cabin. He looked over the covered trunk of the car, could not see Malloy yet, only the side of the porch and not even all of that. But Malloy was still there; had to be. Caster kept low as he moved to the end of the porch, looked over.

Malloy blocked the light coming from the nearer of the two windows in front of the cabin, standing a foot from that window, his back to Caster who could not see the gun but he knew Malloy had one from the position of the arms—up and bent at the elbow. Malloy was peeking around the edge of the window, still waiting.

Caster could not get the gun he had hidden in the root cellar. Nor could he clamber over or under the porch rails from where he crouched, never mind rushing Malloy from the steps.

Too far, too much noise...

He had to separate Malloy from the gun and to do that he had to get closer. The porch was wider than he remembered, but he saw now in his mind how he could take Malloy without climbing over and getting shot point blank.

He crawled on all fours along the front of the porch, rose to a crouch. Enough light spilled from the windows for him to be able to gauge the distance between the lower of the two horizontal porch rails and the flooring.

Plenty of room...

At eye level with Malloy's shoes, Caster snaked both arms under the lower rail and as soon as he touched the bottom of the pants' legs, he lunged ahead, grabbing Malloy's ankles, yanking back hard, pulling his feet out from under him.

The gun went off—*snap*—as Malloy thudded to the porch.

Caster thought instantly: *.22...*

Malloy fell on his belly; Caster did not have to twist him around. He was sure he had heard the gun clatter away. Even if he had not lost it, Malloy could not easily fire at him, not on his stomach, facing away.

He kept pulling Malloy, had him by the belt now. The man flailed his arms—without the gun. He kicked his legs, tried to twist around, to stop the slide, but Caster was too strong. Malloy raised his head, only to crack the back of it against the railing, and Caster hauled him over, lassoing Malloy's neck with his right arm as he tumbled to the ground.

It was not Malloy.

For a moment, Caster could not remember the man's name, only the one he had given him: Glassman.

He was still trying to break free, kicking frantically as Caster tightened his grip on his neck, needing only another few seconds to get enough leverage to break it. But he backed into the chopping block, stumbling, elbow knocking the maul free of the stump. Glassman scrambled to his feet—and did not get far. Caster lunged, bear-swiped his ankles, tripping him. In seconds he was on the man again, dragging him by the feet this time, to the chopping block. He punched Glassman twice, felt him go limp. That triggered Caster's memory: *Robert Tiphook.*

Caster hauled him, a sack of garbage, over to the stump. He did not have the pony-tail anymore, just a brushy stub. For a moment this seemed to Caster the most inexplicable fact of his presence here. What, had he cut his hair to gin up his courage? It would have been laughable if it was not so annoying that the man was here.

He smashed Tiphook's head on the stump just as the loser was rousing. The splitting maul lay within easy reach. He grabbed it now, hefting the weight.

Caster one-handed the maul at half-length. Cleave or smash? Either way, eight pounds of iron…

Light spilled from the cabin doorway, distracting him. How could that be? He had left Helen and Sean bound tightly,

Someone rushed out—thuds on the porch—and Caster did not have time to finish with Tiphook.

Sean leaped from the porch, barreled into him, an arm cracking against the maul handle. He grunted but did not stop, did not look at Tiphook on the ground; his momentum forced Caster away from the stump. Sean pummeled Caster with one fist, was at him too closely for

him to swing the maul. Caster felt spit on his right eye as he grappled with
Sean; finally shoving him away, punching viciously, snapping his head
back. He flung Sean aside, but by then Tiphook was up, staggering away
beyond the pale of the cabin's light, into the darkness.

Caster wiped the spit from his eye, started to run after Tiphook—a
fading shadow in the high grass, stumbling toward the creek bridge—
then stopped.

Helen...

Even as he turned to go back to the dimly lit cabin he saw her, knife
in her right hand...

He sidestepped, avoiding her lunging stab by inches, and recovered
more quickly than she did, taking her off her feet with a sweeping kick to
an ankle. She landed squarely on her back—a loud *huff*—and he hoped
that was the wind knocked out of her. Yet she kept flailing with the knife.
He managed to avoid the wild stabs, pinned the wrist of her knife hand,
yanked it from her. He fisted her hair, hauled her up, twisting her right
hand behind her, the knife his now, at her neck.

Almost as one they walked toward the cabin. She smelled like she had
been...burned.

Sean was curled up, groaning, by the entrance to the root cellar. *Get
him in a minute...*He had to make sure of Helen first before he dealt with
Sean and the Glassman.

Inside, on the way to her bedroom, he saw how she'd done it. The
charred rope lay in a tangle near the hearth. She had backed into the
fire, burning not only the rope—enough to break free anyway—but also
scorching her wrists and singeing her hair. He had made it easier for her,
stoking the fire.

He kept the knife at Helen's throat until he passed the hearth, the table,
then threw the knife into the kitchen, where she could not get it quickly if
something happened in the room; he assumed she would still be difficult
there. The knife stuck in the floor near scattered utensils. A drawer hung
open, evidence of her frantic haste in finding the chef's knife.

He figured she'd go for his eyes or groin and he was right; perhaps
the open window in the room gave her hope. She waited until he had to

handle the roll of tape. She twisted around, getting a knee up, and tried to spear him in an eye with stiff fingers.

He was way ahead of her, batted away her hand, twice slapped her hard to momentarily stun her, then forced her face down on the bed again, one arm crooked behind her back, as before. He managed to tape the one wrist; after that the other was easy. Given the burns on her wrists, it would be painful for her to try to get loose—so much the better.

Part of him was proud of the way she almost pulled it off, as if she shared with him the traits of resourcefulness and determination. The other part of him wanted to end her life now, torch the cabin, and from the forest watch this place—that she shared with Michael Furey—burn to the ground.

After all he had done for her, saving her from the brothers Malloy; after all he was going to do for her, bestow upon her his most precious possession...

He spun, thinking ahead to the time when they would remember this night, and she would tell him she must have been crazy, out of her mind to try and kill him. She would marvel at his forgiveness, his understanding of how difficult the transition from one world to another could be.

Still, he was still angry with her, and there was a need to do something to mark that, short of killing her. He thought of what he was going to do as he used all the rope and the remaining tape to secure her to the bed frame. He would have to reuse the rope when they left in the Explorer.

He closed the window and then, in the kitchen, plucked the knife from the floor. Back in the room he bent low over her. She turned her head—which only made it easier to fist thick sheaves of her hair and hack them off.

"A collaborator's trim," he whispered. "By the time it grows back to what it was, you will wonder why you even tried to get away."

He took the knife, left the room to go kill Sean Malloy.

Robert Tiphook was more than just a glitch that had ruined the final hour at Fado. He could not remain alive to find his way back, go to the police with the description of the Explorer. At some point he could dump the car, steal another car, but a trail would be left.

The Glassman would be making a ruckus out there in the night, stumbling around. Panicked men were not quiet ones, so it should not be too difficult to track him. He would not get far. Caster could not leave Sean alive while he did so, not with Helen in the cabin.

He decided to bring Sean back to the cabin; make that two charred bodies found in the ruins of Fado.

You lose, Michael. Lennie kept her taste for three but it got out of hand, and it seems she killed the other two and set fire to Fado while they slept. After all, she tried to kill me...

It would only take seconds to kill Sean.

Except he was not there by the root cellar, where Caster had seen him ten minutes before.

Inside?

He ran back to the cabin, taking the porch steps in two bounds, to get the flashlight Helen kept hanging on a peg by the door. There was not much room in the root cellar, but he could not go in blindly, have Sean smash a jar on his head, or break one and slash him with the shards. After all this, done in by a mason jar crammed with last year's garden tomatoes?

He took the five steps down to the low door and kicked it open, expecting to see Sean cowering, shivering in a corner, his eyes jewels in the light. Caster bent low, flicking the beam left, right, over...nothing; only the covered containers of ice, shelves of canned vegetables and other perishables.

Helen's gun lay hidden where he had left it, behind the top row to his left. He took the gun, and ran the perimeter of the fence, searching with the flashlight, sure he would flush the man, see him scuttling through the grass, holding his arm. Caster was certain Sean had hurt the arm running headlong into a much bigger man holding a maul.

He speared the light into forest, looking for sparks of eyes. Sean had to have made it beyond the verge of forest—thinking like Tiphook that the forest offered safety. Either that or...

The road.

The only way out.

Both men could hide in the forest yet sooner or later they had to get to the road to escape. Already, one or both of them could be on that road.

And even if they were not, they could be on their way, circling back, or at least trying to.

He had to move fast now.

Take the Explorer? No. He would have to use headlights for the road, and they would see the lights, leave the road like Helen tried to do before, only they would have the time.

He had his plan now and ran back to the cabin to get *The Book of Eric* to put that, along with the necklace, in the Explorer for safekeeping. He quickly retrieved his Black Widow bow—a traditional recurve—and its quiver of five broad-head hunting arrows, plus five extras in a leather case he slung over his shoulder. He would not need even the quivered five but one never knew. He took his hunting knife, stuck the flashlight in his back pocket. He had Helen's gun.

Helen? She wasn't going anywhere. But would one of them come back for her?

*Not likely…*The Glassman would not want to be anywhere close to that chopping log and Sean's arm was hurt, Caster was sure of it. They would not come back to the cabin, believing that he was still in there with her. They would go for help and there was only one way to go for that.

He took the road as fast as he could. The gibbous moon provided just enough light for him to see running shadows; he always had good night vision. With any luck he might hear them over his own breathing and the soft tapping of the arrow case at his side.

After a mile or so he felt sure he would have overtaken them by now. He kept on anyway, slackening his pace a little. He did not want fatigue to be a factor when and if he ran one or the other of them down, or both. Five minutes passed and he slowed to a walk, confident they had not gotten ahead of him. He stopped where the road took its sharpest bend, if he remembered correctly.

He left the road, took his time climbing the scree—the last thing he needed now was to sprain an ankle—until he reached the top of the bluff, about fifteen feet above the road. The moon hung over the precipice on the other side of the road, silvering the twisting cord of the river far below. He gave the stars only a moment, but it was enough to remember the last time he had seen them this clear, beyond the pollution of the cities: at Shadden's, in the rain-shadow of the Olympic Mountains, when he got the idea to name them himself because he had never learned the names like everyone else, and Shadden was dead by then and could not tell him.

He settled in, waiting for them to come his way.

They would. To get out they would have to pass him.

He decided to give it the rest of the night and into the morning— enough of it, anyway, that he could spare. Even if they did not use the road it would be a long time before they got out of the surrounding wilderness. And they might fall, twist an ankle or knee, or even run into a cougar. Out there anything could happen. They had no weapons. If they *did* take the long way out, made it somehow, he and Helen would be long gone.

CHAPTER 15

AMBUSHES

I GAVE IT until midnight before finding my way back to Pattison. Again I slept in the car, the church parking lot, hoping that early-arriving parishioners would be my alarm clock. And so they were.

Still, I'm sure Barbara had opened up the Basket when she said she would—9 a.m. When I got there, she said the coffee had been on for a while, so as she brewed more she gave me directions to Fado. I left with a cup of the fresh stuff, a bag of pastries and a half-gallon of orange juice for Helen and I to enjoy "while we talked." All of it was on the house; she and Joe had won $500 at the roulette wheel the night before.

She told me to drive carefully on that logging road and to be sure to say hi to Helen for her, and ask if she wanted her son to cut more firewood for her sometime.

By the time I found Benson Road—again—the coffee and half the pastries were gone. I couldn't tell you why I didn't open the container of orange juice.

I say I found Benson Road again: I'd already been down a half-mile of it anyway, until the pavement turned to gravel. The night before I'd turned back at that point because of fatigue and the DEAD END sign.

After another mile of gravel I saw the carved Fado sign nailed to a hemlock. The wooden barrier was open, which could only be an indication that she was there, at the end of the logging road beyond.

And Sean?

Not far past that barrier I saw what Barbara Hollner had warned me about. The logging road was more like a dry creek bed than a road. Some of the larger protruding rocks looked as if they'd been gouged and scraped. Every twenty yards—going at little more than a walker's pace—I passed five-foot high sticks with red plastic streamers attached at the top to mark the shoulder—or lack of one. So Helen evidently came here in the winter. I couldn't imagine driving this track in winter, much less being the guy who plowed it for the woman.

The drop-off to my right was so steep the tops of fir trees clinging to the slope matched the level of the road. It was almost 11 a.m. and fog still blanketed most of the valley below—I could see only a few curving portions of the Nooksack. I felt as if I was driving on top of the clouds.

There was evidence of mining in a hollow to my left—rusting machinery poked out from brush and third-growth trees, and narrow-gauge rails ended with some sort of winching mechanism. Trees grew between the rails of this spur, an indication the mines in the area had been long-abandoned. Wildflowers sprouted from a coil of rusting cable that snaked off into the denser woods beyond.

It was hard for me to believe Sean could be at the end of this line…this road. Yet he was *somewhere* other than his apartment unless he just wasn't answering his phone. I'd called yet again from the pay phone outside the Basket.

So two possibilities: he'd driven all the way in here, right up to this Fado, and had done something that could not remain a secret, not this time. Not with me here this time.

I hoped like hell for the other, more likely one: that he simply hadn't answered the phone; that he was, even now, sleeping away a Sunday morning at his apartment. After all, I hadn't seen his car parked on Benson Road near the Fado sign and the barrier, and I hadn't yet seen his car parked on this logging road or the ditch to the side, which would have meant he'd decided to walk in so the woman wouldn't know he was there, and…

And what?

This Fado was isolated. No one would know Sean was here. No one would hear anything. Whatever he was planning—if he was here—he would be thinking this was yet something else that would remain a secret.

If I got all the way in, saw only her car, I planned to turn right around and go back. There'd be nothing to say to the woman, except apologizing for trespassing if she saw me. I couldn't tell her that my brother had been stalking her for days now, maybe even weeks. But I sure as hell would have it out with Sean when I finally tracked him down.

I took a sharp turn slowly—and saw ahead two men in the middle of the logging road, thirty yards apart. I stopped the car.

Neither was Sean.

The closest had his back to me: a big man, walking slowly toward the other, an arrow nocked in a black bow. The second man limped away from him, backing up. He was tall, thin and looked familiar but I couldn't remember where I'd seen him.

The taller, limping man clearly was trying to get away from the other, clearly threatened by him.

Whoever these guys were it was likely they were connected to the woman somehow. They were on her road. They couldn't be trespassing hunters, fooling around, playing a stupid and dangerous game. Only one had a bow. Was he the woman's boyfriend or husband, the other guy a trespasser? If so, he was going *way* over the line evicting him from the property—and he'd be rousting him in the *other* direction, toward me.

At least Sean wasn't a part of this.

I had the gun in the glove compartment, but I wasn't about to get it out, escalate the situation with a guy carrying a hunting bow. I was about to back up the car, maybe go for help, when the bowhunter turned, sensing the car or hearing the idling. He raised the bow, hesitated, lowered it slightly, then raised it again, as if he had to aim for me instead a tire.

I couldn't believe it. For all he knew I'd just gotten lost. The thought spanned two blinks of an eye as he made his pull: *he's going to shoot at me...*

I ducked low and right. The car veered the same way as I accelerated straight at the crazy son-of-a-bitch, heard the *snick* of the arrow glancing off the windshield, where my head had just been.

I rose up, saw it just before the guy dove to his right, into the gully: the marking on his left forearm.

I'd never seen his face, but that night I'd seen the tattoo.

Fifteen feet…and three thousand miles away…and now just the flash of that arm before he rolled into the trough, cradling the bow.

Seconds: that's all it took to realize that Sean was very much a part of this.

He remembered what I'd told him on the phone that time, and saw Shadden…and the woman? And that story about a vigil: *She didn't know—how could she?—that she was bait.*

My brother had led me here to Shadden, but didn't know he had.

I gunned the car over where Shadden had just been, flat-out horizontal in the air. The car thumped up as the left front wheel hit the embankment, then the rear left. I'd wanted to run him over, but saved his life: if I'd been going slower the left wheels, front and back, would've crushed him in the gully.

I felt the scrape and grind of the car's bottom on the edge of the road, but now that I'd missed this chance I kept accelerating.

Don't get stuck…

I fishtailed out of it, which swung the rear end to the other side of the road. For a split-second thought I was going over. But I straightened out, glanced back, hoping to see that somehow I'd skinned him, flayed his top half going over.

He rose with the bow from the gully, and reached into his vest.

Fuck…

He had a gun too. My hands were shaking on the wheel: not the best prospect for getting into a gunfight here. I had to get the hell out of here and there was no place to go but ahead.

I peeled out, tires spitting stones and gravel. Ahead, the other man limped down the road, a parody of a carousel horse. I remembered him now: Sean's photos…the ferry…the woman.

Something behind me cracked at the rear of the car. A taillight? I looked back…

Shadden was fitting another arrow as he ran, gun tucked in his belt. What was he thinking, using the bow and not the gun? Saving his rounds for later?

I braked hard alongside the man. He'd be dead in a minute if I left him here. I opened the door, shouted at him to get in.

He took forever to move six feet—*Christ!*—then fussed with his bad leg like he was at the end of a fucking diving board. I reached over again, grabbed his shirt—"Come *on!*"—and yanked him in just as an arrow *hissed* past, skimming the top of the roof. He banged his forehead, but got his gimp leg in.

I looked back again—Shadden kneeled at the side of the road, twenty yards away, setting a platform to fire his gun now—and hit the gas.

The door closed on the man's right leg before he swung it in and pulled the door shut—a good thing. I had accelerated too fast, had to turn sharply on the narrow road. If the door hadn't been closed, Helen's friend would have tumbled out of the car over the precipice.

He sat on the carton of orange juice, flattened the bag of pastries—and ducked as a gunshot hit a side window, causing a spider-web to blossom around the hole, a foot away from the passenger side headrest.

I drove as fast as I dared. There was no sign of Shadden in the rear-view mirror but he'd be sprinting. My hands kept shaking on the wheel. The guy rubbed his knee but I couldn't tell if he was shaking too, or if it was just the car on that road.

"I don't know who you are but thanks," he said, and started to go on about coming up here because of a woman…and it didn't go well…and the guy who was going to kill him on the road almost did the night before… but he escaped into the forest along some trail and hurt his knee, heard this…*pop,* maybe tore some cartilage…

I cut him off: "How much farther…the cabin?" I glanced at him. One blood-shot eye was almost swollen shut. Shadden had connected; I knew what that felt like. The rest of his face looked like he'd shaved with a bad razor.

"Maybe a mile…less."

"Who else is there besides the woman?"

"Her name's Helen…Helen Sommers. I'm Robert Tiphook."

I took another curve faster than I should have, but Shadden was probably sprinting faster than I could drive on this road. Again: "Who else besides her?"

"There was another man…"

"What did he look like?"

"I couldn't see much. It was through a window. He was tied up, on the floor, curled up."

"Was he alive?"

"He…yes…he was the one to come out of the cabin first to help me. I don't know how…"

"What happened to him?"

"I don't know. It was dark, I just…Malloy was going to use an ax…"

"Wait…you said *Malloy*…"

"He was at my house before. He…he said his name was James Malloy."

"It's not. That's me."

"I don't understand…"

Tiphook was staring at me now. There wasn't time to explain, not that I understood either, other than Shadden setting me up for what he did to the poor bastard next to me. It had to be Sean there with the woman. He was probably dead. Why else would Shadden be out on the road? Maybe the woman was still alive. She was in the middle of all this. If he'd killed her, why stick around?

I took another bend, where a madrona hung over the gully. Up ahead: a white Explorer parked next to a green Toyota Highlander; both adjacent to the cabin. I swerved sharply, skidding, blocking both of them.

"What're we going to do?" Tiphook said.

I reached over in front of him and took the gun from the glove compartment. "Give you time."

"For what?"

I left the keys in the ignition, got out, leaned back in. "For you to get her. And the one you saw with her, that was my brother, I'm sure of it." It was probably too late for Sean; maybe not the woman.

"The other…he's going to be…"

"Real soon. I'll head him off on the road, draw him into the woods. Believe me, he'll follow me. You get Helen and my brother if they're still alive—and get the hell out of here."

"I can't drive, not with my…"

"You can. Either she or you has to. Now get going."

I took off at a run. There was only a couple of minutes to find a place by the road. I glanced back. Tiphook was still in the car, but I didn't have time to wait and see if he'd do what I said or just take off. He'd come here to help her but he'd obviously had it, wanted out.

I ran twenty more yards to a point where the road took the last sharp turn before the clearing and the cabin. The rocky outcrop with the straggly madrona rose fifteen feet and too steeply for me to scramble up with the gun in my hand. I backtracked quickly, entering the woods ten yards behind the rear of the cabin, keeping an eye out to my left where the road widened to the three vehicles. I had to make sure Shadden hadn't gotten there already, maybe getting behind me. He had to be pounding up that road, but I figured I still had enough time to get in position on the little bluff.

It took me less than a minute, using trees to pull myself up. At the top I veered left, keeping low, so he couldn't see me from the road. Soon as I saw it, I crouched even lower, weaving through the brush and trees, snaking the last yards on my belly toward the scaling, rust-red madrona. From there I could see in both directions.

Shadden wasn't in sight. Even if he'd been quicker than I thought, chances were I'd at least have seen him moving toward the cabin. He wouldn't realize I was behind him. I was sure he hadn't gotten past me.

It would be over soon. I tried to get Katie and Sean out of my thoughts: Katie on the bed, looking left, then right for approval, smiling at the unseen clapping. And Sean…dead outside the cabin? Maybe he'd gotten to the forest…

Not now…

There would be time enough later to find him.

I had to relax, get the breathing under control.

He would be coming very soon.

I waited, arms outstretched, elbows a foundation, finger off the trigger so I wouldn't fire accidentally, fuck it up and alert him.

Squeeze it off…

I sighted, seeing him in my mind: a running target but a large one.

Wait for him to get close. Go for the torso…you go for the head, you'll miss…

Then two more shots—*no, empty the fucking gun into him.* He was a big man. I couldn't have him crawling into the gully below. If I missed, or if he managed to make it to the gully only slightly wounded, I'd have to expose myself to his return fire to finish him. And then...what? Go back to the car. Drive back, use the car as a shield and kill him. But what if Tiphook found his spine, got her—and Sean?—took off with them in the car?

Finish it here. Have to...He's coming in a minute...two maybe...twenty yards, no more...

Any moment now.

Squeeze...squeeze them off...

More than two minutes passed.

Should have gotten here by now...

Had he left, called it quits, was even now running the other way? No, that wasn't something Shadden would do. He'd seen me. He knew. He used my name with Tiphook.

Where was he?

Maybe he thinks he'll be vulnerable on the road, in the open. Assumes I've come armed. So...if I come barreling back along the road in the car, catching him in the open, there's no place to go, unless...he goes over the other side, an easy kill if the fall doesn't do it. The other way? Even easier if he tries to climb the slope...No...back where we started...

What then?

He should have been here by now. If he had, he'd be dead; I'd be dragging him to the side of the road, shoving him over where no one would ever...

A jolt of fear made my gun hand jerk.

Suddenly I knew why he wasn't on the road—the only possible explanation.

He was coming, but not on the road. He had to be moving through the woods along the ridge. No problem for a bowhunter.

I glanced to my right.

Shadden stood twenty yards away, flanked by two firs, aiming an arrow at me.

CHAPTER 16

HUNTER AND HUNTED

ANY OTHER ANIMAL would have frozen momentarily when it sensed danger, and died. But Malloy rolled left as Caster released; a dime-shot which would have skewered him in the neck had he not moved. Instead, the broad-tip arrow impaled a young hemlock behind him, a foot above the ground.

Caster darted behind a tree, should Malloy want to finish it here. He was surprised Malloy had seen him since he had not made a sound—no snapping twig, a scuff of shoes. What then? Maybe it was just the gift of the hunt that heightened all the senses. Or Malloy had a sixth one.

He knelt, peeked around the tree, not overly worried about a washed-up ball player making the shot with a handgun at twenty yards, shaking with the realization he should be dead.

Malloy was gone.

The man was quick. Better to know that now. Caster saw not a scrap of the dark red shirt he wore, nothing of him in the forest which closed in thickly beyond the ridge. But if he could not see Malloy then Malloy could not see him well enough for a shot. Still, his quarry could not be far. He moved ahead, veering right, left, darting from tree to tree for cover.

He knelt by the madrona where Malloy had lain in ambush, imagining he could smell his sweat. He had not been sure it was Malloy on the road, but he was a minute ago, squaring up the shot. There could be only one reason why Malloy had stopped to get the Glassman: to get Helen, and leave with her, do later to her what he had with Lissa—the next best thing to killing Caster himself.

For now she was safe—Caster had not heard any shots, however faint. Malloy had set up the ambush instead of killing her. First things first. Yet he had made a mistake in attempting the ambush. He could have killed her and fled into the woods. But, of course, he wanted to do more than just that. Now, he had no other choice but to retreat into the forest and hope to kill Caster there, and then Helen would be all his.

Caster had to decide: go after him, or leave with Helen. He was not worried about the Glassman.

Somewhere out there—no more than sixty yards away—Malloy would be waiting to see what he did. If he did not hear or see him approaching, he would move back to the road, assuming Caster had gone to get Helen before she could escape in a car, thanks to the Glassman. Malloy would be waiting for them above the road as before.

Or instead, he might run down to the cabin before they could get away, trap them inside. Malloy could do anything: set the place afire, burn them alive; pick them off as they tried to get out and flee to the safety of the forest.

Caster figured the other option more likely. He also could not drive the road and shoot at the same time, much less take Malloy down from the opposite side of the car. Helen would be in danger, closer to Malloy, vulnerable to a shot through the near window. Malloy could blow out tires easily with a few shots, trap them in the car. The man would have the elevation. A bullet in the gas tank and it would be all over.

The only thing to do—and what he wanted to do anyway—was to go after Malloy now and kill him. Tiphook and Helen might escape in the meantime, but at least Malloy would be dead. Caster would have time to find her.

There was a good chance he could kill Malloy quickly, head for the beginning of the road, and intercept Helen and the Glassman, but he could not count on that. They would head straight for the police, of course. But Caster was sure he could finish Malloy before they came in force. Then: get the necklace and *The Book of Eric* from the Explorer. He would need only a minute to set the cabin on fire as he had planned, set off into the forest, make his way down the valley. Let Helen flee into hiding; he had a good idea where she might go; indeed he did.

He made up his mind.

Five minutes later, deeper into the forest, he had to alter his plan—a spin move—because he realized the quickest way to Malloy was not straight on, through these firs and cedars, pushing cautiously through the profusion of undergrowth, fallen trees and rocky outcrops. The snowberry and salal were so thick he could not go around them, had to go through. Malloy would hear him even before he saw him; he could be anywhere, crouching behind a boulder, or prone behind any of the red huckleberry bushes growing out of rotting logs.

Caster walked in a crouch another twenty yards and decided: *not toward him; around...*

Malloy had to be close, but Caster was not going to give him another ambush. He fired his gun, directly ahead, then backtracked, moved off to the left, kept going. If Malloy believed he was coming straight on, he would naturally keep moving back into the forest, keeping his distance from a man hunting him with both a gun and bow.

Now, going around, Caster would be able to move faster, not worrying about being heard or seen until he set an ambush for Malloy, from behind.

He moved with a confidence bordering on euphoria. He was in his territory out here. Malloy's? Manicured fields rimmed by lines of chalk.

Kill him first, get Helen later. You know where she will go if she leaves Fado...

A spin move. Even better this way. Let her cross the country by herself, eliminating any problems with a journey of two. Michael, Callan and Petra were only a couple of hours from the red house in the Berkshires.

And while you are in Leary Falls...

Eric Lane Caster plunged deeper into the forest, not worried about Malloy hearing him, catching his movement. Malloy would be retreating but not as fast as Caster was advancing. He was sure his instincts—movement and surprise—had to come from somewhere. He gave himself a brief reward thinking about it. Where had Nathan Bedford Forrest's or Stonewall Jackson's come from? Shadden had books on those brilliant Confederate generals of the Civil War.

Caster felt a particular kinship with Jackson—maybe he once had *been* the man, as Jackson himself might have had a special lineage of resurrections going back to…Scipio Africanus, conqueror of Hannibal. Or even Alexander the Great himself. Spin moves? Alexander created them. Need to take the city fortress of Tyre, located on an island a half-mile from the shore? And you with no navy? Build a causeway across the water for your siege machines and archers.

He took the northern rim at a fast walk, almost jogging uphill through second-growth firs as high as the walls of Tyre, weaving through increasingly rocky terrain, shelving rock shrouded by saplings and cleaved boulders. He figured he was roughly paralleling Malloy, but the man would have a tougher time of it in the lower elevations, going through the basin of dense ferns clustering around dead trees crowded with snags and branches; pushing through brush and briars and middling hemlock and cedar, and always having to stop to listen for the pursuit—and looking in the wrong direction.

Caster loped along the ridge which was twenty feet high in places above the lower ground and kept on for another ten minutes before descending into a basin. He recognized this as prime bear country. There were signs of a fire, not recent, that had reduced much of the tree cover. The vegetation was back but in this vicinity one could still glimpse an approaching man.

When he saw the ruins of the miners' cabins, he knew he had his place. They were tucked into the lee of a hillock, three of them, about forty yards away. The roofs of two had caved in. Moss and ferns grew in the rot of the sagging third.

Here…kill him here…

It seemed likely that Malloy, after slogging through the undergrowth, would instinctively head for the respite of this more open area. Perhaps he might even see the low, ramshackle cabins as *his* opportunity to ambush his pursuer.

Except Caster had gotten here first.

Surprise, Jimmy...

He ran down to the nearest cabin and straddled over a log thick as his waist. He set up at the side of the cabin, smelling the dankness of decay. From here he had a clear arc of fire, perhaps thirty yards.

Give him twenty minutes...

Even if Malloy did not show here, all that would mean is that he had drifted farther south. Caster could continue as he had, faster than Malloy, herding him until finally the man appeared at the end of his hunting arrow, a dead-on shot he could not escape this time.

Caster caught the movement in a thicket of salmonberries and huckleberries. He withdrew an arrow from the quiver, fitted, tracked Malloy's progress, waiting for him to emerge from the tangle. The thicket rose no more than five feet.

He is keeping low...

The movement was not Malloy's.

A black bear appeared, reared up, snout nuzzling the upper reaches of the bushes. Apparently dissatisfied with what it found, the bear dropped again to all fours, hidden again.

Caster had killed one before—an adult male bigger than this one—a few miles north of the Hamma Hamma river in the Olympics, a day's hike from Shadden's. Not a good kill, but then he had not been hunting with a bow for long.

The bear moved off to the right, oblivious of Caster. He followed its path through the trees and brambles. Too bad the bear was not female, with cubs nearby. There was a light breeze which came in the direction from which Malloy should be appearing very soon. The bear might pick up the scent and if it had been a mother with cubs, the bear might have mauled him badly, leaving Caster only the coup-de-grace.

He saw Malloy a minute later, pausing by a shaggy cedar, half-hidden by a sweeping lower branch, looking back. The bear was foraging again, not far from where Caster had first seen it, twenty yards from Malloy. Neither had seen the other yet. When Malloy did, he would likely take off. What did a ball player know from bears, what you should do? He would probably run straight ahead, panicked, looking back. Caster saw it in his mind: the hunting tip pinning him to a tree, hands jerking around the shaft, before falling away as he died. The bear would have first dibs but after a few days, there would not be much left of James Malloy.

Caster watched him move ahead, the gun in his right hand.

He wiped sweat away from his eyes, off his hands. He felt the string tension of the Black Widow, but waited to pull all the way.

The bear dropped, rose again, getting the scent before its weak eyes registered the intruder, facing Malloy now, snout stuttering up and down.

Malloy saw it—froze—then slowly backed off, putting the bear between himself and Caster, who did not have a clear shot anymore. He hesitated a few seconds too long, hoping the bear would charge. It was almost as if Malloy knew Caster was waiting for him, was using the bear to block a shot.

The bear did not charge. Possibly it was too used to people in this vicinity or too young. Caster frowned, hoping Malloy would foolishly fire his gun, precipitating a charge by the bear, or at least use up rounds.

Malloy kept backing away, out of sight.

The bear dropped again, and Caster followed its trundling movement through a gap in the thicket only long enough to make sure it was not coming in his direction. Had Malloy seen the bear's? Caster crept ahead, around the corner of the cabin. If the bear had been Malloy he would have seen him, but Malloy likely was moving opposite to the animal's retreat.

There he is...

Malloy was making a detour from the third cabin in the ruined cluster, pausing by a skinny Douglas fir, hidden to the waist by sprays of ferns, looking across, his heart hammering no doubt at the close call—which was to Caster's benefit.

Caster ducked back out of sight, loped behind the cabins, and stopped at the corner of the third. He picked up Malloy again, coming closer, drawn just as Caster had thought, to the open area around the cabins.

Thirty yards out now.

Almost there...

Part of the bow and arrow stuck out but both were black; Malloy would not recognize them for what they were even if he looked squarely at them, not until he got closer and by then it would be too late.

Five more seconds to get to twenty-five yards; twenty to make sure.

Deer to a salt-lick, the rim of a lake—just like he had bagged that doe a mile from the camp site in the Adirondacks.

Very good, Jimmy, a little more...

Caster drew, stepped ahead, silently parting the ferns at the cabin's corner, expecting to see his quarry in the open, coming toward him, as he had just seconds before.

Malloy had stopped, knelt, gun on the ground, to tie a shoe. A hemlock partially obscured him. Caster was the one in the open now, bow at full draw—with a target diminished, halved by the tree. He waited seconds more, for Malloy to finish, rise, seconds to get the lung shot.

Malloy saw him, gave a startled grunt.

Caster released, felt the string's thrum.

If Malloy had paused to grab the gun, the arrow would have impaled him. He turned sideways and down again; the arrow creased the edge of the tree inches above his head. He lay flat, below the grass, reached for his gun, then rolled away behind the hemlock. By the time he fired the gun, Caster had darted behind the cabin. Malloy fired again; both shots missed. One tore off a scab of log from the base of the cabin, the other hit a small branch two yards in front of Caster, spinning it around as if kicked.

From the sound of the shots Caster guessed Malloy had a .38 or better, not like his own .22. He dropped the bow. To use it now he would have to expose himself for the shot. No way; not with Malloy there, bracing his gun, targeting it at the cabin.

Caster changed his position, moving back, out of sight. He scuttled over to the remains of a huge old-growth stump not far away. He lost a few yards with this, gained a better angle on Malloy. The .22 would not kill him, unless Caster got lucky with a head shot, but it could disable him, let Caster work his way closer to finish him off.

He kept low at the stump—a .38 would tear through the top—and from his belly, around the side, saw Malloy darting through the trees to his left. Caster fired twice but there was too much cover in the way. Malloy stopped only long enough to fire again—a *crack* to the *snap…snap* of Caster's shots.

He belted the .22, retrieved his bow and entered the forest beyond the cabins, north of where Malloy had fled. The firs rose to a cathedral-like canopy here. Below spread a green jigsaw jungle of hawthorn, mistletoe and salal, interspersed with trees fallen at every angle of decay, some at the base, exposing their roots. Caster could have used a machete to clear a path. With every other step he cracked a fallen branch, but he was not worried about making noise. He had moved north so Malloy would be less likely to hear him.

The goal remained to keep herding his prey to the south and get *behind* him.

Malloy could have only a few more rounds, and he would be careful expending them, assuming he had not brought more—a possibility. But it was not likely Malloy had come prepared for an extended hunt. Caster had enough arrows and rounds for the .22 to finish this.

The canopy of firs thinned in a curiously linear way. Here was a track—a mining or logging track much older than the road to Helen's cabin. In the winter it was probably used by snowmobilers. Possibly this was part of the track that began near the start of the logging road leading to Fado; he'd glimpsed rusting machinery among the trees at the beginning of the ridge he took to surprise Malloy.

This was a boon. He followed the track swiftly until it veered away farther to the north and so he avoided increasingly difficult terrain. Soon, he had to leave the track—following it would take him too far away from Malloy, possibly give him the elevation for an ambush and cover behind the rising, shelving rock. The track had served its purpose, speeding him along faster than his prey. If he could find some place on the higher ground, some crevice…

He kept moving up. Through the thick foliage of trees he saw the rock face, the fractured planes and shadows of a steep hillside smothered with clinging bushes and spindly trees, some growing out almost horizontally.

He could not quickly climb the hillside, if at all, and it extended for a long way north and south. Still, if it blocked his way, it would Malloy's.

But again, he'd gotten here first.

Malloy could either go north or south when he came to it. Caster had claimed the north so either Malloy stumbled into a trap, or Caster could keep herding him south, wearing him down, keeping to the base of the hillside, waiting to hear Malloy chuffing, stumbling through the undergrowth. Then, all Caster had to do was wait for the final clear shot.

He stood behind a thick blade of rock that jutted out at face-level, listening, hearing nothing but the staccato thrum of a distant woodpecker.

A rustle: to his right.

Caster knelt, peering into the forest and saw it: a flash of red.

A little more, Jimmy; you can do it…

He fitted an arrow. *Not yet…* The distance was there; the shot was not. Too much in the way.

The rustling grew fainter—Malloy moving away, to the south, but still not far. Caster left his cover. He had to get closer.

His left foot slid off angled rock and, recovering his balance, he snapped a fallen branch. Had Malloy heard that? He stopped behind another outcrop of rock now, but gained a small gap in the trees ahead. If Malloy crossed that, the shot would be there. He ducked low, peering around the outcrop.

There he was, twenty yards away, stepping toward the rock face, knowing now he had to either go north or south.

Caster smiled. Either way, Malloy was dead. At this range it did not matter where the broad-head arrow took him, front or back.

Draw…release, easy, easy…

Two seconds now.

In the few heartbeats it took Caster to rise, step out behind the outcrop, Malloy disappeared.

Caster relaxed his pull.

Where had he gone?

Caster moved ahead carefully—and saw the opening in the hillside, a deep, thick shadow cut against the grain of the shelving rock: the entrance to a mine.

A barricade lay askew on the rocky ground in front, a metal sign fixed to the top, presumably to warn hikers away. Caster stopped.

Malloy had to be in there, just far enough. In his mind, Caster saw him, sitting in the dark, elbows on raised knees for the firing platform, gun pointed at the entrance—assuming, of course, that he knew Caster was outside and close. Malloy had to have heard him. Why else go in there?

He frowned. If he went in he would be an easy kill for Malloy, who would be shooting at short range toward a big, misshapen black bull's-eye silhouetted by the light. Caster could not provide him that, not even with the shield of that metal sign. Malloy's .38—whatever he had—could easily punch through. Even if Caster had matches to set a fire, smoke him out, he did not have the time.

Maybe that was why Malloy went in, believing he could stay in there until nightfall if he had to, knowing his pursuer could not wait him out. And he was right: Caster figured he had maybe another hour before police came to the cabin; at most two before enough of them arrived to hunt *him*, possibly with dogs. Three times now and it should have been all over.

He was running out of time.

So spin again. Build a causeway...

He backed up, looking up at the tangle of trees and bushes smothering the hillside mottled with jutting outcrops, stony ledges. Could there be another entrance at the top, or beyond, where the track curled around?

If the mine went in far enough...there might be one, to provide an escape route in case of a cave-in, or perhaps for ventilation; or a closer shaft used to haul out the guts of the mine shaft, the extracted ore.

He decided it was worth a try since it was the only option he had. He could not go in, could not wait out Malloy or flush him out any other way. If this entrance was the only one, Caster would have to abandon the hunt, go down into the valley, steal a car, return to Seattle. He could not go back to the cabin to get the Explorer. By the time he returned, the police might already have gotten there. So into the wilderness again, back to the city, and begin the hunt anew for Helen. At least he knew where to look for her. Malloy didn't.

He backtracked along the hillside, going north until he found a place where he could climb this scarred ridge: a crevice between a triangular slab of boulder and another the size of a small car. He pulled himself up, using trees growing in the gashes, his bow scraping on rocks, snagging on straggly bushes. It was tough going but he finally made it to the top, his hands smeared and discolored by moss and lichen growing on rocks and tree bark.

He glimpsed the track through the woods to his left, got his bearings. He made his way through undergrowth bearding the summit, roughly paralleling his route from the mind entrance below. He veered away, down the slope. If there *was* another shaft it would be in that direction, closer to the old track revealed by a break in the canopy of trees. He walked on the rim of a gully infested with ferns. Ahead, the hillside now was a sheer face slanting down to within forty yards of the track. A few small trees grew out and up from the rock fissures.

Caster saw it when he came around a slide of rock, tucked below an overhang that dripped with water—and howled his triumph. Malloy, huddled within the other side of the hill, could not hear him. He bellowed again, squeezing his bow tightly.

There had once been a gravel path from the track to this entrance. Bushes shrouded most of the immediate area around the mine entrance and the sagging rectangle of a chain link fence set in concrete blocks.

He hurried ahead, soon saw that he could squeeze through this barricade. Though one side of the fencing was intact, the other had been pulled out, the post broken, the chainlink meshing hanging on itself. Graffiti smeared the smooth areas of the rock flanking the entrance. Bigger than the other one, this had to be the main entrance, not the secondary.

Were the two shafts connected deep within this hill? Of course they would be; it made no sense to have penetrated opposite sides of this mine and not linked the two. Caster felt that this mine, where Malloy would finally die, had a symmetry that could only be another manifestation of fate. There was a reason why the hunt had lasted until this place.

Here is your gift…

Outside, Malloy may have been looking over his shoulder but in there he would be focused on that ragged frame of daylight; he would have his back to the interior darkness, a perfectly silhouetted target for someone coming in from behind him.

One questioned remained for Eric Lane Caser: what part of Malloy, what evidence to take with him after, to give to Helen so she would know how lucky she was that he had prevailed in the hunt and not Malloy; that he had not died in the ambush on the road? Because Malloy would have turned that isolated cabin into a nightmare for her, keeping her alive only long enough for his brother to take his turn with her.

Though he could not use it within, Caster took his bow and squeezed through the opening between the fencing and the rock. Inside he felt the chill envelop him as he moved from light into darkness, stepping carefully, trailing a hand along the wall of the tunnel, his hand his eyes now.

CHAPTER 17
THE SHAFT

I HAD TO SQUEEZE through the entrance to the mine shaft, but six feet in I could stand up and touch both walls with outstretched arms.

The county sign outside on the rusted iron gate had been dimpled with gunshots, marring the warning of *DANGER!*—but it couldn't be worse than Shadden out there with a gun and hunting bow. I had only three rounds left. I was dead-tired; if I'd kept going in the woods, sooner or later he would have killed me.

I crept farther down the gradual decline to the floor of the shaft which angled slightly off to my left. The lack of timbered shoring surprised me—and made me uneasy. Never mind the solid rock all around; there was an entire hillside above me. I tended toward claustrophobia—and probably had since birth, when I came out via a Cesarean, with the umbilical cord wrapped around my neck.

The sense of constriction and pressure of this shaft grew worse the deeper I went in. The light ended after another few feet. The dark maw ahead seemed as solid a barrier as concrete. But as long as I could look back at the misshapen light of the entrance, I'd be okay.

Just a few feet more…

The last of the light revealed a puddle in the uneven floor of the tunnel.

Okay, maybe little more…

I had to be in the darkness, far enough in so that Shadden couldn't see me if *he* entered. I tested the puddle for depth, soaking a shoe. Sure enough: sometimes a puddle is just a puddle. I waded into it, feeling not only its chill but also the sense of being in a gullet. A throat. I couldn't go in farther, even if I had to lie in cold water.

Which I did.

Light from the entrance gave a dull sheen to the puddle, caught the moisture on the walls and the marks of miners' drills or pick-axes. I kneeled, looking back again, feeling better knowing I wouldn't have to go farther in, and telling myself that *here* was better than out *there*—being hunted down by a psychotic hunter who knew enough to stay off the road and turn my ambush into one of his own.

The mine might be a trap, but time wasn't on his side. Helen Sommers and Robert Tiphook were on their way—*had* to be on their way with help. Made the call to the sheriff's from Barbara's Basket. The cops might have already arrived at the cabin, lights flashing.

Help *was* coming.

I could hole up for hours here, but Shadden couldn't wait that long. He might have even abandoned the hunt. The police would finish this, not me. Everything had changed now. The others had seen Shadden. He wasn't just a man with peculiarly high pitched voice for his size, with a bizarre tattoo on his left arm I'd imagined. He existed. He wasn't a conjuring of a delusional paranoid or a guilty man.

They were safe now, Helen Sommers and Robert Tiphook. He had to have gone in to get her, if only because he needed her to drive my car out of there. But it wasn't just a matter now of what Shadden had done to Katie and Beverly Curtiss. There was my brother, possibly lying dead out there somewhere, Shadden's last kill and the one that would put him away—unless he came into this mine and let me finish it after all.

I aimed the gun now at the entrance fifteen yards away, wanting him to come in now.

Don't fire too soon. Squeeze off two. Save the last shot for a bullet to the head, for Seanie…

He hadn't come up here to make another mistake; he'd come up here to see if he could make amends for the one he'd made long ago; a big one, whatever it had been. Had he killed someone, or caused a death some other way? What had Sean written? *Could one life balance out another?*

He'd called it a...*vigil.* He was watching over Helen Sommers, the bait, though she didn't know it. Sean couldn't—didn't want to tell me—perhaps because that was a trail that could lead to what he had done long ago, and his decisive part in shoving Dad out of our lives.

I got on my belly, facing the fifteen yards to the silhouette that might appear in that entrance.

Give it an hour...

If Shadden was going to show—if he even found this mine and thought he'd better check it out—he'd be along in that time. I could endure an hour on the cold, wet floor of this tunnel.

Make that two inches of chilly water.

The claustrophobia had eased off; there was no reason to wait out an hour getting numbed to the bone. Better to get out of it, another few feet.

I backed up, on my knees, to get the space. My foot kicked at something hard. A crate? It didn't move much so I got up, feeling the curve of it in the darkness. A barrel. Still holding the gun I hefted it awkwardly, to roll it away on its bottom rim.

A moment before the barrel left my hands, I felt the edge of a hole in the floor, jerked back, twisting around...and lost my footing, slipping on the edge of the hole. The flare of panic made me drop the gun.

The barrel fell—*thump-thump*—and I followed, knees cracking at the edge of this vertical shaft. I slid off, reached out for something to grab. My legs dangled in the air, pulling me down. The counter-balance of my upper body stopped the slide, but I was now teetering on the brink, scissoring at the waist, legs bicycling in a void.

I struggled for purchase on the shaft's rough wall below me. My feet kept slipping. I scrabbled wildly with fingers, clawing at the rock, but it was too wet, slimy. The points of my elbows were blunt ice picks, the only brake and leverage I had.

Trying to pull myself out, I hit the gun, spinning it back—and into the hole. I heard it clatter and then...a faint splash.

If I fell in I wouldn't be climbing out.

The cold welled up, seemed to be pulling me down into this shaft sunk in the floor of the tunnel. With a flashlight I would have seen that barrel placed at the front edge of the shaft as a warning: the *DANGER!* sign outside.

I was no longer sliding down, but all that meant was a delay to the inevitable. The light of the entrance would be the last thing I saw if—no, *when* I got too tired to hang on. Already I was losing it; the adrenaline couldn't last for much longer. If Shadden appeared in that entrance now, partially blocking the light—the silhouette I'd wanted to see—there was nothing I could do. I was helpless. He could walk up to me, grind his heels into my fingers, and kick me off into oblivion.

I tried to use my elbows to inch back. Useless. I was at right angles. I couldn't hold on for much longer. I had to use my legs as a pendulum—pushing off from the wall, and at the end of the outward arc, pulling myself forward.

That was the idea. But my legs crashed back into the wall and tugged me away from where I had to be. To recover the precious inches took more effort. I was losing strength fast.

There was no other choice but to keep at it while I could: keep pushing off with my feet and trying to raise my legs as high as I could. Each time—*now!*—I reached out, digging with my elbows to move forward at the moment my legs weren't buckets of sand pulling me down. Each time wasn't enough. I kept losing inches and then struggled to regain them.

My back was killing me, elbows getting numb…

Push off…harder…arch your back…

Again…come on! Dig up, dig UP with your feet…

I rested for yet another try, huffing into the stone, feeling the backwash of warmth from my breath.

Again…once more…Do it…hard!…one…two…three…

At the end, with my legs the highest they were ever going to be…I pushed off with my elbows, and lurched ahead, finally gaining the inches before my legs dropped again, feeling the grinding of my belt buckle on the stone.

My legs fell back but not all the way this time, only to my upper thighs, not my waist. I wriggled forward—and collapsed, exhausted, cheek burning against the cold stone, fingers in the puddle now. My legs from knees on down still hung over the hole but I had no strength to move forward. I curled my fingers away from the puddle, the only effort I could make for the moment.

The light from the mine entrance seemed a tether, a lifeline; something I could grab and pull myself through the puddle. I wanted to grab it, get the hell out of here. I couldn't do that, not yet. Shadden might be out there. I had no weapon now. The fact that he didn't know that was all that I had going for me.

Yet the thought of lying here, watching the last light fade, and darkness closing in on me, severing the lifeline—wasn't something I wanted to do either.

All I could do was hope he didn't show up in that entrance within an hour or so—again, he had to be worried about the cops. Make that any time before nightfall, and I'd leave this place. I didn't relish the prospect of trying to find my way back to Fado in the dark.

And if he *did* show up in the entrance, all I could do was retreat farther into the darkness behind me, and maybe he would not see the hole that had almost claimed me.

I crawled ahead to get all of myself on solid rock. The pewter belt buckle scraped on the stone. The buckle was a gift from Katie; I'd worn it every day…since. Hands around the heart, the Claddagh design she loved.

I lay in the puddle, head toward one wall of the shaft, feet at the other, and stayed like that until the cold got too much. I started to get up, to try to work out the aches…and heard something deeper in the shaft behind me, off to the right a little.

A soft rapping. *Tick…tick…*

It wasn't the sound of dripping water. The barrel down there, slipping off some rock? Or had I imagined the sound?

I heard it again. *Tick…*

Bear claws clicking on stone? Bears didn't hole up in a mine during the summer.

Shadden.

You're the silhouette now. Get out...

I scrambled to my feet. The ricochet of the gun shot—explosively loud—sparked off the wall of the shaft, inches from my head. The muzzle flash tore the darkness, but that flaring instant was enough—as I splashed through the puddle—to glimpse him crouching beyond that hole, and for him to see it. In that fraction of a second I also saw the end of the bow at the wall: the ticking sound.

If he had crept ahead another few yards he would have fallen in. Now, the hole saved me. He could have fired quickly again, but that maw must have surprised him, made him hesitate. Enveloped quickly by darkness again, he must have sidestepped closer to the wall of the shaft, to his right, to avoid the hole—and lost his line of fire.

I rushed to the entrance. He fired again now but the shaft angled to the right. If he'd been left-handed...

I made it through as the shot spit at the corner of daylight.

The sun's glare creased my eyes. Eyes half-shut, I slipped on the barricade and fell, scrambled up, cut left into the tangle of trees and undergrowth, arms slashing at the branches, darting past boulders and rocks, leaping over smaller ones.

He wouldn't have time for the bow—too much in the way for a clear shot at a running man. I didn't look back; that would only slow me down. Bushes, small tree branches whicked at my legs and face. I tripped over a concealed snag in a log, but somehow kept my balance. My only hope was the shielding rocks and brush—and the fact that Shadden couldn't run and fire at the same time.

I didn't know where I was running to, cared only about gaining distance. Time enough later for the question of how he'd gotten into that mine.

A fallen branch gouged my left leg. Brambles raked my hands. I slipped again on a log slick with moss, tumbled down, hands scuffing up leaves, got up and took off again—downhill now, into a grove of old growth firs somehow left untouched, plunging through salal choking their bases. I had to stop behind one granddaddy five feet across and dripping with resin. My chest heaved. I wiped sweat from my eyes.

Caster stood thirty yards away, bracing his outstretched arms for another shot. I ducked behind the tree. The shot nicked off a chunk of bark at the gnarled base.

He must have seen my empty hands, confident now he could run me down.

I sprinted away. Thirty yards wasn't going to cut it. I needed something—anything—besides the hope that he was down to his last few rounds.

But he still had the bow.

I ran over the crest of a ridge, down the other side, skidding on my ass, using trees to brake the descent and came to a creek fifteen feet across and moving fast, white water *hissing* and *shusshing* around rocks. Logs and branches littered both banks.

Get across and that would slow him down, give me time to gain distance. But if he caught me mid-stream…it would be all over. Wouldn't matter he used bow or gun.

Let the fast current take me away from him?

Do it…

I braced myself on a rock for the six foot jump down into the creek.

A shot keened off a rock, a furrow in the moss.

Too late.

I bolted, sprinting along the creek, zig-zagging around the outcrops of rock along the bank, not over them; veering from tree to tree, keeping low so he couldn't get a shot. I had to be going faster than he was since he carried the gun, the bow snagging on branches.

The terrain got rockier, rising now. Bushes and straggly balsam choked crevices. Some of the gaps were so wide I had to leap over them. Ahead the trees grew more sparsely, the swatches of sky bigger, the *hissing* of the creek louder.

I was running out of cover but there was no other direction to take. On the left, rocks scaled up too high to climb quickly. The boulder-filled creek—on my right and far below—offered no escape. If I didn't kill myself jumping in, Shadden could pick me off as I struggled in the roaring water, or was caught among the log-infested rocks.

The trees disappeared. I ran onto an expanse of shelving rock scarred with ruts and fissures, the few bushes and skinny trees a mockery of cover. I rushed to the edge thinking I could work my way down the other side.

Forty yards away, a narrow, trestle-like bridge spanned the creek, spars of timber sagging toward the turbulent water below. The creek raced away: bigger, wilder under the bridge. Below, where I stood now, the water had undercut this promontory. Tumbled rocks and boulders formed a craggy chute leading down to rapids.

Nothing here except a long and hard drop into that chute and the tumult of rapids. Nothing around this promontory except a few crumpled beer cans, a charred circle where people had dragged in branches from the woods to make a fire.

I ran back toward the forest, made it ten yards—and stopped, brought up short by a gunshot stinging rock at my feet.

He could have killed me easily as he strode ahead into this fence-less pen. He kept walking toward me, rising up to my level, stepping easily over the fissures, the sun square on him: a man the size of a pro football linebacker, with short blond hair and that splotch on the left side of his face. He smiled as he belted the gun with the hand of his tattoo arm.

He plucked a leafy twig that had snagged in his quiver and fitted an arrow to his bow, the steel broad-tip glinting in the sun.

CHAPTER 18
HEY, FUCKER

THE SOUND OF gunshots echoed faintly over the roiling water below the precipice: *pop…pop…pop…*

One hit a beer can fifteen feet from me, skittering it a few more toward Shadden. The second creased a rock of the fire circle, making a tiny white scar. The third whined off farther away.

He lowered the bow and shouted: "Take a look behind you, Jimmy. She is on that bridge, way from over there. trying to kill you. Seems Helen found the Glassman's gun."

Glassman? I didn't turn. It didn't matter now why the woman hadn't left with her friend. Maybe she and Shadden were lovers, had that sad thing going on where the abused woman turns on the one who intervenes. For all I knew she might have killed Sean, or helped Shadden do it.

I felt a gentle breeze lifting the warmth off this sunny broad ledge of stone. It couldn't have been much past noon.

He was shouting at her now, calling her…*Lennie;* urging her to shoot again, lifting his arms to signal her to elevate her aim. He seemed amused she might get lucky from such a distance and kill me before he did.

But he had moved, so that we were more in a direct line of sight from the bridge, as if he wanted me in between, and I'd be more likely to catch a lucky shot.

Possibly he didn't believe she was trying for me but wanted me to believe that; still trying to pull strings, twenty feet and 3000 miles away from where he began at the house on Fernbank Avenue in Delmar.

I could try to get past him or run off this precipice.

They weren't choices.

I picked up a branch someone had brought from the forest for firewood and never used. I broke it off with a crack. I wanted something in my hands when it happened, never mind it was skinnier than a baseball bat.

Shadden smiled at the branch, saying something I couldn't hear over the water's roar below. Maybe he was telling me he had something in his own hands: the last seconds of my life. He relaxed the bow, wet his thumb, and smeared the saliva on the razor-sharp end of the fitted arrow, saying something now I did hear: about the Greeks being the first to use honey to keep poison on the tip of the arrow.

Behind him, Sean walked up the angling planes of rock.

Never had I done a harder thing than keep my eyes on Shadden and not my brother.

I bore into the splotch on the side of Shadden's face. There was cover here after all—the turbulence of the water below us that masked the sound of Sean's approach. He was twenty feet away now, his jeans soaked, stained darkly to the belt. He'd crossed the creek? He held a kitchen knife.

He altered his path slightly so the three of us were in line, so Shadden would think I was looking at him in the glare up here and not salvation.

Sean stepped over a narrow crevice, close enough now for me to see the chipped tooth in his grin. He'd once misjudged a nose-to-knees curve ball I'd thrown to him in the back yard, hitting him in the mouth. He'd had the tooth capped but the cap was missing now.

I saw in these last seconds what I'd forgotten he once did until Marcy remembered for me. Sean pointed at Shadden, then curled his right hand back to himself, as he did when we were boys, and he saw something he wanted for himself; a silent gesture then as now.

Shadden shouted at me to back up, gesturing with the wicked triangle of that arrow nocked in his hunting bow.

I did so. A few steps.

He shouted louder: "More, Jimmy. To the edge."

Sean took a step to his right, mouthed something, twisting with his knife, pointing. I didn't know what he was saying; maybe I could have if I kept my eyes on him for longer, but I didn't dare.

I backed up; Sean moved with us. With a few steps more he would be close enough so Shadden couldn't react in time.

Not yet, Seanie. Keep going…

He was a lot closer to Shadden than I was, but he wasn't close enough yet.

He didn't keep going. He screamed—"*HEY, FUCKER*"—and rushed at Shadden.

I bolted toward him but the man had already turned from me and shot—and whirled around, dropping the bow. His hand went for the gun at his belt. I swung the branch, knocking the gun away toward Sean.

He reached around, pulled a knife from a sheath at his back, where I hadn't seen it.

That's what Sean had been trying to tell me: *He has a knife…*

I'd never faced one. He held it out, centered, but moving it from side to side, backing me up still more. I grabbed the bow from the ground, all I had to fend off the knife.

Behind him Sean lay twitching on his side Blood frothed with air seeped from his mouth. He tried to reach the gun with a shaking hand but the fletched end of the arrow in his chest got in the way as he bent over to try and get it.

I tried to veer away from the edge; Shadden cut me off. There wasn't much room left and Sean was still trying to get that gun. He pushed with his feet on the edge of a fissure to get closer, curl his body toward the gun. He must have realized he couldn't fire it, not with his trembling and with me so close to the man he still wanted to kill. Sean had the gun now, threw it past me, toward the precipice. I couldn't look back to see where it lay, or if it had skidded over. If I turned my back to Shadden to try for it, he'd have me in seconds. He was going to run me off this rock. Or I could close on him and the hunting knife.

I'd forgotten about the rocks surrounding fire circle near the precipice.

I backed into one of the biggest, tripped, lost my balance—and the bow. I fell on my back, scrambled up. The noise of the rapids hissing through the chute below was so loud I couldn't hear what Shadden was saying. He ignored the bow, useless now, lying near the gun. He walked over to pick it up. Now he had both gun and knife.

I had only seconds to run from him and take a bullet in the back…or wait for the knife.

The black bow lay between us, useless.

Maybe not…

Shadden stepped toward me, grinning now, raising and lowering the gun and knife in his hands, as if weighing them, the gesture unmistakable: which would it be? Which would give him the greater pleasure—a bullet between the eyes or the feel of a knife plunged into my gut?

I kept my head was down, to make him think I was ready to die—so he had to think.

But I was watching his steps.

Now…

I lunged for the curved end of the bow as he stepped squarely in the middle of it with his left foot, and yanked hard—and up—with both hands, catching his ankle, tripping him with the string of the bow. The gun muzzle jerked up as he fell back, fired: a faint *snap* over the turmoil below.

I exploded out of the blocks, driving into him as he landed on his right side, losing the gun. He awkwardly slashed with the knife but I was quicker, my forearm colliding with his. In that instant I felt the man's strength, greater than mine. I had to finish this quickly, keep out of a clench or he'd stab me. Or take me over the precipice with him. His head bobbed over the edge.

He slashed wildly again with the knife, missing me by an inch. I backed off, grabbed his feet. He tried to twist and roll back, then kicked out. I lost one ankle but got the other with both my hands and heaved up…up, with all I had left…and pin-wheeled him over the edge.

I almost went with him, arms hanging over, far enough to feel the rising spray of water on my face and hands; and enough to see his mouth open in a scream masked by the thunder below, before the rapids enveloped him, sucking him down into the cold boil of the chute, the jagged gauntlet that would kill him.

I pushed back, lay on the stone, exhausted, with nothing left except the shakes.

When I finally got up, I hurled the black bow after him. Whatever splash it made was consumed by the white water.

I went over to my brother, my trembling legs scarcely able to support me. I knelt by Sean, brushed his head, but had to look away from his vacant eyes for a moment.

Helen Sommers was no longer on that little bridge.

My eyes flooded. Even if Seanie hadn't been dead, over the roar of the chute he couldn't have heard the whispers.

Why didn't he keep going? Why he stopped too soon?

Blood seeped away into the cracks and fissures of the stone around him. The sun hadn't yet dried his jeans. Like he did when we were boys, like I used to do—copying my older brother's weird gesture that drove our father nuts—I pointed at him and curled my shaky fingers back to my chest. It was all I could think of to do now, besides close his eyes.

The arrow was blurry; I couldn't see it well, but on the third try I broke it off. As more of my brother seeped into the rock, I was telling him he didn't have to stop before he should have, just because of what he did long ago and had never told me, and now never would—and maybe that was the reason.

CHAPTER 19

THE RED MUSTANG

I STAYED WITH HIM.

Had Helen Sommers left the bridge to get the police? Or had Robert Tiphook done that, and they'd be here soon. I wasn't waiting for them, for the help taking my brother back; I wanted to do that myself, though I needed to rest before the carry.

And something else, too: I wanted to be with him here for a while longer because we would never have the chance to catch up and go back through the years like you're supposed to do; slide with him again down the flat, stony terraces of Helderberg Falls back home, carried down by the rushing water, racing to see who'd be first to the big pool below, as if we had any control over the current.

Seanie, what should I tell them if they come now?

I suppose I'll tell them—and Marcy later—I'll tell them you found him all right, the guy who had the tattoo; that he's dead and down there somewhere; go see for yourself.

I'll tell them I came to look for you and wound up here in a fight with him after he killed you. I'll tell them you died trying to save my life.

That's all they get. The rest is yours and mine. The only one who would know any different is Dad, if he's even still alive somewhere, his new name so old now he must think it's who he's always been. His new family—if he started another—would never know any different; never know the choice he made. Likely he would have stayed if it had just been a matter of facing up to the fact that he couldn't keep his pants zipped up outside the home. Was that it? But he couldn't turn you in for what you did, something a lot worse; there had to be a connection to what he'd done. Did you catch them at it, flip out? What?

Could another father have turned his son in? Yes, but ours couldn't. He also couldn't stay, knowing that, and go on like nothing had ever happened.

Maybe someone didn't die. If someone had, surely we would have read about it in the newspaper, or the police would have come to our door.

I suppose there are other ways in which you would have felt you had taken a life. Or was that your imagining?

I'll never know. You took that with you. Maybe that's why you didn't keep going when you could have, when you could have plunged that knife in his back before he turned: so you'd never have to tell me. You gave me the chance to kill the man who deserved to die for Katie and Beverly Curtiss. But Seanie…Jesus…ah Christ, you didn't have to keep on going to where we could never catch up and go into extra innings for the forgiveness and whatever else had to be done…

I CAUGHT HER out of the corner of my eye.

She stopped, gun in her hand, muzzle down. If Shadden had been right about her purpose on the bridge, she could have killed me now, couldn't have missed from ten yards away, with me kneeling by my brother.

She walked to the edge of the precipice and tossed away the gun, like you'd fling a handful of seeds. She stayed there. Sean's head lolled to the side as I got up. It seemed as if she didn't know whether she wanted to step ahead or back. Whatever Shadden had done to her…she'd had it rough.

I walked over and caught her arm gently and she turned. She was crying, the blue eyes reddened like her hands, her black hair ragged, hacked at. I pulled a little on her arm, enough to get her away from the edge, and we wound up holding each other close enough for me to smell her scorched hair. Neither of us said anything; we would have had to shout to be heard over the roar of the chute below. I didn't have enough for that; she couldn't have either.

I left her to go get Sean, lifting him over my shoulder in a fireman's carry. Hefting him I realized carrying him back would be a matter of going twenty yards, resting, then another twenty…and on until we got to the cabin. It didn't matter; I'd get him back if it took the rest of the day. I began walking in the direction I thought was right but she tagged my arm.

"This way," she said, loudly enough for me to hear.

I followed her off the escarpment and into the forest, Seanie's hands tapping a cadence on my legs. She cleared the way, alerting me to obstacles, holding back branches, extending a hand to help me over rises we couldn't go around.

Every ten yards was more like it. When we stopped she helped me slide my brother off my shoulder, and she steadied us both as we crossed the creek at a shallow ford. Mid-stream she said: "It's not much farther." I assumed she meant the bank of the creek because we still had a long way to go, even if he cabin was probably less than a mile as the crow flies.

We rested on the other side. I asked her if we could bury Sean when we got back. I wondered if she realized there was a lot more going on with that request.

"We can bury him at the cabin," she said, "if that's what you want."

"There's no other place for him."

"No better place. I understand." She got up to dip her hands in the creek and then went over to Sean, who lay at my side.

"You must be thirsty," she said, "but we can't drink from here. We'll get something when we get back."

For a moment it seemed as if she was talking to Sean instead of me, as if he were still alive. She clasped his hand, a brief, wordless requiem, and I knew then that she must have seen what he'd done on the escarpment. Her wrists, not just her hands, were reddened. She held them in her lap, one nesting in the other, and I remembered she was an artist and also that photo Sean took of her and Robert Tiphook on the ferry, as she fed seagulls by hand.

I pointed. "Do you have something at the cabin for those?"

She nodded. "The cold water helps for now. They'll be all right. The steering wheel hurts the palms but I got here okay; I'll get us all home."

"Steering wheel?"

"The car," she said, pointing over my shoulder. "It's over there."

SHE'D GOTTEN AS close as she could, she said, taking the track that used to be a mining road where it curled around near to her cabin. The track began near the entrance of the logging road leading to Fado, crossed the bridge where she'd fired the shots, continued around the escarpment and eventually led to a mine south of the cabin, one of three in the area.

She had left the bridge because she realized it was hopeless at that distance to kill Eric Lane Caster—that was his real name, not Shadden, or at least the one he'd given her. By the time she reached the escarpment it was all over. She saw Sean and I, ran back to the cabin, figuring the only thing to do—if I'd been hurt or if Sean remained alive—was to get us back quickly. That meant a car. Caster still had the keys to hers, but there was another one.

She hadn't just driven the car over the old mining track. She'd bulled her way through. I couldn't believe she managed to get here in a classic red Mustang meant for Sunday afternoon drives along good roads in fine weather.

Both side mirrors had been snapped off, one completely, the other dangling loosely. Scratches and deep gouges scored the length of one side of the car; the other had to be ruined as well. Twigs and leaves whiskered the front. The grill's pony emblem had been punched out, a headlight fractured, the bumper dented, the roof clawed and scraped by branches. She'd lost a hubcap. I pulled off a small leafy branch that had somehow stuck in the crease of the trunk, revealing a decal centered on the rear window—a maroon **LF** decal superimposed on the white letters of *Spartans.*

Together we put Sean in the back seat. His blood smeared the spotless black interior. She closed the door with the back of her hand, the long slender fingers—artist's hands—curled back.

I offered to drive.

"Six of one…I'm okay."

"Please, let me. I'll follow the path you made."

She shook her head, got in, and started up the car by the time I slid in next to her. It took her five points to turn the Mustang around. With the car idling—sounding like the muffler was ruptured—she said: "He—your brother—he hid in here after…"

"After?"

"It was the only way, backing into the fire in the hearth, to burn the rope enough to get loose. I freed him, told him to wait, give me a moment to get a knife, anything, to go outside with. Caster was out there. But he didn't wait. I got the knife but if Sean had waited…he might not have gotten out there in time to stop Caster from killing Robert."

"Sean hid in the car after…"

She nodded. "I thought Caster had killed him. He was lying by the root cellar. I thought he was badly hurt. That's the last I saw of him until the morning, after you came and Robert got me loose. He…Sean just seemed to appear and Robert said he'd seen Sean come out of the car—I keep it by the side of the cabin."

Her hands lay palms up at the bottom of the steering wheel.

"He told us what you were trying to do; that you'd said to take your car, go for help. That's what I told them, by the porch, that I knew the area, that we all didn't have to go. I saw the gun near the woodpile—Robert said he'd lost it when Caster surprised him on the porch. I figured if Robert couldn't drive with his leg stiff as a board, well, Sean could. I told them to go get the police while I went to help you…no…it wasn't just that. That's not all of it. I wanted to kill him. All the way out here, I was thinking of that; how I'd have to get close to do it with the gun."

"You followed the shots?"

"Best I could. Sean must have too. When I left, he and Robert were there. I wound up on the bridge, too far away and he…" Helen shook her head. "I don't know how Sean did it, getting to where he did. I saw him coming up behind Caster, and ran from the bridge."

"Let's get him back now."

"I'm sorry…I'm so sorry." She put the car in gear: "I wish to hell I had a rifle on that bridge."

BRUSH SQUEAKED, WHISKED against the side of the Mustang. A low branch scraped the roof with a slow screech. I kept looking at Helen Sommers' hands, and couldn't help but notice the car's mileage: 28,326.

Were those the actual miles or had she turned them back, starting over? A 40 year-old Mustang and almost brand new. Or was.

It must have hurt her to work the stick, but she didn't grimace, said nothing. I wondered if she was punishing herself for something. Yet none of what had happened was her fault. All she'd done was come up to her cabin for a summer's weekend. All I had done was go for a hike with friends in the Adirondacks near Saranac Lake. Now, we were driving through the Northwest woods in a ruined, vintage Mustang, with my brother in the back seat, killed by the man who had brought us together.

Someone would eventually find him, but whoever did wouldn't have been looking—not for someone like Shadden. There wouldn't be much left of him, not out here.

Despite her hands, Helen wasn't hesitant or cautious with her driving. The black tassel of a graduation cap swayed from the rear view mirror as she turned this way and that. She'd already created a path and she retraced it now, banging up, scratching the car even more. If she'd snapped a slim sapling the first time, another lay bent or broken for this return. Whatever else she couldn't drive over she swerved around, plowing through, flattening whatever got in our way.

The old mining road continued to the south, giving an indication of what she'd gone through before. She veered right onto a path she'd enlarged before, and it was about there that we shared our names.

After another five minutes of this screeching, wickering gauntlet I could see, through the trees, a rising meadow and the cabin, then the bridge over the creek. Helen hadn't crossed the bridge; it was too narrow, a footpath's conveyance. But she'd driven through the creek at an angle so she wouldn't bottom out. She'd gone smack through the fence bordering the meandering creek on the meadow side. Now, spinning the wheels briefly on the slick stones in the creek bed, she drove into the break. Two of the fence posts looked as if they'd been rotting but she couldn't have known that before.

She gunned the Mustang up the gentle slope of the meadow, avoiding the furrows she'd made earlier in the tall grass, and drove around the hump of the root cellar, grazing the chopping stump, and stopped over the tarp that lay bunched at the side of the cabin.

Robert Tiphook was nowhere in sight.

She turned off the ignition. A Steller's jay—black and electric blue—flitted away from a corner post of the garden fence nearby and disappeared into the forest verge.

She said: "Is it just you…and your brother?"

"Just a sister now."

"He wasn't married or anything? A girlfriend?"

"Not that I know of. Then again, we hadn't seen each other in a while. But I don't think so." His apartment flashed in my mind.

"What will you say to your sister?"

"What he did here. Anyone else—just what happens sometimes. People go off, you don't know what happened to them…you never see them again."

"You said he has no other place to go."

"No. But Sean…he always thought he did. He was kind of good at moving on. I think this is where he would like to be put to rest."

"You can bring your sister here if you'd like, to see where he is."

"She'll want to do that some time. I appreciate that, Helen."

"Even if I'm not here," she said. "For good, I mean."

"I understand. I'll…well, I'll think of something for whoever is."

We sat there a minute longer and then she said. "Maybe over there. The garden. It'll be better. There are rocks and stones in the meadow; you can't see them, but they're there."

"That's what Yeats said about the 'little people.'"

"Of course. Malloy…you're Irish."

"With one of those useless degrees in English."

She smiled faintly—the closest to what Sean had gotten in those photos, the one with the seagulls. He'd wanted to stay close to her. And close he would be, even if she never came back here to expand her garden beyond where he lay.

AS I CARRIED Sean over to the garden, I saw Robert Tiphook emerge from the cabin. Helen helped me lower Sean to the ground. She pushed over waist-high stakes supporting tomato plants, the fruit still mostly green, to give us room. There was a shovel leaning against the fence.

I watched Tiphook sit his way down the porch steps, then hobble over to the garden gate. Helen stood closest to him, a spade in hand.

Tiphook looked past her to me: "I wish I could thank your brother," he said. "But I can to you. If it wasn't for either of you…"

He turned and limped back toward the porch. Helen insisted on helping me dig the grave. Tiphook sat on the steps, staring off into the distance. After ten minutes I told her I'd finish it.

"Are you sure?"

"Go take care of those hands."

She leaned the spade against the fence, and as she went up the steps past Tiphook she said something to him, lingering for a moment before going into the cabin. When she came out her hands were bandaged, but she gave him one of the two cups she carried. A folded, brightly colored Hudson's Bay blanket was tucked under her arm.

As I drank my cup of water she spread out the wool blanket, smoothing it over the clumps of plants underneath. Then we lay Sean over the blanket.

I went back to digging and when I stopped next, I saw Helen sitting next to Robert on the steps, her arm draped over his shoulder, not the other way around—which couldn't have been what he'd wanted when he came here to help her.

It took me a long time for Sean because the grave had to be deep, so he would rest underneath what someone else besides Helen might plant in the garden. Fado itself would be the only marker he'd have, but I think he would be pleased about that.

Hey, fucker…

He'd been smiling when he said that.

I finished it, soaked with sweat, and when I lay aside the shovel, Helen was at the gate. Maybe she'd been watching me, I don't know. Already she seemed to have a way of appearing—first the bridge, then the precipice, and now this.

She came over and together, each of us holding corners of the blanket, we lowered my brother into the earth.

CHAPTER 20

MICHAEL'S DOLPHIN

H E SENSED SOMETHING tugging—gently rhythmic—at his legs, something chilly. Yet his upper body and arms felt warm. He opened his eyes, seeing first the gravel and rocks close by his outstretched arm, then the forest rising up to a blue sky that hurt to look at.

He lay half in the water—and with consciousness came the pain… pain all over.

His fingers felt like splinters but the roundness of the larger pebbles seemed to ease the pain a little. Someone—a voice within him—told him to get out of the water. If he didn't he might get carried away…again.

Again?

His head throbbed terribly and he was dizzy to the point of nausea. He tried to keep his head motionless as he crawled ahead but that hurt too; his whole body felt ransacked. Yet *someone* had told him to get out of the water. He did, to get warmer—all of him, not just his legs—and to move to a safer place so he wouldn't be carried away again.

He closed his eyes, rested.

The dizziness must have woken him again. It persisted, making a calliope of the trees ahead. He vomited. Gut-bilge. He heaved up more, collapsed to the gravel again, his eyes on the dense green of the forest which wasn't moving like it had before. A breeze helped. He heard birds now in the trees beyond this pebbled strand and, more distantly, the white noise of rushing water.

He wondered if this was where you go when you're dead.

But you don't feel pain when you're dead. Or do you?

With that thought he sat up slowly yet still reeled with dizziness. He felt a tickle on his left arm: a beetle crawling between a nasty gash and purpling bruise that had ruined most of a tattoo. Where had he gotten that? He couldn't remember. He tried to brush off the beetle and missed. How could he miss? Annoyed, he got it the second time, felt the crunch as he squeezed the disgusting thing between his thumb and forefinger, and wiped his hand clean on the gravel.

He moved the arm. Not broken. Anything else? He bent his stiff legs, felt no sharp pain so he hadn't hurt them badly, either. He lifted his wet pants legs to see the cuts, bruises, abrasions—so many it was like he had some rotting disease.

He squinted out over the water. Beyond this large pool—maybe half the size of a football field—the water ran fast, out of sight to his left. Somehow he hadn't gone with it, had fought it, gotten here. Beyond the water, off to his right, he saw a narrow bridge and still more distantly an escarpment of tumbled stones; the source of the burring noise.

He remembered the bridge now. Lissa had been on it.

No, he'd seen someone else—Helen?—before he fell off that escarpment into the noise, pummeled by the water-worn rocks and expelled into the roiling water below. He couldn't remember trying to hold his breath, keep his mouth closed, so he must have been drowning.

Then, nothing more until…the haven of this pool. Compared to the other water where he'd been drowning, it was serene. It had to be the after-life. *That's why she…Helen…isn't here…she's on the other side…*

So he'd floated from there to here, somehow escaping the fast current farther out.

He thought he saw something caught in the current, moving quickly to where he should have gone. The sun hung near its zenith. He blinked, squinted, to focus better on what it was.

It looked like a floating body.

Was it the one who had been up there on the flat rock with him—no, there were two. They were trying to kill him.

Did they?

No, he was sure he'd been alive as he fell and drowned later.

Was that *his* body out there? Who he was before? And now he was...
something else: a conjuring of flesh, nothing more than a ghostly longing
for what he had left, which would soon fade as he began another journey.

Was he looking at *himself*— his corpse floating away in the current—
seeing himself from a distance, one last time?

He had to be dead. He had never learned to swim, could only remember that there were reasons why he hadn't. Even if he had been a good
swimmer, how could he have survived that fall from that high rock over
the water, pin-balling through all those rocks without breaking bones,
crushing his head?

Whatever he'd just seen in the water passed from view. Maybe it was
only a log. The shore here, and farther down, was littered with snags of
branches, trees taken away by the voracious current that kept eroding the
banks where they once grew.

He held up a hand, waiting for the fingers to begin fading away.
Hands, legs first...

Is that how it happens?

He waited.

Nothing faded away.

He had to be alive. Or someone was. He felt the water lapping at his
knees, and he realized he was kneeling by the water. He didn't remember
getting up or crawling back to the water's edge. Time—or was it some transfer of consciousness?—was playing tricks on him, moving back and forth.

You should be dead.

You're not.

But you should be.

Yet the dead don't breathe and hurt all over—these knives in the
head. So maybe he had been—*what?*—resurrected in this birthing pool,
as someone else, given another life?

That's it...

He remembered his name now—the first name, anyway: Eric. There
had been a name before that but it was gone like the beetle.

He was standing now—he couldn't remember getting to his feet, his back to the water. Images were coming now from the flat rock. And other names besides Helen's: Jimmy Malloy; and what was the other one, the brother's? Seanie, that was it. And now the cabin and someone else there. The Glassman. And the carriage, the miracle of seeing Helen…Lennie. He hadn't seen her in so long. How long had it been?

He thought he saw an eagle high above, circling slowly, but he couldn't follow its path because his neck hurt and the movement made him dizzy. He couldn't be sure it was an eagle, but likely it was. The river to the east—the Skagit?—teemed with eagles who had come back from near-extinction. They fed on whatever they could find, mostly salmon and steelhead which needed the struggle against a fast current. Only the strongest made it all the way back to spawn. There were hundreds of eagles along the river in early spring, but they all didn't move on. So it probably was an eagle…like the one near her home, on that island. It was all coming back.

He turned to face the forest now, hoping to see the raptor again, perched on another snag, looking out over the water for prey, maybe even a carcass to feed on, a body. Perhaps even his own, or the other one. Someone had died up there on that escarpment. He didn't see his eagle, but that didn't mean there weren't any here. It was a miracle even to be looking for one now.

Another miracle. They happened for a purpose; they were not dispensed without a reason or purpose. So maybe that was it.

You've been saved for one.

He couldn't even swim, yet he'd been saved. Why?

To begin again…as someone else?

That happened before, he was sure of it.

He realized he was sitting on a log that canted into the water. He had no shoes. Why hadn't he noticed that before? Had they been ripped loose in the churning water out there? Had he taken them off? He didn't recall doing that, a small but crucial act of survival. Maybe he *had* done that, *had* swum, heroically fighting the current to awaken here exhausted, pummeled, disoriented, but triumphant.

Another name came to him. He remembered it as clearly now as his last, the one named Eric…Eric Lane Caster—who couldn't swim, who should have died and maybe he had, to become food for eagles, who took their meat alive or dead and rotting.

But this person was the only one who *could* have taken off the shoes, fought the current, and survived to reach this shore. He'd read somewhere that swimming had been his best sport in high school.

The thought came as quickly as an eagle's kill: *maybe you've been saved to become that person...*

He was up again now, no longer cold any more. He felt eager to move and keep moving into the trees. He noticed shapes on the rocks and boulders scattered along the shore, patterns he'd never recognized before. He went over to one, fully in the sun's warmth, and put a hand on the side of a hulking granite boulder, spreading his fingertips across the fractures and glistening mica stars, thinking of constellations even in the brightness of this day.

Despite his aching hurts, he felt he could move that boulder to the water. That seemed to summon the memory of what Fado meant—the name skipped into his mind. Lennie had never told him, but he knew. He knew for the same reason he had been saved. No, not saved. Reborn. One last and final time, because after him there could be no other.

The pain in his head had subsided with this euphoric revelation and he turned in the direction of the cabin, the starting point: *Fado.* Of course he knew the name; he'd thought of it.

He would have to walk around the water to get there, though he was tempted, in his eagerness to get back, to swim across. No matter, he'd get there with hours to spare before dark. He was confident of the direction he had to go. He'd been in these woods before, hiking out from Fado; knew all about the intense arrivals and wistful departures there; the love-making by the hearth, what it felt like to spread his hands spread over the dolphins. Her moans were not soft; that was not his Helen. Oh, he knew that as well as he knew himself. He'd heard them many times before yet each time seemed like he was listening to them for the first time, hoarding them like artifacts for the times when he would be away from her.

And he would hear them again after he'd taken care of his namesake. One had to fade as the other took his place; one miracle replacing another.

That was his purpose now, why he'd been saved, why he had survived when Eric Lane Caster could not have.

Only Michael Furey could have survived.

That's what his Lennie had said once before, about what he had done far away; and what she would say again when he told her about how he had survived the plunge and the fierce water: *Maybe what you saw was a dolphin out there, gliding past in the water, her work done in guiding you to shore.*

CHAPTER 21

LEAVING SEAN

ELEN AND ROBERT waited in the car while I went into the cabin to get another drink of water before we left. It wasn't just thirst; I wanted to also see the place where my brother had spent the last night of his life.

I was going to drop them off at the car Robert had left on Benson Road, out of sight, beyond the Fado sign. He'd said nothing of what he had planned to do, but it seemed obvious: walk in, surprise Caster and kill him. I had a feeling that Helen hadn't viewed him in the light he coveted. Now, she would be driving to a hospital in Seattle so he could get his swollen knee drained, and get his meds and crutches.

Standing in the kitchen area I could see out the paned window to the garden where Sean lay under a low mound of soil the rain would compact even more come the fall. The blisters on my hands weren't bad, but I still had a hard time ripping a bottle of water from the six-pack plastic and needed a dishcloth to twist off the cap.

They were going to have to wait a little longer for me. I bent over the sink, arms splayed like I was puking, but it wasn't that, or fatigue. I couldn't seem to move.

He'd wanted to do it all by himself, that was plain. He'd seen Helen, then the guy…*with the tattoo Jimmy told me about*…and Seanie knew what he wanted. Follow her and he'd get to him, what he thought was the exit ramp from the past, the way out that he'd never thought would appear; because all that Dad had left was the fucking bequest that some-times there wasn't a way out—one you could live with anyway.

He didn't know where I was, to call me up and say: *Jimmy we'll take care of this motherfucker Shadden together.* But afterwards, through Marcy? *Hey Jimmy...long time, hunh? I got something to tell you and you won't believe it but...it's over. I took care of it. I got him, the guy...Katie. I'm flying back. Meet you at home...we have some catching up to do.*

Two words: *Hey, fucker...*

Through the window I glimpsed the Steller's jay again, alighting on a different post of the garden fence.

I didn't hear Helen come in until she knocked the leg of the table, ten feet away. Once again she just appeared. She had a hand on an oversized book lying on the table near the hearth.

"I forgot this," she said, her tone apologetic, like this was my cabin and not hers. After what had happened, it wasn't a sweet cabin anymore, but it once was, just what you'd want your cabin-in-the-woods to be, with only a few signs of what had happened: the scattering of utensils at my feet, an open drawer, the burned rope by the hearth, scraps of duct tape and the cut lengths of rope in the corner where Sean must have been.

I put the empty water bottle on the counter. "I'll be out in a minute."

She nodded. Then, by the door, she added: "He and I—it's not what you think."

I put up a hand: "None of my business."

"Well, after...I'd say we're all of each other's business. We're friends. He used to be one of the best glass artists around, his glory-hole years."

I took another swig of water. "And what's that?"

"A secondary furnace, where color is fused to the piece."

"What happened?"

"He's an alcoholic for one thing. Besides that, who knows when it stops for an artist. It's not like you get fired from a job. I met him at the Seattle Art Museum. I thought he understood I wasn't interested in the way he was, but I think he misinterpreted my desire to help him, with something else I couldn't give him."

What she'd said about him had stuck in my mind. "A glory-hole... Was that why he came up here?"

"It was a lot more than that. He told me what Caster did to him at his house," she said, and left with a glance at the far wall.

I'd once passed an old mill town smack on the Erie Canal, called Leary Falls. I was on my way to a sectional baseball tournament at Syracuse University. Sean was with me, doing the driving. So maybe that's why, before I left the cabin, I took a minute to check out the wall that her husband—she had a ring—had filled with the kind of stuff that some guys like to put in their man-cave.

This Michael Furey had quite a display: a maroon varsity jacket—#25—and athletic letters had the same **LF**/Leary Falls lettering I'd seen on the Mustang's decal. There were academic awards, a New York State Regents honor, a letter of acceptance from Amherst, some pamphlet he'd written about the Erie Canal. So Helen was probably from Leary Falls, too.

Among a dozen framed photos was one of Helen and presumably this fellow in bathing suits, late teens. His dark hair was cut short; her black hair fell almost to her waist. She was stunningly beautiful, even with her tongue stuck out at the picture-taker. Furey was ripped, a handsome dude despite the gargoyle face he made, curling his lip way up, eyes wide. He'd snuck a V with his fingers behind her head, but she knew he was doing it and had a cocked finger-gun pointing at him.

For various reasons—the awards, the football jersey, the military haircut, the buff swimmer, his absence here?—I thought of the Navy Seals.

I left the cabin thinking that wherever he was—the Middle East no doubt—we all could have used a Navy Seal up here in the boonies. And maybe if he had been, Sean would still be alive.

AT THE CORNER of the porch I could see Robert Tiphook—his arm, anyway, stuck out the window of the back seat of my car, flicking his fingers, like he was trying to shed sunlight. After I got in, I offered to bring Helen back up here if she wanted, so she could get her car. That and Sean, one last time, before I left for home and Marcy.

I couldn't tell if she nodded about Sean or my offer. I left it there, but not the matter of the SUVs—hers and Caster's.

Robert Tiphook stared out the window as Helen and I talked about it. The keys to both those SUVs were probably still in Caster's pocket, where he'd kept them for safekeeping. Maybe they'd fallen out in his long tumbling through the chute that had killed him, but we had to assume they were with him at the bottom of the pool. His body wouldn't rise for days, to drift toward the shore. If and when someone found what remained of him—and those keys—well, the SUVs couldn't be still at nearby Fado.

Robert spoke into the window, but I heard him clearly enough: "Have his towed to my street in Seattle, so I can take a baseball bat and smash a little more of it every night like he—because I know he'll never be coming back for the car. He said he was…he said you were a baseball player, Jimmy. Is that right?"

"It was a long time ago, Robert."

"Well, I'll buy the bat myself, then. Soon as my knee is better. That leaves the Toyota."

"I'll sell it," Helen said. "The Mustang too. Someone will buy it and fix it up."

I said nothing about the other solution. Neither of them would want to go back in a few days to where Caster died and take the keys from his bloated corpse. And neither did I, even if I was not going to be heading home soon to tell my sister that our brother was dead—and where I'd buried him.

I DROVE AWAY slowly and kept the window open for the air. I was so tired I could have pulled over, fallen asleep in a minute. Helen might have been already. She leaned away against her window, eyes closed, her bandaged hands nesting on the back cover of the large book in her lap.

After a few minutes, Robert said, speaking to Helen: "We'll tell them we were horsing around in the yard, and I hurt my knee in a hole the dog dug. You told me you used to have one, German shepherd. Ruckus."

"We don't have to tell anyone anything. You hurt your knee is all."

"We have to tell them something."

"We're going to a hospital, not a police station."

"I was running too fast, and I didn't see where I was going…"

"Robert, it's okay."

"I mean, there was a hole I couldn't see; how could I? It was pitch black out there. The knee popped—I heard it like a gunshot; I thought it was."

He was quiet for the rest of the road. When we came to the end, I turned right, past the barrier and the Fado sign. He'd said he'd parked it near where Benson Road ended, left the keys under the seat.

"There it is," he said.

Through the trees beyond, I saw some sort of excavation, a gravel pit. I pulled up behind the car, and I was surprised to see it was a Mercedes, though an old one. From those glory-hole years?

Helen took her book and got out to help Robert as he hobbled over to his car. When he was in she put the book in the back seat. I walked over to the driver's side, asked her if she wanted a lift back to her home, after the hospital.

"Thanks," she said, "but we could be a while and I'll probably be at his place after, get him set up, make a few meals. I'll take a taxi home."

"Whatever works."

She got in the Mercedes, found the keys. I thought she was just going to drive away but she rolled down the window. I suppose I was ready with answers to questions she had to have, such as how and why two of the four men had wound up at a cabin she shared with her husband—wherever the man was. She knew why Robert had come up here. Caster? All you had to do was look in newspapers every day. But Sean and I?

She sat there, the car idling fitfully, long enough perhaps for her to decide it didn't matter how I had known where to look for my brother, and why.

"What are you going to do now?" she said.

"Fly home. But there's a lot that has to be done before I get on the plane. You?"

"I…well, I just need to get away…touch some bases."

I assumed that meant her husband, and what she was going to tell him. But that was none of my business, either.

"Well, make sure you touch home or it doesn't count."

She smiled a little. "I'll do that." She reached out the window and clasped my wrist: a firm but gentle pressure. I put my hand over hers but not too hard—the bandages. I stepped back and the sunlight was again on her at the car window.

"By the way, that's a great name for a dog…Ruckus."

"I can't take credit for that—Michael named him. He didn't have the room or the yard at his home but we did at ours. It was a big house, three floors, used to be a rooming house way back when. We taught Ruckus not to bark at the boats that went by in the canal—take care of yourself, okay?"

"You too."

I watched them go, then turned my car around, stopped by the Fado sign, got out again and closed the gate; it seemed like a thing that should be done. Likely Fado would be someone else's before the year was out. I was sure this Michael Furey—the high school sweetheart she'd married?—would see the need for that, after Helen told him what had happened. Maybe before they sold the property there would be time to bring Marcy out, to see where Sean was buried, though the garden would probably have been let go, to become part of the meadow again.

I stayed for a little longer, not wanting to go, not yet. I mean, Seanie was down there at the end of it all. A Steller's jay flitted past, a flash of blue. There was no blue like that, except for those welkin eyes of Helen's.

Who knows if it was the same Steller's jay I'd seen by the garden. I wanted to think so. The bird took off in the direction of Fado, more or less. Before I lost sight of him, I did Seanie's thing, the point-and-scoop, one last time.

CHAPTER 22
MICHAEL'S RETURN

EVERYTHING WAS THE same yet so different when he got back to Fado; not the least the furrows in the high meadow grass.

Someone had taken his Mustang into the woods and come back. He'd seen signs on the way here. He frowned at the car's condition. All that work to save the money to buy it from Wick Houser and the car looked like it had just been hauled out of the lake—except for the sluicing water.

Malloy's car was gone. And was that freshly turned earth in the garden?

The low mound was unmistakable. Who had Malloy buried—his brother or Lennie? Or had Lennie killed him, buried *him*?

In the cabin he smelled something medicinal. There, on the kitchen counter: a tube of antibiotic. Of course. Lennie had singed her hands and wrists in the hearth, trying to get free; rushed outside after the brother— what was the name again?

Sean...

And she had a knife. Anger flared but then he also remembered that she hadn't *really* been trying to kill him. She'd been trying to kill Eric Lane Caster.

And he was almost gone now.

Whoever had driven the Mustang out into the woods must have taken the brother back, the one Caster killed on the ledge, a point-blank lung shot. So most likely it was the brother, Sean, in the garden. Malloy wouldn't have put ointment on Lennie's hands and then killed her. Even if they'd left together, that didn't necessarily mean she still wasn't in great danger from Malloy. She may have gone to get the brother, but Malloy could have still secured her while he buried his brother.

Perhaps Lennie's helping Malloy had earned her a reprieve. Undoubtedly he was going to take her back East where he lived in upstate New York, near Albany. He'd left thinking Eric Lane Caster was dead—not so far off the mark—and he was scot-free now, *up the canal,* to do whatever he wanted with Lennie.

Well, Malloy would be in for a surprise, but nothing like Lennie's when she realized who had come for her again; this time for keeps. No more distance, no more leave-takings.

There had been books on the table here, important books. He didn't see them. Something else was missing too.

He sat down at the table. He sensed he had done something special here. Then he remembered the books: the one she was writing and illustrating about him. And his book.

Right, the testament…that artifact of his life…

So she would know all about Eric Lane Caster.

Say goodbye, Eric…

But what was the other thing, besides the testament, Eric's book? He stayed at the table for five minutes, then ten, trying to recall. It was only when he saw the picture, the big framed one on the east wall of the cabin, that he remembered the curve of her neck, how the…*necklace*…rose with the swell of her breasts when he placed it there, to see how the gift would look on her.

Her?

Lennie or the One before her? Lissa, that was her name…

And there been another One too.

Where were the books and the necklace? Malloy must have stolen her book, taken it with him. But Eric's?

*There…out there…in the car…*The one Caster drove here. *That's right…*

He'd put the testament and the necklace in Caster's car there for safekeeping because Sean and someone else had gotten loose, the ones who were trying to take Lennie from him again, and he had to set up and kill them before he and Lennie left forever.

He went outside to get his artifacts. The Explorer was locked but…he still had the key in his pocket. The key hadn't fallen out; another indication that he'd been saved so that he could give the necklace to her when they were together again.

The book and necklace were in the back, below the seats. Eric had scribbled *The Book of Eric* as a title. He took the thin stack of its pages, along with the necklace, back to the cabin, put them on the table. He rolled up the pages. *That's better, like an artifact…*

The necklace would be magnificent on her, the gold filigree and bright jewels such a stunning contrast to her dark hair that would in time be long enough to reach the dolphins he'd named Les Deux and…*never mind she shouldn't have tried to kill me with that knife, but all's forgiven now…*

The book was a paltry relic of the past but he decided he would take it with him and give it to the canal. It wasn't just priests who offered sacrifices to gods who bestowed those rarest of gifts—purpose and rebirth. And what had he once said to Lennie, long ago, wondering about what they'd find if somehow the canal could be drained? That they'd find skeletons of canal men and coins—you name it.

And soon the book would settle among all those artifacts too though it wouldn't last long. Not the necklace, however. That was Lennie's, for when they were together again.

He felt like this place was home, belonging to him now, with all his things on the wall; more of a home than any other place he'd known. Everything else had been a waystation—including Shadden's. That was the old man's name. But he hadn't been so old he didn't realize he had to prove his usefulness or he'd be dead, and he had been useful.

Fado was a home more than even Mrs. Comoy's place in the Berkshires, that old red farmhouse that had the ramshackle barn where her cats caught most of the mice.

She was pushing ninety, still freakishly vigorous, though she did have the habit of naming the throw rugs scattered about her home. Little wonder that no one ever came to visit her though she'd kept saying her son would be visiting soon from San Francisco—which never happened. After he dumped her, all but two of the cats, and the filthy throw rugs into the pond out back, he had the place all to himself for a month. Well, he and two of the cats; he needed those to cull the mice in the house.

He couldn't recall if someone else had helped him bring—what was her name?—*Katie*...to that old farmhouse. That didn't matter now. But he did remember having to break the ice on the pond to drop Katie next to Mrs. Comoy and her cat-hair-matted throw rugs, because that winter had been cold and snowy.

This cabin was different. Maybe even a place to come back to, with Lennie, since it was possible someone else had taken over Mrs. Comoy's place by now.

He knew this place as well if not better than the others; knew how well the hearth drew, how the windows in the back room worked, how long it took for the sun to move across the front windows. He knew each one of his possessions displayed on the far wall. He knew the best moments by heart, events that mattered, currents that flowed through the years faster than those that took Eric Lane Caster away.

He knew how much he'd paid Wick Houser for the Mustang, and who took his favorite picture on the wall here: Petra. He knew where they went after the picture—back to the big, white frame house by the canal; and how he once climbed the big oak in the storm, reaching the third floor dormer where the girls were, and tapped on the window to scare the bejeesus out of them.

Even now he could hear Ruckus barking...until Helen shushed the dog so he wouldn't wake the parents. He'd taken the German shepherd puppy from a friend trying to dispose of the litter, but his parents wouldn't let him keep the puppy so he gave it to the girls, and they kept the name he'd thought of, too.

The view from his own bedroom window was blocked by the high, close fence of a neighbor but from another, favorite window of Lennie's big house—where you could see the canal for half a mile in either direction—he'd once told her: *Either way; all we gotta do is get up and go...*

And he knew that the young man in the picture, now a man, was still in Leary Falls. Everyone thought he'd take the world by the scruff of the neck, but to the surprise and disappointment of so many, he had stayed.

But that Michael didn't deserve to stay, not any more. One had to die so the other could live, because he—*he*—was the one who couldn't live without her close by. Oh, Lennie would see that! She'd understand that the other had forfeited her long ago, that she deserved better than long-distance. Surely that would be her own resurrection, would it not? Perhaps they could sacrifice a jewel from the necklace to fashion a ring, and in time they would come back here, where Michael should be, always, with her. And she would say: *This is Michael...my husband. We grew up together back East but we're living out here now, and he gave me this necklace as a wedding gift.*

There would be no one to disbelieve, or take her away again. James Malloy would be back East too, back home. The...Glassman? If Lennie ran into him, she would tell him: *Michael's with me at Fado.* Michael Furey would be the last person the Glassman would ever want to see in person, no question there. Or perhaps they would invite him up to Fado, and this time he would never leave.

There would have to be another accident, of course, in Leary Falls. He had all the time in the world, driving back across the country, to think of how he would do it. After all, he was the one who always came up with the ideas; and coming up with an...accident of some sort would be a breeze for someone gifted with a *passing lane*. But this time neither the old Michael or Petra would survive, nor Callan. Such a tragedy, everyone would say in the paper. But he'd be there for Lennie to console her, tell her they would have another child to replace the one who died in the accident, and this time he would name it.

He realized he was sitting in the Mustang and couldn't remember going back out, and bringing the necklace and that book, the artifact he would throw into the canal after it was all over.

She'd left the keys in the ignition—such an odd thing to do. But who was ever out here in the wilderness to steal it? Anyway, the keys could only mean one thing: she had given her blessing. His Mustang started right up, purred beautifully, except for the muffler. He'd have to get that fixed, the headlight, clean up the car, especially the blood staining the back seat.

Otherwise, she'd left it, well, maybe not in *perfect* condition. But close enough to get him to where his One would be.

CHAPTER 23
GONE

OVER THE NEXT few days I booked a flight into Kennedy for early Thursday morning and cleared out my apartment and Sean's. The story I gave Sheldon Watson brushed the truth: my brother had met a Bellingham woman and wouldn't be coming back. He'd asked me to settle up for him. So I did.

I had a Salvation Army truck take away most of his clothes and furniture and tossed the rest at the city dump at the north end of Lake Union. I packed up the rest of his belongings, much of it the beautifully painted Warhammer figures and terrain for Davy.

I took Sean's journal and the photos of Helen Sommers with me. They were all I'd have to show Marcy when I saw her after I got back.

My apartment took much less time. I wound up with two boxes that I'd ship, along with Sean's, the day before I left. Everything else I could take with me. I never had a checking account so I paid the utilities in person as usual. I planned to drop an envelope with the balance of my rent in the after-hours slot in the apartment complex. There was no time for the rigmarole of selling my car so I gave it to Kira Petraznik.

Marcy would get the boxes after I arrived. I'd called her, knowing she'd be at work, and left a message that I was still looking for Sean. It stunk to lie, but she'd understand later when I told her that I didn't want to tell her about Sean over the phone.

I called Helen and Robert from the Fiddler's, got no answer from either.

Wednesday afternoon I mailed the boxes from the post office on 35th, and called Helen again. Nothing.

There was nothing else to do but drive, keep moving, until I had to go. The apartment was empty, everything was in the car, ready to transfer to the taxi I'd take to the airport.

I was going to miss the steep hills here, the water everywhere and the mountains, especially Mt. Rainier majestically looming over all, making you forget it's still an active volcano. Past the University District, on Route 520 over the floating bridge, you get to see Rainier to the south and Mt. Baker to the north, much farther away but snow-capped as well, the volcano closest to Sean and Fado.

I swung around Lake Washington, telling myself as I neared the Island Crest exit on I-90 that she wasn't at home, anyway, so why not? But I passed the exit and kept on, into Seattle, through the city and along the western edge of Lake Union and over the drawbridge spanning the Ship Canal linking Seattle's inner lake to Puget Sound.

Trees lined the canal but from the street you couldn't tell there was one. All I saw were the masts of a schooner gliding through on its way to the Sound, as if the ship was moving through the land. People watched the passage, among them a couple walking a scruffy black dog with white paws.

What had Helen said about her German shepherd? *We taught Ruckus not to bark at the boats that went by in the canal...*

So she must have lived in Leary Falls, close by the Erie Canal.

I wound up on 45th, a straight shot back to the neighborhood and the Fiddler's Inn. I could have crossed 1-5 there at 45th, near the Blue Moon, where I'd waited for Sean. I turned left onto the northbound entrance. There was plenty of time before I had to go, time enough to say goodbye again to my brother. Because I might never get back. I might get caught up in starting over and...it just doesn't happen. Or if I did come back, whoever was there at Fado might not allow a visit.

In truth, it wasn't just Sean. I wanted to see Helen Sommers again. She probably wouldn't be there, getting her car, whatever. But maybe she would; maybe Michael Furey would be there by now, and that was fine.

Perhaps he'd gotten a call from her, rushed back from wherever he'd been. Besides, I was curious to find out why the man hadn't been there with her: a beautiful and formidable woman who ruined a vintage cherry Mustang driving through the woods with burned hands to bring back two men she didn't know, and help bury one of them in her garden.

THE GATE WAS fully open—which could mean only one thing.

She'd come back.

I drove through, took the road faster than I had going out a few days before. The Nooksack valley below seemed sharply etched, the river glazed with the late afternoon sun. Had she returned with her husband? How else would she have gotten up there? I wondered how he would handle the fact that Helen and I had shared something he had never shared with her, and hopefully never would,

I expected to see another car there at the end, the one they'd driven up here, his car.

There was only Caster's white Explorer.

I parked, thinking about the possibilities: she and Furey were off somewhere; she was visiting Barbara Hollner; she'd come and gone, forgetting to close the gate at the end of the road. I decided to wait a little while, to see if she'd be back and if not, perhaps swing by her house on Mercer Island before I left and say goodbye. Again.

I got out, greeted by the scent of cedars and firs. The sun was low enough now to darken those Mustang-furrows she'd made in the meadow. As I walked around the front of the cabin, I stopped short. I might have walked into a wall.

The Mustang was gone.

My first thought: *she's driven it back, to sell it…*

She'd said she was going to do that, yet it had only been a few days. Selling the Mustang certainly wouldn't be at the top of her to-do list after what happened; getting away had been.

Maybe Furey had gone off in the Highlander on some errand, and she was inside. At the porch steps I shouted; and again, at the door: "Helen?"

I knocked loudly, waited a moment, opened the door, and stepped inside.

She'd been here, that was obvious. The place had been tidied up, utensils gone from the floor, drawers pushed back in, the rope gone.

Gone, too, from the showcase wall to my left were her husband's memorabilia.

Had he done that or had she? Packed all of his things, put them in the Mustang or Highlander and driven back to Mercer Island?

She sure hadn't wasted any time.

Something didn't seem right.

My impression had been that she wanted to get away for now and—*Jesus*—who could blame her? The last thing she'd want to do is come up here so soon...after. And that the other things—like selling the Mustang—could wait. Still, maybe her husband had wanted to do that, however, after she'd told him. Or done it himself.

Michael, I can't go back up there right now. Will you do it?

I'll go, honey. I'll take care of things...

But no, they both must have come up here, since both the Mustang and Highlander were gone.

I left the cabin, stood on the porch—along with the feeling that something wasn't right.

I went over to the garden.

What gives, Seanie?

One thing was certain: Robert Tiphook hadn't been up here, hobbling on crutches. One thing that wasn't: the odd relationship Helen had with him. She was married; she had the ring on her finger. Was Michael Furey away so much that Robert Tiphook felt he could ask—and Helen would accept—an invitation to go on a date to Bainbridge Island and feed the seagulls on the way over?

Were she and Furey separated or otherwise having problems?

I said it aloud this time: "What the fuck, Seanie? Who the hell's been here?"

Hey, fucker...

I don't know why I'd missed seeing that the low door to the root cellar was open when it hadn't been before. Why would Helen or her husband have gone in there?

Fado suddenly seemed too quiet. If there had been a breeze before, I saw nothing moving in the forest beyond the meadow, all around the cabin. The needled branches were still. No one approached the bridge over the creek at the end of the meadow, but I kept looking there anyway, in the direction we'd come from where Caster fallen to his death.

Seanie, got to go now...

I picked up a splitting maul from the ground near the chopping block, the solid weight of edged iron reassuring in my hand. Walking back to my car I kept turning, feeling foolish yet unwilling to give my back to any part of the forest for more than a moment. I had to fight the urge to move faster to the car. I didn't want to give in to the instinct that all was not as we'd left it days before—except for the low mound of earth over my brother's grave.

I put the maul in the car, passenger side, handle slanting up from the seat well and drove away, keeping an eye on the bluff to my right where I'd waited for Shadden—Eric Lane Caster—to show; where I narrowly missed being killed when he trumped the ambush. I passed the spot and the fear receded. I had the axe, the car. I could run him down if...

No way...not a chance...

He couldn't have survived that fall, the jagged rocks of that chute. Even if he had been only stunned, incredibly escaping injury, he still would have drowned in that roiling water.

Yet someone had been at Fado after we left—maybe even Helen.

But she wouldn't have taken the Mustang...

Okay...calm down...

Maybe that someone had been a hunter or several of them.

No...

Coming across an empty, unlocked cabin, they might have trashed the place, or stolen things, but they wouldn't have cleaned it up, taken another man's high school varsity jacket, pictures of him and his girlfriend. Would they have stolen the Mustang? Not in its condition.

It had to have been her, with or without Furey. So...she changed her mind. Decided before going away to clean up, take the personally meaningful stuff to give back to an estranged husband. What she'd been meaning to do for a while? Furey would certainly want her to do that. The stuff was his. And take the Mustang, get what they could for it. Clean the slate now, instead of leaving it for later. Was Helen that sort of person?

I hoped so because the only other alternative was Eric Lane Caster being alive.

All right, okay, say he had survived somehow...

Surely he would have been hurt badly. Getting to the cabin...from there? And then cleaning up the cabin, taking Furey's things, the Mustang. Why? More likely he'd have been in a rage—if he was physically even capable of that—and burned the cabin to the ground.

Helen...had to be Helen...

But...what if she had done what she said she would? *I just need to get away...touch some bases...*

What if Eric Lane Caster *had* survived, against all odds?

I sped up the logging road.

I had to find out if she'd been back here. If she hadn't, then she had to know that Eric Lane Caster was still alive.

IT WAS EARLY evening when I passed the stadiums south of downtown Seattle, and headed east on I-90, over the Lake Washington bridge. This time I took the Island Crest Way exit for Mercer Island, stopped off at a convenience store to get her address from a phone book.

A couple miles south on Island Crest, I found her home, behind a church—another clearing in the woods—and expected to see a once-cherry Mustang in the carport at the end of the gravel parking lot.

The carport was empty.

That meant—I hoped that meant—she'd already disposed of the Mustang, and taken off in her own car—to leave at the airport, or just pick a point on the compass and drive. Sometimes mileage helps.

I knocked on the door. No answer. The door was locked of course.

Before I got back on the interstate, I called Robert Tiphook from the same convenience store pay phone, thinking maybe she was with him. No answer.

I found his address in the book, drove to his house in Seattle, the Wallingford neighborhood north of Gasworks Park on the edge of Lake Union. His old Mercedes wasn't there, either. I knocked anyway. Nothing.

She wouldn't have gone off with Robert Tiphook.

The only thing left to do now was get on the plane, rent a car with what little money I had left, and drive up to Leary Falls and find some-one—family or old friends—who might know where either Michael Furey or Helen Sommers might be. Someone— anyone—who could give me a number to call, to ask the question. And I hoped like hell that Helen would be with him, and she would answer: *Yes, we went back to Fado afterwards to get the Mustang and Michael's things…*

She'd said she had to get away…touch some bases.

The only bases I could think of were in Leary Falls, about an hour and a half from where I was going anyway, to tell Marcy our brother was dead.

CHAPTER 24

THE LOCKSPOT

I ARRIVED IN Leary Falls shortly after 10 p.m. that Thursday, weary from the crowded flight and the drive up from Kennedy on the Thruway. I found a Best Western motel at the corner of Route 5 and Ann Street, not far from the Conrail tracks that ran through what had once been the industrial heart of the town, close by the Mohawk River and adjacent canal.

A blue Leary Falls police car cruised by a small group of teenagers at the corner. Even at this hour the air was still heavy and humid, so unlike the summer crispness I'd gotten used to in Seattle. Across the street from the motel a couple argued at a laundromat as I got my suitcase from the rental car:

"...And you're also twice the bitch Lenore is."

"Then do me a favor and go fuck her for a change."

Welcome to Leary Falls.

After settling into my room, I got a local map from the lobby and took a look at the area directory at the pay phones next to the ice machines.

There was no *Furey* listed, which wasn't a good start. So much for assuming any Fureys still lived here. There was, however, a *Donald G./ Betty Sommers, 17 Old Paradise Road.* I decided face-to-face would be better than a phone call, and jotted the address on the map, found the location—off Route 169, about four miles north of the town.

Helen had lived by the canal—*we taught Ruckus not to bark at the boats that went by in the canal*—and this address was far from it. Still, maybe they'd just taken the dog for romps by the canal. Or maybe they had, in fact, lived by the canal, but the parents had moved, downsized after their daughter left the nest. *It was a big house, three floors, used to be a rooming house, way back when.*

I took a shower and went to bed with the white-noise of the air-conditioning, thinking about what I would tell Donald and Betty—if Helen was not, in fact, with them. If they didn't know where she might be other than her home, surely they would have an address and phone number of Michael Furey. Whatever their situation, he and Helen were obviously still a couple; and even if she wasn't with him now, it seemed a reasonable assumption she might have called him. He would know where she was.

One way or the other, the question would be answered: did she or Furey go to the cabin afterwards?

Thinking about the other possibility kept me awake a lot longer than I wanted.

THE MAID WOKE me up at 11:30 the next morning. I cleared out by noon, got some gas and a cup of lousy coffee at a Stewart's convenience store a few blocks away.

Leary Falls seemed to be a familiar story for these parts, more than a hundred years past its prime and the heyday of industrialization and canal traffic—and far removed from the colonial heroics at Oriskany and Fort Stanwix resurrected in *Drums Along the Mohawk,* book and movie.

The neighborhoods I passed through on my way up the hill were full of rundown 'widow's-walk' homes that would have been stunning if fixed up. In a park at the corner of Gansvoort and Monroe, workmen were repainting a pergola. Red, white and blue Fourth of July bunting lay in a pile nearby on browned grass, ready to trashed. It was anyone's guess why they were painting now instead of before the recent holiday.

Monroe turned into Route 169 up the hill and I followed it past one of those old-time water towers with a conical roof. I fell behind a Walmart semi gearing up the hill—yet another one. I must have seen ten Walmart trucks on the Thruway coming north and then another from Albany west to Leary Falls. They were everywhere, like the trucks carrying the pods in

Invasion of the Body Snatchers, the original that Seanie and I liked better than the do-over.

Past the entrance to the high school—*Home of the Spartans*—the grade flattened out, then rose into uplands that had metastasized from dairy farms to housing developments. If I kept going north I'd be back in the Adirondacks, where it had begun.

From up here you couldn't look back and see the town itself or the Erie Canal that cut through the lower, labial folds of land. Nor could you see a canal lock that adjusted the level of water, making possible a passage. Lock #17. That was Leary Falls number, just one of dozens from Albany to Buffalo.

Upper Paradise Road branched off the main thoroughfare—Trinity Avenue—and led to a development called Heaven's Acres. Given the names, I was not all that surprised to see a modest church centrally located among the residences—and wondered how holy-roller-ish Donald and Betty might be. Enough to send their artistic daughter fleeing across the country? That she'd up behind a church on Mercer Island was probably a coincidence, given what Barbara Hollner had said about Helen's disdain for people who believe that one hour on Sunday gives them the excuse to ignore the rest of the week.

Their house sat at the end of a cul-de-sac. I pulled into the driveway next to a blue Ford-150 pickup and parked behind a Winnebago with a fish decal at one end of the bumper, a haloed Good Sam Club sticker at the other, and in between the anchor-through-the-world Marine Corps decal.

The door opened so soon after I rang the bell it seemed as if the woman who answered had been waiting for me. She kept the door open wide enough for me to see the cell phone in one hand. Her fingernails glistened with red polish. She wasn't much older than Helen—mid-thirties—and five feet tall, if that.

She was also Asian—Korean perhaps.

Okay, well, maybe Helen's father had remarried.

"Yes?" she said.

I introduced myself, told her I was a friend of Helen Sommers, visiting in the area from Seattle and…would she know where I could contact Helen?

"I don't unnastan," the woman said.

"I'm looking for Helen Sommers."

From within, a man's voice: "Who is it, Betty?"

"Sommon for an Ellen."

"What?" The man appeared, looming over Betty in the foot-wide crack in the doorway. He was in his sixties, with a full head of slicked-back white hair.

"Sorry to bother you, but I'm looking for a Helen Sommers. I have…"

"I got two sons in the Marines, but no Helen," he said, and pulled his wife back.

"Semper Fi," I said to the door after he closed it.

I DROVE BACK to town thinking that all I could do now was get to Marcy's and call Helen and Robert; and if neither were home leave a message to call me immediately. The Furey and Sommers families didn't seem to be in Leary Falls any longer.

It was close to 2 p.m. I decided to get something to eat before heading east to where Marcy lived in East Greenbush, across the Hudson from Albany. I found a restaurant called the Lockspot, near a defunct 19th century factory that still had on one side, in huge faded letters: *Fowler Manufacturing.* The newer signs said: *Leary Falls Arts and Crafts Center and Mohawk Antique Mall.* There was plenty of parking where other factory buildings had been demolished. Crossing the street to the restaurant, I passed a poster stapled to a telephone pole: *Leary Falls Canal Celebration—August 11-13. Low Bridge, Everybody Down!*

The Lockspot made the most of the connection, full of old photos of the canal era and even a couple of framed quotes from Melville, who evidently had once traveled on the Erie Canal, adventuring west before he signed on with that New Bedford whaler.

One quote was from *Moby Dick*: *…One continuous stream of Venetianly corrupt and often lawless life…*

The other came from *Billy Budd*: *…At the tiller of the boats on the tempestuous Erie Canal or, more likely, vaporing in the groggeries along the towpath…*

There wasn't much vaporing going on in the Lockspot at this hour—the lunch rush, such as it may have been—was gone. When I went into the bar there was only the bartender and an older man sitting at the end, his pint of beer half-full. We nodded to each other as I sat down six stools away.

I ordered a ham and Swiss and a Saranac lager from the bartender, a young guy, mid-twenties. After he brought me the beer and sandwich, he went over to his other patron, obviously a regular by the familiar way the bartender leaned closely. Above the back-bar to my right, closer to where the two men chatted, there was a framed print of a painting, the lower part obscured by a tip jar, computer terminal and liquor bottles. But I could make out the title: *American Aqueduct*.

I was no art expert, but the piece seemed beautifully done, the original probably a water color given the play of shadows and early morning—or evening—light on the arches of the aqueduct supporting the canal as it crossed over a creek and marsh. The towpath wasn't visible, yet most of the mule was, as well as the rope leading to the bow of the canal boat. Three people had gathered by the stern, as if watching the observer of the painting on a following boat. Two stood, one pointing right at me; the other leaned on a rail.

I left my half-eaten sandwich, which wasn't very good anyway, and slid down a few stools to get a better look, leaning over the bar.

"Need something?" the bartender said.

"Just looking at that painting. You know who did it?"

"Well, let's see. I've been here six months and never really took a look—you know how that works."

He shifted a few bottles around. "There's a name down at the bottom. Looks like..."

"Helen Sommers?"

"Hey, that's it! How'd you know?"

"Lucky guess," I said. So she was here—a print of one of her paintings anyway.

"Jeez, how're you with lottery numbers?—I'm still paying off my college loans."

"Way out of my league. But I have another question for you. Any chance you've heard of a guy named Michael Furey, used to live around here?"

A car horn sounded. The bartender nodded toward the window. "Your cue, Cully."

The man drained the last of his pint, got up shaking his head. "Time was I'd get at least two beers waiting for Donna to finish up with the wife's hair, but she's losing it faster than I am. Go figure."

"See you next," the bartender said. "Don't do anything I would."

"I already have, Joey." Then to me: "You were asking about Michael Furey?"

I swiveled around on the stool. "You know him?"

"Used to. Hard not to. A kid we all thought we'd be planning a homecoming for, smack dab down Albany Street, and not like the one come back from Iraq not long ago. Kids hereabouts mostly leave; can't blame them. Not much to keep them."

"Thanks, Cully," Joey said.

"You didn't grow up here so don't count. Anyway, you just gave your notice."

"Not yet I haven't. Said I was *thinking* about it."

"Cripes, I'm not talking about you, anyway. This one was before your time. This kid we really wanted to leave."

The wife blared the car horn again and Cully limped toward the door—something wrong with his left leg, couldn't straighten it out all the way. "It was a damn shame," he said to me. "You're about fifteen years too late but it was about this time it happened."

Cully was already out of the bar, heading toward the door, too late to answer the question I never thought I'd be asking.

Joey said something I didn't hear, either. I was looking at the old fellow getting into the car in a way that reminded me of Robert Tiphook getting into mine. Soon, his wife made a left turn, out of sight, but what I was seeing was that wall in Helen's cabin 3000 miles away. I heard Joey this time, and swiveled on the stool to face him. He leaned close, elbows on the bar: "This guy, he was a friend of yours?"

"No. I…we never met."

Joey left it there, maybe because I was staring at the painting and not looking at him when I answered him. You work behind a bar, you hear... *places* where maybe you'd better not go—like a guy asking about another who sure as hell seemed like a friend but saying he wasn't; and this guy reacting like he'd taken a two-by-four across the chops.

So you tap the pint glass.

"Another?" Joey said.

I shook my head. "I'm done, thanks." I asked him for Cully's last name.

"That's his last name. Culbertson. I couldn't tell you what his first is. Always been Cully."

"I'd like to talk to him some more. Does he live in town?"

"On Gansvoort Street, across from the Carnegie library, I think. You'll have to wait till Monday, though. He just headed off to Schenectady for the weekend. Family deal."

I paid up and as I was leaving, Joey said: "So that painting...you know the woman who did it, then?"

"We spent some time together in Seattle, but it was still a guess. She used to live around here."

"Soon as my girlfriend finishes up at Syracuse, that's what I'm looking forward to saying too."

I left him a ten-buck tip. You have to take care of your own and besides, at his bar I'd gotten the answers to two questions. The first? Michael Furey sure as hell wasn't the one who'd gone back to the cabin, with or without that beautiful young woman who'd had a finger cocked like a gun at his head in that picture on the wall.

The second?

Joey had given me an idea of where I might find out why Michael Furey had never left Leary Falls fifteen years ago, if not why Helen Sommers kept his high school varsity jacket on a wall of a wilderness cabin a continent away, then took it down—took everything of Michael Furey's down, and put it all in a banged-up Mustang, and drove away.

Or had she?

CHAPTER 25

HOME

H E DROVE IN from the west on I-90, getting off near Herkimer, New York, and continuing on Route 5. He ate the last of the Freihofer doughnuts he'd bought when he stopped for gas, and tossed the box in the back seat along with all the other crap he'd accumulated from the cross-country trip. He reminded himself he'd have to clean the car up once he got to Leary Falls, now only six miles away.

He couldn't remember ever having come into town this way, in the Mustang. Then again, he'd only had the car for less than a year after buying it from Houser. But he, Lennie and Pete had gone pretty much every other way in the car, which included Lake Shendego and Bannerwood State Park there—thank God Helen hadn't gone with them that Friday. He almost hadn't been able to get Petra out before the car sank. If Lennie had been with them…if it had been the three of them, as usual, one of the Sommers sisters wouldn't have made it.

They'd taken other road trips in the Mustang: to Glimmerglass State Park at the north end of Lake Otsego, and once to Cooperstown at the southern end. Another time they drove east to Schenectady and Union College, heard William Styron's talk at the Nott Memorial and then watched Billy Burke—a high school friend who'd graduated ahead of them—play in a freshman basketball game. He wondered what had happened to Billy, all 6'6" of him and juiced with the quickest wit of any person he'd ever known. He'd have to ask Lennie; maybe she knew. She was the fount of all, probably had read more during the months of her pregnancy than he had at Amherst.

Houser paid for the repairs on the Mustang. Following his recovery, every chance he had he drove the resurrected Mustang home from Amherst. And that, too, became part of the lore: that Michael Furey could get back into the same car after what happened, to be with the young woman who was carrying his child.

Well, the distance from Amherst to Leary Falls wasn't *that* far; he would have driven much farther to visit her, to feel their child kicking. And he was at her side for the birth. After a couple of years, Pete and the parents would drive out with her and Callan for the weekend, once seeing him score three touchdowns—one for 95 yards—in the Little Three championship game against Williams his senior year.

If he had a buck for every prediction that they wouldn't last as a couple who'd had a kid way too early, he'd be rolling in money. People just couldn't understand how it was, how it *always* had been between them. When you're all but born with someone who turned out like Helen, there was no other place to go. She didn't even think of what she had done as a sacrifice. She promised him, her family—and herself—that she would take her turn once he'd graduated.

And she had, with help from family and friends.

But in earlier years, he'd mostly taken the Mustang to get from the house his parents rented a few miles from town, to the Sommers' big home. It was a little west of Leary Falls, not far from Lock 18, a stone's throw from the canal—the New York State Barge Canal really, part of the Mohawk River, but it would always be the Erie Canal to him.

Soon, they'd finally be leaving Leary Falls in the Mustang, both of them this time. *Finally.* Distance and time away was taking its toll. Pete and Callan would have to stay, of course; nothing to be done about. In time Lennie would understand.

There was no way around the fact that there could only be the two of them now. When they had played hide and seek among the glacier-sculpted rock towers and potholes of Moss Island, close to downtown and across from Lock 17, it was always either he or Helen who found the other. Pete might be close but she never was the one who found where anyone else had hidden. He knew Lennie so well he could always guess where she would hide, and she always seemed to know the places he chose.

When you have that awareness and perception of another, there can *be* no other. Not when you've found your One.

Funny how the closer he got to home, the more impatient he was to say goodbye to it and leave for good this time—like everyone had always wanted him to, *expected* him to, so he could live the life that most everyone else in Leary Falls never would.

The Mustang had performed well going across the country, but there was no reason why it shouldn't have, given the low miles. Lennie had taken good care of it—well, mostly. The exterior looked like crap but the car still had the horses. And he still had his *passing lane*, going 700 miles or more every day, and not once did he turn on the radio. He slept on some of Lennie's blankets he unrolled by the car in those isolated places he always had a knack for finding.

He was getting looks now from a couple of kids on bikes and an older couple on a porch. The kids seemed curious about the Washington plates, the scratched and dented exterior. Grandma and Grandpa? Maybe they remembered the red Mustang from long ago, and the handsome young man with his elbow stuck out jauntily, on his way to see his girl and her sister.

He was almost home, and what mattered now was that Lennie couldn't see the car, not yet. He'd come a long way to surprise her and so he would.

She was here, he was sure of it. Where else would she come to besides Leary Falls? Surely she would want to be with them after what happened. He had hours to find her, and even if she wasn't at the house where he'd spent so much of his youth, he wanted to see it before they left for good. Everyone had always assumed they would wind up together, far from Leary Falls, and so they would, fulfilling predictions that were voiced so frequently they seemed like community property.

He'd spent as much time at her house as he had at his own. After all, his mother had brought him to the Sommers' house when he—and Helen—were only months old. The nanny deal: Mary Furey watched over her son as she watched over the Sommers' first child; and then in a couple of years, the next, Petra. Even after the three of them grew old enough so that a nanny wasn't really necessary, his mother stayed on. And so at least until he, Helen and Pete began to have separate after-school activities, he could always be found at the Sommers' house. No one ever thought it might be a good idea for him to go elsewhere after school. Someone might as well have told the moon to alter its phases.

There it was: Kenyon Road.

It seemed as if he'd never left.

He remembered the signs for the boat launch and Lock 18. But here was a new one—some things had to change of course: a sign and arrow for the Towpath B&B. And there were some homes in the area that hadn't been there before. The trees were bigger but some had been cut down, so he could still see the top of the three-story house, always his home away from home, there by the Erie Canal.

He knew a lot about its history and stages of enlargements. The original, begun in 1817, was only four feet deep and forty across. Now, what passed by the Sommers' house was a constant reminder of possibility that still seemed more exotic and palpable than the invisible routes of airplanes, the crude paving of highways.

Hell, he knew more about it than anyone, maybe even more than Canvass Henderson at the museum. He'd done his senior year project on the Erie Canal, got an A+. He wasn't just a three sport jock—football, swimming and baseball; he could write, too. Henderson had published the 'book' as he called it—printed it up fancy, cover and all, and put it on the counter at the town museum—corner of McKenna and Wilson Streets—for anyone to buy. Everything about the canal was in there, including his ancestors who emigrated from County Clare to work the canal and stayed on after it was finished.

By the time he went off to college, he'd sold 126 copies at a $1.50 each, proceeds to the museum which was scarcely bigger than the Sommers' two-car garage. Wick Houser bought a dozen, but that was to be expected.

For all he knew it was still selling.

Lennie, of course, read the forty-page paper even before it was published. She was particularly intrigued by the fact that many taverns, stores—and brothels—had been located on the towpath side of the Erie Canal in those first years, *the mule-side,* where certain necessities were more accessible. It was a matter of convenience for the canal-men and therefore precious time—and time was money with a boatload of freight or passengers; usually both. The Sommers' home was located on what had once been the mule-side.

He came up with a catchword that only he, Lennie and Pete shared: *feeling mule.* Or sometimes *fool for mule*—which Lennie certainly was, you betcha.

And was he ever *feelin' mule* right now!

Before the night was out, he'd have his *mule-city kitty* once again. Lennie had thought of that one herself. Never mind she disliked cats, always had. He loved it when she called herself *mule-city kitty.*

That's my girl…

He might start something, but *oh yeah,* she sure knew how to take it from there.

He slowed as he neared the fork in the road, catching more of the Sommers' house through the trees. He stopped the car. She—all of them—could be there; the place was plenty big enough. If he drove right up in the Mustang she'd see it, or one of them would. Even Callan might remember. He was what?—sixteen now?

He couldn't have Lennie know he was here, that he'd come back for her—not until nightfall.

Kenyon Road continued on toward Lock 18, past the ruins of the aqueduct that once carried the early canal over Sumas Creek, where they used to jump down from the top of one of the four remaining arches—used to be eight when the mules still pulled the boats over the span. Water over water. God, he loved that concept.

He and Lennie were always ready to go for it but Pete always insisted on testing the depth of water first, as if they hadn't jumped before in the same place. To tease her sister Lennie would yell, each time they jumped, something she'd read in a book—White-Jacket, that was it: *And if ever we drown, it will be in the raging canal!!*

He drove along a short way, stopped again, the Mustang mostly obscured from the house, now fifty yards away. He got out and leaned against one of the maples, feeling the afternoon heat, the heaviness of the air. A bluebird flitted past. He hadn't seen one of those in a long time, heard the warbly *churr-i-lee...churr-i-lee...*

He spied the oak tree next to the house, the same oak he climbed up once in that storm, to tap on their window with the stick. He picked out the window of the room the girls shared, one of the four windows on the second floor. They could have had separate rooms but they wanted to share the one. That was Lennie and Pete, his *insepara-belles.*

Four cars were parked by the house. The sound of a power mower grew louder and from around the corner of the house came a teenager cutting the grass, long blond hair sticking out from under a reversed baseball cap.

Callan?

Then he saw her, the black hair unmistakable, though much shorter than when she was young. She appeared on the wrap-around porch, near the swing where he used to brush her hair—Pete's too—and to hell if his buddies came by and saw him. She was talking to a woman too old to be Petra. Lennie gave her a wave as she walked down the steps, past her son—their son—mowing the lawn, and went on to her car.

Neither she nor her son seemed to acknowledge the other, not even when he stopped the mower to unload the grasscatcher. Perhaps they smiled and nodded—he couldn't see that from this distance. But still... they acted like they didn't know each other; no stopping to talk, appreciate the work on a hot and humid late afternoon. Which was something Lennie would certainly do, not having seen her son in a while.

It came to him then: *the kid's not Callan..*

And if he wasn't their son...then this might not be her home anymore. He moved quickly, ten yards to his left, saw the sign now that had been hidden by the cars. He couldn't read it from here but he realized it had to be the sign he'd seen before and hadn't connected to the house: *The Towpath Bed and Breakfast.*

So she was visiting, staying with the others somewhere else in Leary Falls.

Was she going there now?

As she backed her car up, he got into the Mustang, made the U-turn, still screened by trees. He was careful not to follow too closely. She took Kenyon Road back to Route 5, then drove east into town and pulled into a parking space in front of a row of shops on Albany Street. He stayed back, a block behind, next to a Fleet Bank.

Pedestrians clotted the sidewalk so he didn't see her come out of a store ten minutes later, but he caught her blue rental backing out and followed: left on Fox, right on Main, then past the park across from the huge red brick edifice of Jameson Hall Academy, circa 1890, refurbished while he'd been away.

On Monroe he'd always taken the left to go back home, girding himself for the steepness of the long hill if he was on his bike. Lennie took a right, and he matched that to Salisbury Street. He tried to remember what was up in this direction. McManus Field was around here, where as a kid he'd played in the outfield when he wasn't pitching. Left-handed Billy Burke always played first because of his reach. Lennie and Pete were often in the rickety stands. But what else was here besides the municipal golf course and the Nostrand Nursing Home where the girls had volunteered during high school?

She turned left again a quarter-mile ahead. As he drove past the stone gateway of Holy Trinity Cemetery, her car was already deeply among the oaks and maples, moving slowly toward a pickup truck and a workman preparing for a weekend funeral.

He kept going on Salisbury and turned around in the driveway of the nursing home, then parked on the shoulder of the road, facing the cemetery. Lennie walked from her car which she'd parked near a stone obelisk at the far end of the drive, the flowers she cradled in her arms mere spots of color at this distance.

When she finally drove out and headed back toward town, he followed—but not for long. As he approached the cemetery entrance he slowed, curious to find out with whom she had just spent almost an hour. It wouldn't be a problem to find out where she was staying. Petra Sommers and Michael Furey would be in the phone book. And the number would be the same, since they were living together with Callan.

He turned into the cemetery, parked where she had, walked in the direction she'd taken, drawn to the markers by the flowers she'd left.

HE STOOD OVER the graves, in a rift not unlike the one he'd been in at the pool of his rebirth far away. He glanced back at the Mustang yet didn't feel up to driving it quite yet, going through the mechanical motions of key to ignition, pedals, shifting, turn signals. But if he'd had an eagle's wings he would have soared, canal to mountains and back.

His Helen had been waiting for him all along; waiting for him to come back and take her away.

Here, etched in granite, was the proof of his resurrection. It was no easy thing to leave its presence, but finally he did.

CHAPTER 26

SHOOTING STAR

T HE LEARY FALLS *Spotlight* shared the ground floor of a brick building on Douglas Street with the smaller offices of an attorney named
Flesinger, and the R.V. Stubbs Realty Co. Half an hour after I walked in, I
left with a sheet of paper I copied from the weekly newspaper's morgue of
back issues. There was a fee for reproducing articles but the receptionist,
wearing a Flogging Molly T-shirt, just glanced at the single sheet, waved
me out with a smile and a "have a nice weekend." She looked about the
same age as Petra Sommers might have been, working her first summer job.

It had taken me fifteen minutes to find the newspaper's office. Walking
back to my car took longer. I must have taken wrong turns. I wasn't paying attention. My mind was far away, the distances merging: Fado and
Leary Falls.

The car's interior was a furnace. I don't know why I opened the window instead of cranking up the air-conditioning. Maybe to pour my stale
coffee out the window. A rental truck backed up to the entrance to the
antique mall.

I unfolded the sheet of paper to read the article again. The date was
July 15, 1991.

LOCAL TEENS KILLED IN CAR PLUNGE
By Stephen Lubis
*Two Leary Falls residents died last Friday evening as a result of an ac-
cident that caused their car to skid from Route 28, west of Richfield Springs,
and over a bluff into Lake Shendego.*

Michael Furey, 18, was pronounced dead at the scene by Otsego County rescue workers who recovered his body from the lake an hour after the accident occurred. Police said it took several more hours for divers to be summoned and extricate the body of Petra Sommers, 16, who had remained trapped in the vehicle.

Rescue workers searched the lake for other possible victims but police later confirmed that Furey and Sommers were the only passengers in the car, a 1965 Mustang, which was not removed from the lake, a popular area destination, until late Saturday morning. Police estimated the depth of the lake where the car sank at approximately thirty feet.

According to a member of the Sommers family, the pair were driving to Bannerwood State Park at the lake, to attend a social gathering with friends.

George Gillivray, 38, of Oneonta, witnessed the car's plunge as he was sailing with a companion: "We were heading back to the dock and we saw this red car skid off into the lake."

Gillivray said his boat was about forty yards away from the car as it began to sink. "We saw a man surface from the water, from the driver's side, disappear, then resurface and go under once more, and that was kind of it. I think he was trying to get another person out, but he couldn't; the car was sinking too fast."

Gillivray's companion, Susan Peterson, 34, also of Oneonta, said they had difficultly tacking the sailboat closer, and abandoned the effort. She swam to the scene but "that car was long gone by the time I got there."

Although a full investigation of the accident is pending, Richfield Springs Police Lt. Edward Petrollo said that prior to the accident a motorcyclist had lost control of his vehicle and that the car, driven by Furey, may have swerved to avoid hitting the skidding motorcycle ahead of him.

At that point on Route 28 there is only a wide shoulder. William Manson, a county highway official, said that the recently defeated bond issue would have included funds to install guard rails along that portion of Route 28.

Lt. Petrollo declined to comment on whether the gravel spill on that stretch of road earlier in the day possibly contributed to the chain of events, nor would he identify the motorcyclist, who was taken to Otsego County

Memorial Hospital with injuries police said were critical but did not appear to be life-threatening.

Both Furey and Sommers attended Leary Falls High School. Sommers was a member of the junior class and a daughter of Charles and Rebecca Sommers, 18 Kenyon Road. Furey graduated last month. He was the son of John and Mary Furey, 345 Hillview Drive.

According to high school principal Patrick McKenna, Furey had been president of the Class of 1991. A three-sport varsity athlete and editor of the creative writing magazine, he was to have attended Amherst College in the fall.

I folded the sheet of paper again, staring at the two men unloading antiques, thinking of the candle Helen Sommers had kept lit—*seriously* lit—for Michael Furey at a place he'd never seen.

I'd known her for only a few hours. I couldn't list ten mundane ways she moved through her day; if she smoked, liked white wine more than red, or neither; preferred tea over coffee; if she was the kind of person who wept at injustices but never really liked people, or if it was the other way around. But there are people who have known each other for a lifetime yet have never taken the kind of measure we did at Fado.

She was an accomplished, beautiful woman who'd undoubtedly had suitors a lot younger than the spurned Robert Tiphook. What would such men make of that wall of Michael Furey's? What would she say to them or any friend she brought to Fado?

I had the feeling there were few, if any, who had seen the inside of that cabin. Because if they had, what answer could she give them? This feeling—and it was strong—seemed akin to violation. Because if true it was something I had no right to know, a secret that was hers alone to reveal if she chose.

She appeared to be a successful artist—a difficult gig—but it was likely she didn't have to deal with rush hour commutes, time-clocks, office cubicles, and overseers pounding the corporate drum. She had the house on Mercer Island. She had her refuge—Fado. She had a print of one of her paintings in her home town. Were there others around Leary Falls? I'd seen a gallery near the tavern. She seemed to possess that grail so many seek and few find: living life on her terms.

All that, and the solace of time and distance—fifteen years and 3000 miles—hadn't seemed to be enough for her. Did she carry within her that big home by the canal, and the one room within she couldn't seal off?

We all have that room. Seanie did. He walked into his and chose not to come out again. I had mine. Fifteen years from now, I'd still be seeing Katie on that bed, hearing her sing softly to the man who, moments later, would kill her and the baby conceived by rape.

One thing hadn't changed. Contacting Helen and asking her if she'd gone back to Fado afterwards and, for whatever reason, decided it was time to extinguish the candle. If she hadn't, then one or the other of us would have to call the Whatcom County sheriff's department.

I drove away from the canal, through the town. It seemed to me how little things must have changed since 1991. Some new homes and buildings here and there, sure. But everything else—as Michael Furey and the Sommers sisters had seen it—was still present: abandoned factories; the ever-present canal and river; the train tracks, the buildings—old even when the three were growing up—etched with the years…1895…1916…1876…1794…1933… on cornerstones and bronze plaques.

Today was Friday, the same day it happened and the same time of the year; the air still hot, something you didn't just breathe but felt, like the softest of garments; the same pergola and trees in the park. Some must have been taken down, but others had grown to replace them.

I took the steep incline of Route 169, glancing at the map. The street was there all right.

He'd have come the other way that evening in 1991, but he would have passed the same water tower and maybe he knew who'd climbed up and painted the class year above the girdling catwalk, next to other, more recent years. He might have even climbed up to do it himself, this Michael Furey, #25 for the Leary Fall Spartans. His football or baseball number? He wouldn't have done it drunk; he would have known he had too much to lose. He would neither have acceded to a dare nor taunted someone else to do it. That didn't seem like the guy.

He would have been on top of the world that evening. Work-week done, a fun softball game with the Sommers sisters and friends with whom he'd grown up, Michael Furey still would have been keenly aware that he'd never see them very often after they went their separate ways after high school. Perhaps driving to the Sommers home he had wondered what was going to happen to Helen and him; that had to be the only cloud on his horizon. They must have talked about it. He'd be in Amherst; she'd be…where?

Where was Helen going to be?

Someone once had the idea—I think it was Jack Finney in a novel he wrote—that if you could duplicate the exact details of a specific time and place in the past, you could return to that time, such was the fluidity of past and present.

Or at least what we keep in our hearts—what might have made Helen Sommers not all that surprised if her Michael Furey had walked into that cabin late one night, with an armload of wood for the fire in the hearth, eager to share the wonder of the brief spray of shooting stars he'd seen in the sky over the meadow, far from the glare of city lights.

She'd put Michael Furey's constellation on that wall.

Hillview Drive meandered through a neighborhood of newer, modest homes that never had the splendor of others closer to town, where the Victorian wealth had once been. The Fureys never could have had much money, if this was the street where they'd lived. For some reason I assumed Michael had been an only child, and it seemed likely the local Kiwanis and Rotary had vied to see which could give him the most scholarship money to add to all the financial aid Amherst had promised.

Most of the 300 block, including the Fureys' address, was gone, replaced by a school district bus depot, with a small, new-looking building and maintenance shed adjacent to the rows of fallow summer buses.

I drove back down to find the Sommers home. I couldn't leave Leary Falls without seeing that house, assuming it was still there by the canal where Petra Sommers waited for Michael Furey to pick her up in the red Mustang, to go to the lake that Friday evening. It was possible that the two were boyfriend and girlfriend, but it didn't seem likely that a young man about to head off to college in September would have a sixteen year-old sweetheart.

So Helen had to be the one. Why would she have bought another vintage Mustang—or fixed up the *other* one—and kept that shrine at Fado for the boyfriend of her younger sister? But where had Helen been that day in July? Why hadn't Michael picked both of them up?

Only Helen could answer that. Whatever the reason was, it had saved her life—and changed it forever. I had no business asking her that question, but I wanted to.

And though I still intended to try and contact her, the other question—the reason why I'd come here—*seemed* to have been answered in the back-issue morgue of the Leary Falls *Spotlight*. Because of Eric Lane Caster, Fado was no longer a place where she could imagine Michael Furey walking in with an armload of firewood. So she had taken him away, gone away with him.

To where?

The map of Leary Falls showed Kenyon Road west of town, off Route 5. That's where I headed now. Of course she wouldn't be there. When I got to Marcy's later in the day, I'd make another call to see if Helen had returned to her home on Mercer Island. And if she wasn't, I intended to keep trying. Wherever she was, sooner or later she had to come home.

But first I wanted to see the one she'd never really left.

CHAPTER 27

HELEN FOREVER

H E DROVE THE Mustang along the road leading to Lock 18, slowly passing the house in the distance. Helen had returned all right; her car was parked close to the lamp-post by the walkway leading to the porch.

He sped up, and in a few minutes went by the shallow lake, with a scrubby islet in the middle. Once when they were young, they swam to the islet and buried a Mason jar of pennies, nickels and a single two-dollar bill. Even when they were much older they still called it Treasure Island.

The Mason jar still had to be there. The thought pleased him.

He passed the ruins of the aqueduct that had carried the old canal over what had not been a lake in the 19th century, but marshlands and a creek.

He didn't want to go all the way to the lock, another half mile ahead, so he turned left on an access road leading to a heavily wooded park that bordered the dry bed of the old canal. On the other side was the bigger, modern one that bore pleasure boats and, less frequently, barges. Trails connected the old to the new, the best one paralleling the latter for miles in either direction. It was about a mile from the access road to the Sommers house, located a little east of where the enlarged canal diverted from its abandoned predecessor.

The park was mostly empty, people having gone home for the dinner hour. He parked the Mustang near a picnic bench, under branches of a beech tree, at a corner of the parking area. From there, beyond the wide strip of cut grass, he could see the canal, the water glistening in the

lowering light. Lawns of homes on the opposite side led down to the canal. He breathed all of it in deeply—freshly mowed lawns, charcoal smoke
drifting over from someone beginning the weekend with a cook-out.

He opened all the car doors, cleaned out the interior, threw the trash
in a nearby litter barrel. All his belongings he'd taken from Fado were
safely in the trunk, including the pages of what Eric had written there,
a kind of *old* testament really. He'd changed his mind, intending to keep
the scroll of pages as proof of his resurrection from a past life, or at the
very least as an artifact. He'd always liked history—hadn't he written his
little book about the Erie Canal and visited the ruins of Hisarlik/Troy and
Ephesus? He planned to start a new book, of course, to record the new
beginning with Lennie.

As he left for the walk, he glanced back at the car with the thought
that this was also new—the Mustang parked here. They'd never taken the
car here or anywhere else close by. Always they'd walked—he, Lennie and
Pete—even when they were old enough to drive. But it was fitting the
Mustang should be here.

The trail back was *mule-side*, all the way. He felt a sense of complete-
ness, knowing that he belonged here, connected to the past every way
you looked, the last of the Fureys in these parts. Those Fureys had come
a long way from County Clare—*you betcha*—packed into steerage across
the Atlantic, just a few out of all the Irish micks recruited straight off the
boat to work the ditch.

The evidence surrounded him, down to the trough of grass through
the trees—all that remained of the cycle of sweat, aches and thirst; then
mud, chill and the steaming breaths of men and horses; then the swel-
tering heat again, through all the seasons of labor. But always there'd be
the promise of the night to come, the few hours of drinking, fucking or
both, before you did it again in the morning with your shovel or pick-axe
still slick with dew or frost, the air fractured with the shouts and curses
of crew bosses.

Now, Lennie would be his fifth season, like he always told her she was.

The Fureys dug, and some of them—like Callan's namesake—did not
move on to the cities or out west. They found homes where they could

along the canal, and stayed to work the boats or drive the teams of mules or draft horses that pulled them. The progression became shovels to tow-lines skimming the canal water. And always the thoughts—as the crickets burred, as you swatted mosquitoes—of the night ahead, and the women from Albany to Buffalo come out to dance by the light of the moon, as the old song fancied.

Oh, it was wild in those days! Often, with only a single lock, you fought for position, and sometimes you did what you had to do to move up, get to the lock first; get to where you had to be—and that included getting to your special one up ahead, before anyone else could claim her for the night, because she wouldn't wait for you; she'd take the first ditchlicker to come along if he was clean and had the silver.

He crossed over to the Lock 18 road, keeping the Sommers home to his right, and kept going past Kenyon, making his way through a con-struction site of half-finished homes set around a cul-de-sac, the hardhats gone for the weekend. This had once been a field where he, Lennie and Pete had played, making jumps for their bikes and catching fireflies on summer evenings like this one. Helen used to call them lightning bugs. You couldn't see them but they were there. They'd be out once it got darker.

Near the canal he paused to wave, as they always had, at a sailboat motoring past, its wake breaking against the canal banks, sail tightly furled around the mast that stretched horizontally for the length of the boat; otherwise you couldn't get past the low bridges.

He read the name on the transom: *Idylling.* The boat was probably the last to go through Lock 18 for the day, to tie up at the little marina closer to town, near Lock 17. You couldn't keep a boat moored along the canal banks, at least not during the day, but you could come and go.

There were homes—he could see several from this vantage point—which were as close to the canal as the Sommers home, the back yards extending to steep stairways leading down to small docks set back from passage lanes of the canal. Lennie's family had no such dock—the side lawn just ended at a fence along the bank. He remembered the three of them sneaking over to these modest docks at night and swimming and giggling in the moonlight, playing 'Crocodile.' He'd first touched the girls' bottoms during one of these games. Even then, Lennie's was rounder and fuller than Pete's.

He walked along the canal-side path, away from town, the sun in his eyes, and stopped when he could see the house through the bordering trees. Her car was still there, parked by the lamp-post. For the next few hours he would keep a vigil until darkness fell—the least he could do after all these years she had kept hers for him.

What was the worst that could happen? He'd see her come out carrying luggage, heading to the airport to fly back to her home on that hump-backed island in the middle of—what were the names? *Mercer Island… Lake Washington.*

No matter if she went back. She thought he was dead. So he'd follow her there. The Mustang would make it. His car looked like hell, but it still had the low miles. Oh, he'd need money to get back, gas prices being what they were. But he knew what to do when he ran low on the moolah. After all, he'd done things he hadn't told her about, even though they'd been necessary, and never mind the story of saving the dolphins near that Turkish resort. A man, young or old, had to survive, didn't he, when he was far from home, any home?

He wouldn't sell the necklace he got in Turkey. He hadn't told Lennie about that either for obvious reasons, since to get it he'd done something neither she nor Pete would have believed him capable of doing.

He'd been saving the necklace to give her. Of course, he hadn't had the chance to give it to her yet. But he'd figure out a story to explain how he'd come to possess it, something she'd believe. He always had. She always believed he was capable of doing anything he wanted—that *passing lane.*

So her leaving tonight wouldn't be the end of the world.

If she didn't leave?

Bed and breakfasts didn't offer dinner, so she'd have to go out for that. When she got back it would be dark, and he'd be waiting for her, sitting on the ole porch swing—he could see it now. All he'd have to do is hold out his hand and say: *I'm back, Lennie…*

Once she saw him that's all he *should* have to say.

She would stop crying after a while, and they'd sit and rock in the swing, holding each other as she kept whispering: *Michael, oh my God…I can't believe it…I can't believe you've come back for me…*

What if she didn't believe him?

Well, *of course* she would believe him.

Who else but her Michael could ever say: *Shhh, it's all right now. I've returned. We're mule-side again, baby. Hey, you been taking care of our dolphins for me, Les Deux?*

Who else but Michael would even know they existed, and where they were and know how to make them move?

She'd believe him, even if…*what?*

Even if she didn't *quite* believe him at first. But she would in time, like the others. Sure, he'd had others while they'd been apart, though he didn't like it that she had, too. After a while his *others* had come to believe he was who he said he was. Of course, Lennie was not like them, not even close…

A car pulled in next to hers now, and a couple got out, stretched. They held hands as they walked toward the porch steps to check into the B&B for the weekend. The woman pointed toward the canal.

Something was bothering him, a thought that shouldn't be nagging him, not now, but already it festered. What if she *didn't* believe him? Not now. Not in three months. Not ever. What if she *never* believed him, never accepted that it was truly him—Michael—who had come back for her after so long a time away?

Could he risk that?

"*No.*" He said it so loudly he looked around to see if anyone had heard him, but there was no one else on the path, no boats on the canal in either direction.

Okay, well…I'll just have to do something about that, if she doesn't believe me…

And do it now.

She wasn't like the others; she was capable of so much more. You don't spend more than half your life seeing someone almost every day, without knowing what she was capable of. At first she might say she believed him,

TwO GRAVES FOR MICHAEL FUREY 317

but only to fool him, bide her time, wait for the opportunity and then—
ffftt—she'd be gone.

That had happened before with another One, and he couldn't bear the
thought of *her* leaving him, going away. Again. She did it once. She could
do it again.

Yup, better to do something about that now...

He remembered that Eric, the one who had died, had a name for a
change of plans: a spin move. He knew all about those too.

All right...what then?

Always he'd thought of something, always. You name it, he got there
first.

What has to happen?

He knew.

*Lennie, you gotta stay canal-side forever. Right here. It's the only way,
baby. I'm here. You're here...*

It made sense. The parents—his and hers—had always worried about
the canal from early on, what could happen, so they'd taught their kids
to swim at an early age. And he'd been the best of them learning at the
municipal swimming pool close to where he lived—about the only thing
they'd ever done close to his crapola house where you couldn't even see
the canal or much of the town either.

So when she was found in the canal, everyone would have to think it
had been something more than an accident, since she was a good swimmer. What else could it be, except a suicide.

They all would say she never did get over what happened at the lake,
poor thing and...*do you know she kept a Mustang, just like the first one,
at a cabin she had way up in the boonies north of Seattle? She came back to
die in a place she loved more than any other. Terrible. But such a gift, don't
you think, to be able to choose your time and place to die?*

He'd drive the Mustang back and fill their cabin with what he would
take from her home on Mercer Island, and she'd have her own wall next
to his, again. And he'd spend his nights starting anew with his own book,
a better one of what *should* have been, just like she'd done with hers.

His search would go on. Hadn't he told her that it wasn't so much the end that mattered but the getting there? How else do you get through all the years it takes to build a canal?

In time he'd find another One to give the necklace to, who would most definitely believe, without a doubt, that he was who he said he was: Michael Furey. He'd give her the pick of names for the child they'd have. And she'd say: *Such lovely names you thought of, Michael! Callan's fine for a boy. But you know, if it's a girl, I like 'Chelan' better than 'Helen'.*

He clapped twice, excited about what he had to do now. He felt he was thinking so clearly, the clearest he had in a long time. It was like he was on a boat in a canal lock, waiting for the water to rise so he could continue on to the next one, then on and on…

Lennie had to die—*finish up the lemonade, baby*—because only she could say to him: *You're not Michael. Michael's dead.*

She'd be so very, very wrong.

The beauty of it? In the new book he'd write, he could resurrect her in the way he wanted.

She, of all people, would understand that sometimes to keep on living you had to die first.

That would be his last gift to her, maybe even more wondrous than the necklace.

Death, like birth, was the penultimate artifact.

Surely in the moment before she died she would understand what he had to do, so they could always be together, perfectly.

He'd tell her she showed him the way.

She'd written that book, one of a kind like her, the drawings so beautifully rendered from nothing more than her memory and imagination and a refusal to accept what had happened. She'd written it about him. Oh, herself too, and Pete, and all the others who brushed their lives, but mostly about him…*Michael.*

Could he do that, too?

Of course he could. Hadn't the Fureys helped dig the ditch? Not a problem. Can of corn. That's what everyone had always said about him: *That Michael Furey, he sets his mind on something, he can do whatever he chooses.*

They always had said it with envy or wonder and sometimes both, with a headshake that meant that maybe it wasn't so fair that one person had a bigger bucket than anyone else to take to the well.

He said aloud: "Can of corn, Lennie."

SHE CAME OUT of the house, a shoulder bag dangling down. He heard the faint rap of the screen door closing, or thought he did. Did it matter?

When he used to wait for her outside, even with the Mustang idling, he could always hear the whack of the screen door closing behind her, and again if Petra was coming too—a sound that decisively signaled the beginning of another summer evening they would share. Sometimes he'd press on the accelerator, gunning all 286 horses under the hood. The day might have been exhausting, working on one of Houser's landscaping crews but then, as now, the sound of the door, the sight of her, seemed to make time speed up. When she wasn't with him, he was often too conscious of the hours to go before he would see her again, and so they passed slowly.

She was dressed for a walk, not departure: jeans, running shoes, a blue T-shirt. Even from here he could see how she filled it out. *So maybe one last time?* He knew secluded places near the aqueduct. After all, they'd used them before, just her—his *mule-city kitty*—and him.

One last time to make the dolphins move?

She had cut her hair short and he remembered now how it got that way and why. She'd tried to kill that Eric. Malloy might have pushed him over the edge, into that chute; but it was really Lennie who killed Eric— and kept Michael alive, when everyone else thought he was dead. And why did she do that?

The answer was so obvious he had to laugh. *Here I am, Lennie!*

Pete had told her the morning after they'd sparred in the storm, she inside and he high up in the tree outside the window: *You two are either going to be married someday or you'll kill each other.*

And Lennie had replied: *Maybe it will be both.*

Well, she had it almost right. What she meant was that they would always be together. It was her turn now to die and *his* turn to keep her alive, always.

She headed straight to the canal path. He didn't move back to conceal himself among the bushes and trees lining the canal path. He knew she wouldn't come this way. They never had before. Always they'd go toward the aqueduct ruins, to where the path widened out into the park, toward Lock 18; or to the dry shallow ditch where the old canal had been, where they used to have foot races and where, until they were fourteen, she invariably bested him.

The sun was in his eyes and he remembered she never liked sunglasses and neither had he. It wouldn't take much time, not with the canal so close by, and no boats in sight. She wouldn't hear him on the path. It would be better if she had something plugged in her ears, like everyone else these days, but that was not his Lennie. He reminded himself that she was strong, though to look at her you wouldn't immediately think that.

He decided to let her get far enough to see the Mustang, turn around, and then he'd appear, blocking her way back to the house. There was nowhere else for her to go once she saw the car. Once he had her, they would jump from the aqueduct, one last time, together he hoped. But if not, then her first, and he would follow, keeping her under, to drown like she always said, *in the raging canal.* Could there be any other reason why she'd come back, to wait for him to return to their special places, so he could take her away to the most secret one of all, that only he would know about?

CHAPTER 28

THE AQUEDUCT

I PARKED NEXT to the sign carved in wood: *The Towpath Bed & Breakfast*. The letters were dark green, matching the trim and shutters of the house. Set against a white background, and below the name: a mule, drover and iconic canal boat.

I was surprised to find the Sommers place was now a business, but maybe the owners would give me a few minutes, share what information they had about the family. Then I'd leave.

No doubt this big house with the third story dormers had been their home. The brass number, 18, gleamed by the door, confirmed it. Someone had just watered the flowers flanking the walk to the wrap-around porch, the soil splotched damply. A guest had left a book and a bottle of water on one of the Adirondack chairs on the porch beyond the swing closer to the front door.

I went in to the tinkle of a bell, shivering a moment with the chill of the air-conditioning. Past the entryway and a side table stocked with tourist brochures was a Dutch-door with a small office behind. To my right a stairway railing curled around a landing. The hallway opened to a large living room dominated by a hearth of gray stone. Magazines fanned out around a vase of flowers on a coffee table set between two couches in front of the hearth. Two paintings flanking the hearth drew me a step into the living room.

Even at a distance it was obvious these weren't prints. One showed a towpath, the two mules, drover and a boat backlit by a setting sun; the other a canal lock of the present day, with three people peering down from a catwalk above the massive, creased gate, surrounded by machinery.

I couldn't see her name but it had to be there, in the lower right hand corner, as it had been in the print at the restaurant in town. Had Helen done them as a gift to the people who now owned her childhood home? How else could they afford these originals in a place like Leary Falls? Given that I knew so little about her, it seemed odd to feel so sure that she had given these paintings as a gift.

"Can I help you?"

I stepped back into the hallway, toward the voice, saw the man leaning over the counter of the office area. He said as I walked over: "I heard someone come in, but then you disappeared."

"I was just looking around—those paintings caught my eye."

He peered over the rims of his reading glasses. "They're quite nice, aren't they? I'm Ken Carruthers, by the way. Pleased to meet you…"

"It's Jim Malloy. And likewise. You have a nice place here. Too bad I found that motel in town first."

Carruthers scratched his beard, one of those Amish-style rigs that frames the jawline. "Well, perhaps tomorrow night, if you're going to be around for the weekend. We should have one or two vacancies, if you can do without a TV in the room. It's an ongoing thing with my partner—Tim thinks those might help business. I don't."

"You have my vote. Does it count if I'm not staying?"

Carruthers winked. "All votes are counted here so long as they match mine."

We chatted a bit more. I told him I was a writer, doing research in the area, then asked him how long he'd had the place.

"Long enough for second thoughts to have come and gone," he said. "We were lucky to find it, though the circumstances were sad."

"How so?"

"Well, we bought it from the woman who did those paintings. Her parents had died in a plane crash—maybe you remember that one, went down near Cancun; just a handful of survivors, one of whom wrote that book. It was terrible—what happened, not the book. I didn't read it, but

Tim saw her on Oprah—we do have a TV in our room here. They were going to Cancun for their anniversary."

Charles and Becky...

How soon before she lost her parents had she lost her boyfriend and sister in the accident?

"That...that's a rough one."

"And then some." He rapped a knuckle on wood. "I never asked her but that's probably why she moved out to Seattle. She's doing okay now, though. Says the rain doesn't bother her a bit, even helps her stay inside, get her painting done."

I was still reeling from that woman's losses; I heard myself asking him what I already knew: "Those paintings in the living room...they're hers?"

"They are indeed. She's very talented. Comes here to stay every year." Carruthers leaned forward. "I suspect it's to make sure we're taking care of the homestead."

"So far so good?"

"I think so, though Tim and I are a little worried. She was here only a few months ago. At least this visit she hasn't said anything about..."

"Wait...she's here *now*?"

"You look like I said something wrong."

"No...not at all. I'm just...surprised. I was thinking how I'd like to meet the one who did those paintings and...she's here."

"As a matter of fact, I think she stepped out—at least I didn't see her come back in. If you'd like to wait, she should be back soon. Probably took a walk by the canal—our guests always like to do that, it's so close, you know." Carruthers smiled. "I could introduce you if you'd like."

"That's okay; thanks anyway. I'd like a walk myself. Maybe I'll see her by the canal."

"It *is* an evening for that."

I was at the door when he called after me: "Mr. Malloy..."

"Yes?"

"I didn't tell you her name."

"That *would* help, wouldn't it?"

"It's Helen. Helen Sommers. She's carrying a shoulder bag—haven't seen her without it since she got here. You see her, you can't miss her.

Tall, lovely woman. Black hair. She always kept it long; at least every time she's been here it's been long, but it's shorter now and whoever cut it in Seattle…well, maybe he had too many Starbuck's espressos. But heavens, don't tell her I said that!"

"Got it."

As I walked past my car, I heard the door open and my name called yet again. "That's her car, I think," Carruthers said, pointing. "So she's probably taking that walk, like we thought."

I waved at him, didn't look back to see if he was still on the porch and maybe wondering why this guy was running to meet a woman whose name he'd just been given.

HE WAITED FOR her among the trees and thick undergrowth along the old canal bed. He couldn't see the Mustang from where he crouched but surely she would be coming from that direction. She had no other way to get back to the childhood home she would never see again.

Besides the night, this was the time of day he liked most, after the sun had set and darkness not yet fallen; when shadows were deep enough to set everything in sharp relief. He'd never been one to confuse brightness with clarity.

He remained hidden even after he saw her; she was too far away. If she saw him now she might run, perhaps make it back to the park, if not Lock 18, where there might be people. He saw none in the immediate area. He frowned, puzzled at her pace—not a leisurely one yet not fast, either. One hand rested on her shoulder bag, the other swung freely.

She must have walked far enough to have seen the red Mustang. If so, wouldn't she at least be walking quickly to get back to the house? Perhaps she *hadn't* seen the car; that had to be it.

He waited.

When she approached the barricaded entrance to the aqueduct, no more than thirty yards away, he rustled through bushes, emerging from his hiding place. Here was the old canal bed. Long ago he would have been walking through chest-high water.

He got fifteen yards before she saw him. She froze: a startled grunt. He thought she'd dart ahead, or back. Instead, she bounded up the edge of the low stone wall bordering the outside rim of the towpath and began climbing the broad, wooden slats of the barricade near a sign: *Aqueduct Unstable—Please Keep Off.*

He and Lennie always ignored that warning, though Pete—ever cautious—always hesitated, as if maybe for once they should heed the warning.

He ran after her, shouting: "Helen, wait! It's me. Michael."

She was at the top of the barricade, straddling it now, swinging her long legs over. The shoulder bag snagged; she quickly freed it.

Too late to pull her off...

No matter. He had her now, could catch her on the other side. In her panic she'd forgotten that there was no place to go beyond. The towpath ended where the middle of the aqueduct had collapsed long ago.

She was making this easy, trapping herself on the grassy berm of the old towpath. If she jumped to one side he'd go after her, as they always used to do, and take care of it in the water.

As he clambered over the barricade, he knew she wouldn't dare go off the other side, into the mess of brambles, bushes and small trees that masked the collapsed ruin of the granite blocks that once supported the canal bed itself, carrying boats over the creek, useful water over useless.

He jumped to the towpath grass, so close now to holding her in his arms one last time before he said goodbye to her, breaking her neck either here or below in the water if she jumped. He didn't run; he didn't have to. She was trapped. He called to her, more softly this time.

"Lennie, it's me. Michael. I've come back for you."

She stopped running, but she wasn't looking back at him to see if it truly was her Michael; and if he had any doubts about what he had to do, they vanished. It seemed as if she was hiding something from him. She couldn't be; her hands were empty.

She stood near the end of the aqueduct's narrow, grassy towpath and *still* didn't look back at him. After all they had shared, after all the miles he'd traveled to return to her, she had turned her back to him. She was spurning him. She had decided he didn't exist after all, that he wasn't who he said he was.

Over time and distance she'd changed, like they all had changed.

Here was proof she'd never been worthy of the necklace.

He saw no one on the water to his left. He glimpsed a house on the far shore, but it was too distant for anyone there to see what was about to happen here.

Now...

ONE MOMENT THERE was no one in sight, no sound except for crickets, nothing on the bed of the old canal that curled away from the new.

Then, a man emerged from the trees and brush to my right, thirty yards ahead. His back was to me. He began walking fast, as if he'd just done something worse than piss in the bushes, and headed toward a barricade blocking what looked like a ruined old bridge.

Even when I saw Helen on a course along the path that would intersect with the man, it still didn't fully register that this was Caster—until I heard him shout: "Helen, wait. It's me. Michael."

She ran to the barricade, climbing over. Caster was at the barricade quickly, scrambling over too, holding no gun or knife. Or did he have something in his pocket?

I sprinted toward the barricade and the sign—*Aqueduct Unstable— Please Keep Off*—and climbed up stone blocks splayed out at the entrance. I swung around the end of the thing—it was a long way down—and back onto the granite edge of the grassy towpath. Caster was fifteen yards ahead; Helen twenty beyond that, her back to him, as if resigned to her fate. We were all facing in the same direction.

I didn't call out, not wanting to lose the surprise and have him pull a weapon out from a pocket as I closed on him. He should have heard me, but he was focused on Helen. He weighed the air with outstretched hands—*what are you doing?* Then: "Lennie, it's me. Michael. I've come back for you."

I ran full bore at him. He heard me at the last moment, spun around. I caught him below the waist as he turned, lifted him off his feet, driving him into the ground so hard my hands popped off him. I slid over him, knuckles crunching into the stone border of the towpath—and scrambled up, screaming at Helen to run.

She didn't.

Caster rose now—one knee then the other. She lost her chance to escape. I'd forgotten how big he was, those hands. I kept it tight, snapping off punches, but not at his head—I'd break my hand. He shifted quickly for a man his size, blocking the punches with his arms. I had to tie him up, keep him on me so Helen could get away. He kept moving sideways, feinting a punch, then kicked high. I was zeroed in on his hands; I didn't expect him to use his legs, not with those hammers.

He kicked me so hard in the gut I lost air, fell back toward the stone rim again, one arm flailing in the air over the edge. Caster went for a leg to topple me over.

I was about to roll into him, grab anything I could, take him with me, but he turned toward Helen when she screamed the name: *"MICHAEL!"*

She stood behind him, the flap of her shoulder bag open now. He reached out as she fired the gun—a single *crack*…

His head jerked back. A hand rose to his forehead, as if there was a mosquito bite and not the dark, neat hole above his right eye. I felt the kick of a foot at my side—his reflexive intent to push me over the edge. The kick had no force. He tripped over me. I grabbed his twisting body, heard the lesser crack of his knees hitting the stone. Still kneeling, he toppled over the edge. I heard the closer yet faint thud of gun to grass a moment before the louder splash below.

CHAPTER 29
THE CORNER ROOM

HELEN SANK TO her knees, hands quivering at her mouth. I kneeled next to her, my chest heaving, heart galloping. The taint of the gunshot lingered in the air. She dropped her hands to her lap, the fingers still tinged red in places; it hadn't been that long since Fado.

"Jimmy…"

I gathered her in, her tremors mingling with mine. A siren wailed in the distance but it couldn't be for us, so soon. The shaking—hers and mine—gradually subsided. Crickets resumed their burring.

There had been only the one shot, the snapping of a branch. If guests had been on the porch swing at the house, savoring the evening, they would have heard it distantly—perhaps a neighbor's kid using up the last firecracker from the Fourth.

We didn't move. A light winked on in one house across the water, then another.

I suppose we were waiting for the stabs of flashlights, sounds of anyone at the barricade.

No one came, nor did sounds of splashing and groaning from below. He'd fallen near the end of the towpath. We could have gone down to make sure, pushing through the tangle of bushes and trees on the shore, climbing over stony debris, and then swimming out to the far arch right below us. Perhaps we should have. We didn't; not in the gathering darkness, not now.

When we finally got up, my foot nudged the gun. I picked it up carefully, muzzle down.

"I didn't miss him this time," Helen whispered. "I know I didn't."

As we began walking slowly toward the barricade, she said: "I didn't miss him, did I?"

"No."

"We don't need it anymore, but don't...let's not get rid of it...not yet."

"We won't leave it here."

I climbed over the barricade more carefully than she did, since I had the gun. I assumed we were going back to the house. She touched my arm, gesturing the other way. "The car's this way," she said.

"You didn't drive here."

"He did. Across the country. I saw it...before."

The Mustang was parked in a far corner of the park alongside the canal, the only car in the area. Lights shone from homes fronting the other side of the canal. Music drifted over: Billy Joel's *Piano Man*.

We couldn't leave the Mustang here, an abandoned car near where the body of a man would be found, sooner or later; a man who hadn't just ignored the warning and fallen to his death from the aqueduct—not with a bullet hole over an eye. Even if we stripped the plates there was a good chance the Mustang could be traced to one Helen Sommers, of Mercer Island, Washington, who happened to be staying very close to where the bloated corpse of the man was found, along with...the keys to the Mustang.

"Helen, we forgot; we're going to have to go back and get the keys from him."

"I've got the spare set," she said, next to me at the car's driver's side. She dug into her shoulder bag. I heard the faint clinking, then: "Shit," she said. "I dropped them."

I found them first, unlocked the driver's side. She pushed away my hand when I offered the keys to her.

"You drive. I can't...I don't want to even get in..."

"You don't have to. I'll take the car somewhere far from here, meet you back at the house."

"No…no, it's all right."

The interior reeked of his sweat, and coffee. I leaned over to let her in. We both rolled down the windows. I slotted the key in the ignition—on the second attempt.

I drove slowly, couldn't have done it any other way.

The keys were a spare set from the cabin. She said she hadn't intended to go back but she got a call at home from a friend from Pattison who was in town with her husband for a Mariners'game. She got a ride back to the cabin with them, and gave her the best story she could think of to explain why she'd left her car there. Barbara Hollner winked at her husband and said something about a nice young man, a writer who wanted to do an article about her…and was that his Explorer by the cabin?

I told her I went back too, that we must have just missed each other—and Caster. And why I came here trying to find her, or someone who could tell me where she was.

"He took everything there," Helen said. "Maybe it's all in the trunk."

It was the book—the big one I saw on her lap as we were leaving Fado with Robert—that led her to think Caster would go to Leary Falls.

"He read it," she said. "He read all of it, and he *remembered it*. He remembered *everything* on those pages."

"You knew he'd follow you here…"

"I couldn't come back here believing he wouldn't."

"The gun?"

"Buffalo. I flew to Buffalo. It took me most of a day and six pawnshops to even pay for the name of someone in Tonawanda who sold me a gun on the spot, no questions asked. I've been waiting for him, hoping he wouldn't show up—and hoping he would."

"So was I. Looking for him, I mean, in Seattle, even before I came up there looking for Sean."

"You'll tell me?"

"Yeah, but let's do what we have to do with…Michael's car."

"You know it's not…you know what happened?"

"I know."

"It was a long time ago…"

She said it in such a way that she thought I might think she was crazy. I didn't.

"Maybe too long ago," she added.

"Helen… maybe sometimes that isn't enough," I said, thinking of my brother, too.

BY THE TIME we pulled up in front, I had told her how I knew about Michael and Petra.

How many times had he done this with her—the love of her life, and she his—the young man who, long dead, had saved my life when she called out his name on the aqueduct?

There came a moment when I imagined a curtain to be pulled aside and, within, Charles or Rebecca Sommers saying to the other: *It's Helen. They're back.*

A few lit windows spotted her darkened home—guests or Ken Carruthers and his partner in their inn-keeper's room

In the trunk we found two Washington State apple boxes filled with Michael's things and brought them up to her room on the third floor. Then we went back down again to take care of the Mustang.

She said she'd follow me in her car. It didn't matter where we were going to abandon it, so I just drove through town, turning left at the fork of Routes 5 and 167, toward Dolgeville—for no other reason than the name seemed familiar. Then I remembered.

I'd always used a bigger bat, an Adirondack. Coach V thought my hands were sometimes too quick, and a heavier bat would slow them down, help me stay back on the ball for the breaking stuff.

Dolgeville was only six or seven miles, but far enough away from the aqueduct, or so we hoped. I drove past the Rawlings/Adirondack bat factory off McKinley Avenue, turned right onto a side street and parked. I used my locking pen knife to unscrew the plates, wondering why I hadn't thought of the knife, small as it was, out there on the aqueduct.

Helen drove around the block. I got into her rental, put the plates on the floor. I'd thought of taking the keys to the Mustang, but decided to leave them in the ignition. She said when she got back to Seattle, she would report the Mustang as stolen. But a car like that, even in its condition, would probably be stolen again, and wind up in someone's garage, another secret to be fixed up like new, over time.

BACK AT THE house she parked next to my car. We walked to the porch, as if we'd done this many times before, as if we'd already decided about that on the way. We hadn't, though the need to be together for one night at least, had been a third companion in the car. She talked about her sister; I talked about mine, how I would be driving to Albany the next day to tell Marcy about Sean.

The bell didn't jingle. Perhaps Ken and Tim disengaged it for the night. This wasn't a motel, after all, with all-night clerks. The carpeted stairs still creaked in places: Helen, no doubt, remembered every spot from the times when she sneaked into her home after being out too late with Michael Furey. For a moment I wondered about Petra. Would she have winked—the co-conspirator—and left for another room?

A dormer made the third floor corner room seem bigger than it was. They'd painted the walls a light blue, with a darker blue spread on the four-poster. The Mohawk Valley pastorals were not Helen's. Earlier we'd put the apple boxes on the dormer's padded ledge.

She didn't leave the light on very long. There was an overstuffed chair in the corner between the dormer and window with an air conditioner. On the side table, next to a reading lamp, lay her book, as if she had been reading it before. There was enough light from outside for me to see the title—*The Book of Michael*—and a Celtic motif on the cover.

The room was hot. Helen turned on the air-conditioner. As it hummed to life she sat on the end of the bed, facing the chair, but not in total darkness. Light seeped through the window from two spotlights illuminating the B&B's sign near the cars. The illumination was enough to cast a pale nimbus around her. I sat in the chair and for a while we sat there in silence, until she began telling me about this house, that the room we were in had always been closed off after a while, to save money on heating.

"The whole third floor was," she said. "I don't know why my parents bought such a big house. I think maybe they wanted to have more children, try for a son or two, but that never happened. The place was pretty rundown when we got it, with all sorts of stories about its past, the old rooming house close by the canal. Dad liked the price, and Petra and I liked the stories.

"She and I would come up here, sometimes with Michael when we were younger, and we'd make up stuff; it was easy to do way up here, with everyone else way downstairs."

She shifted on the bed. "That's all I was doing with the book over there—what we all had done before. I was going to work on it some at the cabin."

"You said he had read it."

"Yes, but he just didn't *read* it. He *recited* it back to me from memory—entire pages. I couldn't do that and I wrote it. And he didn't stop there. He thought—did you hear him keep saying Michael's name—that he'd come back for me. My God, did he really *believe* he was Michael?"

"He must have at the end. If you hadn't said Michael's name, made him truly believe for one instant…"

"It just came out."

"Well, I'm sure as hell glad it did, for the both of us."

"Jimmy…"

"Yeah?"

"I need you here, for a while…is that all right? I can understand if… well, this room is pretty crowded, isn't it?"

I reached out for her hand and soon, together on the bed we turned away from the window. She lay on her side, and I behind her, arm draped over her. She took the hand, snugged it tightly under her breasts.

She was right, the room was crowded, yet quiet enough to hear the faint conversation in the adjacent one. That ceased after a while, giving way to the white noise of the air-conditioner.

"Your book, then…you kept them alive."

"I had to. But I didn't know it until my parents sent me away after the accident. They had me on a suicide watch before they decided to send me to a place near Geneva, in the Finger Lakes. It wasn't even on the lake but they called it the Shorewood Institute. I was there for three months. Part of the therapy was keeping a journal. The girl in the room next to mine just smeared shit over the pages of hers.

"What began with a journal became something more, a kind of life-line that seemed like the only way I could surface again—to make believe it hadn't happened."

"That probably wasn't what they had in mind when they said that writing about it could help."

I felt her nod. "I'm sure they thought I'd come there in one basket and left in another," she said. "Their name for it was functional delusion, something like that. I didn't care. I'd found a place I could go to—for an hour, a day, a weekend—where I could believe Michael and Petra and I were living out our lives, like we were supposed to.

"Outside of that place you live with what you *have*. You have your friends, you have lovers. You pay your bills, do your work, swear at idiots using cell phones when they drive, you vote the clowns out of office though the circus remains the same.

"Sometimes I've thought I was lucky, and sometimes I thought I was really fucked up. But either way I've always had that place to go to, for years; page after page, sketch after sketch. Some of it are things that happened, and some that didn't but I wished to Christ they had. I kept adding pages to that book, one that would never have an ending."

She said no more for a few moments. Then: "You said you were looking for him…in Seattle."

"I'd still be looking if Sean hadn't seen him first."

"It wasn't just your brother…"

"No, Caster did something before, that Sean knew about. He found him first…and you."

"So one led to the other. What—would you mind telling me what it was?"

I did. Everything: Katie, that night, Beverly Curtiss, and back to my brother.

"I'm sorry," she whispered. Then she asked me if I would tell her about what Katie had been like, where we met. I told her about the phone number written on the baseball. I told her more than I thought I would.

"I think I would have liked her," Helen said.

She fell asleep not long after that. She had to be as tired as I was. But I couldn't get to sleep, not yet. The room was still so crowded—with what we'd done out there—and hadn't; with all that she'd told me, and I her; with Michael Furey and with Katie.

Katie used to hum a song, frequently enough that I finally asked her about the words. She seemed embarrassed to tell me what they were, but finally she did, after we'd known each other for a few months. It was an old Chad Mitchell song. She said her Aunt Jean used to play it a lot. The melody was gone but the words came back to me now:

I have a quiet room…a room nobody can see…a secret place…that's all my own…and only I have the key. Sometimes I sit in my lonely room… and think how fine it would be…if you could come to my quiet room…and share its treasures…with me…

"Without a doubt you would have liked her," I said, not knowing whether I was talking to Katie or Helen.

I WOKE UP thirsty during the night, and cupped water from the sink in the bathroom down the hall. Someone snored in a nearby room. Back in ours, I turned on the reading lamp by the chair, waiting for the light to wake her but Helen remained asleep. It occurred to me she might have left it there for me to read.

The Book of Michael was big as an atlas in my lap, with thick paper that gives such fine weight to the whole; makes you feel it's no small thing to turn the page. I wondered at what point, after her stay at the Shorewood Institute, she decided to transfer what she had begun there, to this. And if she'd kept her parents alive somewhere in the pages.

I had no trouble reading her handwriting; it flowed precisely as calligraphy. She'd used black ink, without the benefit of lines on the paper:

What if one of us had to make a choice that Friday in July, when dolphins swam in Lake Shendego? That is the one thing we've never talked about since, because there should have been the three of us, together, as always…

CHAPTER 30
ARTIFACTS

THE ROOM WAS steeped in gray pre-dawn light before I finished *The Book of Michael*.

Helen had made a wondrous, beautiful work of art from something many of us do to one extent or another I suppose: try to replace what has been lost or reconfigure the past. They're pretty much the same thing.

I got up to put the book back where she'd left it on the table by the bed—and saw her lying on her side, looking at me.

"How long have you been awake?" I said.

"For a while."

I put the book on the table. "I hope you don't mind."

Helen shook her head and got up from the bed. We held each other for a long time before we kissed, and longer still before we began to undress one another. We swayed a little, amid the debris of our clothing. I thought of things to whisper to her. Perhaps she did too. Neither of us said a word.

I lifted her up; she did the rest, hooking her legs behind me, guiding me into her. She moaned as loudly as I did, pulling her in deeply, as close as could be. She lay her head at my shoulder, arms wrapped tightly around my neck, fingers dug into my back.

We slowly turned as we kissed—once, twice—a carousel of two, and ended up at the edge of the bed. I put her down gently, and that's when I saw the delicate chain circling her ankle—gold, silver? And something attached to it.

"Pull it off," she whispered.

"Helen…"

"Please do it."

I did—a quick yank—and gave the chain to her. When her hand came back it was empty.

She turned on her belly, raising herself up, and brought her hands back, fingers sliding over tattoos of dolphins that faced each other below the dimples of her bottom.

She parted herself, and before I entered her, I glazed first my fingers then my lips and tongue with her wetness.

The dolphins shuddered with our collisions.

I NEVER LEFT her; we were careful to make sure I wouldn't slip out of her. Maybe she, too, believed that's the closest thing to a home, to perfection, that there can ever be. I kissed her, everywhere I could reach. She kept my hands curled in hers. I could feel her breaths on them, and maybe that was why I fell asleep after she did.

The last thing I remembered was rocking gently with her, and the moistness of her hair, the moisture in the vale between her breasts where she cradled my hand in hers, as if that was something necessary for the dreams ahead.

I WOKE TO an empty bed, heard the door closing, and thought she was going to the bathroom down the hall. I must have drifted off again, but not too deeply because I was waiting to her to come back. She didn't. I glanced at my watch: 11:20.

The boxes were gone on the dormer ledge, in their place a piece of paper. In the chair where I'd read *The Book of Michael* was a plastic bag with handles.

I got up to read the note but before I did, I looked out the window and saw her talking to Ken Carruthers as he watered flowers along the path. One of the boxes was at her feet, the other by her car.

They talked for another minute—perhaps she was alerting him to my presence up in her room—and hugged. She picked up the box and walked the short way to her car.

From our different vantage points, Ken Carruthers and I watched her drive away. I doubted he was surprised that Helen Sommers had taken to her bed the stranger who admired her paintings. But I wondered what Helen said to him about the boxes she hadn't had when she arrived.

I unfolded the note—a piece of paper she'd creased and ripped neatly from her book; there had been empty pages at the end.

Jimmy,

Last night was ours, too. I'll never forget it and not just because it was the last time I'll be back here. You're home now; close enough I guess. I have to go back to mine and do something there with what remains, now that it's all over; something I probably should have done a long time ago. Well, that's hindsight; what my mother called the devil's wisdom, and she wasn't even religious.

I'm sorry to leave that bag on the chair for you to do something with, to leave that up to you. I didn't even want to touch it again.

Take care of yourself. That sounds so—I don't know what it sounds like—but I mean it. Please do that. If you ever get out to Seattle—you know, for Sean—give me a call, and we'll make that happen, one way or the other.

Helen

I didn't look in that plastic bag—not in the room—but I took it with me to the car when I left, with Helen's note tucked in my pocket.

I DROVE TO the parking area from where we'd driven away in the Mustang. It was just past noon and there were plenty of people about. A canal tour boat was filled with more. As it passed I could hear a guide with a microphone talking about the now extinct wonder of the canal that had once linked the settled East to what passed for the West in those days. He pointed in the direction of the aqueduct, relating how many of those had been constructed, and asked the folks to imagine, beyond the ruins, what it must have been like to ride a boat on the water, over water.

The guide pointed to where Caster had to be dead, his body snagged against the base of the aqueduct that had proven stable enough for Helen—for us both—to finish what had begun for me when I came home that night, another Friday, and saw Katie for the last time.

I could have gone into the dense tangle of trees, bushes and stony debris underneath the aqueduct, to make sure, but Caster *was* dead. I saw the bullet hole above his eye.

The guide's narration receded as the canal boat moved on, and I hoped now for another recession: the song Caster made Katie sing before he murdered her. Scarcely a day had passed since I heard it the first time that I didn't hear it again in my mind.

I couldn't tell you why I lingered in the park. If Caster hadn't been dead—if I'd mistaken that fatal wound in the twilight—he would have come to the house in the night, or waited for us somewhere the next day.

Still, he'd survived once before. So perhaps I was waiting for *him*, just to be sure: another vigil like my brother's to make sure Helen would be safe. Or perhaps it was simply a matter of doing something with what she had put in that plastic bag, which now lay on the seat next to me.

A family of three passed by on the trail, heading toward the aqueduct. The father pointed at the sign. The child, a boy, broke free, seeing something that had caught his attention in the water. But it was only a Frisbee someone must have skimmed too far out for recovery and now had floated back to shore.

The boy hooted with delight at his prize—a boy much younger than Helen's child would have been had she not lost it. Some of what she'd written had happened, she'd said; and some hadn't. Yet I believed she *had* been carrying Michael Furey's child and she'd lost it. She never would have given it up for adoption. After what had happened, there seemed little doubt that a miscarriage was the truth, and that he and Petra had never known she'd been pregnant.

But in *The Book of Michael* she'd never lost the child or the father, and they had all been together for that race, the four of them, on the peat-black water of Doon Lake in County Clare.

THE NECKLACE I took from the half-cent plastic bag had the weight—and intrinsic worth to me—of a tablespoon, as it must have had for Helen; as it would have been for Katie had not Eric Lane Caster wore her down, twisted her into someone else before he killed her. It had to be the same one I'd seen her wearing on that bed, as she sang a song in the last moments of her life.

I felt like throwing it in the canal, this thing of gold ribbon, pearls and emeralds, ages old, and no doubt worth on the antiquities market the price of a down payment on a house much bigger than I'd ever lived in or ever would. Few people could ever have in their possession something worth so much and desire so little.

I didn't throw it in the canal. Caster had stolen it from somewhere and there were undoubtedly people to whom it would have historical significance. As I put it back in the plastic bag I decided to send it anonymously to some museum and let curators squabble over its provenance. There was no doubt about the provenance of the other thing in the bag.

Helen said he'd written it. He'd rolled up the pages in a thick cylinder, as if he'd liked the idea of an ancient scroll. He'd tied a hard knot of twine in the middle. I slid it off, uncurled the pages.

All I had to read was the title on the first page—*The Book of Eric*—to guess that he had read Helen's first, and for some reason felt compelled to mimic hers, in an obscene attempt to match what he had read.

I've seen yours, now you will see mine…

Was that what it was?

His handwriting was nothing like Helen's, but it was surprisingly legible given the circumstances.

Circumstances? He'd tied up Helen and Sean before he began writing, both of them knowing what was going to happen when he finished. But Robert Tiphook showed up and he never did.

There were no lines through words, no mistakes. It was as if Caster had been merely copying what someone else dictated, whispered to him over his shoulder, hour after hour.

I READ IT IN ONE.

After two more, I'd passed the exit I would have taken to get to my sister's, and I kept heading east on I-90.

Because now I knew that I'd been wrong about hearing only the one voice in my house the night I saw Katie for the last time. Maybe only Caster had spoken so that was why I hadn't heard someone else; maybe it was my panic and fear and rage that masked the other's voice. But there had been another man with Eric Lane Caster that night: his brother Kurt, who lived in a red house where they had taken Katie.

CHAPTER 31
FATHER AND SON

IBOUGHT A copy of the *Berkshire Eagle* in Nuzzo's General Store in South Linfield, Massachusettes. The town, tucked in the southwest corner of the state, was typical enough for these parts: quaint shops, a village green, a few monuments and white-steepled churches. Cars crowded the area around the larger of the two—a Saturday afternoon wedding in progress.

I drove a mile out of town, pulled over near a sign with an arrow indicating the direction of The Taconic School, waited for a few cars to pass, and opened the trunk to get the gun. I put the gun on the passenger seat, the newspaper over it. I was getting close now, and the gun had to be where I could get it easily, not in the trunk.

I had the town. I had the private school where, according to what Caster wrote in the *Book of Eric*, his brother Kurt worked as a groundskeeper and maintenance guy. Caster had also mentioned that Kurt could walk to work. That meant that Byron Road and the red house where they lived—had taken Katie—couldn't be too far from the school.

It wasn't.

Byron Road branched off from the wider road—the two lane highway leading out of the town—less than a mile past the entrance to the private school. Caster hadn't given a number for the house, just its color. And there it was, about thirty yards from the road. I saw no cars in back of me and I slowed, pulling off to the shoulder. There was no house on the other side of the loose stone wall to my right, just swells of fallow fields.

The late afternoon sun burnished another field and trees on a ridge-line beyond the property. Shrubs and bushes shrouded the front porch almost to the roof line. On the side of the faded red house a deck, filled with junk, jutted out from a second-story door.

Where had they kept Katie? In the room whose shutter-less window looked out over the front porch? On the DVD there had been a window, the hint of snow falling, and a tree in the distance. There was a maple in the front yard. Or had Katie's window looked out to the back?

As I slowly drove on I could see more trees in the back, and a child's swing set that looked like it hadn't been used in a long time. Not far away, a small RV canted toward a partially collapsed barn. Patches of grass and weeds grew in the middle of a gravel driveway that curled around to the back, the rear of a car just visible.

Someone was inside.

A pickup truck slowed behind me. I pulled over to let it pass and moved on, but not far. Looking back at the red house I knew where I'd have to go, to wait for Caster's brother. His car, an old Ford Taurus, was about ten yards from the rear door, the RV another twenty from the car. I had no intention of going up to the house now, nor at night. I had to get him when he was away from the house, surprise him on his way to his car or from it, to see he had nothing in his hands.

There was only one thing that had to happen before I killed him: he had to see me. I didn't know what he looked like. But he knew me. He and his brother had watched Katie's and my house in Delmar, seen me go in with her, charting the rhythms of our days.

That night he had seen me inside. All I needed was that one moment of recognition—my face, my name, or both; that moment when he would realize I'd come for him.

Hey Kurt, remember what you and your brother did to Katie Walsh? Remember me?

He might break for the house or car. It didn't matter if needed more than the one shot that killed his brother. I had enough chambered rounds in the gun Helen used.

Farther up the road, out of sight of Kurt's house, I found a place where I could leave my car, walk back and hide between the barn and RV. There was enough light left. If it didn't happen today then tomorrow morning.

I drove on for a few more miles, to make sure there was no other red house.

There wasn't. This was the one, close by the school. This was where Kurt and his brother had taken Katie, raped her for months, then killed her. Yes, Caster had written about another house somewhere in the Berkshires, where she had been buried. But this one was Kurt's, and he'd been in mine to switch the DVD.

COMING BACK I slowed when I saw him walking toward his car with a slight limp. He carried a yellow plastic jerry can—water for a leaking radiator? I didn't get a good look at him before he got in the car, but he was a big man, though not his brother's size.

If he was carrying water for his car that could mean he'd be driving for a distance. The day's heat still lingered. I decided to follow him, having missed one chance now that he was leaving the house before I could set myself up as I'd planned. If I stayed with him perhaps another, better opportunity might present itself elsewhere. And I didn't know how long he might be gone. If I was careful, following him eliminated the risk of staying in the immediate vicinity and having someone notice and remember a new white car that seemed to be loitering near the house where a man was shot to death.

He turned right. I gave him distance, settling in for what I had assumed would be a longer drive.

It wasn't.

Within a minute he turned left into the drive of the school down the road. I slowed but had to go past the entrance and a green and white sign: *The Taconic School. Founded in 1907.* What was he doing here on a late Saturday afternoon?

If the boarding school had a summer program in session, it wasn't evident by the empty playing fields to either side of the winding drive. There may have been a few people in the school's buildings on this summer weekend, but those buildings were far in the distance, closer to the high, forested hills beyond.

I made a U-turn up the road, and as I approached the entrance I made the decision. The grounds were deserted. There was no one on the football field or the field house beyond. Trees lined the school's drive farther up and spread out as the lane branched off to the various campus buildings, where a security guard—maybe two—would be.

He had parked his Taurus on the right side of the drive, about a hundred yards from the road, near a stone bridge which seemed more a portal to the school since it spanned no creek I could see.

I figured I'd need two shots to make sure, even at such a short range— no more than the width of the drive. The shots would echo, but by the time anyone looked out from a building, I'd be long gone. A car passing at just the time I killed Kurt Lampron? I'd take my chances.

I drove slowly, close enough now to see him leaning into the car, one knee on the seat, getting something; close enough to see the bumper sticker on the rear fender: *Mac-Haydn Theater. Chatham, NY.*

Kurt the actor, the stage-hand, the clapper.

He backed out of the car. I drove on, deciding to turn around up ahead, do that first, and come back. I'd then be closer, driver's side, so that after I shot him I wouldn't have to take the time to turn the car around.

Near the stone bridge I looked in the rear-view mirror to see him walking from the Taurus, carrying the yellow jerry can. I turned the car around in the empty parking lot of the Henry C. Mills Alumni Center and drove on a ways before stopping. From this distance, should anyone glance out a window, all he or she would be able to note—and remember—was the color of the car, not the make or license.

I slid the newspaper off the gun underneath, checked it one last time. At the bridge again I kept the gun in my lap, the muzzle pointing toward the driver's side door handle. It would take only a few seconds to fire through the open window at Caster's brother, the amateur summer-stock actor, who loved his home movies, and one in particular.

They're gonna put me in the movies/they're gonna make a big star outta me…

He stood by a few saplings staked not far from the far end of the stone bridge. There was a metal plaque set on low wooden posts between the young birches. A wooden bench completed the rough semi-circle. He paused from watering the trees when I stopped the car in the middle of the drive, put it in park. His car was up ahead, on my left. He couldn't see my right hand bringing the gun up just shy of the bottom of the open window.

He stood there with the jerry can of water in one hand, twenty feet away, squinting with the lowering sun, looking right at me now: Eric Lane Caster's brother.

He was old enough to have been my father.

Caster had been late-thirties, give or take. Kurt was at least twenty years older than that. Deep creases lined the narrow face. He didn't have much hair in front. The long sideburns were gone to gray.

Why hadn't I noticed his age before? A trick of fading light? Distance? Or just seeing what I wanted to see—the man who took turns with his brother raping Katie.

What I saw now was a man pushing sixty who gave no indication he'd recognized me.

He went back to watering the last of the three birch saplings, doing it a lot more slowly than he had to, as if wanting to prolong the process.

I lowered the gun, the muzzle now resting on my left thigh, still pointing at him as I waited for him, the actor, to remember me any second now, the pretense abandoned because he had the summer stock playhouse bumper sticker, he lived in South Linfield, Massachusetts in the red house on Byron Road, close enough to walk to work at the school…

It was all in that plastic bag on the floor of the car: Caster's *Book of Eric*.

And it was all wrong.

All wrong? Or just some of it?

I put the gun on the seat, covered it with the newspaper again, and got out of the car. He heard the car door close, glanced at me as I approached to have a closer look at the inscription on the plaque:

In Memory of Kurt Califf
Class of '05

"Did you know my son?" he said.

When he spoke, I was thinking about the East Hampton mansion belonging to a man named Califf who had a secret hoard of priceless antiquities; who'd bought for his wife a son named Kurt—and what Jacob Califf's real name was, if he even existed.

I said: "I met him only once, but it was enough for me to want to find him again. I was… told he worked here at the school."

"He did. The new fellow doesn't keep the fields as good as Kurt did. They liked him a lot, the kids here." He pointed at the memorial. "It was good of them—they didn't have to do that. People think they're all spoiled brats, a school like this, but that's only a few."

"You live around here?"

"We did but just me now, down the road—he used to eat his lunch here in the good weather, keep an eye on things; you know, what he still had to do for the afternoon. Sometimes I'd walk over and take my lunch with him."

"I'm Jim Malloy," I said, and shook the hand of the man I was going to kill only a few minutes before.

"Jordan Califf. Sorry," he said. "That was a little wet."

"Not a problem."

"Name doesn't ring a bell, but then Kurt had a lot of friends, always did."

"Like I said, I only met him once." I nodded at the plaque. "Would you mind me asking what happened to your son?"

He put the jerry can down. "I'm guessing you're not local."

"Albany. I've been away for a while."

"Albany, hunh? Kurt used to go over there for the weekend sometimes. That's where it happened; north of there, anyway. Saranac Lake. The four of them went up there. Kurt and his girlfriend; his sister. They did a lot of things together, even walked to work here and before that the bus stop for grade school. She worked in the library here. This place is kind of a family affair."

"You said there were four?"

"There was the man my daughter was seeing. They all went up for some camping, bowhunting—this guy was into it too, like Kurt was. Only one of them came back—my daughter."

He picked up the jerry can. "Now, why don't you tell me why you really came here. I thought I was all done with the reporters, leastways the fellow from the *Eagle*."

"I'm not a reporter."

"Hope not because if you want to talk to my daughter, that's not going to happen. Lissa's in a safe place, where he can't find her, like she said he'll try to do. He can try me, but he won't get it out of me."

"Which name did he use with all of you—Richard Lampron or Eric Lane Caster or Shadden?"

Jordan Califf stared at me as I turned to go back to the car. When I returned he was sitting on one side of the bench. I sat down on the other—and put the necklace in between us.

"My daughter used to wear that—where'd you get it?—from Lampron?"

I nodded. "She's safe now. There's only one way I could have gotten that. Do what you want with it—give it to a museum, sell it, throw it away."

"You're saying he's dead?"

I looked him straight in the eye: "Yes."

"You?"

"I was there."

The necklace made no more of a sound than an empty fast-food container would have when he brushed it off the bench.

"For a moment there—when you went off to your car—you looked like you were going to be sick."

"It's better now."

"Lissa will want to know how you came to be here, and so do I."

I told him.

Then he took his turn, as the twilight deepened down here below the hills that still caught the last light of the day. He said he had to walk, said his leg stiffened up with too much sitting. So we walked up to the school and then around the fields.

IT WAS KURT who met him first, got talking to him at a tavern in Great Barrington, noticing first the tattoo which the man—who introduced himself as Richard Lampron—said he'd gotten in Amsterdam on leave from his unit based in Germany. He was an intelligence officer, or so he claimed. Kurt was into bowhunting, his father having taught him, but after he'd hurt his leg he couldn't go out with his son. But this guy, Lampron, was into it too, had done some bowhunting out west. He'd come back to live in the area, convenient for business he had in Boston and New York, though he never elaborated on what that business was. He said he'd bought an old farmhouse and five acres from an old lady.

Lampron and Kurt went out hunting a few times, probably where they shouldn't have. The man had money, that was for sure—at least he drove a car that cost more than Kurt made in a year cutting the grass of the playing fields, marking the lines, doing maintenance, working as a stage hand for school productions. And even that wouldn't cover it; you had to throw in what Lissa also made acting in various theaters in the area during the summer season. They were close, these two Califf children.

Lissa met Lampron at one of theaters. Soon enough, Jordan Califf saw something with his daughter that he'd never seen with the other boys she brought home, a kind of "sunrise" in her eyes, he said. Lampron said he'd briefly taught history at some college; and he talked like it, for sure, though he never named the college.

Still, something didn't add up for Califf. Maybe it was the bizarre tattoo and that burn mark on his face that he said he got fighting wildfires in California a few years after his stint in the army. At first he said that he had a girlfriend, then one day announced they'd broken up; said he'd done it for Lissa. He told her she was the one he'd been looking for all his life, and he'd been plenty of places.

Califf always wondered where this ex-army guy got his money but Lampron never divulged that. Lissa didn't care. When you're a 24 year-old woman and a lot of money is being spent on you, you don't always persist in asking where it comes from. He gave Lissa a pendant that had to be worth a year of her salary, explaining that he'd gotten into antiquities in Europe, where he stayed on briefly after the military.

And on a trip to Cape Cod he showed her a necklace he said he was going to give her as a wedding present. He even bought Kurt a new Black Widow, a traditional recurve bow, top of the line. The gifts made Jordan

Califf uneasy, but then when he needed help with medical bills, Lampron took care of those.

As far as Califf knew, Lissa never went over to his home—Lampron said it was getting remodeled. But the two would go to New York to see plays, or up to Lake George, staying at expensive places. She was smitten, bowled over by her luck, certain this guy was the one. He certainly kept telling her she was. She wanted to finally leave the house she'd grown up in. She wanted a life of her own—which was fine. But she wanted to spend it with Richard Lampron.

Looking back, what could you do? Califf said. Maybe if his wife had still been around—she'd died of breast cancer—she could have given her daughter a better perspective. They'd been close. Califf had serious doubts about Lampron but at least the man had money to give his daughter a better life than her last boyfriend, a UMass Art major dropout who wanted to try organic farming. Lissa was old enough to make her own decisions and stubbornly insist that her father's doubts about Lampron weren't hers.

Still, when Kurt told his father that Lampron and Lissa were planning on going up to the Adirondacks together, with Lampron footing a fancy hotel finale in Saratoga, Califf asked his son to go along, maybe work in the bowhunting thing. Kurt said he would; he'd been having second thoughts about this guy too. But three would be weird, so Kurt got his girlfriend Rachel to go along, too.

The second day up there, Lissa twisted her ankle horsing around with her brother and Rachel, and didn't feel up to going with the others to shoot the bows, so she stayed at the camp. She probably was content to do so, since she was immersed in *Lonesome Dove*, a birthday present from her brother. So Kurt, Rachel and Lampron went off with the bows.

They left in the morning and by late afternoon still hadn't returned. Lissa was getting worried. She found Lampron's keys in their tent, thinking that if they weren't back soon, she was going to hike to the trail-head, sore ankle or not, and drive the car to get help. But around 5 p.m. Lampron came back, alone, saying they'd gotten separated, but all it was, he figured, was Kurt and Rachel wanting to be alone—*wink, wink*: they'd be back soon.

The two fixed dinner. Lissa told Lampron about a man she'd talked to briefly on the trail. Small world: he was from a town near Albany—Delmar—where her best friend now lived. Lampron went off on her big time, making accusations about what she had "done" while he was gone. She got angry—and then scared, because Lampron seemed to truly believe she'd fucked the guy. He was acting in a way she'd never seen before. Or at least, Califf said, in a way that she hadn't told anyone about. Admitting you made a mistake is tough to do. Young or old, didn't matter.

Kurt and Rachel still hadn't come back. It was getting dark. If Lissa hadn't already known something was very wrong, she did when Lampron told her: "Well, it would seem it is just you and I now except for the old man in that shithole he calls a home. So there is no point any longer in waiting to take you away, is there?"

She hadn't known he'd brought the necklace on the trip and he showed it to her again, telling her that it was going to be hers, a gift to mark their "bond." He said he "forgave" her for what she'd done. Lissa said later that probably scared her the most.

She knew she had to get away, go for help. She couldn't do that with him there. She waited until he'd gone to sleep, then crawled out of the tent, thinking she'd tell him, if he woke, that she was going to pee. But he didn't stir, and she got away, taking the keys to his car, a flashlight and nothing else except the fear that he would wake up and come after her on the trail.

She made it to the trailhead by dawn, bruised and bloody from falls and stumbles. She drove to the police in Saranac Lake, called her father, who drove up to get her.

They never found Kurt or Rachel, though the search lasted a week. No one knew what Lampron had done to them. There are plenty of lakes up there, large and small, and they couldn't check all of them if he'd weighted and sunk the bodies.

They never found Richard Lampron either.

Money can buy anything—false names and addresses; illusion and deception. He obviously had enough money—cached somewhere off the grid—to help create the shadows, the prisms he needed to bend his light the way he wanted and disappear, as surely as if he had never existed at all.

But he did exist. Lissa was terrified he was going to come after her. So she went someplace that only her father knew about, where Lampron could never find her…they hoped.

BY THE TIME Jordan Califf finished we had crossed the stone bridge and returned to his son's memorial. From the ground he picked up Caster's necklace and for a moment I thought he'd pocket it after all: a thing you can hold, feel the weight that will never be more, or less than what it is, secure with the constancy of its design, the brilliance of the gold and jewels.

He handed the necklace to me. "Do what you will with it. I don't want it, and I seriously doubt Lissa will."

When Jordan Califf was talking on our circuit of the school ground, it had occurred to me that perhaps he, too, was a master of deception: a father protective of what his son had done as an accomplice of Richard Lampron, or what little he knew about it anyway.

Maybe he suspected Kurt was leading a life unthinkable to the Taconic School Class of '05 which ponied up for his memorial. He hadn't mentioned Lissa being pregnant, as Caster wrote; nor had he mentioned that pendant the man had given her. Maybe Jordan Califf didn't even have a daughter.

Still, I had little doubt that what he said had more truth to it than what Eric Lane Caster had written at Fado.

I suppose we like to think that truth is a possession, a grail; or perhaps even a destination, requiring only the journey to get there. And sometimes it is, like the necklace Jordan Califf gave back to me.

Before we left, never to see each other again, Jordan Califf offered a handshake that became a brief embrace. He asked me where I was heading now, and I said I was going home, to tell my sister something that couldn't wait any longer.

"And then?" he asked, like a father who wanted to know what else his son planned to do.

"I'll be getting on a plane," I said. "There's someone at the other end."

"So you're not coming back?"

"That's why I'm going there, to find out."

ON MY WAY to Marcy's I threw the gun—and the necklace—into the Housatonic River.

And the last thing I did before getting on that plane was meet with John Walsh at Vincent's in Albany, and give him Eric Lane Caster's scroll of pages, and tell him the man wouldn't be doing to anyone else what he had to Katie. He and his family deserved the closure.

We sat in the same booth where he'd offered the bribe to get me out of his daughter's life. Neither of us wanted anything to drink when the waiter asked.

I was sure he'd grill me with questions. I thought he might even ask me for a sample of my handwriting he could take to the police for comparison to what lay before him. I would have given him one. But all he did was stare at those pages before looking away. And it was then that I almost regretted bringing them.

"You don't have to read it," I said. "You can trash it, or let the police read it instead. But I... it was the only way to let you know that Eric Lane Caster took a bullet in the head."

John Walsh looked at me, and I thought he was going to ask me if I was the one who shot him. "*Yes*" was on the tip of my tongue.

He said: "I'm sorry...about before. I know you did, too."

It took me a moment before I realized he was talking about Katie.

"I did. I loved her very much."

EPILOGUE

I NEVER RETURNED from Seattle. The police never showed up at the door to the apartment in Ballard, not far from the Locks, that I lived in for three months before Helen asked me to move in with her.

She kept Fado. When we're up there we always stop by the Basket to see Barbara Hollner. The cabin might as well be Robert's, for all the time he spends up there. He's assumed the role of caretaker and every time Helen and I visit him, there are always flowers from the meadow over Sean's grave.

But Robert wasn't at Fado the day Helen and I dug the other that is close by Sean's in the garden: Michael's second grave, in which Helen interred *The Book of Michael* and everything that had been on that wall. I left a few things of Katie's with Michael, too, including the baseball with her phone number on it.

Call it a groove or a glory-hole but Robert has it back; Fado is as good a reason for that as any. Before he sold his Wallingford house, I saw what someone once said about his work, that he was a "master of motion in glass." Maybe it's more than that, if you think of time as a kind of gravity, pulling you ahead. You can try to stop the flow, or alter it, or even go back, but that's only a catch—the interruption of a ball's descent. In this new series of sculptures Robert has done, called 'Rapids,' he's suspended everything permanently. Inside the white, flowing glass is a speck of darker glass; something caught and sealed forever in turbulence.

He gave Helen and I the first piece of the series as a wedding gift. His latest work, called 'The Pool,' sold for almost as much I make in a year teaching English at Mercer Island High School—I got my Master's at the University of Washington—and that includes the extra I earn as the freshman baseball coach.

Two months ago I finished the follow-up to *Angel's Share*. Neither book has sold yet but it helps—sort of—to keep a quote of John Ruskin's close at hand: "The highest reward for man's toil is not what he gets for it but what he becomes by it."

Marcy has been out three times, twice with Davy, and each time it hasn't rained a drop. And each time she crosses Lake Washington to Mercer Island, she marvels at the sight of Mt. Rainier rising in the distance.

At Fado, the first time she went up there with us, we took a walk—just the two of us—and I told her what I hadn't before: about taking a gun to kill a man in South Linfield, Massachusetts, and the note that our father left.

IT'S EARLY SUNDAY morning here on the island, so the ball fields at the park near our home are empty except for a couple walking their dog along the outfield fences. Helen returned yesterday from a show of her latest paintings at Iwano Associates gallery in San Francisco. I couldn't join her for the trip down there because someone had to stay with little Sean.

He was conceived during our honeymoon in Ireland. Helen believes she has the exact hour—also a Sunday morning—and the location: Doon Lake in County Clare. We rented a rowboat from Tommy Toher, who got in hot, unholy water from his wife for doing business when he should have been at Mass. Helen and I rowed out to the Bronze Age ringfort on a small island in the middle of the peat-stained lake water. I spread out the dark wool sweater I bought on Inishmore, the largest of the Arans. Later, we took our time rowing back since there was no one alongside to race us to the shore.

Right now I'm thinking about the ball I hit, or pretended to, with an inside-out swing to the opposite field; and about how fine Helen looks as she smoothly—and slowly—rounds first base, holding the wee hand of our child. There is another on deck, four months along.

There is also an imaginary guy on second. Sometimes you have to do that if you don't have enough players for a game. I figure #25 will be able to score from second if he hurries, and I wave him on home.

ABOUT THE AUTHOR

BRUCE FERGUSSON'S other suspense novels include *The Piper's Sons*—nominated for best novel by the Pacific Northwest Booksellers' Association—and *Morgan's Mill*, which weaves history of the Civil War and Underground Railroad into a contemporary narrative of suspense.

The first two novels in his Six Kingdoms fantasy series—*The Shadow of His Wings* and *The Mace of Souls*—were nominated for Nebulas and the former was also a finalist for the genre's Crawford Award for best first novel. Robin Hobb, New York Times bestselling fantasy author, said this about the 3rd book in the series, *Pass on the Cup of Dreams*: "[It] quickly immerses the reader in the imaginatively detailed fantasy world of the Six Kingdoms. Fergusson's writing is excellent, the plot relentless, the characters wonderfully complex. If you enjoy gritty, dark fantasy you will find a feast here."

The 4th book, *Kraken's Claw*, will be published in 2016. A companion volume for the series to date—*The Six Kingdoms Codex*—features an introductory story, extensive glossary and background to the world, and a color map by cartographer Pieter Talens.

Bruce lives with his family in Edmonds, Washington.

Find out more about Bruce and his books at www.brucefergusson.com.

www.ingramcontent.com/pod-product-compliance
Lightning Source LLC
Chambersburg PA
CBHW020928260626
47169CB00006B/1625